ONE WITH THE DARKNESS

"Superb writing, vivid narrative combined with complex plotting, and intricate characterization make each novel by Ms. Squires an absolute winner. Don't miss this exciting chapter in this unique and captivating vampire series."
                    —*Romantic Times BOOKreviews*

ONE WITH THE SHADOWS

"Full of colorful characters, romantic locales and vivid details of 1820s life, [*One with the Shadows*] has a delicious pace and plenty of thrills, and her vampire mythos is both mannered—almost Victorian—and intriguingly offbeat. Bound to net a wide audience of paranormal fans, this one may even convert devotees of traditional historicals."
                    —*Publishers Weekly*
                    (A Best Book of the Year)

ONE WITH THE NIGHT

"Superb...captivating...With her usual skill and creativity, Ms. Squires has crafted a novel that is passionate, heartbreaking, suspenseful, and completely riveting."
                    —*Romance Reviews Today*

"Few writers combine a sensual romance within a supernatural thriller as well as Susan Squires consistently does. Her latest is a terrific Regency vampire romantic
                    MORE...

suspense starring two courageous heroes battling one hell of a meanie." —*Midwest Book Review*

"This is an incredibly unusual take on historical vampire stories. Susan Squires delivers an exciting story."
—*Fallen Angel Reviews*

THE BURNING

"A terrific tale...the story line is action-packed."
—*Midwest Book Review*

"Blazingly hot and erotic."
—*Romantic Times BOOKreviews*

"Marvelously rich, emotionally charged, imaginative, and beautifully written." —*BookLoons*

"A fantastic erotic vampire thriller." —*Fresh Fiction*

THE COMPANION

"A darkly compelling vampire romance...the plot keeps the reader turning the pages long into the night."
—*Affaire de Coeur*

"Bestseller Squires charts a new direction with this exotic, extremely erotic, and darkly dangerous Regency-set paranormal tale. With her ability to create powerful and tormented characters, Squires has developed a novel that is graphic, gripping, and unforgettable."
—*Romantic Times* (4 ½ starred review)

A TWIST
IN TIME

Susan Squires

St. Martin's Paperbacks

This is a work of fiction. All of the characters, organizations, and events portrayed in this novel are either products of the author's imagination or are used fictitiously.

A TWIST IN TIME

For information address St. Martin's Press, 175 Fifth Avenue, New York, NY 10010.

ISBN: 978-0-312-94354-7

Printed in the United States of America

St. Martin's Paperbacks edition / March 2010

St. Martin's Paperbacks are published by St. Martin's Press, 175 Fifth Avenue, New York, NY 10010.

10 9 8 7 6 5 4 3 2 1

This book is dedicated to Fred Williams, neighbor and sailing instructor *par excellence* who graciously (and heroically) taught me to sail and trusted his twenty-five-foot sailboat to me in some pretty impressive swells. He also looked over my sailing language in crucial parts of the book. The mistakes are mine. The fact that there aren't more belongs to him. And, as always, this book belongs to Jen, *editor extraordinaire*, who makes me think twice. Second time is a charm.

Chapter One

It was okay to be a little obsessive, Lucy Rossano told herself, trying to breathe. Perfectly normal. She clutched the shoulder bag that contained the book to her chest. It was the most valuable book she'd ever acquired in the eight years she'd been dealing in rare books. So of course she couldn't bring herself to sell it, no matter the price, or donate it to a museum, or even lock it in the safe at the store. It was by frickin' Leonardo da Vinci. Who wouldn't want to carry it around all the time?

And sleep with it.

"I can't *believe* you have a book that shows a picture of the very machine I'm working on." Brad could hardly contain his excitement. He pushed past the guard's desk at the Super Collider Lab. "Hey, Wally. Just in for a quick check on the power levels."

The guard's eyes widened. "Uh, okay, Dr. Steadman." His stare shifted to Lucy. She could feel him registering the really red hair. It was the only reason anyone ever noticed her.

"Oh. Uh, Lucy's my . . . my new research assistant. Lucy, why don't you sign in?"

Lucy moved to the loose-leaf binder as if in a dream. This couldn't be happening. Brad was wrong. Maybe the whole thing was wishful thinking on his part. Right. Wishful thinking—*Brad*? Practical, subatomic-particle-expert Brad? He'd been her father's research assistant at Stanford. Wishful thinking wasn't in Brad's gene pool. She signed her name. The guard passed her a visitors' tag. She clipped it to her black knit jacket. Her hand shook.

"You sure work all hours, Dr. Steadman," Wally said, waving them through.

Brad grabbed her hand and practically dragged her through two double doors. When the doors were safely shut, he said, "And you showed it to me only hours after I'd had a breakthrough in powering the thing. What a co-incidence!"

Yeah. Just a coincidence. But she'd had the book for months now and hadn't told a soul. So why had she felt so . . . so *compelled* to show her friend Brad the book to-day of all days? The urge had haunted her at the Explor-atorium. It should have been just like any other visit. She and Brad had gone to the Exploratorium every few months since her father died. Brad was trying to interest her in the hands-on exhibits meant for children. He thought she'd be happier if she went back to school and got a degree in some kind of science, preferably particle science so they could work together. Like that was going to happen. Her doctorate meant nothing to him, both because it was in comparative literature and the because it was from Berke-ley, not Stanford.

Still, she liked the Exploratorium, as much for the pic-nics they always had at the Palace of Fine Arts next door as anything else. The classic semi-ruin built for the 1915 Panama Pacific Exposition held a strange attraction for her. Today the place was all torn up because the city of San Francisco was retrofitting it to withstand earthquakes. But the mysterious basement they'd uncovered below the Rotunda floor only seemed to make the attraction stronger. Why had it been built? Why was it empty? In the middle of her speculation, the urge to show Brad the book began to feel like she'd ordered Thai food extrahot—a burning sensation she couldn't control. Finally, as the November fog rolled in through the Golden Gate and down the colonnade, she'd pulled out the book and let Brad page through it in the overhead light of the car.

Now, here they were, hurrying down the long corridor of the Super Collider Lab to see . . . what? An impossibility.

"I *knew* this was important, no matter what Casey said." Brad had been under a lot of pressure since some guy from the government had come in to supervise his project. "He doesn't give me the respect I deserve." Brad glanced back to her. "Just like someone else I could name."

Lucy mustered up a smile. Brad was a strange mixture of rampant ego and insecurity. It was kind of nice to have a friend who needed you as much as you needed him. And she had been needy after her father died. "You know I think you're brilliant."

Brad's eyes darkened. He set his lips. "Yeah. You think I'm smart. That's why you bother to hang around with me."

That was only part of it. They did have good conversations. But she also hung with Brad because he'd known her father. Now that she was alone in the world, Brad was a kind of connection to her father. And Brad had been a friend indeed, helping her with the funeral, arranging to sell her father's boat so she could keep the store going. "You know it's more than that."

A little glimmer of something flashed in his brown eyes. "I know."

That was puzzling. But this whole thing was puzzling. When Brad saw the picture of the machine in Leonardo's wonderful book, he freaked out. He said the machine actually existed. The Italian government found it under Il

Duomo cathedral in Florence and asked Stanford's Super Collider Lab to find a way to power it. No one knew what the machine actually did.

Except Lucy. Leonardo's book told her.

It was supposed to be a time machine.

Therefore, it wasn't real. She couldn't be hurrying down some corridor of a lab in the hills of twenty-first-century San Mateo County to see a time machine built in 1508. Impossible.

But that's not what her bones were telling her. She'd always known that Leonardo's treatise, which had such a hold on her, was no ordinary book.

It had all started with a girl named Frankie Suchet.

"I've got a book I want authenticated," the beautiful young woman said. Her blond hair was spiked out and tipped with coal black. Her blue eyes glowed in translucent white skin. She was lean and boyish, dressed in tight leather pants and a skimpy sweater that showed her flat belly. Just the kind of body Lucy always wanted to have. "Professor Lambeth over at Berkeley said you could do the job." The woman began unwrapping a brown paper package tied with string.

"Don't you want to know how much I charge?" Lucy asked, taken aback by the girl's abrupt demeanor.

"Charge what you want. I need to know if it's real." Her voice was hard.

Lucy sighed. It would be some diary found in an attic trunk, worth no more than its sentimental value. That's what usually walked in her door. The bookstore was just creaking by, yielding only enough income to hold body and soul together. She'd charge the woman a hundred bucks just to make the service seem worthwhile and tell her the bad news.

The large book revealed on Lucy's counter had a

*beautiful tooled leather binding. Who would do some-
thing so expensive for a diary? The style was almost High
Renaissance, with scenes of angels swirling up toward a
radiant cloud. Lucy ran her hand over it. Not stamped.
You could clearly see the mark of the awl in several places.*

*There was no title page, only a dedication . . . in ar-
chaic Italian:*

> *For Contessa Donnatella Margherita Luchella di
> Poliziano, from her friend Leonardo da Vinci. I
> dedicate to you my greatest work.*

A chill ran down Lucy's spine. It couldn't be. Get hold
of yourself. *A fraud. The writing was certain proof. She
turned a page. Her eyes scanned the note.*

> *What you see before you is a time machine.*

*Right. Somebody was trying to put one over on the ac-
ademic community. They'd probably go for it, hook, line,
and sinker, too. Who didn't want to believe that Leonardo
da Vinci had built a time machine? She scanned again.
Something about only the Contessa having enough power
to make the machine run. . . .*

> *You are asking yourself how it works. If you care to
> read the journal, you will know. But if you are in
> haste, know this, time is not a river but a vortex,
> and with enough power a man can jump into an-
> other part of the swirl.*
>   *So, my dear Contessa, pull the lever. Think of the
> moment you want to be in as you leap into the mael-
> strom. You will end in the moment you imagine.*
>   *Be warned: The machine will go with you, but it
> cannot stay long in another time. To return, you*

*must use it again before it disappears. I do not
know how long it can stay. I do not know what will
happen if you make it back to the time you are in
now, or what will happen if you don't. I give you
only the means to change your destiny, or perhaps
all of our destinies. Use it if you will.*

*But the book wasn't Leonardo's. She'd known it from
the first words of the dedication. She turned the page.*

My God.

*The writing of the central text was done from right to
left. Each letter was written backward. It would read
correctly in a mirror. Exactly how Leonardo wrote his
notebooks—why, no one knew for certain. Diagrams,
calculations in the margins, long batches of text that
would take many hours to translate . . . it all looked
amazingly authentic. And on the final pages, there was
an intricate picture of a machine with incredibly complex
interlocking gears.*

"What do you think?"

*Lucy looked up at the girl. The look in those blue eyes
was cynical, but only on the surface; underneath there
was a terrible, wrenching . . . hope.*

*Lucy managed a shrug. "Well, if it's fake, it's one hell
of a fake. The paper is made from macerated rags rolled
out in a press. The writing is in the manner of Leonardo.
There's a chance it's real. I'll know in a couple of days."*

Frankie Suchet had left her name and address. The book
had been real, of course. But that wasn't the strangest part
of it in some ways. When Lucy had told her, three days later,
the girl had taken a gigantic breath and said, "Well, that's
it then." And she had turned around and made for the door.

"Don't you want to take the book with you?" Lucy had
called after her.

The woman had turned in the doorway. "You keep it. I have what I need from it."

And she'd walked out.

That was the last Lucy had seen of her for five months. And then one day, she walked in through the shop door, accompanied by the most drop-dead gorgeous man Lucy had ever seen. At least Lucy *thought* it was Frankie Suchet. She had to look twice. Gone was the spiky hair, the air of cynicism. . . .

"It's you! I've been looking for you." Lucy's eyes slid to the guy. She tore her eyes away and back to Frankie. *"You look . . . different."*

The girl ran her hands through her hair self-consciously. "Where are my manners? Lucy Rossano, this is Henri Foucault." She pronounced it in the French manner. "Ahn-ree Foo-coh."

Lucy nodded to the guy and felt herself blushing like every other woman probably did when confronted with that man. "A pleasure, Monsieur Foucault. Am I to credit you for the change I see in Ms. Suchet?" Lucy glanced to Frankie. The soft expression was the real change.

"I like to think so," the hunk murmured.

Frankie's blush joined Lucy's. "Never mind that. I've come about the book."

"That's why I've been trying to find you. No one had heard of you at the address you gave."

"I've been . . . away. Do . . . you . . . have . . . the . . . book?" Frankie spoke each syllable slowly.

Lucy realized she was staring at the couple. She ran her hands through the thick mass of her hair. "Yes. Yes, of course. But someone has made an offer on it. A . . . a million dollars."

The couple glanced at each other. "We'll match whatever you're offered," Foucault said.

Lucy's mouth worked, but she couldn't manage any sound. She couldn't sell it to the woman who had given it to her. She wanted to say she'd just give it back. But that would mean giving it up.

Frankie leaned over the counter, blue eyes burning. "There's more to it, isn't there?"

Lucy felt trapped. But this woman would know about the book if anyone did. And Lucy needed to know. "I've started to dream about the book. I think about it every waking moment. Is . . . is it cursed or something? I mean, the way you just left it here when it was so valuable— were you passing it on to get rid of it?"

Frankie smiled. Suddenly she seemed sure of herself. "No, I had already decided to use the knowledge it contained to make me happy. I had all it could give me."

"You do look happy," Lucy whispered.

Henri looked to Frankie, then spoke to Lucy. "If you're short of money, we know some influential people in the arts in San Francisco. We'll spread the word about your shop."

"Keep the book." Frankie looked into Lucy's eyes. "You're meant to have it just as I was."

And they left her a treasure. Sometimes she wished they hadn't. The book had hold of her, no matter how much she pretended she wasn't obsessed. She'd begun to make up fantastic stories about Frankie Suchet using the machine to make herself happy and what that might mean. She'd daydreamed about using the machine herself as if it really existed. Because ever since her father died, Lucy had been drifting, waiting for . . . something. She wanted what Frankie Suchet had. Certainty? Happiness? Lucy wanted that. She wanted her life transformed into something meaningful, even though she didn't know what that meaning would be.

And now the whole sequence of events seemed like destiny. The feeling was overpowering. The book had been left to her. Frankie believed it was meant for her somehow. The Italian government sent the machine to America to give it power. Her friend Brad was assigned to the project. Too many coincidences. The book and the machine were coming together with power only the Super Collider Lab could provide.

And they would be used.

Tonight.

Maybe it wouldn't work. This could all still be some elaborate hoax.

But Lucy no longer believed that. This was destiny. Her destiny.

A guy with a ramrod-straight military bearing and a brush cut stepped out of an office directly into Lucy and Brad's path. She could practically feel Brad cringe. The guy had an intense look about him.

"Colonel Casey, just the man I wanted to see." Brad wasn't an imposing man, maybe five nine or ten, lean from being a runner. He dressed precisely in pressed chinos and Bruno Magli loafers, maybe too precisely. He wasn't God's gift to women. But he and Lucy had their common looks in common. She wasn't God's gift to men. Maybe that drew them together—a lifetime of being everyone's second choice. There was no way Brad was fit to stand up to Casey.

"I heard you made a breakthrough, Steadman. About time. Though what this retro bunch of gears is supposed to do is beyond me." His eyes never left Lucy's face. They were the palest blue she'd ever seen. Even though his hair was blond, they seemed unnatural. "Trying to impress your girl with a government project that requires special clearance?" The sneer in his voice was evident. "Not smart, Steadman."

"As a matter of fact," here Brad cleared his throat, "Miss Rossano is my research assistant. I've located a book about the origin of the machine and its purpose."

Lucy tried to relax. This guy would never let the machine be used, destiny or not, by some girl he didn't know. She was off the hook. She had no desire to succumb to some fate over which she had no control, regardless of the feeling in the pit of her stomach.

"Okay. Give me the book. I'll take a look. *You* wait in the lobby, Miss Rossano."

Like hell. She wasn't giving up her book. She leaned forward and stuck out her hand. "That's *Dr.* Rossano. Nice to meet someone else who reads sixteenth-century Italian."

Casey stared at her. Boy, if reptiles had blue eyes . . . He didn't take her offered hand. He shot a disgusted glance to Brad. Then he gestured down the hall.

She saw Brad swallow as he led the way. Casey fell in behind them.

Brad opened a door at the end of a long hall. Lucy had memorized each detail of the diagram in Leonardo's book. But that didn't prepare her for the sheer size and weight of the machine standing on a platform across the lab. It gleamed faintly in the tiny work lights that still left shadows in the cavernous lab. The whole experience was like the first time she'd seen Rodin's *The Thinker* in the sculpture garden at the Norton Simon Museum. Everybody knew what it looked like from pictures in countless art books. But that never prepared you. It was that dense occupation of space that gave it emotional resonance.

The giant, brass gears towering above her, immensely heavy, made her catch her breath and struggle for air. The gems that studded the wheels coruscated with emerald green, ruby red, and the blue of sapphires as big as your fist. Where had Leonardo gotten such jewels? A fortune winked from among the interlocking wheels, none bigger than the huge diamond that formed the knob of a control stick. Everything looked just as it was in the book, except for the lunch box–sized metal box bolted to the frame just under the largest wheel.

Could this medieval machine really send someone to another time? On the face of it, it was ridiculous. Yet if anyone could build a time machine surely it would be Leonardo da Vinci. Half scientist, half artist, in some ways he was more than either—a magician, perhaps. Was it that possibility that had fueled her obsession?

Both the colonel and Brad watched for her reaction. She thought Brad might explode with excitement. "It's Leonardo's machine, all right." She couldn't help that her eyes filled.

"Da Vinci?" Casey's voice was sharp.

Lucy nodded. She could hardly see his light eyes in the dim room.

Brad tried to calm himself. He cleared his throat. "If the book is right, this machine could be more important than you've been thinking, Colonel." Was Brad excited only to prove himself to Casey? Maybe.

Casey's hard eyes reassessed her. "And *you*, Dr. Rossano, know what it is."

She nodded slowly. Well, at least he'd never believe her. "Yeah. It's a time machine."

"A time machine," Casey snorted. "Right. Are you crazy, Steadman?"

"No, you've got to see the book, Colonel," Brad protested. He hurried to a long table that faced the machine and switched on a small work light. "Luce, bring the book and show him."

Lucy hefted her bag off her shoulder. The book wouldn't help a military guy believe. Huge girders loomed in the ceiling far above her. The place had that peculiar sterile environment that left only a faint metallic odor. She pulled out the book and spread it open. Casey leaned over it. Lucy pointed. "Leonardo's signature." She flipped pages to show the diagrams on assembly, key notes in the margins, mathematical equations. Then she flipped to the full drawing. Casey drew in a breath. She paged back. "Here's where he says that time is a vortex. And here . . . he says the jewels focus the power."

"How do I know that's what it says?" Casey asked softly, his eyes darting over the text.

"You can check it with another expert in archaic Italian." There. That would buy time. She could feel the machine looming above her, heavy with . . . with purpose. That was bad.

"How do you select a time? There are no dials or settings we could see."

Lucy smiled. This would seal his disbelief. "It says in the book that you pull the handle and just think about the time you want to be in."

Casey blinked once and chuffed a disgusted laugh. "Oh, great. I get the really good assignments."

"Okay. I know it sounds a little out there," Brad admitted. "That's why we've got to try it. If we've spent a lot of someone's money powering a machine that doesn't do anything, better to know that now. If it's a hoax, all the Italians have is a fortune in tourist dollars when they put it on display in the Uffizi. But if it's not, then we've got something *everybody* is going to want."

Lucy was dismayed at Casey's look of speculation. He couldn't be considering powering up the machine, could he?

"And then this wasn't such a crappy assignment after all," Brad continued. "In fact, you can probably name your next one." Brad really struck a chord with that. Casey thought he'd drawn a crappy assignment and he was now thinking how nice it would be to come up with something incredible no one ever expected. "So why don't we test it out? Right here. Tonight."

No, no, no. Definitely not. Lucy looked around wildly. The machine seemed to be vibrating in satisfaction. "Wouldn't . . . wouldn't that be bad scientific method? You should do a . . . a controlled experiment." Brad was always talking about controlled experiments.

"Well, we've got a problem," Brad said, his eyes on Casey. "We can't go to my boss, or your boss, and tell them we've got a time machine. We'd be laughed out of the office."

"Well, yeah," Casey said, dripping sarcasm. "I guess we would."

"Unless we had proof. Come on, Casey." Brad was on a roll. Sure of himself. "You want prestige and power. If it works, you're in like Flynn. A time machine built by Leonardo da Vinci and powered by our project?" It must have killed him to share the credit for the project.

Casey was becoming convinced. He'd gotten that speculative look, in spades. "Your little lunch box over there works?"

"Of course it works," Brad said through gritted teeth. "We successfully moved the gears today using a fraction of the power it's capable of."

"Could you go to the future?" Casey stared at the machine, even though he was addressing Lucy. He was caught by the possibilities. He would be the one to use the machine tonight. Maybe that was okay. But it didn't feel right. She shook herself mentally. What was she thinking? She had to get out of here or something . . . momentous would happen.

But she answered anyway. "I don't know. Leonardo was more interested in understanding the past. I guess if time is really a vortex you could go either way."

Casey continued to stare. "What if you can't power up the machine again once you're there?" Oh yeah. She'd been through that possibility in her mind a thousand times.

"According to Leonardo, the machine can't stay in another time forever. It's too much pressure on the flow of time. It'll snap back to where it came from with you or without you."

"If he knows what he's talking about. And if he doesn't?"

She took a breath. "You get stuck there, along with your machine." There. That should make them think twice about using it.

Brad looked desperate. He wanted the project to succeed that much. "Look," he said. "There's always risk. Somebody has to be first. Chuck Yeager had to go up and fly fast even though nobody knew what would happen when you broke the sound barrier. John Glenn had to go up in Friendship I. Sometime, somebody just has to do it."

Casey peered at the illustration in the book, then straightened. "I agree." He turned to Lucy. "How about her?"

Both Brad and Lucy were stunned. "She isn't even part of the team," Brad sputtered.

"She's perfect. She's obviously read this book a hundred times. She knows how it's supposed to work." Here Casey looked at Brad. "And we have plausible deniability. We were doing tests and she pulled the handle while our backs were turned." He'd gone through all the permutations in his mind. One: It didn't work. Nothing lost. Two: It did work and she went back and returned. He won big. Three: She went back and only the machine returned. He won. He didn't care about her. Four: She went back and neither she nor the machine returned. That was bad. They'd have to admit that she hoodwinked them. But it was one in four. Odds were with Casey. *Really* with Casey with how big the odds were that it wouldn't work in the first place.

Lucy felt the lab almost tremble with intent. Brad's face was a comical combination of eagerness and guilt. He wanted so badly to try the machine. Badly enough to risk her life? Apparently. "Brad?"

He took a long breath. Fear flashed across his face before he pulled down a mask over both the fear and the eagerness. "You'll be okay, Lucy."

So that was it. He did want it that bad, but he didn't have the courage to use it himself.

Casey looked at her. Brad looked at her.

It all came down to this moment. The months of obsession, the feeling of her life being without purpose, stale, and tasteless since her father died, her fascination with how happy Frankie Suchet had been. If she walked out now, what would she be walking out *to*? She had nothing out there. A successful business, maybe even wildly successful since Frankie and Henri had directed all their friends to frequent her shop, but it didn't *mean* anything to her. She had no friends except a crazy old loon of a landlord and Brad, and Brad didn't look to be a great friend right now. She had nothing but her obsession with the book. And if she walked out, they'd never let her take the book with her. That left . . . nothing. Her life beyond the walls of this lab had not a shred of magic in it. But here, in this sterile place, magic hung in the air, delivered across time by a magician named da Vinci.

A thrill of . . . expectation made it hard for Lucy to breathe. How long since she had had expectations of life? A feeling of rightness washed over her. Everything was about to change, and that was as it should be. Her breathing calmed. "Okay." She turned to the machine. "Rev up your lunch box, Brad."

Brad looked back at Casey. Casey nodded. Brad took a

breath and turned to the machine. "Get me more light," he called over his shoulder.

"Nix. That'd attract attention," Casey snapped. He turned off the light on the table. "Only the work lights."

Brad knelt in front of the machine without further protest.

"Let me watch you," Lucy said, leaning over him. "I'll have to start it up myself to make it back." She watched him flipping lighted switches and murmured the pattern to herself. "Blue, then the two whites from left to right, twice, and then the red."

The machine began to hum. Vibrations just at the edge of her awareness filled the room. She steadied her breathing. She was going to do this. How . . . miraculous was that? The right feeling pushed her fear behind some kind of curtain in her mind. She knew all the things that could happen. She could get stuck in the past. She'd probably be burned as a witch. A red-haired witch. It was an insane risk. She just didn't care anymore. All this was meant to happen. "Okay, to you two it will probably seem as if only a moment has elapsed before I reappear." She closed the book, tucked it into her bag, and slung the bag on her shoulder. "Let's get this show on the road."

"You should leave the book here." Brad was trying to sound like Casey. Not.

"Hey, I'm not going back to who-knows-when without my references."

"Let her take it," Casey said. "Does us no good if the thing doesn't work." He nodded to her. There was respect in his eyes.

"I'll go back far enough that they'll be in awe of me and my machine." She was wearing the outfit she'd worn to the Exploratorium, a flippy knit skirt and matching slinky jacket over a green shell, and ballet slipper flats.

"Better pick summertime," Casey said, echoing her

thoughts. "Hate to see you ruin those shoes in snow." Was Casey kidding? How did you know with a guy like that?

"You got it."

"Give her all your change," Casey ordered Brad. "Just in case she's there long enough to need to buy food and lodging. Silver is good." They each piled a handful of coins into her bag.

"I won't be there long. I'm going to figure out where I am, grab something to bring back with me as proof, and hightail it back here." Was that true? She stepped up under the machine in front of the lever topped by that impossibly huge diamond.

Brad knelt by the lunch box again. "After you do the switch sequence push this chrome button here, and that will start the power." It was a rounded pad you pressed with your palm.

She nodded and put both hands over the diamond knob. Brad slapped the button. The power hum passed out of hearing range, but she could feel it in her chest and throat. She pulled the lever down. No gears moved. The feeling of power in the air made it difficult to breathe. At last the big gear in the central portion of the machine creaked.

God, it was going to happen! She had to think of a time period. The small gears began to spin, faster and faster. Shakespearean England? Fin de siècle France? She spoke French pretty well. The gears whirred until they were only a blur. She couldn't decide! A white glow filled the room. She thought Brad was shouting, or maybe it was Casey. She couldn't make out the words.

What she really wanted was to go back to a time when magic was possible. Any time, it didn't matter—a time when people believed in magic and it transformed their lives.

The gears seemed to stop; time hung suspended. Oh no! Did Brad's lunch box not provide enough power? Or

was Leonardo's design flawed? The glow was cut by a
hundred beams of light, colored like the jewels. They criss-
crossed the ceiling, illuminating the girders above. What
was happening here? She felt that possibility of magic
she'd imagined receding. A sense of loss suffused her. . . .

Then everything happened impossibly fast. The sensation of time slowing changed in an instant to a feeling of
being flung forward from a slingshot, and everything was
a blur and she was screaming, only she couldn't hear herself scream. . . .

Chapter Two

Her breath was knocked back into her as she hit the ground. Grass, punctuated with great gouged muddy places. The earth shook as the machine thunked in behind her. She blinked, disoriented. Around her shouts and screams reverberated. Dim figures leaned forward through the smoke. Were they peering at her? And what was that other smell? Like a butcher shop.

It was blood.

Lucy got to her hands and knees, clutching her bag. *My God, it actually worked!* Leonardo had built a time machine. In spite of all her obsession, all her daydreaming, she hadn't really thought it would. Figures loomed out of swirling smoke, frozen, peering at the machine. Where in God's name was she? A single bulky figure brought up a sword and cleaved another in the neck. The bearded man dropped to his knees with a scream. All around her men sprang into action. Steel clanged on steel.

She'd landed in the middle of a battle. And the fact that she'd appeared so suddenly had meant but a moment's interruption in the carnage. She staggered to her feet. Giant men in chain mail and leather greaves with huge sharp axes and swords that looked impossibly heavy surged around her. Hair and beards flowed out from under peaked helmets with nosepieces. Saxons? Vikings? Maybe she was in the time of King Arthur. The smell of blood and sweat and smoke was almost overwhelming. Lucy choked as a giant of a man lunged for her. She screamed and pulled away. He turned to parry a sword thrust by another giant. She scurried to the shelter of the machine. *Get this thing started and get out of here, wherever and whenever here is.*

She crouched beside the silver lunch box. "Blue switch. Check. Two whites. Check, check." Her voice trembled. She looked up at a shout and saw a man lose his head. She screamed. She'd seen it in movies a lot. But real was something else entirely. No comforting latex, no soothing CGI. Blood spurted. The body staggered forward even as the head thudded to the ground and rolled. The attacker whirled away, beset on all sides.

The eyes are still blinking. It felt like someone else was thinking that. She was frozen, staring at the head as, behind it, the body toppled. Her breath started to come fast and shallow. Darkness threatened at the edge of her vision. *Get hold of yourself, Lucy. Got to get out of here.* With a wrench she pulled her gaze away from the head. The lunch box began to hum. *Be quick. Please be quick. Quick. Quick.* Now for the chrome button.

A hand on her shoulder pulled her away from the machine. Hard eyes examined her from behind the battered helmet. The man had bad teeth and worse breath. She struggled, but this time the grip was iron on her arm. He said something guttural. German?

"Let me go," she screamed as though he could understand her.

A shadow loomed out of the smoke behind her attacker. The shadow roared something, and her attacker turned and met the descending sword by thrusting up his small, round shield. As the two engaged, the one who had been gripping her thrust her away. She plunged back to the power box and pushed the chrome button. The feeling of energy in the air thumped in her chest. She pushed herself up and went to the lever. The two giant men were hacking at each other, parrying and thrusting not two feet away. The younger of the two, who had attacked the one with bad teeth, seemed to be getting the better of the struggle. The rest of the battle was closing in on the machine. Huge men everywhere, sharp edges of steel, leather and sweat and blood. She reached up and pulled the lever down. The gears began to spin. Several men staggered away from the machine, pointing. But any lapse of attention could be punished with a killing blow, so the fighting sputtered but didn't stop. The two giants stumbled even closer.

Machine! she thought. *Get me out of here.* The gears were really whirring now. In moments she would just disappear the way she came. *November 9, 2009.*

Beside her the two men grappled with each other. The younger one thrust the one with bad teeth away. He fell right at Lucy's feet. The younger one hurled himself on top, but the older man got his axe up and the blade cut the younger one's thigh. Blood seeped through a long cut in the leather. They rolled and staggered up. But now the older man was like a fury, swinging the axe again and again. A white glow from the machine permeated the smoke. The older man picked up a mace lying over a dead body and swung it at the younger man's helmet. It clanged. The helmet drooped. The older man reached across the body of his adversary for Lucy. His axe dripped blood. But the younger man pushed up with his sword and it found his adversary's hip joint. The younger man struggled to his feet in front of Lucy and faced the one with bad teeth, now bared in rage. Was he protecting her?

Things began to slow. Oh, dear. It was happening. She had to focus. *November 9, 2009.* She hadn't brought anything back with her. Except the bruises she'd have from that guy's grip. The colored beams of light crossed wildly through the smoke like a demented circus. The old guy thrust at the dazed man between them and sliced his shoulder. The younger man fell slowly against Lucy. Warm blood soaked her. In this time a wound like that was a death sentence. No S.F. General Trauma Center to stitch up those arteries. The older man raised his axe. It came down toward Lucy, oh, so slowly. She ducked, even more slowly. The axe head hit the huge diamond on the lever and crashed down onto the lunch box. The axe reverberated, sending the attacker back a pace.

Then everything sped up.

November 9, 2009. She looked down at the man leaning against her, gore welling from rents in his chain mail. He really needed a hospital. The sensation of being flung forward engulfed her. All was light and sound and whirling vortex. . . .

"That story is . . . is balderdash." Brad could see Jensen's veins bulging on his forehead. Jensen ran the Super Collider Lab, but he was about to retire. Brad had thought by delivering an actual working time machine he'd become a shoo-in to get the job. That wasn't exactly how it was working out. "There is no such thing as a time machine, and no mere girl could have stolen it."

"Then how does a fourteen-foot machine just disappear without anyone noticing?" Brad was fighting for his professional life here. "No guards saw it being taken out, no reports in the neighborhood of trucks hauling huge cargo. But the guards did see Lucy." Blaming it on Lucy was the only way to get clear, he told himself.

"I want him off the project." Casey's voice was calm. "He brought her in."

"I can't put him off the project until we're sure there is no project." Jensen ran his palms over his thinning hair. "On the off chance your story is some twisted version of the truth and the damned thing reappears, he's the expert. You *did* say Leonardo da Vinci, didn't you?"

Brad breathed again. He shot a glance to Casey. "I did. Miss Rossano had a book that showed its design, written by da Vinci in 1508."

"You brought in a double agent," Casey was sticking to their story that Lucy had taken the machine when their backs were turned as a matter of self–defense. But that didn't mean he couldn't spread a little blame around to Brad.

"You didn't even know what the machine was until our research turned up the book."

"*Our* research? Hers. She played you like a violin, Steadman."

"Innocent Lucy who always has her nose in a dusty book? She's lost somewhere and can't get back. You can sneer all you want, Casey. You just don't want to admit I was right about this project all along. It's the most important discovery since space travel."

"*Was* the most important discovery—" That was why Casey was angry. Brad knew how he felt. So close to the brass ring . . .

"What am I going to tell the Italian government?" Jensen practically wailed. "Or the police? They're looking for Lucy Rossano, who has apparently disappeared into thin air."

"We told you—"

"I'll take care of the police," Casey grunted, interrupting Brad.

"Find a way to get that machine back, Steadman," Jensen threatened. "Or you'll never work in any government-funded project again." He spun on his heel and stomped out of the room.

Like energy leaves a trail through time you can track. Brad sighed. But he had to get Lucy back somehow. She needed his protection. She'd been just on the verge of realizing she was in love with him. She'd said he mattered more to her than just a friend, hadn't she? Everything was spoiled now, just when all his patience with her since her father died was about to pay off.

"I'll get her picture to Interpol. She must have taken it somewhere."

Brad grimaced. "Or some time." They both knew that if da Vinci's machine was a time machine, she could take it where they'd never find it.

Casey's eyes glittered. "In the meantime we'll turn her life upside down. Let's find out just who this Lucy Rossano really was."

Lucy squeezed her eyes shut as though that would stop the headache. Had she been drinking? She never drank to the point of having a hangover.

She was lying on something cold and hard. She blinked her eyes open. Cement. A fluorescent light blared from somewhere close. She smelled oil. She raised her head gingerly. Lines were painted on the cement. Parking structure. She was lying in a parking structure. How had she gotten here? She'd had a wild dream. She'd been at Brad's lab. The machine turned out to be real. One *very* scary battle in some other time. It all seemed so clear. One hell of a dream.

The parking structure was empty except for one car down at the end that looked like it had been there awhile. A tire was flat. She pushed herself up, squinting against her headache.

The machine glinted in the fluorescent light, quiet, heavy, utterly real. And about ten feet to the right of it lay the young bearded guy from another time who'd been wounded in the battle.

Lucy couldn't breathe. It wasn't a dream at all. She'd traveled in time and now she was back, though somehow she wasn't in the lab, and she'd brought something with her after all, a guy who was Saxon or German or maybe from Camelot. She'd probably just changed the fabric of time or the course of history or something. He'd fallen against her just as she was disappearing. Inconvenient timing. Worse than inconvenient. This was *awful*.

She eased her bag off her shoulder and crawled over to the man. Was he dead? He was lying in a pool of blood. His chain mail, made of small interlinking loops of metal, was rent over his shoulder and covered with gore. She dared not look closely at the flesh beneath if she wanted to avoid fainting or, worse, vomiting all over him. Even as she reached for his throat to feel for a pulse, he groaned and rolled his head. His helmet clanked against the cement. Okay. He wasn't dead. Was that good or bad?

She pulled off the helmet. His hair was darkened with sweat and matted against his head. Two small braids hung from his temples. He was at least six feet—probably really tall for back whenever she'd been—and big through the shoulders.

His eyes fluttered open. He muttered something. German? Scandinavian? She couldn't understand. She shook her head. He tried again. This time he sounded vaguely like a reading of *Beowulf* she'd heard once at a coffeehouse in college. He tried to raise his head. That made his shoulder ooze redly. *Great.* Whatever blood he had left would end up on the cement at this rate.

She looked around, panicked. At least she was in the right century for medical help. This was apparently the

underground part of a parking structure. A green exit sign
glowed in the corner. Probably stairs. She'd never get this
guy up stairs in his condition. She peered the other way at
a sign fizzing weakly. Did it say: *Elevator*? She scrambled to her bag and fumbled for her iPhone. If she could
get a signal down here, she could call the paramedics and
use the map locator function to tell them where to pick up
the injured guy. She hit the button at the bottom, but no
screen came up. *Great.* She'd charged it earlier today . . .
apparently time traveling took the charge out of her
phone. No phoning the paramedics.

"All right, buddy," she said with false cheer. "You have
to rally round here. If I go for help, you'll probably be
dead by the time I get back." She knelt beside him and
wormed her arm under his shoulders. He got the idea and
with her help he managed to sit up with a grunt. He was
woozy with loss of blood. *Hope this parking structure is
on a busy street.* Maybe they could flag down a passing
Samaritan.

"On your feet, soldier," she ordered, putting as much
grit in her voice as she could and pulling on his good arm.
He managed to get his feet under him and shoved himself
up. His leather breeches were soaked with blood on one
side under a long rip in the leather. She pulled his arm over
her shoulder. Could she do this? If he fainted, it was all
over. She staggered as he leaned against her and she put her
arm around his waist, slender for the width of his shoulders. They took a few tottering steps. Abruptly he stopped.

"What's the deal?" She tried to tug him forward. Like
that was happening. He just braced his feet, peering
around. He spied his bloody sword and pulled her over to
retrieve it. He almost toppled over on her as he straightened.

"Okay, you've got your sword." He gripped the grue-
some weapon as though it was salvation. There was some

kind of engraving on the blade. "No more stops." They staggered to the elevator. When the doors opened, white showed around his pupils. No elevators in whenever he was from. "Trust me. We need the elevator." Like he could understand her. But he let her drag him inside. When the doors closed, his lips went grim. She punched *Lobby*. The result of her disastrous foray into history braced his feet wide and brandished his sword as they rose through five floors. Yeah, elevators felt weird even if you realized what was happening.

The first thing that greeted them when the doors opened was red and white cycling lights across an asphalt drive in front of a huge building blazing with light. The guy stiffened and held up the wavering sword. Two ambulances were backed up to wide glass automatic doors under a sign that shouted: *Emergency Room* into the cold night air. It was drizzling.

"I . . . I know this place," Lucy whispered. It was San Francisco General. They had come back through time to the parking lot in front of the only trauma unit in the city.

How wild was that? Had she been thinking about that at the moment the machine slung them forward? Whatever. The General was just what her guy needed now.

"Hey!" she yelled to two paramedics just pushing their empty gurney out the doors. "Help me. This guy is bleeding."

One thing about paramedics, they decide quickly and they don't waste any time following through. One big blond ran across the asphalt, dashing in front of a car on its way to the parking structure, and the other one pushed his gurney over at a trot. Her time traveler started to put up a struggle. "It's for your own good!" she yelled. The paramedics finally wrestled him onto the gurney as he weakened. She put a hand on his chain mail. "It's all good," she said, softer this time. He looked up at her. Even in this light she could see that his eyes were really blue. He was breathing hard, but under her hand she felt him stop his struggle. When one paramedic tried to take his sword, her Beowulf guy growled something and gripped the hilt.

"Better let him keep it," Lucy advised. She lifted the blade to lay it on the gurney.

"Hey, was this some kind of reenactment?" The blond pushed the gurney over the asphalt. The other pulled and steadied it. "This chain mail is really authentic looking."

"Reenactments hardly ever result in actual blood," the other observed as they rushed the patient in through the emergency room doors.

"Got a live one, ladies. Ready, camera, action." The blond pushed the gurney past the women at the registration desk and through the big double doors to the emergency room. Lucy trailed after them in time to see the patient roll his head and try to sit up.

"Bay three." A big black nurse in green scrubs pointed. "Doctor! Trauma."

The paramedic at the big guy's head pulled him back down. "Take it easy."

A doctor stuck his head out of a curtained bay. "Type him and get an IV going. Epinephrine. How's our blood supply?"

"Depends on his type." The black nurse directed people who appeared from everywhere. "Page a gas passer," she ordered a young girl.

"I . . . I'm O positive, if you need blood," Lucy said into the hubbub.

"That's good," the big nurse said, but her attention was elsewhere. "Let's get those wounds prepped. I want a tourniquet ready for his leg just in case." She beckoned impatiently to a harried tech pushing a crash cart.

Lucy watched with wide eyes as orderlies and nurses swarmed her guy and began pulling off the chain mail.

They cut off a sleeveless leather jerkin sort of thing he was wearing and then his shirt. Another pulled off his boots and cut the leather strips that held his breeches on. One ripped open some sterile packaging and produced a needle. The big man started to struggle again at the sight of the needle. He was shouting in what sounded like a Scandinavian language again.

"Hey!" an orderly yelled as he took a balled fist in the eye.

"Get me some gas," the doctor shouted as a nurse pulled on his gloves. "I want this guy out now!" Another man in green ran up and pulled down a plastic mask as he checked some dials. The mask was shoved over the patient's face. He struggled harder, right until he went limp.

A tech tightened some rubber tubing around her guy's bare thigh just at the groin.

"Don't tie the tourniquet, for God's sake," the big nurse snapped. "He'll lose the leg. Leave it loose, so it's there if we hit an artery."

Lucy started forward as though she could help. The big nurse strode over, took her by the shoulders, and firmly turned her around. "You," she said to the paramedics. "Take her outside."

The blond paramedic took Lucy's arm and guided her back out to the registration area. Lucy noticed for the first time that there were several gurneys in the hallway with patients on them. "They got him now. They know what to do. He couldn't be in a better place."

"You just fill out the paperwork. Let them do the tough stuff," the other one said. They sat her down in front of a tired-looking Asian girl behind a glass barrier with a round hole for speaking and a slot at the bottom. "We're outta here."

"Good luck to you." They disappeared. Lucy was left staring at the expectant Asian girl.

Paperwork. On a time traveler.
Not good.

The girl's nameplate said: *Bernice*. Not exactly Asian, but in San Francisco she could be a fourth-generation immigrant. Bernice pushed a clipboard through the slot. "Just fill these out."

"Well, uh, that's going to be a problem." The truth wasn't going to do anybody any good here. It might get her locked up, with people feeding her happy pills.

"Just the basics. You don't have to know his Social Security number or anything. Did they give you his personal effects? An insurance card from his wallet would be great."

Lucy was tempted to say she'd just found him somewhere in an alley. He had no ID. He could be a homeless person. But with no connection to him, they'd never let her see him, and she had to keep him close until she could get him fixed up and back to his time. Okay. She'd make up a connection. And how to explain the chain mail and the very big sword? Best to go with the paramedic's first impression. Reenactment.

"He's a cousin visiting from . . . from . . ." *Someplace obscure.* "From Finland. I don't know what kind of insurance they have there." Was Finland a socialized-medicine state? The girl frowned. Lucy rushed on. "I'd be glad to guarantee payment for his care, though." She wasn't sure how charity cases worked, but she didn't want them kicking him out if he couldn't pay. "I'll give you a credit card." She began digging through her bag.

"Social Services can contact his family and find out the details. I'm sure you won't be on the hook for it." But she took the credit card. She ran it through the machine.

Lucy glanced around at the waiting room full of old people of several nationalities, mothers with crying babies, Mission District denizens looking entirely zoned out.

Those patients on the gurneys must have been waiting for admission. "You're really busy."

"Tuesday nights are usually slow, but tomorrow being St. Patrick's Day, we're almost up to weekend busy. I wouldn't want to be here if St. Patrick's Day was on a weekend. We're the official knife and gun club."

What did she mean, St. Patrick's Day? Lucy concentrated on filling out the forms. At least she could manage the date. She had that one memorized. November 9, 2009.

"Okay, we're good." Bernice handed the card back.

Lucy wrote "Bjorn Knudsen" in the space for the name on the form. That sounded Finnish. Knudsen was the name of the local dairy that made her favorite ice cream. Now for a town. She couldn't think. *Make one up. Helgard. Yeah. Why not?* "I can't remember his street address."

"We'll get details from him when they're done with him."

Good luck with that. "I can give you my info. He's staying with me." Was that a mistake?

"Put that down under the 'Responsible Party' section."

Lucy printed her info carefully. She shoved the clipboard back through the glass.

Bernice scanned the sheet. "You put down the wrong date." She looked up at Lucy, curious. "It's March 16." She raised her brows at Lucy's blank look. "St. Patrick's Day tomorrow?"

Lucy felt her stomach drop. She opened her mouth, but nothing came out.

"Two thousand ten," Bernice said slowly, careful now, as though she was dealing with a crazy person. "You . . . uh . . . lost a few months there."

Lucy managed a shaky smile. "Oh. Of course it is. I . . . I guess I'm more shaken up by all this than I thought." She not only hadn't come back to the place from which she'd left. She also had lost four months of time. Brad must be crazy with worry. She'd better call him. And he was just the one to help her get her time-traveling companion back to his own year. Of course her phone had no charge. "You have some pay phones around here?"

"Sure. Down by the cafeteria." Bernice pointed down a hallway absently as she changed the date on the form.

"Thanks."

Lucy headed down the hall following the overhead signs to the cafeteria. She spotted the phones. But suddenly she felt as though she wanted to vomit. She held out her hands. They were shaking. She needed to sit down, pronto. She headed to the cafeteria, filled with neon lights too bright on orange and purple plastic furniture. Enough to make her stomach turn flip-flops. She sat in the nearest chair and put her head down. Shock. She was just shocked by all this traveling through time and battles and bringing back a half-dead warrior and lying to everybody.

She took deep breaths until she felt like sitting up. She needed something in her stomach, even hospital food. She bought some onion soup and a Diet Coke and loaded up on crackers. She sat at a table by some windows, black now with night. The soup wasn't half-bad. Or maybe it was the Diet Coke that settled her.

She found herself staring at her reflection in the dark window as if it were that of a stranger. She was short and . . . curvy. That was the kind word for it and the main reason she always wore black. Why hadn't she gotten her father's wiry build along with his height? Brad was a runner and was always urging her to take it up, presumably to transform her into someone with a runner's body like his. Wasn't going to happen. What she did instead was walk. She had walked the hills and hollows of San Francisco as if she was looking for something ever since her father died. She just didn't know what she was looking for.

Her hair wasn't the dark auburn fashionable at the moment, either. It was red. Really red. Carrot red. Well, darker than carrot. But still really, really red. And curly. She wore it long because she'd grown tired of watching some poor stylist try to make something of it. Now it tumbled to her waist and she could trim it herself. She always wore it in a long braid to confine it at least, but curling tendrils popped out around her face, especially in San Francisco's damp weather. And then there were her freckles. If you were a redhead with very pale skin you couldn't escape them. She may have gotten the Italian name from her father, but her looks were from her Northern European mother, dead now for . . . what? Sixteen years.

A wave of shame washed over Lucy. Once she would have known to the hour how long it was since her mother had succumbed to ovarian cancer. Sometimes Lucy missed her as sharply as if she'd died yesterday. Lucy missed her mother's balance. Her life had been slowly gyroscoping out of her control since she was fourteen. Her father had tried so hard to make her into his own image even though she had no interest in physics. Then, with his death, everything just seemed to fall apart. Maybe because she had no purpose to replace the one her father tried to give her. Brad too. But Brad was easier to resist than her father. True, she liked her work, searching across history and cultures for connections between people, their thoughts, their emotions, through the books they wrote. It wasn't that. It just didn't seem like enough.

"Miss?"

Lucy looked up to find the big black nurse in green scrubs from the ER.

"We stabilized your cousin. He's going into surgery now."

At least he wasn't lying on a gurney in the hall. "Will he be okay?"

"The surgeon is very good. Does lots of shoulders. We'll admit him afterward. You can be there when he wakes up. Seeing a familiar face might keep him calm. He's a fighter."

"I'd like that. Do you have enough blood for him?"

The nurse patted Lucy's arm. "You go down to the basement and tell them you want to donate for a patient going into surgery. Give his name. It'll make you feel better."

Lucy nodded. Calling Brad could wait. She was responsible for ripping this guy out of his own time. The least she could do was donate blood for him.

As she came back up to the emergency waiting room, she sported a sticky label on her chest that said she'd donated blood today. She should go back down to the cafeteria and call Brad, but she could hardly think, she was so tired. She wandered back into the crowded waiting room. Here, too, the lights were too fluorescent and the magenta and orange flowered carpet relentlessly cheery. A large industrial clock over the reception area said it was now nine.

The problem with calling Brad was that she'd be calling in Casey, too. She didn't trust that guy as far as she could throw him. Would they understand the danger of kidnapping a man whose deeds might be an integral part of history? Brad would think of him as a prize. He'd want to "debrief" him (and her) when they should be getting the guy back before his absence changed things too much. And there was a chance Brad and Casey wouldn't want to risk using the machine again.

But wouldn't taking him back, all repaired and dosed with antibiotics and germs he got in a modern hospital, maybe change the course of events, too? She had so blithely used the machine because she thought it was some kind of destiny, she hadn't thought what could happen. And now she couldn't think what was right to do. She had to

be sure what she should do before she called Brad, or he
and Casey would just take over and do whatever they
wanted with the guy. She tried to think. It was all so con-
fusing. . . .

"Miss . . ." The black nurse was shaking Lucy's shoulder.
"Your cousin is out of Recovery. We're taking him up to a
room."

"Is he okay?" Lucy rubbed her eyes. She hadn't meant
to fall asleep. The waiting-room clock now showed nearly
midnight.

"Groggy and weak. He lost more blood than we could
replace. But the doctor said the surgery was successful.
He should be back in action and ready for physical therapy in a few weeks. He looks like he's normally healthy
as a horse," the nurse laughed. "Say, where's he from?
Nobody could figure out what language he's speaking."

"He's . . . he's from a remote village in Denmark."
Were there remote villages in Denmark? It was a pretty
small place. Uh-oh. She'd told the receptionist he was
from Finland.

"Well, go on up to Room Fifteen-oh-six and talk to him
as he comes out of it."

Yeah. Like she spoke Beowulf, or whatever it was.

Galen Valgarssen opened his eyes slowly. At first he
couldn't make out anything. His vision was blurred. The
place seemed to be all white. He hadn't thought Valhalla
would be white. The skalds told of a jolly great hall with
wenches and drinking and a huge fire over which roasted
haunches of venison. His shoulder throbbed. And his
thigh. Wounds were supposed to be miraculously healed
every night in Valhalla. Well, maybe it took a while. He
was lying in a bed with the head raised. It was night outside. The window was black. But inside the room a round

disc by his bed gave off a cone of harsh white light very unlike candles or oil lamps. The place smelled foul, like urine and something acrid. The blankets were thin but tucked tightly around him. It made him feel like a prisoner. This wasn't his idea of Valhalla at all.

Maybe he was in Hel's domain instead—a wintry land below the surface of the earth, according to the Old Religion. That fit with the harsh white and hard surfaces, even if he really wasn't cold. But he had been an honorable man and a brave one who died in battle. He expected Valhalla. He turned his head. In another bed a very old man with skin like yellow, wrinkled wax breathed laboriously. That one had not died a warrior's death.

A clear bag hung above Galen on a metal pole, a flexible sort of tube going into his left arm. That wrist was circled with a leather cuff lined with fleece and chained with short links to the metal frame of the bed. His other arm was held to his chest with an elaborate sling, immobilizing it as surely as a shackle. Panic surged up from his gut. Now he remembered. The cursed man in the soft green clothes had tortured him by poking needles into him. They had made him breathe foul air through a mask over his nose and mouth until he passed out. He was definitely in Hel's realm. He peered down. He was dressed in a thin tunic, pulled over his heavily bandaged shoulder, under the sling.

He had to get out of here. He yanked the chain with his good arm. . . .

"Whoa there, guy, steady."

The woman had braided red hair and fair skin and very green eyes, not unlike some of his people. He couldn't understand her, but she took the hand of his shackled wrist and stroked his forearm, making soothing sounds. Her hands were delicate, with very clean nails worn longer than any woman he knew. She smelled like blood, though. Her clothes were black, in stark contrast to all the white around her. He remembered her now. She had appeared at the battle with the great contraption made of brass mill wheels like a Valkyrie come to take him away, and Egil had attacked her, so he had to defend her, and then . . . then he must have blacked out. When he woke she helped him to . . . wherever he was. It was probably his blood he smelled on her. "Are you Valkyrie? Am I dead?"

The only word she apparently understood was Valkyrie. Her eyes lighted up when he said it. A Valkyrie who didn't speak Norse? She shook her head. "Not Valkyrie." She smiled. When she smiled, he thought he might be in Valhalla after all. You'd want your Valkyrie to smile like that. She put her hand on her breast. "Lucy. Lucy Rossano."

"Galen Valgarssen."

"Not exactly the name I gave you." She shrugged and raised her brows. "Finn? Norse?"

Finn and Norse he understood. He nodded. She was asking his nationality. "Danir and Saxon." Half of each, curse be it on him.

"You are Viking?"

That he got. He nodded. "Half."

She looked frustrated. "I wish I spoke Danish."

Something to do with Danir. He had many questions he would ask her. He rolled his eyes around the room. "Where is this place?"

She shrugged again to say she didn't understand.

He tried Englisc. "*Hwaēr es min sweord?*"

She looked surprised. "Your sword?"

She understood Englisc. This was good. "*Bring hit to mē,*" he ordered.

"I don't think that's a good idea."

That was no Englisc he had ever heard. He recognized two words—"think" and "good." He shook his head to signal that she wasn't being clear. "*Unsael thes racetēāg.*" But she only echoed his frustrated shake of the head. Did she or did she not speak Englisc? Or would she just not release his shackle?

The man who had tortured him earlier appeared behind her. Galen started to sit forward and demand that she release him, but pain washed over him and he almost fainted. She made a gentle shushing sound and pushed him down, smiling reassuringly. She began talking to the man very rapidly. He could understand nothing. That could not be Englisc. Were they deciding how to kill him? Were they discussing tortures? He balled his hands into fists. He was helpless here, weak with his wounds, bound to the bed, and unable to understand what they said.

Suddenly, from out of the haze of unknown words, several rang very clear. The man said, "*Umerus humerus.*" The Latin word for shoulder. Then he heard the word for loss of blood. They spoke Latin.

"You speak the tongue of the Christ Cult?" he asked in Latin.

The man didn't stop talking, but the beautiful woman turned to him, surprise and relief glowing in her face. "I study—studied—Latin. I speak a little," she said with a horrible accent.

Galen sighed in relief. This would make things easier. "Good. Is this the Christ Cult heaven? Are you an angel?"

She looked amused. "No."

"Well, whoever you are, get me my sword now."

"That is a bad . . . idea." She turned to the man in green. "He speaks Latin, Doctor." He recognized only the words "he"and "speaks."

"I've called the police," the man in green said, whatever that meant. "They'll be here shortly. You can translate their interview, since I'm sure none of the city's finest speak either Danish or Latin. He can check out tomorrow in the early afternoon. I'll leave prescriptions at the nurses' station. He should see a primary-care doctor for follow-up tomorrow." He turned and left.

Whatever the man said, it made the girl look worried. "What is it?" he asked in Latin.

She shook her head. "Someone will . . . want . . . to know who hurt you."

"That bastard Egil," he snorted. "He never could have laid an axe on me if not for that chariot of iron wheels appearing out of nowhere."

She looked appalled. "Did I change . . . the . . . the battle only by being there?"

Of course she did. He chuffed a bitter laugh. "*Ja*." But he had more important concerns at this point. Like where he was. "What is this place if it is not Valhalla or Christ's heaven?"

She pressed her lips together. "That is difficult." She chewed on one of those very clean fingernails and finally shrugged. "Where was the battle?"

She must mean "is," not "was," since the battle was no doubt going on without him even now. She spoke haltingly and sometimes had to search for words. "Anglia, in the Danelaw," he answered. "Egil Ingvansen rebels against Guthrum's son."

"And when was it?"

"Are you feebleminded, woman? It was, *is* 912 as Christians count years."

She took his hand. Hers were soft, uncallused. She had not done the hard work of a serving maid or a peasant tilling the land. Was she nobility or perhaps a prostitute or concubine? No decent woman would wear clothes that clung so to her body. Or maybe she wore the garb of a sorcerer. For if she was not angel or Valkyrie, she must be a *wicce,* to own such a chariot of bronze wheels. "Listen

to me. This is the year of Christ 2010," she said. "And you
are in the . . . land beyond Iceland. Uh . . . Vineland your
people call it."

He stared at her in shock. "You lie. There is no land
beyond Iceland."

"Oh. The discovery of Vineland was after your time.
But there is land beyond Iceland."

"Why did you take me here? Get me back to the battle."

"It was a . . . mistake. I did not . . . What is the word? . . .
Intend it."

"*Where* is my sword?" Whether she lied or whether he
was truly somewhere no man had any right to be, he was
in deep trouble.

"I know not." She looked around, then went to a tall
cupboard and opened it. "Here, and your clothing." Then
she murmured in her own tongue, "What's left of it." He
got the words "what" and "of" and "it," but not the sense.

"Bring them, woman. I must return to the battle."

He saw by the mulish set of her jaw that she was about
to protest when two men in strange dark clothing with
short sleeves and golden broaches walked into the room.

Great. Police. Just what she needed. She couldn't have
them arresting the Viking for vagrancy or something.
She'd never get him back to 912 if he was sitting in jail.
And he sure looked like a homeless person. Tangled
blondish hair with crazy braids in each side, and a close-
clipped beard—he had no address, no money, no labels in
his clothes. He would give his name differently than he
was registered. He was a mystery they'd love to unravel.

"Officers." She smiled. *Deceit, thy name is woman.*
She was about to lie through her teeth to the police. Way
worse than lying to the registration girl. "Thank you so
much for coming." The nurse who had escorted them

pulled a curtain around the bed that held an old man and left. Lucy turned back to Galen, meaning to tell him who these visitors were, but instead she just stood there, blinking. Even weak and woozy from the anesthetic, he exuded strength and masculinity. What did they call it in martial arts movies? *Sai.* Of course he was a Viking. What else would he be? Just now he was gritting his teeth and looking very dangerous. She smiled and patted his hand. Wow. That sent shivers through her. Then she turned to the police. "This is my cousin Bjorn Knudsen from Finland. Do either of you speak Finn?" she asked with feigned hope. "No? Neither do I, but we get by in Latin. I'll translate."

"Looks like he ran into a little trouble." The fresh-faced young Hispanic officer flipped open a notebook.

"Gangbangers broke up a battle reenactment down in Golden Gate Park. Bjorn and his friends were doing the Battle of . . . of Anglia."

"You were there?" The other officer seemed to be the senior partner. His dark hair receded on each side of his forehead, and his face was pocked with old acne scars.

"Yes, I saw it all." At least that was true.

"Anybody else hurt?"

Oh, lots of people. But she couldn't tell them that. "I don't know. These guys took weapons. They attacked Ga—Bjorn. Then they squealed out in those low-slung cars. When I saw how bad he was bleeding, I hailed a cab and yelled to the driver to get him to the General."

"Front desk says no insurance, no ID."

"No wallets allowed in reenactments. His backpack got left in the park. I'll vouch for him, and I told the hospital I'd pay for his care. He's staying at my place." She took out her wallet and showed her driver's license. "That address is correct. And here's a card for my store."

The young officer took down the information while

the older one asked, "Did you see what kind of a weapon was used? "

"It was an axe." The shudder she gave was real as she remembered that blade coming down on the man lying in the bed over there. "They took it off one of the other reen-actors."

"Ouch." The young officer winced.

"Did you get a look at any of them, Miss Rossano?"

"It was just getting dark. Everyone was packing it in for the day. And it all happened so fast. I'm afraid I couldn't identify anyone."

"Does your cousin have such a weapon?"

Lucy recognized the trap. She sighed. The staff prob-ably already told them. She didn't dare lie. "He has a sword."

"And would it be in this closet?" The one with the scars was already opening the door. He whistled, then took out his handkerchief and picked the sword up just under the hilt. Even in this dim light it looked fearsome. A hilt wrapped with leather over a bloody blade engraved with writing of some kind. Behind her, Galen growled and clanked his restraint. The guy sure wasn't helping. Could he possibly seem not crazy for a minute? She put a hand on his chest to steady him. The feel of hard muscle be-neath the thin hospital gown was . . . interesting.

Now the one with acne scars had gone hard. "Looks like this thing's done some damage. Like maybe assault with a deadly weapon."

"That blood is fake." She managed a half laugh. "Re-enactment. Remember?"

"We'll see about that." This from the young officer with the notebook.

"In the meantime we'll be looking for someone else in an emergency room tonight who might have been on the receiving end of it," his partner added. "If your cousin was engaged in more than reenactment, he'll be prosecuted."

They'd find out the blood was real, though no one would turn up who'd been wounded.

"Don't leave town, Miss Rossano. Or Mr. Knudsen, either." The young one snapped his notebook shut. "We'll be in touch."

She was going to get in *so* much trouble over this. Even if they didn't arrest Galen, they'd want to ask him more questions. And, if she could get him back where he belonged, he wouldn't be around, or traceable. If he was still here, then they wouldn't like his answers. *Loony bin for him for sure. Great. Just great.*

The two turned out of the room, taking the sword with them. Behind her, Galen roared.

"They shall not take my sword!"

The officers turned in surprise. He spoke in Latin, but the sentiment was clear. Lucy shrugged apologetically. "Authentic period weapons are hard to come by."

"He can pick it up down at the precinct, *if* we clear it of being involved in a crime." The acne-scarred officer frowned. "If not, you'd better find him a lawyer who speaks Finn." The officers closed the door behind them.

Lucy let out a breath she hadn't realized she'd been holding.

"You let them take my sword." Galen was outraged.

"You are . . . fortunate they did not take you also."

"Loose this shackle," he commanded. "I need my sword."

"What would you do, fight with them?" Was that the right word for fight? Her study of Latin in order to translate texts wasn't exactly "Conversational Latin for Time Travelers." And he spoke it with a rhythm and pronunciation very unlike hers. Possibly because Latin was a dead language and no one now living knew how it sounded.

That was also probably the only reason they could understand each other at all. Latin was a language frozen in time. She noted the rebellious look in his eyes. He was so in over his head. If he attacked the officers, they'd just pull their guns and shoot him. He wouldn't even know what had happened. He'd be no match for Colonel Casey, either.

She was suddenly certain that Casey would lock Galen up. He would not be interested in just letting a living, breathing Viking go back where he came from. And the effect of snatching him out of his time, losing whatever things he would have done in his life, outweighed the danger of sending him back. She made a decision. She'd have to risk it, hospital germs and all. And she had to do it by herself.

"You must go to your time. You want that, yes?"

"*Ja*. This is a place for feebleminded discards of the gods. I go back to the battle now." He tried to sit up and went white as the pain struck him. His breathing got shallow and sweat broke out on his forehead. He'd never make it out the door.

"I don't think so." That was a problem. Someone was going to discover the time machine sitting in the bottom of the parking structure, and soon. They must use it tonight.

"This place is evil," he insisted. But he lay back down, causing him to wince anew.

"I'll get a nurse," she muttered in English. She left him looking disgusted with himself.

She found a slight woman with mouse-colored hair writing in charts at the nurses' station. "Excuse me, ma'am, my cousin seems to be in quite a bit of pain."

"Oh, the big guy? Let me do something about that." She checked the chart and then went to a locked cabinet and got out a vial and a syringe. "He's one tough cookie.

Put up a real fight in the recovery room." She glanced to Lucy. "Sorry about the restraints. Must be hard when you don't know the language and people are doing painful things to you."

Lucy hadn't thought much about that. She'd been thinking he was a disaster for her and possibly for the fabric of time, but she hadn't thought about how he might be feeling about this whole thing. Pretty insensitive of her.

"What's his name?"

"Bjorn Knudsen."

"Where's he from?"

"Denmark." *Uh-oh*. She was losing track of her lies.

The nurse bustled out from the station and across the hall. "I'll have to put it on my list of 'must-see' places." She grinned at Lucy and pushed in through the door to Galen's room. "We cleaned him up as best we could in Recovery, but orderlies and nurses will be fighting over bath duty tomorrow before he's discharged."

Galen eyed the nurse and her syringe with glaring rage. "Will you join them in torturing me?" he accused Lucy as he tugged in vain at the restraint.

"She will stop your pain," Lucy said. The nurse opened a valve on Galen's IV and stuck in the syringe, plunged, and twisted it shut.

"There. Should take effect almost immediately." She smiled at Galen. "That'll hold you for a few hours, handsome. Get some rest."

"Will it put him out entirely?"

The nurse shook her head. "It's just Demerol. It'll make him groggy. With what he's been through, he'll probably sleep." She blew out a breath and shook her head as she took one more longing look at Galen before she left. To the police he probably looked homeless, but to the nurse he looked good enough to eat. Women were always suckers for blue eyes. And cheekbones. His hair was lightened by the sun so it was a dozen shades of light brown and blond. The narrow braids could be interpreted as exotic, not crazy. His arms were big and muscled under the thin hospital gown, his skin tanned. Lucy could imagine him at the prow of a dragon ship, stripped to the waist.

What was she thinking? She shook herself mentally. "Feel better?"

"Flax in my head," he slurred. "No weapon . . ."

"Rest. Then we'll go."

"Your promise, wench?" But his eyes were closing.

Was that the Latin word for . . . for wench? Or had he just called her a slut? "The name is Lucy, not wench." God, she was glad she hadn't lived in 912.

"Looshy . . . ," and he was out.

Chapter Three

"Okay, sleeping beauty. Time to wake up."

Lucy turned his head toward her by his bearded chin and watched his eyelids flutter. It was four in the morning. She dared not wait longer if she was going to take him back to 912 tonight. She'd filled his prescriptions at the all-night hospital pharmacy: a batch of antibiotics and a big bottle of Vicodin 750s for pain. She'd bought some bandages and surgical tape and some hydrogen peroxide to send back with him. Who knew what dirty rags he'd end up binding his wounds with in 912? Even the antibiotics wouldn't help him if he didn't keep them clean.

The question was whether she had to take him back herself. She'd had four hours to think about it. She sure didn't want to. He could go alone and the machine would come back to the present in two or three weeks. But who knew what could happen to the machine in that time? Losing Leonardo's machine would be a tragedy.

Then there was the question of exactly what time to return Galen to. If she went back to before he was wounded, would there be two of him in the battle? That couldn't be good. All the time travel stories or movies agreed that having two of you in one place and time was very bad.

Great. Using sci-fi as your only guide? She really was in unknown territory.

But she couldn't send him back to a time later than the battle, either. What if the locals thought he had died of his wounds instead of disappearing? When he reappeared they'd think he'd been resurrected or something. She didn't want to be responsible for starting a new religion. Changing things in ways she couldn't foresee was the most frightening thing of all.

"Do you want to go from this place?" She switched to Latin.

"*Ja.* We go now." He blinked away his sleep, though he was still groggy.

She bent over his forearm and carefully peeled back the adhesive tape that held the needle flat. "Do not move." She slid the needle out. A drop of blood oozed. She tore off a little bit of gauze from the roll in her bag and pressed it against the needle-stick, then sealed the tape across it again. "Not bad if I do say so," she muttered in English as she surveyed her work.

Galen clanked his chain. "Unbuckle this, woman," he ordered.

"Don't you ever say 'please' and 'thank you'?" she grumbled as she worked the leather straps. She couldn't manage the sentiment in Latin. When he was free, he rubbed his wrist, though the restraint had not been tight. Maybe he just wanted to rub away his helplessness.

He sat up, carefully this time, his jaw clenching. Boy, she sure hoped he could make it out to the time machine. She let down the side rail of the bed and got him sitting on the edge. The nurses had put blue socks with rubber treads on his feet to keep them warm. He looked over his shoulder. The hospital gown tied loosely in the back but would leave a clear view of back and buttocks. That gown

would be no match for a San Francisco March. She turned
to the closet.

Behind her, she heard a grunt. *"Hwāet unnytt hemeth
is this?"* She turned just time to see him rip the hospital
gown from his back with his good hand. "Bring my clothes,"
he ordered.

Lucy just stood there, a blush creeping up to her face.
Even marred by the bandages on his shoulder and thigh
and the red and bluish bruises that were forming in several
places, the man's body was . . . well . . . impressive. Broad
chest, heavily muscled, and lightly covered with blond hair.
His abs undulated across his belly. His thighs were massive
and . . . and he was very well endowed in the reproductive
department as well. There were old scars here and there—
hip, chest, right arm. He'd been in battles before.

He raised his brows at her and then a self-satisfied little smile crossed his lips.

She shook herself and turned away. Damn that little
smile. The phrase that came to mind was "cocksure of
himself." "They cut your shirt. It's useless," she said by
way of punishment for the smile. She rummaged through
the closet. "You have only your breeches." She put the
armload of leather and thongs on the bed beside him. It
looked like they'd cut the thongs near the knots, so there
was probably enough leather to rewrap them. He'd better
be able to dress himself, because she sure wasn't going to
do it. She turned back for his boots and pretended to
brush the clots of dried mud from them. They were soft
leather that bunched at the ankle and were soaked with
blood. She could hear him grunting and breathing hard.
But, finally daring to glance over her shoulder, she saw he
was standing with his sliced and bloody leathers on trying to tie the laces to the crotch piece at his waist with
one hand. At least the important parts were covered.

"I'll do that." She set the boots next to him and took the leather thongs. Her knuckles brushed his belly as she tied a bow, and that brought the blush up again. It also brought feelings between her legs that made her hate herself. She looked up to find him glaring at her. "What?"

"Not a manly knot."

At least that's what she thought he said. "Then you tie it." She held up his leather jerkin, but it was stiff with blood and cut in several places. She sighed.

"No need for shirt or tunic," he said.

"It is cold here."

"I have been colder."

He had stepped into a boot and she tugged it up his leg. "San Francisco is very cold."

"Colder than Danmork or the lands of the Volga River?" He stepped into the other boot.

Well, that put things in perspective. She pulled his boot up ruthlessly. "Now we go." She hoped he didn't faint on her. She took his good elbow, and in spite of his bravado, he leaned on her. Since the room was just across from the nurses' station, she'd have to brave the hospital staff.

"Where do you think you're going?" the mousy-haired nurse asked, hands on hips. Other nurses and orderlies either behind the counter or down the hall turned to look.

"This place is making him crazy. The doctor said he could go home tomorrow, and I think we'd better head out a little early."

"You're the one who's crazy. He was in shock when he came in. He's had surgery. He needs to stabilize before he's discharged."

"He's strong as an ox and he was fussing at those restraints," she pleaded. "Really, he'll be better off at home. The receptionist has all my information." She fished in her bag. "Call her if you want. We're not trying to sneak out without paying." She could feel Galen holding himself ramrod straight beside her. He'd better not collapse. . . .

"Let me call a doctor."

"The doctor won't say anything to change our minds. You can't hold him. He'll sign whatever you want." Could Galen even write his name?

The nurse pursed her lips. She knew Lucy was right. "Okay," she finally said. "It's on your head." She fished out a clipboard and slapped a pen on it. "You're signing out against medical advice. You know what that means?"

"Yup. You aren't responsible for anything that happens." Lucy signed her name on the form with a flourish.

Before she could hand the clipboard to Galen the nurse snatched it back. "He doesn't speak English and I don't have forms in Danish, so his signature wouldn't be legal. You're the one on the hook for this." She motioned an orderly to collect a wheelchair.

"Okay." Lucy handed the clipboard back. Galen didn't put up a fuss at the wheelchair. In fact, he looked relieved. At least they might make it out to the parking lot.

"Get him to his primary-care doctor today for follow-up," the nurse called after them.

Lucy waved acknowledgment. Galen was so glad to be leaving he made no protest at the elevator, though he held tightly to the arms of the chair. Out through the thinning crowds of the emergency room. There were no ambulances or cars to dodge. At four in the morning, the place was finally quieting down. Now to get rid of the orderly. "I'll take it from here," she said, smiling.

"Can you get him into the car?"

She nodded. "And I'll bring the chair back to the ER." Almost before he had saluted and disappeared, Galen pushed himself up to standing. They left the chair where it was and headed across the driveway to the parking structure.

Galen stopped so suddenly she stumbled. "We will get my sword now."

Oh, good. Not this again. "The . . . the army has your sword."

"I need my sword to go back to the battle." His lips were set in a stubborn line.

"It is far. They are many. Therefore—no sword. " She could be as stubborn as he was, even in broken Latin. "Do you want to go to your time, or no?"

He gritted his teeth and glared at her for a long moment, then started across the asphalt.

It seemed a really long way to the parking-structure elevator. Galen's breathing was getting ragged. The machine had begun to seem like a figment of her imagination. She couldn't believe the elevator doors would open and there it would be, on the bottom level of a San Francisco hospital parking structure.

But it was. Both she and Galen stood and stared at it, gleaming in the flickering fluorescent light. Lucy swallowed. They'd go back to a time after the battle. Better chance him looking like a miracle than running into himself. And she had to go with him. She couldn't in good conscience send him back alone. *And* Brad would kill her if she left the machine back in 912 for very long.

Brad. She tried to imagine Brad mourning the loss of his friend. All she could see in her mind's eye was his triumph that the machine worked, his obsession with why it hadn't come back in the next minutes. Boy, that would be driving him crazy. And now he didn't have either the machine or the book that told how to build it. He'd be kicking himself for experimenting prematurely. He'd chastise Casey for letting her take the book with her. Casey would be on Brad's ass to figure out how to get the machine back and keep them both out of hot water with whoever was funding their project.

She had sure screwed this up. She'd brought back not a small piece of cloth or some kind of writing that could be dated to prove she'd been back in time, but a Viking, for God's sake, a real, difficult, actual man who was very obsessed with weapons.

So she had to take him back and pick up that souvenir, then get the machine back to the lab in the present. Or close. She'd missed by four months the last time. She'd contact Brad when she had put things right and Galen was safely back where he belonged.

"Are you ready?" She looked up at Galen.

His blue eyes examined the machine. He nodded silently.

"Then we go." She knelt beside the power source and started flipping switches. The lunch box began to hum. She motioned Galen to her side. "Hold to me." She moved to the lever.

He stood behind her and put his good arm around her waist. She felt his warmth pressed against her back, acutely conscious that his torso was bare. "Here we go." She grabbed the huge diamond with both hands and pulled.

It came off in her hands and bounced to the cement, where it rolled away under the machine. The end of the lever, several prongs bent and broken, shot out a jagged blue streak of power. She gaped and they ducked and rolled to the hard cement. Galen grunted in pain. The blue bolt had barely missed them. Ozone drifted in the air, reminiscent of lighting. Gears, barely moving, ground to a stop. The parking structure was silent except for a faint sizzling sound from the lunch box. For the first time she noticed that it was dented.

"Odin's eye, what was that?" Galen gasped in what must be Norse. But she got the sense.

Lucy blinked. "Egil hit the . . ." She couldn't think of a word for lever or lunch box, so she just waved a hand toward them. ". . . with his weapon. The machine is . . . damaged." Was that the right word?

"But you made it come here."

"Maybe that's why I'm four months off," she muttered to herself. She got to her hands and knees and collected the diamond. "More damaged now," she said in Latin to Galen.

"What do we do?"

Lucy looked around. Galen was ashen and shivering. "We ask Brad to fix it." The sigh that thought elicited felt dusty.

"Who is this Brad?"

"My . . ." What was the word in Latin? "My friend."

Galen examined her face, reserve settling in his blue eyes. "Can he fix it?"

"I do not know." She made a decision. She had to get him someplace warm, and she was *not* going back into the hospital where she had spun a host of inconsistent lies. "We will go to my house and . . ." How to say this? "Call out to Brad." She might have just said "shout to Brad."

"Is your house far?" Galen must have realized his strength was waning.

"Across the city. We will take a . . ." No Latin word for cab. Or car for that matter. "We will hire a . . . cart." It was the closest she could come. He nodded and she pulled him to his feet with his good arm. Better hope there was a cab in front of the hospital at this hour.

Galen limped down the strangely paved road, leaning on the girl. He was half-glad the metal wheels had not worked. They might come down in the middle of the battle, with him wounded and without a weapon. He would not have lasted long. And Egil would kill the girl or keep her as a concubine slave. Galen wasn't sure what would be worse for her.

But to be stuck here . . . wherever here was, was equally bad. He looked up at the stark hall where they had stuck needles in him. It was impossibly tall and made of steel like his sword and glass like the little bottles noblewomen kept their scent in, great sheets of it. One got up and down such huge buildings not with stairs but with boxes that moved by themselves. Rooms were lighted by discs that glowed like the moon. Who built such miracles? Gods? But he had seen no gods there, only men and women who tortured him, and this girl.

They walked down a white paved path. He heard a roar and turned. A metal beast with glowing eyes rushed down on them. He crouched and thrust the girl behind him. She shrieked. But the beast passed without attacking them. As it went, he saw that a man sat inside it, both hands on a wheel. He straightened. It was no beast. "What was that?" he muttered.

The girl brushed herself off, looking disgusted. "It was a cart."

"That was no cart. It moved by itself without a horse."

"There is no Latin word for it. We call it a 'car.' Now come."

She grabbed his good arm and pulled him toward a "car," painted yellow with black letters and Arabic numbers and a lamp on the roof that glowed white. She raised her hand in salute, and the car growled like Fenris, the wolf who ate the world at Ragnarok, and its glowing eyes blinked open. It took all his courage to stand his ground.

"Where to, lady?" the wizened man who sat inside the beast asked.

The girl opened a door behind the man, and said, "Sixteen Thirty-two Filbert, a few blocks off Van Ness." She motioned Galen to get into the cart. He hesitated. To put himself in the grip of magic seemed . . . foolhardy. "You cannot walk," she said with a frown. "So enter." She didn't wait but sat on the seat and pulled her knees in, then scooted across the bench to make room for him.

He was at her mercy and he hated that. But what choice had he? He did not want to linger in a place where they chained him and stuck him with needles. Gingerly he sat and hauled his legs in. The place smelled like old smoke, body odor, and something greasy. She reached across him and pulled the door shut. "Turn up the heater, would you?" she asked the wizened man.

Immediately the cart moved off, picking up incredible speed. The noise whined up and down the scale. Galen braced himself on the seat ahead as the cart careened around a corner. His heart jumped into his throat. The thing would surely overturn and kill them all. But the woman called Lucy was very calm. She buckled a belt around her waist that kept her in place, then reached over and did the same for him. The man in the seat ahead of them began to whistle. Hot air came from somewhere. Apparently this terrifying experience was an everyday occurrence. Galen watched and became sure the man was controlling the cart with the wheel, for he turned and held it in the direction the cart turned. The cart appeared to be run by some kind of power generated in the vehicle itself rather than relying on a beast or a water-wheel.

Galen calmed enough to look out the window. The streets outside the glass were nearly empty, but occasionally another cart passed, going at equally incredible speeds. The halls were grander than any he had ever seen. Some were of familiar stone. Others were needles of black reflection that touched the sky. None were of wood. They towered everywhere. Colored lights blinked in squiggly designs, some of which looked almost like runes or the Latin alphabet. Some flashed lighted paintings of people real enough to capture their soul. The designs changed before his eyes. It felt like many people were shouting at him, competing for his attention.

This city must hold millions of people. It had very steep hills. The cart did not hesitate but went up and down the hills without appearing even to strain, except for a change in the noise it made. As they came over a hill, he saw the glint of black water some way away. Enclosed like this he couldn't smell the sea, but there it was. He could make out a gigantic bridge hung from a huge rope looped between towers, to hills on the other side of the water. Lights moved across the span. It looked like a spiderweb, delicate but strong. He had ordered his men to make such bridges, much to their amazement, when the Danir army needed to ford streams. He thought the design his own. But here was just such a bridge, and bigger than he could have imagined.

"Who built this bridge?" he asked the woman.

"I . . . I do not know. We call it 'Golden Gate.' It goes over the . . . the mouth of the bay." The name was not in Latin. She must not know the words for it. Her Latin was awful. It sounded almost like she said "gylden geat" in Englisc. That was a good name for a bridge over the mouth of a bay. She leaned over to see what he could see out his window. Her braid brushed his chest. It made his nipples pucker. And not with cold. She would be a welcome bed-mate after he had rested. "That island," she pointed, "is Alcatraz. It was a prison."

"There are many wharves."

"This . . . bay is a large port." Her Latin wasn't up to saying more.

The car careened down the hill, jolting his shoulder. He swallowed but managed not to make any sound.

"Next left," Lucy told the driver. "Three blocks down on the left corner." The car screeched to a halt. Lucy fumbled in her bag and came up with some dirty and wrinkled green paper she handed over the seat to the driver. "Keep the change."

Had she paid the driver only with this tattered paper? But he seemed to accept it willingly. "Thanks, lady, you're a peach," he said. Thanks. Was that related to the Saxon "thonc to thu"? It was tantalizing. He could recognize some words, no matter how wrong the rhythm was, and yet the language was not Englisc.

She opened her door and slid out, beckoning to him. He fumbled with the cursed belt with his good hand, but it didn't have a proper buckle.

"Sorry," she mumbled, and leaned in. The buckle released itself at her touch. He pushed himself out, ignoring the sear of pain in his thigh and shoulder. The night air slapped him after the warmth of the cart. Now he could smell the sea, along with bread baking somewhere and that greasy, oily smell again. The air did not smell clean. The woman ran to the glass doors and he staggered after her. His limbs felt like they weighed a hundredweight. This house was big, taking up what must be the length of four or so halls, but had only five levels. Not like the place where he had been tortured. Still it was taller than any building he knew. Windows poked out in bays over the street. Lucy punched some buttons labeled with Arabic numbers outside some glass, and a buzz sounded. She opened a door in the glass and dashed in.

It was warmer in here. She went to stand near two sets of doors he now recognized. He gritted his teeth and stepped into the claustrophobic box. As it rose, he noticed that the Arabic numbers lighted. They stopped at 5 and the door opened. He followed the girl down a dim hall. She took out a ring with strange keys on it and used it on a door at the end.

The girl turned the key this way and that, but the door did not open.

Suddenly she stepped back, struck by something.

"This might not be my apartment anymore," she whispered to herself in her own language. She looked up at Galen, and her green eyes were a little frightened. Then she straightened her back. "I'll have to wake Jake."

He reached out and grabbed her arm. "Who is this Jake?"

"A friend."

How many "friends" did she have? Women did not have male friends. Was she a prostitute, to have so many "friends"? She strode down the hall and banged on a door at the other end.

When no one answered, she called softly, "Jake, it's Lucy. I know you're awake. Open up." She stepped back, in clear view of a tiny peephole in the center of the door, and just waited. Galen leaned against the wall for support.

"He is not there."

"Oh, he's here." She folded her arms under her breasts. They swelled into her neckline. She *must* be a prostitute to dress so.

She was right. There was a clanking behind the door and then the knob turned. The door opened only a crack. A chain crossed the opening. A gnarled face appeared. "Lucy!" The door shut with a snap but opened wide a moment later. "Lucy, girl. Where have you been?" The man limped out and threw his arms around Lucy. Galen didn't understand the words, but the sentiment was unmistakable. The man was big but wizened, with a full gray beard and bright, hard eyes. He had been a warrior in his time. Galen knew that immediately. "I've been so worried about you." He glared at Galen. "Who's this?"

"Long story, Jake. Can we come in and tell it?"

Jake peered down the hall in either direction, then motioned them in. Galen limped after the girl. His vision had begun to blur around the edges. He steadied himself against the wall just inside the door. Lucy turned around, saw him, and said, in Latin, "Galen, come. Sit down here." She guided him to a soft, long bench with a back, and he sank into it, easing his shoulder against the cushion. His wounds throbbed. The house was very strange. Many books on shelves. Was this man so rich? Strange objects hung on the walls. It had thick rugs but no tapestries. The whole place was warm, though he could see no fire pit.

"Got some water, Jake?" Even he recognized the word for *waether*. That must be universal. The old man scurried away. Lucy sat beside Galen. "Jake will help us. I have known him for a long time. Be calm and rest." She squeezed his hand. He liked when she did that. He leaned his head back against the cushion. This bench was as soft as any bed he had ever slept on. How long since he had slept in a real bed? When the old man returned with water, Lucy produced several small white tablets of various shapes, offered them to him with the water.

"What are these?"

She replied to his Latin, "For your pain."

"It will make me sleep," he accused. A drug. Like the woman in the white room had given him. It was not safe to lose himself to drugged sleep in such a place of peril.

"It is just Vicodin." Whatever that was. "You will not sleep." When he started to protest, she held up a hand. "Just take it." She was exasperated.

She had been only kind up to this point. Except for taking him away from a glorious death on the battlefield and delivering him to the man with the needles. Still, someone had sewn his wounds and bandaged him. That might be the only reason he was alive. He gritted his teeth and took the tablet and the water. "Odin's eye and Thor's hammer. You are a trial, woman."

Chapter Four

Jake had been her landlord ever since she moved out of her father's house eleven years ago. He wore an old serape along with huaraches and jeans that had seen better days. His ponytail was as grizzled as his beard. Jake limped from 'Nam. She wasn't quite sure how he'd been injured, but he'd had multiple surgeries since. Jake never said exactly what he did during the war. Now he was pretty well set. He owned this building, though he employed a service to make the toilets run and fix the garbage disposals so he didn't have to bother with the tenants. After his hip replacement a few years ago, she'd practically had to force her way in with casseroles so he wouldn't starve, but she could be stubborn. After a while, she didn't have to force her way in. They'd become friends. Jake was a fascinating character, interested in everything, a real jazz buff with hints of a dark past. What was not to like? He didn't seem to have other people he trusted. A bookshelf held a picture of a daughter, but Jake would say only that she'd died.

"You speak Latin to him?" Jake asked from where he leaned against the archway to the kitchen. The sweet smell of cannabis hung in the air.

Lucy glanced over as Galen took the pills, looking disgusted with himself. "He speaks Danish. Latin is the only way we can communicate." How much was she going to tell Jake?

"Looks like he got in one helluva fight." Jake's old eyes were flat, revealing nothing. He was waiting for an explanation as he studied Galen.

She didn't want to tell Jake the truth. Problem was, Jake was a difficult guy to lie to. "Can I use your phone to call Brad? If you'll just let us wait for him here . . ."

"Brad?" Jake's eyes searched her face. "I wouldn't think you'd want to call Brad."

"Why not?" Lucy frowned.

"Well, *Brad* and that Casey guy, who is a spook if I ever saw one, came round here and cleaned out your apartment and questioned everybody in the building like you were on the Ten Most Wanted list. They confiscated everything you owned. Went to the trouble of getting the Quantico dirtbags involved."

"The store . . . ?"

"Closed. Your whole inventory boxed up and removed. They 'questioned' Amy until she practically had a nervous breakdown. Couldn't stop crying."

Amy was the girl who helped her on weekends. "My God, why . . . Why would they do that?" She was asking herself more than Jake.

"You tell me. Brad seemed pretty mad about something. I have a feeling it's about this guy you got here who you speak to in Latin but who swears in what I think is Old Norse, not Danish. He's wearing breeches handstitched with gut and cut with a laced-in crotch piece like they used to wear about a thousand years ago, except for that stupid bow, which I expect I can lay to your account since he's only got one good hand. His boots are deer hide. Don't see *that* much these days except on those nuts up in the Utah mountains waiting for Armageddon. And he didn't get those muscles in a gym. Looks more like he got them on battlefields over years, along with the scars. That fits with the callused right hand. And he's been cut up bad, all those bruises . . . looks like he met up with an axe or a sword real recently. So what do a spook and your wussy scientist friend want with you and Mr. Anachronism here so bad that they're willing to get the FBI help to tear up your life?"

Lucy felt like she'd been slapped. Galen started to heave himself up, glaring at Jake. She turned and pointed. "Sit," she commanded in Latin. She sighed as Galen set his jaw rebelliously. "Please. Please sit." She shot Jake a rueful smile. "He thinks he can take you even in his condition. He doesn't know what a rugged old coot you are."

"He's got a protective streak." Jake softened. "If you're in trouble, Lucy, you came to the right place. But you've got to tell me what's going on." He folded his hands over his chest, waiting. When the only result was her chewing her lip, he said, "What you need is breakfast."

"I couldn't eat." Lucy pressed her palm against her forehead. She had an awful headache.

"Well then, I'm going to make *him* breakfast, because I've got a feeling he doesn't chew Vicodin real regular and on an empty stomach he's likely to throw it up all over my rug." Jake turned and went through to his kitchen.

Lucy glanced to Galen and shrugged. "He will give us food."

Galen pushed himself up. "I will watch. He could use a knife as a weapon."

Galen didn't recognize the many guns, antique and modern, mounted between the bookcases in the living room as weapons. Jake had a license for every one of them. He wasn't really a whacko, just a guy with definite opinions, mostly involving the government.

"You are wounded. You should rest. He's a friend."

"I am Danir. I fight whole battles wounded. I will rest later." He stood, a little shaky.

Lucy was too tired to argue. She trailed into the kitchen, Galen stomping after her.

Jake's corner unit had views out to the bay on two sides. After he'd recovered from his hip replacement and could get around, he'd remodeled two units into one larger living space. Instead of bare walls and linoleum, his apartment was filled with things he loved. In his kitchen he'd put up open-fronted cabinets to display his handmade pottery collection. It was a cozy place of earth-tone tile and wood, except for the stainless-steel restaurant-grade appliances. Jake liked to cook. A big butcher-block dining table doubled as a cutting board. Lucy slung her bag over one of the spindle-back chairs at the table and sat. Galen took another. He was wavering. The fool. Trying to prove something. Food was probably a good idea.

"So tell me the story, while I whip up a couple of omelets."

Lucy ran her hands through her hair. What did it mean that Brad and Casey had removed the contents of her apartment and her store? Could they think she'd stolen the machine by bringing it back to some other location? Like she could hide it in her apartment. Maybe he was looking for the book, or a clue to where she took the machine.

Jake retrieved an armload of eggs, cheese, and vegetables from the Sub-Zero. Lucy followed his glance to Galen and saw a watchful furrow in the Viking's brow. "Begin at the beginning."

"Well, it began with a gigantic coincidence," she started.

"No such thing as coincidence," Jake growled as he cleaned scallions at the sink.

"It sure seemed that way to me. I had a book, my most prized possession. It was by Leonardo da Vinci, and it showed diagrams of a machine he wanted to build." She swallowed. Here was the tough part. "A machine that could travel through time."

Jake pushed his lower lip up and nodded his head. "Maybe that's what they were looking for—book must be worth a pile."

That wasn't the part that was hardest to believe. "Yeah. It's worth a pile. I never told anyone about the book. It was too precious to me. Until one day we were out at the Palace of Fine Arts, and . . . and I had the strangest urge to show it to Brad."

"And the coincidence was . . ."

"He was working at the lab on getting power to a medieval machine in partnership with the Italian government. None of them knew what the machine was supposed to do. I knew right away, in my gut, that it was the machine from my book. Leonardo had actually built it."

Jake grinned as he chopped scallions at the table with a huge knife. Galen tensed beside her. She put a hand surreptitiously on his good thigh under the table and gave it a pat. "Bet it frosted that ole spook's ass that you knew what it was and he didn't," Jake said.

"Maybe it did. Well, anyway, we went down to the Super Collider Lab and there it was, all gears and jewels. It's a beautiful thing. Colonel Casey—"

"Got to be CIA or NSA or some damn thing. I recognized him as special ops right off." Jake straightened, hands on his hips. "So you tried it and it worked, right? That's where you got your friend." He looked like the cat who'd swallowed the canary. Leave it to Jake to accept the unbelievable. Galen never took his eyes off that big knife.

"I thought I was going to have to show you the book."

"Hell, if you got the book, I'd love to see it. But let's eat first. Wouldn't want to get egg all over it." He put down the knife, right within Galen's reach, and cracked eggs into a bowl. He swung round and got out a small Calphalon pan and turned on a burner of his Viking range. Viking. That was rich. "So, was it you who went back?"

"Yeah. Boy, was I stupid. But it felt . . . I don't know. It felt like my destiny or something."

"Those two are real heroes. They get plausible deniability and you take the risk." He swung back suddenly. Galen flinched and grabbed for the knife on the table.

"Whoa!" Lucy held up her hands. "I told you. Jake is a friend," she continued in Latin.

Jake had gone still. "That's right. A friend. Maybe you want to sharpen that for me?" he asked slowly, nodding to the knife.

Galen narrowed his eyes in suspicion. But he said, "Freond?" It sounded like "friend." Maybe that was a Norse word that had been absorbed into English. In graduate school she'd learned that English took on words from all England's conquerors, first Vikings, then the Normans. The structure had grown simple and strong with the invasion of the Danes, able to collect words of all kinds. Maybe she was understanding the words they had in common.

Jake turned carefully to a drawer and got out a sharpening stone. He held it up, and Lucy saw recognition in Galen's eyes. Jake held out the stone. "A man needs to feel like he's got a weapon when he's in a bad place, and I expect that's just what this seems to you."

Galen nodded once. "*Wǣpn,*" he said clearly, though with an accent.

Jake set the stone on the table and slid it across. Galen began to sharpen the knife, holding it with his bad hand and smoothing the stone along the blade with long, slithery strokes. The muscles in his shoulders bunched and relaxed with the rhythm. He seemed to relax as well.

"You're a kind man, Jake. Let's just hope he doesn't use it."

Jake ignored her. "So, looks like you landed in some trouble."

"Right in the middle of a battle. I'm not sure who was fighting whom."

"That where you were aiming the machine?"

"This is going to sound so crazy. Leonardo says you just think about the place and time you want to be in and the machine takes you there. I . . . I thought about going to a time when magic was still possible."

Jake was silent at that as he watched butter sizzle in the pan. Finally he turned to slap two slices of bread into the toaster. "You're lucky you weren't killed."

"Galen nearly was. A fourteen-foot machine made of bronze gears all whirring that appears right in the middle of a battle is . . . distracting, I guess." She gave a helpless chuckle. "This sounds insane on so many levels. I think he was protecting me from a guy with really bad teeth. Anyway, Galen was wounded. He fell against me right as the machine took off and we came back together. But the teeth guy hit the control lever of the machine with an axe just at the last minute and damaged it. I guess that's why I'm four months late."

"Where'd you get him patched up?" Eggs sizzled in the pan and he sprinkled some chopped Brie and avocado and scallions on top.

"We landed in the bottom level of the parking structure at the General. Can you believe it? Right outside the only trauma center in the city. I guess I was thinking he needed medical help or he was a dead man." She chuckled. "You'd be proud of the lies I told. Boy, Richard Nixon has nothing on me."

Jake's eyes crinkled. "Let me guess . . . a reenactment."

"Yup. I said he was a cousin from Denmark, or some-times I said Finland." She grimaced. "Okay, maybe I'm not a *great* liar. Anyway, the police took his sword. If he hadn't been restrained and groggy from surgery, he would have fought them for it right in the hospital room." She chewed her lip. "I took him out AMA to get him back to his own time before someone found the machine. But it's broken. Brad is the only one who can fix it—"

"Don't call him, Lucy." Jake slid the omelet onto a plate and put it with . . . surprisingly, a big serving spoon in front of Galen. That seemed all right with Galen. He dug in with the spoon.

"*Gōd*." He pronounced around a mouthful of eggs. "*Thonc to thu*."

"You're welcome," Jake said. He slapped another pat of butter into the pan and poured in another batch of eggs.

"I've got to get him back before his absence changes something. I'm not sure man was meant to mess around with time."

"I guess we're going to find out."

"What do you mean? If Brad can fix the machine—"

"If Brad and the spook can fix that machine, you can bet they'll use it. Whether or not they agree to send your friend home."

"They might want to keep Galen for a while. But we can send him back to the exact time he disappeared and not change anything." She stared into the night at the lights of the bridge. "Would it be so bad if Brad used the machine in some controlled experiments? It'd be amazing if you could go back to another time, just as a visitor, without changing anything, and solve mysteries. Like who really killed Kennedy. You'd like that. . . ." She looked up.

Jake stared at her, his eyes hard. "Don't be naïve. You can't just visit. You found that out. And that's not what the spook wants with a time machine. You just think what he could do with it. He could go back and assassinate people he didn't agree with. Maybe he doesn't like the New Deal, so he goes back and assassinates Roosevelt. Or maybe he thinks he's a 'good guy' and he wants to eliminate Hitler. Doesn't matter. These guys are going to change history big-time."

Lucy felt like she was sliding down a rabbit hole into the twisted warren of conspiracy theories Jake inhabited. "They don't have the machine."

Jake looked under his brows at her. She felt stupid. When someone found the machine in the parking structure they'd call the police. And the FBI or the CIA or whoever would have put out a call for information about it. Casey and Brad would have the machine back in no time. Though of course it didn't work now. But they'd fix it and do what they wanted with it. And she'd made this possible. Would Brad let Casey use it for whatever he wanted? It was Brad's project. But she knew in her heart that Brad was no match for Casey. Whatever Casey wanted, he'd do.

Jake sat at the kitchen table. "Let's get serious. You call anyone since you been back?"

Lucy shook her head. "You're the first person I've been in contact with. My phone doesn't work."

"You give your real name at the hospital?"

"Yeah. I listed myself as the responsible party, to be sure they'd give him surgery."

Jake just stared at her. "Tell me you didn't give them a credit card."

Lucy's blush answered the question.

"Then we don't have much time." Jake looked grim. "But you came to the right place. You can use my setup."

"What are you talking about?"

"You and your friend here have got to go off the map for a while. New identity, the whole nine yards."

Lucy blinked as she tried to follow his logic. Galen

examined each of them in turn, alerted to the change in the tone.

Jake set his lips. "I know it's a lot to absorb, Lucy. But our friend Colonel Casey is going to want to eliminate anybody who knows about his little project."

"Eliminate, as in . . . kill?" She laughed. She had to remember it was Jake she was talking to here. "Jake, no one wants to kill me. I'm a bookseller, for God's sake."

But Jake didn't laugh.

"They'll want to find me, but not to kill me, just to get these," she continued. "I've got the book." She reached around to her bag and hauled out the book and set it carefully on the table. "And this." She fished out the diamond slightly bigger than her fist.

"Shit, howdy." Jake stared at the diamond. Lucy realized that for him, it was this impossibly big diamond that made the whole thing resonate in his gut as real.

"From the lever. Machine doesn't work without it. They could get another one—"

"Those don't grow on trees." He glanced out the windows. The sky was lightening. You could see the stream of headlights from early commuters coming over the Golden Gate. Lucy could just make out the rotunda of the Palace of Fine Arts far off to the left. "They'll find you, take what they want, and then they'll kill you both. Or maybe they keep him, while they question him about his time. Captivity isn't much better than death. Take it from me. Nothing for it, babe. You got to take your Viking and disappear."

"Brad would never let anyone hurt me." Why didn't her voice sound surer?

"Look." Jake reached across and took her two hands in his. "I know you think I'm the crank down the hall. But it takes an ex-spook to know a spook, and I worked on enough conspiracies in Southeast Asia to know conspiracies are real. The world is filled with bad people, Lucy. Humor me on this one. Drop out of sight for a little while longer. Better safe than sorry."

Lucy felt an actual pain in her stomach. If once you started seeing evil everywhere, pretty soon you'd be wearing huaraches and a serape and collecting guns. And yet she herself had already had doubts about turning Galen over to Casey. She started to shake her head.

"Okay, let's do it this way," Jake interrupted. "You said you felt it was your destiny to use the machine. You wanted to go to a time where magic was possible. So you travel through time and some wounded guy leans up against you and comes back with you. Sounds like magic to me. Or maybe destiny. Then again maybe not. But you land in the one place that can save him, then you come to the one guy in fifty miles who knows how to go off the map, which, believe it or not, you need to do. If that isn't destiny, it sure is something. Ask your gut. Your gut knows."

Lucy was about to protest or maybe just get up and go to the phone she saw hanging on the cupboard to call Brad. But she didn't. Her gut, as Jake called it, was doing flip-flops. She looked around wildly for something to hang on to.

Galen raised his head, sensing her distress. He stared at her, frowning. Oh, those blue eyes. Even she was not immune. She steadied, searching his face.

Jake receded. The kitchen seemed far away. And she felt something . . . emanating from Galen, like he was his own vortex of true and right. Her stomach eased. A feeling of . . . she could only describe it as . . . as wholeness flashed through her and was gone. And its loss was the most devastating thing she'd ever experienced. Her eyes filled.

The room came flashing back. She blinked at Galen as a breath shuddered through her. It felt like the first breath she'd ever taken, that screaming first breath of a newborn babe, howling at the loss of sanctuary, the harshness of a new reality dawning.

Slowly she turned to Jake. She had no idea what she would say. But the words came anyway. "He needs to heal. Then things will be all right."

"You agreeing or not?" Jake demanded, examining her.

"I'm agreeing."

"Good." Jake rubbed his hands together and stood. "I've been preparing for this day for a lotta years. I've got a car registered under a false name and a forty-four-footer in a slip up north on the bay registered to another one. Not traceable. You can stay there. No phone calls, no letters, and for God's sake no credit cards."

"Won't they look for me here?"

"You'll be gone in ten minutes. If they come looking, everyone in the building will say the same thing I do. Ain't seen you. Their part'll be true."

Ten minutes? He went to the pantry, scooped away some containers of flour and beans to reveal a safe, and twirled the knob. He pulled out a gym bag and tossed it on the table, zipped it open, and fished out a key ring. "Car's in the basement. Blue Chevy, nothing special. Runs like a dream, though. Here's fifty thousand in twenties and a nine-millimeter Glock with no registration number."

"I can't take money from you, Jake. And I wouldn't know what to do with a gun."

"The money's a loan. I'll charge you some usurious rate of return." She didn't believe that, and he could see it. "Look, girl. You saved my life once. You probably don't even know that." His smile was rueful. "No. You didn't pull me out of a swamp, or get me out of a bamboo cage. You did it with casseroles. Even though I didn't want to be saved. I was about ready to call it a day what with my daughter dying a day after that last surgery, knowing there would be other surgeries, that I'd never be the man I was again. You didn't know that."

He'd never said a word about his daughter dying only two days before Lucy had barged in with her first casserole. "That's what friends are for," she said softly.

"Exactly." He cleared his throat and moved back to the table. He raised a tiny camera and held it up. "Smile." He clicked a picture of her and one of Galen. "Two passports will be delivered to the Quik Stop up where the dirt road turns off Highway 37 day after tomorrow. That's where the mail comes for the marina. Now give me your cell phone."

She dug in her bag. "Jake, this is the latest iPhone," she pleaded.

"Not anymore. You been gone four months. There's a new version out. And from now on, cell phones are out, along with all Internet. The minute you hook into the Net to do a Google map, they've got you." He took the phone, laid it on the table, and went to one of his kitchen drawers. He came back with the kind of wooden mallet you used to make paillards. Lucy sucked in a breath. She glanced to Galen. He seemed unfazed by the impending violence. He just looked gray. Jake brought the mallet down on the phone. Again and again, until little circuits shot out over the tile floor. "I'll dispose of the pieces."

Jake scratched on a grocery list pad with a stubby pencil, tore it off, and stuck it in the bag. "Here's the slip number and directions. Don't fraternize with anyone on the boats around you, or the nosey little gossip up at the Quik Stop. Only the diehards will be up there in March, and they're a suspicious lot. The boat's got everything you'll need except perishable food. If push comes to shove, take it out the Gate and sail west. You're a good sailor."

"I only crewed for Dad." She couldn't just head to Hawaii in a forty-four-foot sailboat. "And I can't do it alone."

"Two can crew her." Jake nodded toward Galen. "Bet he knows how to sail."

Lucy made a face.

"Ask him." Jake pushed past her.

"He wants to know if you can sail a boat," she said in Latin to Galen.

Galen looked at her as though she was . . . what did he call it? Feebleminded. "I have been *vikingr* on the whale road. I know water and wind."

Okay, so he sailed. That didn't mean he'd know anything about a modern sailboat. He was in no shape to haul sails anyway. And she couldn't let Jake give her fifty thousand dollars. She'd have no way to get it back to him if they did go "off the map." Which they were *not* going to do. But Lucy had caught Jake's urgency. She gnawed at her lips. Jake seemed so sure of himself. And he was not going to take no for an answer. Jesus! Was she really going to try to hide out just because Brad and Casey had come looking for her when she didn't return?

And brought the FBI? And confiscated everything she owned?

Jake came back in with an armload of clothes and a gym bag. "I had some overshirts that might fit him, but no jeans even close. There's a Target in Novato and a Macy's." As the last of the clothes were being stuffed into the bag, a long samurai sword was revealed. "And this . . ." He hefted the curved black scabbard inlaid with intricate gold work. He held it out to Galen. "This is for you. My pa brought it back from Okinawa."

Galen pushed himself up. His eyes slid along the scabbard. He knew what it was. He looked up once at Jake to make sure he wanted to give such a precious gift. Jake nodded. Galen took the scabbard reverently and pulled on the gold-worked hilt with his good left hand. The blade emerged, very slightly curved and lethal. It was much lighter than his sword. But that didn't seem to dismay him. A small smile played over his lips as his eyes caressed the blade.

"It's a killer all right." Jake said. "At least in some men's hands."

Galen nodded, that curt acknowledgment he always seemed to give, and shoved the blade back in. "*Es gōd . . .*" And then he said in Latin, "The steel is fine." He switched back to his own language. "*Thonc to thu.*"

"Just don't let anything happen to her." Jake jerked a thumb to Lucy.

Galen glanced to Lucy and nodded again, just once.

As if he knew what Jake was saying or as if he could protect her in his condition. "Well, if you two are done with this testosterone fest, I think we'll get going." She put Leonardo's book back in her bag along with the massive diamond. "I will pay back every cent of that money."

"I have no doubt." Jake zipped the bag and went to the door.

Lucy stopped. "He's going to need a doctor, you know."

"Not unless he gets infected. Did they give you antibiotics at the hospital?"

She nodded. "Yeah, Keflex, but—"

"You can change bandages and take out the stitches yourself."

"Jake, I don't know who you think I am, but I am not that person."

Jake smiled at her. "Yes, you are, Lucy Rossano. You definitely are." He swung around.

"Wait," Lucy said as he threw the bolt lock. "How will I know it's safe to come back?"

"If nobody's been around in a month, I'll send you word. You won't hear from me until then. If they do come around, they'll be waiting for me to try to contact you. If you haven't heard from me in a month, then something's happened. If anybody shows up at the marina asking questions, the same. Just take the boat and sail west."

She was about to protest, but he put a finger to her lips. He smiled again, but this time his eyes were sad. "No questions. No doubts. You go off the map and you don't ever come back on it. Sail around Borneo. Visit Sri Lanka. These buggers never forget. They'll never quit looking. And there's nothing you can do about whatever they decide to do with the machine. You're a bookseller and he's a tenth-century Viking. You are no match for them. You understand?"

This speech frightened Lucy as nothing else had. "Jake . . ."

He swung the bag off his shoulder and pulled it up onto hers. "Now you go. I've got to clean up. There can be no trace of you here." He took a handkerchief out from somewhere under his serape and pushed her out the door. Galen grunted and followed. The door shut. She heard the bolts snap into place.

Chapter Five

Wednesday

"Okay, now we can make some time," Lucy muttered as they cruised onto the Golden Gate. The traffic was backed up at the tollbooths coming south into the city, not heading north to Marin County. Car lights made a broad white ribbon snaking away onto the bridge itself. She glanced over to the half-naked man in the passenger's seat of Jake's Chevy. As she accelerated, he gripped the center armrest with his good left hand. His lips thinned into a grim line.

"Drive this cart more slowly," he commanded.

Any slower and she'd probably get arrested. But any faster and Galen would probably lose Jake's omelet. "It's okay," she said as she turned her gaze back to the road. Stupid. Like he would understand that. What was "okay" in Latin? "Es good," she finally said, in what she hoped was whatever language he'd been using. It occurred to her that he didn't know why fast was a good thing. She kept the car at fifty and eased over to the right-hand lane. She was probably the only person on the bridge actually going the speed limit.

"We must go fast." Her lack of fluency in Latin was really annoying. And her accent was definitely different from his. He seemed to have trouble understanding her.

"Jake—my friend Jake? Jake thinks men will come to . . . take you." How was that so bad to him? "They would take you to a prison." Sort of true. They'd hear about Galen from the hospital staff. And they wouldn't let a treasure like an actual man from the past run around loose on the streets. They might be right about that. This whole thing was really bad. "We must go." The word for escape escaped her. "Fast. Before they . . . find us."

He was breathing through his mouth. "You did not send for Brad to fix the metal wheels. How will I go back?"

Tricky, especially in Latin. "Jake thinks Brad will take you to prison."

"Your lover would imprison me?" He almost relaxed. "I will tell him I do not want you."

"Gee, thanks." That cut a little too close to the bone. She'd always known she wasn't movie star material. But did he have to be so blunt? "He is not my lover."

Galen shot her a look that might have meant she must think him stupid. "Woman," he insisted. "We will go to this Brad. I will make him fix the metal wheels."

The hills rose up around them north of the bridge. The sky had lightened to that pearly quality it got just before sunup. The grass covering the hillsides showed itself vibrant green. Sausalito would appear down to the right at any minute. Why couldn't Jake have moored his boat there instead of way up at the top of the bay? Probably because the docks at Sausalito had turned into a cozy neighborhood. People lived on houseboats that hadn't moved for thirty, forty years. Not the first choice for a secrecy and paranoid specialist like Jake.

"It is . . . of no matter that you do not want me. Brad has a bad friend. They want you because . . . you are from another year. They will not . . . let you go back." Was that true? Was she doing the right thing, running away? Then she remembered Colonel Casey's cold eyes. This time, Jake might be right to be paranoid.

"I will fight them with the sword of Jake." He stated it simply, as if she would be a fool to think he wouldn't win such a battle.

"You are not . . . enough strong. They will bring . . . other men. We . . ." What was the word for hide? "We go far. You heal. Then . . . you can fight." Except they would have guns and he had a sword. She couldn't let him face off with Colonel Casey, ever.

Running away was difficult for him. She could see his jaw working. In the end, he took in a long breath and let it out. His shoulders sagged a little. "Until I heal. Where do we go?"

"We go to the boat of Jake."

"I will heal. Then will I fight whoever comes. Brad will fix the metal wheels, and I will go back to the battle." He nodded to himself and sat back in the seat. Apparently he felt better now that he had a plan. It made him feel in charge of his fate. Like anybody was in charge of that.

She'd love to have a plan besides just hiding out. While Galen healed, Brad would be working to fix the machine. Maybe Casey could get another diamond. Would Casey care about finding her and Galen if he had the working machine? Jake thought so. If they did escape Casey, Galen would never get back home to his family, to the woman he probably had waiting there, to the battle that seemed so important to him. And Lucy's life was gone, too. Who was she, without the bookshop, with her only two friends in life, Jake and Brad, lost to her, too?

How foolish was it to decide on an impulse to power up a frigging time machine and visit the past? How had she gotten so obsessed with Leonardo's book and his machine and the possibility of . . . escape? Was that what she'd really been obsessed with all along? Escape from what? Was her life so bad? Or was it just . . . ordinary?

What matter? It was all gone forever now.

The whole world might be changed if Brad and Casey used the machine. Would she even realize it? Maybe she'd never know the way it should have been. Jeez, but she hated these time-travel conundrums.

The sky was fully light now. She glanced to Galen and saw that the rocking motion and noise of the car had sent him into an exhausted sleep. Gone was the hard warrior. His expression was soft. His long eyelashes brushed his cheeks. He had dark circles under his eyes. He'd pushed himself to exhaustion, wounded as he was. She'd been practically carrying him by the time they got down to Jake's car. And he was a load.

She wished she could indulge in the luxury of sleep. He might have fought a battle, time-traveled, and had surgery in the last twenty-four hours, but she hadn't slept in she didn't know how long. And time travel really took it out of you. Or maybe it was just the constant rush of adrenaline. Not exactly the quiet life of a book lover. To keep awake, she consulted the directions she'd gotten from Jake, scribbled on a pad with a Realtor's name and picture at the top. The exit was off Highway 37 all the way at the top of the bay. It wasn't technically even San Francisco Bay up there, but San Pablo Bay once you got past the narrows at Point San Pedro.

They had maybe an hour before they got to the marina. Not far.

But not far to what she didn't know. What the hell had she gotten into?

Someone was attacking! He hit out with his right hand and felt pain stab through his shoulder as he came fully awake. A sling prevented him from landing the blow.

"Hey, you almost got me, buddy." The woman jumped back, red blooming in her cheeks. Her eyes were the clearest green he had ever seen. Just now they were snapping in anger. What was she saying? Why couldn't the woman speak Latin?

"Do not wake a warrior in this way," he grunted, and pushed down the pain from his shoulder. He sat forward. The cart was stopped, thank Loki. She had been leaning in to wake him through the open door. Behind her, masts dipped and bobbed against a blue sky. Good. They were at the mooring of Jake's boat. The torture of this Helbegotten cart was ended. He struggled out, pushing her anxious hands away. The woman was always trying to control him.

But when he stood, the rocking masts wavered and blurred. Before he could protest, she slipped in under his good shoulder and steadied him. "I can walk, woman," he grunted.

"If you fall, how will I . . . take you to the boat?" She seemed exasperated. She was right. Tiny as she was, she'd never get him up if he passed out.

He realized in that moment how dependent he was on her. He did not speak the language of this cursed place. He knew nothing of the workings of the carts. He had no coins with him. How would he eat without her? Beg on the streets when he did not speak a language any here could understand? The empty feeling in his belly was not from lack of food. He gritted his teeth as she pulled him forward, but he did not push her away. He would have to put up with her for now.

How difficult was it to put up with a comely wench? They were always willing to do his bidding, as long as he satisfied them in the bed box. He was good at that. The masts steadied as his head cleared. He limped ahead, leaning on her as little as possible. He would bed her and bend her to his will as soon as he was able. Then she would do his bidding. Perhaps this Brad had not Galen's broad experience with pleasing women and that was why her temper was so bad. This Brad probably did not know what the women of Gaul had taught Galen.

She had taken out one of the small, serrated pieces of metal that were actually keys. She opened the lock on a metal grid fence and pushed open the gate, then closed it behind them and pulled him down the dock to the left. He was breathing hard and sweating. He hardly recognized the shiny, sleek white craft moored here as boats at all. There was little wood in sight. His mind registered their lines, how they rode in the water. They would be fast. Very fast.

She paused and compared her scrap of parchment with the signs in Arabic numbers at the head of each dock. "Wonderful," she muttered as she did when she spoke her own language. But he knew that word.

"*Thu understandath* wonderful?" Surprising.

She looked up at him in equal surprise, her arm around his waist still supporting him. "I understand that." And he understood her. It was the third time they had truly communicated. She spoke Englisc, no matter how warped.

She nodded and he could feel her relief. "Better than Latin. We might have a chance."

He understood the first part. "*Gōd. Betra thone* Latin," he repeated. Her inflections were different, but the words sounded the same. When she talked fast, like to the man in green, it wasn't just that so many words were unfamiliar. It sounded like gibberish, as if she didn't know that words should have the emphasis only on the first syllable.

She looked around and pushed down the dock. She counted under her breath as they passed each boat. His leg was dragging. He wouldn't make it much farther, and if he fell he was like to crush her. "*Hwāer is se bāt?*" he panted.

She looked up to him, blinking. "There," she said, nodding at the last dock. She must have understood him.

He might have known it would be the farthest away. He got there. Barely. The boat looked to be more than forty feet long, shiny white, with bright canvas dyed blue with woad covering what must be furled sails. It was moored to the dock with surprisingly light ropes made of some slick, bright yellow material. He slung his leg over the light lines that formed a small fence at the edge and stepped down onto the rocking deck with his good leg. At least he didn't fall. He did not want to humiliate himself in front of the woman. Still, he leaned against the cabin as she used another key to unlock a hatch.

She pushed it open and peered inside. "Uh-oh, ladder," she said, looking worried.

She must think him weak as a mewling babe. He could negotiate a *hlāeder*. He pushed her aside. But he gripped the small rail with his good left hand until his knuckles were white as he descended into the cabin. It was surprisingly spacious. He didn't have to duck his head.

"Learn some manners," he heard her mutter just behind him in her own language. That he didn't get. Didn't have time to try because his legs didn't want to obey him. He stumbled to a bench with a cushion at a small table and sat heavily.

"Okay, big boy. We're getting you to bed." Then she switched to Latin. "Stay here."

What an ungrateful wretch. Pushing her aside like that. Like she wasn't the one saving his hide. Now where to put him? Jake's boat was a tidy affair, an Irwin with a center cockpit. It had been completely refitted. Forty-four feet was big enough to live on and just big enough to sail in heavy weather. It was like Jake to have called it the *Camelot*. Lucy glanced around at the rich, varnished teak that formed shelves and drawers around a galley much bigger than the one on her father's Catalina 30 and lined the salon. She headed forward, past the head, and found only half of the usual V-berth. The other half had been converted to storage. The Viking was a big man. The narrow half V-berth didn't look promising. She peeked behind the louvered doors where the other berth should be and found a generator, extra batteries, and floor-to-ceiling storage shelves. Jake didn't apparently hold with the "sleeps seven comfortably" part of every yacht maker's brochure. This vessel was outfitted for long voyages. She slid back down past Galen and the galley through the passage around the center cockpit and found a queen bed in the stateroom with a big locker and bookshelves and another head. Okay. That was better. He could have the big bed, and she'd take the V-berth at the opposite end of the boat. Far away, was good, too. She pulled back the spread. The bed had fresh sheets and several blankets. The dirty and blood-soaked leather of the Viking's breeches flashed through her mind. Those breeches would have to go.

When she got back to Galen, he was looking ashen. "Bed," she said in Latin, and nodded to the aft cabin. She grabbed his good left arm above the elbow and helped him up. The bulge of his biceps under her fingers, hard under the smooth skin, was . . . a little shocking. More than a little if she wasn't lying to herself. Helping him down to the boat, with his arm over her shoulders and his bare ribs pressed up against her, had been difficult. Okay. That was natural. The heat from his body had seeped into her until she was hot, too. But even holding his arm was doing things to her she didn't like in places that shouldn't be reacting like this.

Her lack of foresight was soon evident. The little passageway wasn't built for two to pass. She looked up at him and heaved a sigh. He was on his own. "Go there." She inclined her head to the aft cabin.

He nodded, set his lips, and staggered through the passageway, his broad shoulders caroming off the varnished teak paneling. He stumbled to the right side of the bed and slowly collapsed onto his good left side. Lucy hurried forward and knelt to pull off his boots. She didn't even try to explain. What she was doing was trying really hard not to think about the fact that she was stripping a very virile man. Or about what that was doing to parts of her body she hadn't paid much attention to lately. He was injured. What kind of a human being was she to be turned on by a wounded man? She pulled at the strings of the bow she had tied at his waist.

"Are you so eager for my services?" he rumbled in a tired voice.

Conceited lout! Did . . . did he know what she was feeling? He couldn't. A small smile curved his lips. Was that self-satisfaction, or was he . . . was he teasing her? Did Vikings tease? There was a kind of self-aware humor around his eyes that was . . . incredibly attractive.

"Dirt." She pointed. "Blood." She pointed to the crisp white sheets. "Clean."

"Women." He shook his head. Was that mock despair or real disgust? She motioned him up so she could get his breeches off, but he lay on the bed, propped on one elbow, making no effort. His complexion was so pale she thought it might not just be rebellion. Maybe he couldn't do as she bid. She pulled the thongs from around his legs. All that was left was to pull his breeches off. She wouldn't blush. She wouldn't. She wouldn't even look.

She looked.

Darn it. The flush moved up her neck to lodge intractably in her cheeks. She pulled the covers back. He dragged himself up to the pillows, and she drew the covers over him. That was better. Much better. She couldn't see the ribs move under the skin on his flanks. Or the taut abdominals, for that matter. The bunching curve of his buttocks was concealed and the corded muscle in his thighs and even his nipples puckered in the cool morning air. Not to mention his . . . genitals. *Big deal.* All men had them. She wasn't a virgin. She'd had two relationships that included sex. She'd seen men's genitals dozens of times.

Without the reaction that this man was causing or anything like it.

This was bad. Very bad.

"Sleep," she said, her voice tight.

His eyes were already closed. *"Thonc to thu,"* he muttered.

She fled.

Lucy took her mind off her charge and their situation by getting their bag in from the car and exploring the boat. Jake had provisioned it down to the last piece of silverware. The cupboards held everything from noodles and vacuum-sealed entrées to powdered milk and coffee. Cans of juice filled one whole cupboard. No scurvy on this command. Soap, shampoo, cleaning supplies; the boat had it all, including a ham radio and two small high-def flat screens, one in the aft cabin and one in the salon on the cockpit wall that could be seen from the dining table and the sofa across from it—even from the little galley across the bar from the dining table. Strange of Jake to have left the televisions. She wasn't even sure he had one in his apartment. She turned one on. It worked. Maybe if you were on the run or there'd been some kind of disaster newscasts were handy. She'd seen the little satellite discs provided by the marina on the lampposts by the fence. The boat also had no GPS, no computer, and no phone hookup. Guess those would be too easy to trace. *Jeez*. Was she beginning to think like Jake?

She climbed outside and hooked the boat up to the power box with the heavy cord provided by the marina. At least they wouldn't have to run the generator. She hung Jake's loaned shirts in the locker and hid the money and the diamond in a narrow space she found behind the trash compactor in the galley. But where to put the gun? She couldn't imagine sleeping with it under her pillow. She decided on a drawer in the galley with the knives where it was handy to the ladder down from the hatch. Like that would make a difference if some of Casey's friends came to get them. And as for the sword Jake had given Galen—that she *did* put under her mattress. There was no way she wanted a Viking lurking around with a sword. And maybe it would be protection, in case someone came into her cabin in the night. Like the Viking. Could she hack at him? Maybe she wouldn't have to. Just brandish it . . . maybe.

And then . . . then there was nothing left to do. She pulled off her flats. Her flippy knit skirt had seen better days. She smelled like blood. Too bad Jake didn't have any clothes she could borrow. Macy's in Novato tomorrow. Or maybe Target. Target was one-stop shopping. Definitely good. But first she'd rest. She lay back on her bunk. Just for a few minutes . . .

Chapter Six

Brad stood looking up at the impossible. The machine that had become the center of his life over the last year gleamed in the artificial light of the lowest level of the parking structure outside San Francisco General Hospital. Relief washed over him.

The last four months had been a nightmare. Jensen and Casey had made Brad's life miserable. It wasn't just the endless speeches berating him. No, Brad's downward spiral was rooted in the feeling that his future had been ripped away, the knowledge that an opportunity that only comes once in life was squandered. He couldn't eat. He couldn't sleep. He couldn't run or play tennis or date anyone. The pitying or revolted looks from his peers hadn't helped.

Lucy made him crazy. He thought about her constantly. Could she be the wily spy who played him like Casey said? Could Brad have been wrong about her growing to love him the way he had always loved her? Casey searched her apartment, her store. Confiscated everything and went through her life with a fine-tooth comb. Brad had given Casey one of the hundreds of photographs he'd taken of her to show around. But Casey and his shadowy friends never found anything to suggest she wasn't what she seemed. And Brad was left in doubt, his purest longing for her polluted. But now the machine was back. Had she come back with it, or had it come back alone? And why to a hospital? Maybe she was hurt, dying. His panic surged.

"Get it back to the lab, pronto." Casey had come up behind him.

Brad started. The guy was quiet on his feet. "We'll need a crane."

"So? And for God's sake cover it up. Preserve *some* secrecy. Not that half the hospital staff wasn't out here gaping before we cordoned off the parking structure." Casey sounded bitter.

"I've got a tarp coming from the lab. We'll have to cut major sections of concrete out of the entry and prop up the outside wall with girders to get it out."

"Can't just take it apart?"

Brad gave him a withering look over his shoulder. "Maybe if I had the book to show how to put it back together. But you told Lucy to take that with her."

"So disassemble the parking structure. I'll get in the Corps of Engineers."

"Going to cost an arm and a leg. Jensen will freak."

"Money is not a problem. Get back to the lab. The Corps will take care of everything."

"I don't want to go back to the lab." Brad stared down Casey's dismissive glance. "And right now I get to do anything I want. Notice anything about the machine?"

Casey jerked his focus to the glowing golden gears. "Shit." He broke into a run. Brad followed, watching him look around frantically for the diamond.

"It's not here. And just so you know, the power source is damaged, too."

Casey squatted to peer at the box that had occupied

Brad's thoughts for nearly two years. His shoulders slumped. "Can you fix it?"

"Maybe. Without the diamond it's no good, of course."

"I'll take care of getting the diamond." Casey's voice was as hard as the subject of his sentence. "Your girlfriend has it."

Girlfriend. He liked the sound of that. "Any sign of Lucy?"

"Oh yeah. Everybody who saw her remembers the red braid."

"Was she hurt? Sick?" That had to be why she hadn't called him right away.

"She had a guy with her."

"What?" Brad turned on Casey.

"Apparently a strapping specimen. Spoke some Nordic or Germanic language. Guy was cut up pretty good. Big sword. Chain mail. My men think the clothes they cut off him are from the Middle Ages. She used her credit cards to pay for his surgery. Said he was her cousin from Denmark or sometimes Finland. Left business cards all over the hospital. Stupid bitch."

Lucy came back with a man from the past? Brad's brain reeled. What the hell had she been doing back in time for four months? A feeling of betrayal circled in his gut. Had Casey been right about her? Had she been playing Brad all along? "We've got to find her. Them." And get rid of this guy, whoever he was. It made Brad . . . angry. So angry he felt nauseous.

"Check. I'd like to have a little talk with both of them."

Brad started pacing. "If your guys had been watching the credit cards twenty-four/seven like they did in the first days, we'd have gotten her." He was tired of Casey pushing him around.

"We're only a couple of hours behind her and she's got

a wounded guy with her just out of surgery. They gave him transfusions, but he's still weak. She needs to go to ground."

Had Lucy . . . had she done it with this guy? The *f* word inserted itself in that thought. Brad knew he was spiraling out of control here. He never used the *f* word.

"My guys are checking her apartment, the shop, even though she can't get in. Not sure her shop assistant would take her in with a medieval warrior in tow, but we'll check. Hotels, too."

"She can't use credit cards." Brad thought frantically. "She never carried much cash."

"Unless she was going to steal a time machine." Casey's voice was flat. It was the same taunt Brad had been hearing for four months. "Then she might have prepared very carefully. And taken cash." Brad could see in the working muscles of his jaw that Casey was remembering how they'd scraped together their change and given it to her, how they hadn't even searched her bag. Casey didn't like being made a fool of.

"Can't have it both ways, Casey. She can't be a cool, calculating Mata Hari *and* a stupid bitch who leaves her business cards all over the hospital." Brad didn't mind taking his anger out on Casey. Either way, Lucy had brought a man back with her. She hadn't even called. So whether she was a traitor or a stupid bitch, she'd pissed all over the love Brad had given her so unselfishly. He didn't like being made a fool of, either. The loss of his innocent, pure love for Lucy left a void that ached to be filled.

Casey flipped open his phone. "Get the Corps of Engineers down to San Francisco General. I want a full crew in here within the hour." He motioned to a guy in a black suit and gray tie who stood at the stairwell. The guy had an earpiece. He trotted over. "Reports on the hour about the search for this little bitch and her knight in not-so-shining armor." The ice in Casey's voice used to scare Brad.

Now let it scare Lucy. "Go for it," he muttered.

Lucy opened her eyes on darkness. Where was she? What time was it? The gentle rocking of the boat at the dock grounded her. She sat up, rubbing her eyes. Had she slept so long? She pushed herself up, that horrible grogginess that daytime sleep always gave her making her head thick.

She'd better check on her Viking.

If she'd slept this long, he'd probably slept even longer. He was the one who'd lost blood and had surgery and should be in the hospital. If she had to wake him to eat she'd call his name from the doorway. Shaking him awake was dangerous. But when she entered the cabin, he was nowhere to be seen. The covers were crumpled at the foot of the bed, along with his boots and his discarded breeches. And his sling.

Panic surged up inside her along with wild thoughts. Had Colonel Casey taken Galen from under her sleeping nose? Was he trying to escape from her? She'd come straight through from the forward cabin. He wasn't in the galley or the salon. She checked the head that opened on both his cabin and the passage. Nothing. A series of thuds sounded on the deck above.

She dashed up the ladder into the cold air of evening on the bay. An icy March wind had kicked up. She stood in the cockpit and surveyed the deck above. The outline of his naked form at the prow was just visible against the black of the water beyond. He teetered at the line railing, holding on to the shrouds with his good hand at the edge of the deck. His other hand was at his groin. A trickle hit the water. She sighed in relief. He snapped his head around.

"You should stay below," she said in Latin, hugging her arms against herself. He must be freezing. Lights were on in one or two of the boats moored at the little docks. Across the bay, the lights of Vallejo and Richmond made a glow. Somewhere behind her she could just hear the faint sound of a truck up on the 37 over the creaking of the docks.

"You like linen clean. I like linen dry."

"Sorry." She should have showed him the head. She shouldn't have fallen asleep. Fine fugitive she was. And now he'd probably fall overboard trying to relieve himself. But decency and her own embarrassment required that she hang back until he was finished.

His flow went on and on. He'd really had to go. At last he shook his penis and turned, wavering. Thank goodness she couldn't see him well in this light. She climbed up out of the cockpit and took his good arm. It was trembling either with cold or with the effort it had taken to make it outside to pee. Or both. That should have been only a reminder that he was sick, but the feel of warm flesh and hard muscle had what was becoming a familiar effect on her.

"Down the ladder, big guy." She felt so helpless as she watched him stagger down into the cockpit and then down once more below decks. No way to help him. She got down after him as fast as she could and squeezed ahead to flip the light switch. Too close. She was definitely too close to a really big, naked man. He made the boat seem small. And hot. She opened the door to the head and demonstrated how the lid opened with a foot pedal. What was the word for pee in Latin? "Do that here," she said, and pointed.

He raised his brows. "Inside?"

She flushed the toilet to illustrate.

He started back as the water swirled around the basin

and down into the holding tank. A small smile dawned and he nodded thoughtfully. "*Es gōd.*"

"Now, to bed." She gestured forward. She expected protest, but he was obviously exhausted by his foray up the ladder. He eased himself into the bed while she turned on the bedside light. In the golden glow, the fact that his wounds had seeped fluid into his bandages was obvious. That could not be good. She went to her shoulder bag on the table in the galley and pulled out the white paper bag of pharmacy supplies she'd meant to send back in time with him.

First things first. He hadn't had any painkillers all day. How had he made it through? She would have been screaming. No wonder he'd been trembling. She poured a glass of water and grabbed the pharmacy bag and headed to the bedroom.

Could she do this? She was no nurse. But soiled bandages had to be bad. And how hard could it be to change bandages?

It would be harder if she had to stare at his impressive male equipment. She set the water down and resolutely pulled the covers up to his waist. There were lines around his eyes and between his brows. He might be a stoic, but the pain was taking its toll. She poured the contents of the bag onto the table. Pill bottles, bandages, surgical tape, some Betadine. She read the directions, then shook out two Vicodin and a Keflex. "Take these." She held out the pills.

He looked suspicious.

"For pain." That didn't make him relax. "No sleep. But no pain."

When he still looked rebellious, she decided on threats. "No pills, no food."

His glower said he was thinking about the deal. Why she didn't know. He had no choice. She was his lifeline in this time. And then she saw a strange expression cross his face. Shame. He was ashamed. Of what? He set his mouth in a grim line as he took the capsules and the proffered glass. He downed the pills and made a face. The Vicodin was bitter.

She wasn't sure what was going on with him. Who knew what a Viking thought or felt? He seemed like a creature from another planet. At least he responded to threats.

"Okay. Got to keep those bandages clean and dry," she muttered to herself. She sat beside him like he wasn't staring at her and leaned over to work at the surgical tape that held the bandages in place. Her braid slid over her shoulder onto his belly. "Sorry," she murmured as she pulled carefully at the upper tape. As it came away, it pulled at the skin. Was she pulling at the wound? She glanced up. His lips were set and grim. This wasn't feeling great, obviously. Should she wait until the Vicodin took hold?

She sat back, unsure.

"Dō hit," he said through his teeth. He was too distressed for Latin, but she understood.

She swallowed. "Okay." She bent back over his shoulder and pulled at the tape. "I know this hurts," she murmured, refusing to glance up at his face. "But all this oozing can't be good. I'm afraid getting you to the car or the boat maybe opened something up. Or climbing up on deck instead of lying in a hospital bed where real doctors and nurses could take care of you." So what if he couldn't understand? She wasn't talking to communicate but to keep her mind off the fact that she was totally inadequate to care for him. "But I'm all you've got, and Lord knows, I'm not much." She peeled back the pad.

Jesus, Mary, and Joseph.

Lucy couldn't help her intake of breath. The swollen

wound, held together with stitches like black caterpillars, wound across his inflamed flesh diagonally from the point of his shoulder across his collarbone to the top of his pectoral. A small tube inserted in the bottom was the culprit for most of the oozing. Maybe it was supposed to ooze. What did she know? She began to shake her head convulsively. "That looks really evil."

He peered down at his own shoulder. *"Ne yfel,"* he said.

That was pretty clearly "not evil." She looked up at him, her panic receding. Funny. Just the fact that he understood her made her feel not quite so alone in all of this.

"Ic cnāwe wundes." He grimaced.

She took a breath. It sounded like he said he knew wounds. With a pronounced accent, of course. Surprising that the words were the same, or almost. He said "ic" for "I." But not surprising that he knew about wounds, what with all the scars on his body. She soaked some gauze with Betadine and daubed at his shoulder. It made the skin around the stitches a sickly yellow-orange.

"Hwāet thes es?"

That was pretty clear, too. "For infection?" He didn't understand and she didn't know the word in Latin. "For rot?" That word she knew.

Rot he understood. He nodded again. *"Ilca acetum."*

Yeah. That was what the Romans used on wounds. They might just be able to communicate in English sooner or later. What a relief that would be. Her Latin sucked for actually talking. Reading and translating were entirely different from speaking. Where could she get a Latin dictionary? Jake had said she couldn't go online. A library? She couldn't apply for a library card. Maybe she was no longer destined to own any kind of identification, even a library card. Sad, really. If she didn't know herself, no one else would know her, either.

She daubed at the wound. Nothing she could do about the sticky gray streaks of adhesive the tape had left. She used the Betadine to loosen the tape on the bottom of the bandage. They'd shaved some of his right pectoral, or ripping off the tape might have hurt even more. How long until the stitches could come out? How would she know? Could she pull them out? Her stomach threatened rebellion and she pushed down the thought. Time enough for that later. She made a pad with the bandages and put it over the stitches, then took his good hand and pressed it against the pad so he could hold it in place while she taped it. She was going to need a lot more gauze, for sure. Target had a pharmacy. Definitely a trip to Target tomorrow.

Now for his thigh. She took a deep breath and pulled back the covers. God, did she have to blush at every turn? Another curse of red hair and fair skin. Target had boxer shorts, too. This bandage was bound with strips of gauze. She rose and went to rummage in the galley. She couldn't find a scissors, so she got a paring knife. That would have to do. She tested the edge, but she needn't have bothered. Of course Jake's knives would be sharp. She stalked back to the bedroom. She was not going to let the fact that Galen was naked get to her anymore.

His eyes widened as he saw the knife. She glanced down. What was the Latin word for cut? She couldn't remember, so she just pointed to the bandage on his thigh. "Be calm." That was as close as she could get to "relax." She stalked over and sat beside him. Vowing to keep a firm hold of herself, she cut the bandages and pulled them away. But she could feel herself getting redder and redder. She knew he was staring at her. She would *not* look at him. But when she saw his flat belly shake ever so slightly, her head jerked up in anger.

"You think this is funny?" She didn't bother with Latin.

His lips straightened, but his eyes refused to sober. "*An wif nīedeth an gōd mon.*"

"I am not your wife, and I do *not* need a good man. And in case you haven't noticed, you are wounded and in pain, and you should act like it. Am I going to have trouble with you?"

That sobered him up, though how much he understood was doubtful. She saw again that look of chagrin. No, more than chagrin. It *was* shame.

Finally he shook his head. The words he might not have gotten, but he sure understood that she was angry with him.

"Good." She was ashamed herself for speaking sharply to a man in pain. But really! He had a disgustingly high opinion of himself. She pulled the bandage back with a little less concern for his comfort. The long, straight line of stitches was much less swollen than his shoulder, though this wound was draining, too. The skin around it was inflamed. Was that okay? She daubed at it brusquely. They had shaved the whole front of his thigh. The rest was dusted with light, curling hair. *Sheesh.* She was going to have to wrap his thigh. She wouldn't be able to avoid having to touch him, his inner thigh, right next to his . . .

Her lips tight, she made a pad with fresh gauze and laid it lengthways over the stitches. "Hold it," she ordered. He put his hand over the bandage gingerly. She pulled up his knee and wrapped the gauze around his thigh. Yep. Her knuckles brushed his flesh. His genitals were in clear view. It was awful.

And her reaction to the whole situation was worse. Was she becoming some kind of sicko that a wounded man could make her feel like this? She'd have to go change her underwear if she wasn't careful. As if she had any to change into. When she had taped the ends of the gauze in place she rose, thankful to put some distance between them. She was about to leave as quickly as she could when she spotted the sling on the floor. She sighed.

Picking it up, she turned back to him. He had pulled the covers up. He was looking more relaxed. The Vicodin must have kicked in. She held up the sling. How did this thing work? Okay, this strap over his head. Lay his arm in here and buckle this little strap around his torso to keep his arm close. She pushed a breath out through pursed lips. Couldn't do this from across the room.

"Ready?" she asked. Was she asking herself or him? He was looking mulish. "Don't start." He didn't have to understand the words to realize the meaning.

He nodded, disgusted.

She laid his arm in the sling, then leaned over, very conscious of how close her breasts were to his face as she lifted the strap over his head. She heard him hiss in a long breath. Was he inhaling her scent? For God's sake, was the man an animal? Or maybe she was hurting him. . . .

She pulled him forward. There was nothing for it but to rub against him as she reached for the strap to fasten around his ribs. Surely he would feel how her nipples were peaked. She fastened the little buckle with fingers that weren't quite steady and practically dashed from the room. And to think she was stuck here on this tiny boat with him until he healed.

Whoa. And when he healed she might have an even bigger problem. Good thing she had a sword under her mattress. Now if she only had the skill and the stomach to use it . . .

Chapter Seven

Galen's body relaxed against the pillows as the pain receded. It was not gone, but it was better. Her tablets were more effective than the best valerium. The boat rocked against the dock, sealed against the biting wind outside. The blankets were warm, the bed soft. The glow of the strange lamp that did not burn at least wasn't the stark light of the white room where he had first wakened. But his mind could find no comfort. He could hear the woman moving around in the area with the washbasin and the table. The sound of chopping drifted into his room. Occasionally she passed in front of the open door as she looked inside cupboards, sometimes retrieving a brightly colored container. She was barefoot, her red braid swinging. She had taken off the strange, tight jacket she wore and her arms were bare. Her skin was fine and pale. She must be rich to have skin so white. She had never worked outside. What would the soft flesh of her upper arms feel like in his hands? She carried a good weight, not like a starving peasant. She must be a noblewoman as well as a witch. He could not deny she was beautiful.

The battle seemed far away. Too far. The woman said that this strange and fearful place, full of so many things he could not understand, was in the future and beyond the great sea from his life in the Danelaw. At first he was sure she lied. But what else could it be? This place might have carts that needed no horse to pull them and halls might be made of glass that stretched into the air, but this was not Valhalla or the realm of Hel. It was just . . . just a place where people lived. The woman's friend Jake had swords and made food, though he could turn the fire on and off without a flint. That was not natural. But they had boats and clothes Galen mostly recognized. And there was the language. It was the same as the Saxons in the Danelaw spoke, but changed.

As though by time.

It was the very fact that this was familiar and yet strange that argued she told the truth. And if she did, then . . . what was to become of him?

He had left behind the battle to unite the Danes that he was sure was his destiny. He had not inherited his Saxon mother's magic. His mother had told him, even unto her death, that someday his gift would come to him and he must be on the lookout for it. She had special hopes for him, since he had been born a boy and all the priestesses of the horse goddess Epona, like his mother, gave birth to girls to take their place. She had said that one day he would do great things.

That had just been her desire to fill the hole in her heart left by his older brother's death. It was Eric who was special. He had their mother's magic. All Galen had was what he could push a mere man to be. He had always been on a quest of one kind or another, looking for his value. He went *vikingr* up the Volga River with the Rus and up the Seine. He learned to read and write from monks, that he might serve his people better. He drew the plans for a system of dykes and ditches that drained the fenland though they had not yet been built and invented the bridge that hung from towers and ropes. He had figured out a new way to smelt iron, so the steel for swords and plows was stronger. In honor of it, his mother engaged an artisan to make the sword lost now to the army of this time and carve on it the runes that haunted him. He bound the Saxons and the Danes of his corner of the Danelaw together with strong leadership and fair, in the manner of his father. He was magistrate and defender of their territory. Even though he was so young, skalds sang of his prowess in battle, in judgment, and in a woman's bed.

Thus had he found a purpose. The battle from which he had been snatched was fought in the name of the second King Guthrum to keep the Danelaw strong. Egil Ingvansen wanted to break the Danelaw into North and South. The Danelaw occupied the entire eastern half of the island, the part closest to the shores of Gaul. One day the Northmen who had settled in Gaul would attack the island. They were Norwegians. You could never trust Norwegians—greedy bastards who were bound to covet the green island sooner or later. But if he was stuck in this time Galen couldn't even win the battle that would keep the Danelaw united. The Danelaw, split, would be vulnerable. His people would be subjugated. And he, who should be their defender, would have failed even in this most mundane of unmagical efforts.

He must get back his strength and return to his own time. Here he had no value. He did not speak as these people did. No one wore swords, not even Jake, who owned one, so Galen's skill with one would not be valued. Maybe those men he had seen so far were only peasants who owned no swords. But they did not act like peasants. No one bowed or pulled his forelock, even to the man who wore soft green, who was clearly giving orders. Galen did not understand this place.

The smell of food wafted into his room and he realized

he was famished. That stabbed a knife into his belly. He was totally dependent on the woman. She cared for his wounds. She had practically carried him to the boat. She translated for him. She was about to feed him. Was this the way of a Danir warrior?

She obviously despised him for his weakness. Her tone was clearly ordering. She had actually threatened him with starvation if he didn't take her hellish tablets. He had to admit that he was grateful for the surcease of pain. But to be forced to submit . . . He normally liked strong women. Danish women could inherit property, and many a widow who ran her holdings without the advice or dominance of a man had beckoned him to her bed. But in this woman independence was most annoying. She treated him with such disdain.

She *did* covet his body. Her blushes were certain proof. That was natural. All women wanted a strong and well-made man. It was a point of pride that he had never paid for sex or taken a woman against her will. What need? But this one resisted her attraction. She grew angry when he laughed at her struggle not to admire his male parts.

She came into the room, holding a bowl heaped with steaming food and a glass of water. "Hope you're hungry."

"*Ic eam hungrig.*" The food smelled wonderful. His eyes strayed from the bowl to her face. She was . . . soft. He liked that. He pushed himself up to sitting.

"That sounded just like 'I'm hungry.'" She placed the bowl on his lap. It was a glazed pottery, not wood or pewter. A stew of carrots and potatoes and beef steamed in the center.

"I'll go out and get bread and salad stuff tomorrow." He didn't understand that, but she handed him a spoon and he dug in, left-handed. The stew was strangely spicy. Probably to cover how bland the meat tasted. And the carrots and peas did not have the sweetness of the land in them—almost as if they had not ripened before they were harvested. He could taste the salt. And was that pepper? Only the richest could afford pepper on their food. It came from the farthest trading posts. She must be very wealthy.

She went away and got a dish of her own and a glass of water. She sat with one foot tucked under her on the very end of the bed and ate. But he could feel her watching him.

"More?" she asked.

He hardly had to translate to *ma*. He got it from the context and nodded.

She set her bowl aside and left to fill his. "*Bring meodu*," he called after her. She poked her head back in. She obviously didn't understand. "*Wīn? Bēor?*" He'd rather have mead, but they would do. A man didn't drink water except if he was on a fast march or was too poor to afford a better drink.

She shook her head. "The boat does not have beer or wine." She seemed too tired to speak Latin consistently, but even in her strange Englisc he got the meaning.

He could not hide his disgust. It looked like it was water or nothing.

By the time he was halfway through the second bowl and had drunk the glass of water she brought, he was able to slow down and watch her eat. She was very dainty. She wiped her mouth with a fragile piece of cloth. Was it cloth? He couldn't help noticing that her neck and her chest were bare since she'd taken her jacket off, as well as her arms. Her skin was almost translucent. Her hair was the color of banked coals. If she would but let it loose down her back it would flow like a river at sunset. Her lashes were thick and dark. They only made her skin seem whiter. The fact that she seemed not to care that her legs and arms were bare argued that she was a prostitute as he had first guessed. Yet wantons did not blush in embarrassment about their desires. She was a puzzle. A beautiful puzzle.

She glanced up from her food to find him watching her. Her eyes were gray-green like the sea now, but in the morning light at the docks today they had startled him with the green of rich summer grass. This woman could have any man she wanted. Would she stay with a wounded man?

"*Es gōd*," he said, indicating his bowl. "*Thonc to thu.*"

She was even prettier when she smiled. She handed him the cloth to wipe his mouth. But it wasn't cloth. Could it be very thin parchment? He wiped his beard and mustache, acutely conscious that he had gulped the stew. He watched her brow crease in concentration. "You are very welcome," she said slowly in her heavily accented Latin. "I have sorrow my Latin is poor. You speak three languages, yes?"

He nodded and mustered an answer in Latin: "Danir live beside Saxon in the Danelaw. They must learn the words of both. And the priests of the Christ Cult have influence. It is good to know their language also." A thought occurred. He would give her something to do while he healed, keep her busy so perhaps she would not chafe at staying with him as long as he needed her. And he would become independent of her into the bargain. "You will teach me to speak the Englisc of your time," he ordered. "My tongue loves words and yours are kin to ones I know. I will learn quickly."

Her eyes lighted up. "If I am not . . . having obligation to speak Latin, I am . . . made glad." She slipped out of Latin to mutter, "No. That's not right." She started again. "I want to teach you."

"You can tell me of your world."

She smiled. "You be . . ." She searched for a word. "You will be not happy with my world when you know it."

"It is good to know your foes."

Her eyes opened wide. "I am not your foe."

"No, you are not." He mustn't frighten her. "But you say foes would keep me from my home." He wanted nothing more than to go home.

She heaved a sigh. A crease appeared between her brows. He liked it better when she smiled. "Jake thinks we have such foes."

"Jake is a wise man."

She rose and took his bowl, spoon, and napkin. "Can you sleep? Did you sleep today?"

"No." How could he with so much pain?

She bit her lip. "I am sorry. I will set the . . ." She apparently couldn't think of a word. "I will wake in the night to give you . . . to take away your pain."

He was very tired. He slid down in the bed. She pulled the blankets up, then put the bowl down on the little shelf next to the bed and adjusted his pillows. The linens were finer than any he had ever seen. He was glad for her tablets. They kept the pain at bay. Perhaps he should not have made her threaten him with starvation before he agreed to take them. . . . There was one more thing he needed. "I would have the sword. Bring it to me."

She bit her lip, then gave a tiny shake of her head. "Later," she said. "You are too weak."

He felt his brows draw together. That was true. A fierce fire lighted inside him. He would not be weak long. And then he would show her what it was to serve a warrior leader of the Danir.

She turned out the light. "Sleep well," she said in Englisc. He understood. The words were nearly the same now as then. But he didn't know if he could do as she bid. . . .

* * *

Lucy finished washing the dishes in the tiny galley and put everything back in its place. She took one of the large flannel shirts Jake had sent along for Galen with her into the head just off the salon. She stripped off her knits and she pinned up her hair. In the little mirror she saw her breasts rise as she lifted her arms. She wanted a different body. Now that was a transformation she couldn't make, short of radical surgery. Maybe it was the comparison between her softness and the Viking's hard body that made her more wistful than usual. She'd never been a woman a man lusted after. She'd gotten used to that.

She pushed the wistfulness away and stepped into the shower. Hot water had never felt so good. The muscles in her shoulders unwound as she washed her body, twice. She was quick about it, though. Hot water was precious on a boat. Stepping out, she dried and donned the soft flannel shirt. Then she rinsed out her knits and her underwear with liquid soap until the water was no longer pink and rolled them in her towel to squeeze out the water. When she emerged from the head, she draped them over the little table in the galley to dry. At least she wouldn't smell like blood tomorrow.

This whole situation seemed unreal. She was hiding out on a boat with a Viking from A.D. 912 because someone might want to kill them because they knew the secret of a time machine. It sounded like a bad sci-fi movie. And Brad? Brad the ultrapractical, driven scientific geek, was part of all of this? How could she believe that?

As well as she could believe that a Viking was asleep in the aft cabin.

And she was going to teach him English.

But first, in the morning, she would head into Novato and buy him some boxer shorts.

* * *

Galen watched her through the lighted passageway from the dark of the bedroom, moving about putting dishes away, getting things from cupboards. Did the woman always have bare legs? Even when she was wearing her skirt he could see her knees, and now that she wore only a brightly colored man's shirt, even her *thighs* were visible. It was amazing she wasn't raped half a dozen times before she could make it to the daily market. All men were not like him, who had no need to force a woman. The men of her time must be eunuchs. The only time one saw a woman's body was when one swived her, and sometimes not even then, if she only pulled up her skirts. Perhaps this Brad who was Lucy's lover protected her from attack. But then why had he let her go back to Galen's time alone? If Galen weren't so cursed weak, he would show her the result of tempting a red-blooded man in this way. He would make her *want* to bed him, and then he would show her such pleasure that she would want it many times before she broke her fast each day.

But now he was tired. All day he had lain in pain, unable to find any position to give him relief. Now . . . now the pain wasn't so bad. And that was good. He breathed softly. In. Out. In. Out. Yes. It was definitely better. . . .

"Bring those rollers over here!" Brad yelled at the team from the Army Corps of Engineers unloading them from the flatbed truck that later would carry the machine back to the collider lab down the peninsula. Brad had gotten no sleep, not just because he'd been reporting in to Jensen, who was *not* a happy camper and facing the fact that his project was still in the toilet. He hadn't slept because he couldn't get out of his mind the fact that he really hadn't known Lucy at all. She'd betrayed him by taking the machine and hooking up with this medieval guy. Brad had wanted to marry her for God's sake, even though he could probably have gotten women better looking, or who at least pretended to share his interest in scientific method and pursuit. He'd almost been ready to overlook Lucy's shortcomings. She was kind of a project, just like the machine. He wanted to make her into all she could be. And the ungrateful bitch threw him over for some dumb-ass Neanderthal? Unbelievable. How she'd strung him along, taking advantage of his love for her. . . .

"Dr. Steadman." The big guy with the florid face held out his hand. "Captain Fred Erli. I'm the supervisor on this job." The man's handshake was as bluff and hearty as he was.

"Just get it out safely and quickly."

"Gonna have to take that tarp off."

"Absolutely not."

The man raised his brows. "Look. That tarp'll get caught in the rollers. And we've got to see the structure clearly to know where to hook the cables so as not to damage it."

Brad looked both right and left, disgusted, before he snapped, "Do what you have to do."

Erli gestured to the workmen putting the rollers in place. "Tarp," he called. They ambled over to pull off the heavy canvas.

"Steadman." Brad turned. Casey's eyes were bloodshot. His suit was wrinkled.

"Have you found them?"

"She and the guy took a taxi from the hospital to her apartment. Her fingerprints were on the doorknob. Took a while to talk to everybody in the building. They were at work or whatever. Nobody saw her. Nobody found anything missing." Casey shoved his hands in his pant pockets. "No sign of her at the shop. She'd have seen that it's vacant, so she might not have tried to get in. No taxi with a fare pickup at either the apartment or the shop. We confiscated her car months ago. He couldn't have walked far. Maybe she called someone to pick them up. But her cell phone contract was cut for non-payment, and the only all-night drugstore around there didn't sell any disposables. We checked with her assistant. She says she didn't get a call. Phone records confirm that, but we'll sweat her a little more anyway."

They'd lost her. "Great." He'd thought Casey was invincible. Looked like he was wrong.

"What's even better is that is that I had to spend time cleaning up the trail she did leave." Casey spit onto the concrete. "The hospital called the police because it looked like the guy was a victim of an attack. They confiscated a nasty-looking sword with blood all over it. She told them he was taking part in some battle reenactment and the blood was fake. Of course an event like that would have to get a permit, so it didn't take long to find out she was lying on all fronts. That got everybody excited." Casey shook his head. "I had to call Felton over at the FBI again to get the sword back and take over the case. Don't want the thin blue line tangling things up."

"You got a drawing of him circulating? Someone's got to recognize a half-naked medieval guy."

Casey glared at Brad's questioning his competence. "Not sure what he is. We sent the clothes and the sword down to Stanford for analysis."

The tarp sighed to the concrete floor in big folds. The men gasped at the great golden gears studded with jewels. "I thought you said the clothes were from the Middle Ages."

"The professor down at Stanford said on first glance he thought they were Dark Age."

"When was that?"

Casey frowned at him. "Education a little narrow there, Steadman? You should have gone to the Point. Dark Ages were roughly A.D. 500 to 1000. Rough times. Coupled with the Nordic or Germanic language witnesses report he spoke, looks to me like we have a Saxon or a Viking on our hands." The workers dragged the rollers into place and hooked a cable to the base of the machine.

Brad flushed. Lucy had fallen for a primitive Viking, the kind who pillaged all of Europe? The original terrorists. Saxons weren't much better. They just got there earlier. Brad lost it. "Great. He's probably the one who sabotaged the machine just to get the diamond and you can't find them even though he sticks out like a sore thumb in modern San Francisco."

"We'll find them," Casey said through gritted teeth.

"And you think that, why?"

Without another word the colonel whirled away and strode to the elevator.

Thursday

"Rise and shine," Lucy said, bringing a bowl of oatmeal into the Viking's cabin, along with another dose of Vicodin and Keflex. She'd found an alarm and set it to get up and dose him with Vicodin in the middle of the night. The alarm meant he'd been crouched on the bed ready to attack or defend by the time she opened the cabin door. But at least he'd been awake enough to recognize her and relax into a disgusted grunt instead of taking a swing at her.

"*Gōd mergan*," he muttered now, pushing himself up. She'd heard him giving small, unconscious groans as he tried to get comfortable in the middle of the night. She was afraid the Vicodin wasn't getting all the pain. But she was already giving him two seven-fifties. She couldn't give him more. And this bottle was going to have to last. It said no refills and Jake had said no doctor. If Galen had still been in his own time, he'd have had to live in terrible pain for weeks and weeks, or until he died from infection. How did people live with such hardship? She didn't like seeing him in pain at all.

She set the oatmeal on the nightstand. First things first. "You need to pee? Urinate?" she asked in English because she didn't know the Latin for it. Not happening. He looked blank. She gestured at the door to the head in the corner of the master cabin. "Privy? Bathroom?"

"*Baeth*?"

"Not exactly." But close. Another word that seemed the same in both the English he spoke and her own version. He must have gotten the connection between bath and toilet, though. He got out of bed carefully and made it to the door to the head, giving her an X-rated full frontal view and then a long look at the muscles moving in his back and those round and totally lovely buttocks. He disappeared inside the head. *Thank goodness*. After a while she heard the toilet flush. He was a quick learner. There was a shower in there, but he probably shouldn't get his bandages wet. She'd give him soap and a wet cloth and let him wash himself. What to do about his hair? The sink in the galley, maybe.

He came out, X-rated all over again, seeming unconcerned about his nudity. She wished she could be. "You have a fine mirror. It is glass and not polished metal?" He was back to Latin.

"Yes. Glass."

"Everything here is glass, even the grand halls." He sat heavily on the bed and maneuvered his way to sit against the pillows as she pulled the covers up to his hips. She was probably fifteen shades of red.

"I must go to buy food and clothes. Stay here." It made her a little nervous to leave him. A horrible thought occurred. What if he got bored sitting here with nothing to do and went outside? He was weak, but he'd made it outside to pee last night. She looked around. Okay, well, there was the flat-screen television on the wall. What did parents call it? The electronic babysitter.

She found the remote as he wolfed down his oatmeal. This might be a shock. She stopped his spoon in midair and took his bowl. "Wait. Look at this." She motioned with her head to the screen on the wall and pointed the remote at it. The television flickered to life. He stiffened, his eyes wide as the images settled into a morning newscast. The good-looking guy and the perfectly coiffed girl were talking about the traffic. "It's okay," Lucy murmured. He didn't look soothed.

"What is this magic? Are these the things that are, or that will be?"

"This is like . . . like a mirror. But it shows what . . . happens far away." Drat her Latin.

He seemed to get it, though. He nodded thoughtfully. "You are *wicce.*"

Even she knew that Old English word. "I am not a *wicce.* All people here have these. They are called 'televisions.'"

"I will call it 'far-seer.'"

That kind of said it. And it was poetic, too. Way better than "television." "This," she held out the remote, "changes the . . . the painting." "Painting" was as close as she could get. She showed him volume and the channel control. Fear in his expression was replaced by curiosity. He took the remote and waved it as he pushed one of the buttons. An old western movie appeared. Indians chased a wagon train that had begun to form a defensive circle.

"*Hors,*" he said approvingly. "*Waegen.*" He raised his brows at her. He was testing to see whether she understood the words in Old English.

She nodded, smiling. "Horses and wagons, yes."

"Deathcwealm?"

Whoa. She shook her head. "Sorry."

He shrugged, looking past her at the television. Well, she didn't need to be nervous about leaving him. She was definitely of secondary interest. "Keep the door . . . locked."

He didn't answer but nodded, never taking his eyes from the screen.

"Don't bother to see me to the door," she muttered, and headed for the hatch.

Chapter Eight

Lucy drove the Chevy slowly up the dirt road to Highway 37 past the little convenience store Jake had told her about. She'd brought about a thousand dollars of Jake's cash, but she resolved to spend as little as she could and get back to the boat as fast as she could, before her Viking could get into trouble.

She hit the Target in Novato with a long wish list. Conditioner. Jake's provisioning was pretty basic when it came to hair care. Some hair dye to get rid of the too-conspicuous red. Scissors to cut hair and bandages. There were razors in the bathroom, so she didn't need those. Boxers. She guessed at a size 34 or maybe 36. He was a big guy. Better too big than too small and gaping open, God forbid. She picked up a pair of sweatpants and a sweatshirt, because you didn't have to know sizes. Extra large was close enough.

For herself she found some Nikes for traction on wet decks, some jeans, and four or five long-sleeve and elbow-length-sleeve stretchy tops she could layer. A jacket and some socks, undies, and some bras and that would pretty much do her. She also got a sleep shirt—she wasn't big on pajamas or flannel nightgowns, and the little camisoles with short-shorts looked *way* too skimpy to wear around a Viking who was probably used to raping and pillaging.

She rolled her lips between her teeth. She wouldn't think about that. But she did. The thought of cutting his flesh or shooting him made her ill.

Pepper spray! That would take his mind off any raping and pillaging he might have in mind but not cause permanent damage. Not something they sold at Target, though. No Internet research on her missing iPhone, either. She'd have to ask.

She wound her way over to the pharmacy part of the store. She scooped boxes of gauze bandage and rolls of tape into her cart. The shelves had about fifty kinds of disinfectant. When it came down to it, she didn't know anything about caring for wounds. His were still draining. Her fresh bandages were wetly pink and yellow this morning. That couldn't be good. She needed some help. But she couldn't go to a doctor.

Pharmacist! She couldn't ask too many questions without arousing suspicion. But she might be able to get some help. She went up to the counter that said *Pickup* over the window.

A young Asian woman with long hair and a name tag that said "Pharmacist" looked up from her computer screen. "Can I help you?"

"Uh, sorry. What would you recommend for cleaning wounds? My . . . my husband . . ." Conjugal images rose in her head and had to be thrust forcibly down. "My husband has some stitches in a cut, and I was wondering what to use to keep the area clean." She wouldn't mention just how many stitches. Or the drain.

"I like hydrogen peroxide at half strength. Just mix it with water. Finish with Betadine."

"Thank you." Lucy smiled in relief. Too bad she couldn't ask when to take the stitches out. She'd just get told that his doctor should decide that. But there was one thing a pharmacist would absolutely know. "The doctor gave him Vicodin seven-fifties, but he still seems to be in pain."

"Add some ibuprofen. The combination is really effective." She continued to stick labels to pill bottles. "I can't believe doctors don't routinely prescribe a cocktail. It's really accepted therapy at this point. But no worries. Give him four over-the-counter strength at a time along with the Vicodin. Have him take it with food. That stuff does eat away at your stomach lining."

"If I can get him to take it at all. I had to threaten him last night."

"Men!" The pharmacist rolled her eyes. "So macho."

"*Oh* yeah." *Who was more macho than a Viking?*

"He's probably afraid of getting addicted. Tell him from me," she said with a wicked smile, "that as long as the drugs have something to do, like relieve pain, he won't get addicted. He'll stop taking them naturally when he doesn't need them anymore. Their whole purpose is to let him sleep so he can heal. And don't let him chase the pain. Steady doses, that's the trick. Doctor's orders." She winked. "He won't know we're talking Doctor of Pharmacy."

Lucy had to chuckle. "Thanks." She waved and returned to aisle three to scoop up extralarge bottles of hydrogen peroxide and Betadine, a huge bottle of ibuprofen gel caps for fast action, and a big bag of cotton balls. This Target didn't have perishables, so she'd hit a grocery store on the way out of town. So much for one stop.

She moved to the registers. The girl who rang her up was hefty, with a blotchy complexion and too many earrings. "Know where I can get some pepper spray?" Lucy asked as casually as she could. Now she'd be up to three stops.

"Gee, no," the girl said. "What do you need that for?"

"I live alone in a kind of out-of-the-way place. You just feel better with some protection."

The girl glanced to the boxer shorts Lucy was putting into the bag. Oops, the living-alone thing was maybe not the most believable choice of lies. "He gets out of line, does he? I had one like that. Pepper spray's good. But I've got no idea where to get it. Why don't you go online?"

"Yeah. Yeah, I will," Lucy muttered. Over Jake's dead body. And maybe hers.

"That'll be four hundred and sixty-six dollars. Debit or credit?"

"Cash, actually." She counted out twenty-four twenties from her roll.

The girl's eyes were big. Oops again. "Don't see cash for anything over twenty bucks anymore," she murmured.

"My mom had a fetish for paying cash. Got it from her mom, who lived through the Depression. I guess for me it's kind of a genetic aversion to credit cards."

The girl made change. "You know." She cleared her throat. "You can leave him. There's a hotline that will find you a place to stay where he can't get you. Just call information and ask for the Family Violence Center."

Lucy smiled, sad as that made her feel inside. "You're very kind. Maybe I'll call."

She left feeling guilty. That girl had been in an abusive relationship and made it out. She found the courage to be generous to others. Lucy hadn't had it tough at all. Her life had been pretty okay. So she'd traveled in time and was on the run with a man from 912 who might enjoy raping and pillaging.

But on the whole, things could be worse.

Are you crazy? Strange as it was, she had the strongest feeling she was in the right place, doing the right thing. She found herself standing in front of the newspaper box outside the Target exit. Why didn't she feel more panicked about the whole situation?

Of *course* she was panicked, underneath. She was just too tired to feel it. That was all. She flicked quarters into the machine for a copy of the *Chronicle*. Better look for news of the time machine and any search for her and Galen. She wanted to just sit on one of the benches near the store entrance and scan the paper immediately, but she had to get back to the boat before Galen got up to anything. She loaded her bags in the Chevy's trunk and tooled out of the parking lot. Besides, why should she panic? No one was going to come looking for them in a marina down a dirt road in this backwater. They were safe, as long as he didn't kill anybody or something.

Tempted as she was to just go straight back to the marina, vacuum-packed meals weren't especially attractive. If Galen was going to get his strength back, he needed to chow down. What did Vikings eat? Fish probably, and pretty simple food. No kung pao chicken. There was a Safeway a few blocks down.

The two little fridges were going to be packed. . . .

Galen waited until he heard the growl of her "car" recede before he got out of bed. The far-seer was fascinating, but there were more important things to do at the moment. He wanted his sword. She must have brought it in from the car. She would not leave so precious a thing where others could steal it.

He shoved himself up, cursing his weakness. Had they done something to him in that place of glass and steel to make him weak? But then, he had lost much blood by the time the men had pushed him onto that rolling metal cart. By all rights he should be dead. He leaned against the wood of the passageway, limping past the indoor privy.

He knew full well that she had hidden the sword from him. She wanted him to remain in her power.

He opened each cupboard, each drawer in the kitchen, whether it seemed large enough to hold a sword or not. They held strange boxes or slick-feeling bottles not made of glass. He found the place where pots and pans were kept, glass tankards for drinking, and the bowls out of which he had eaten stew last night. One cupboard contained small, round canisters brightly painted with pictures of food, including round red fruit with tiny stems he did not recognize. Then he found it. A drawer with many knives. He sucked in air suddenly sweet with satisfaction. He picked the biggest knife and concealed it in the sling over his forearm. Not his sword. But good.

He pushed into the sitting area with a soft, long bench chair and another far-seer, the table and bench that he had collapsed upon when he first came down the ladder, and beyond that . . . another passageway. It must lead to the place where she slept, since she had not slept in his bed, though it was plenty large enough for two.

He opened a door in the passageway. It led down to a room filled with the smell of grease and much metal in convoluted shapes. He peered around in the dim light from the open door. He could not tell for certain the sword wasn't there, but he could not find it. Back up in the passageway, he found another door to a shallow closet that held boxes of strange metal tools, and spare rope, boxes of soap. He pawed through everything. No sword,

Too bad. The closet would have been a likely place for her to store the sword. At the far end of the passage, he pushed into the room she had taken for her own. It was tiny, with barely room for a narrow bed on one side. A little box-table like the one beside his bed held a lamp. There was a chest under the bed. He pulled open the drawers. Bedding, but no sword. He looked around. Across from the bed was another cupboard. Inside on a hook on the door hung the shirt she had worn last night that left her legs bare. He could not resist. It seemed to draw his hand. The cloth was almost furry, soft to the touch. He could imagine it against the white skin of her arms and her breasts. He lifted the cloth to his face and inhaled. It smelled exactly the way she had smelled when she leaned over him to fix his sling last night. But now there was the added scent of soap. She had bathed just before she donned this garment. How he would like to bathe her. He imagined his palms, slippery with soap, sliding over the generous mounds of her breasts. . . .

No sword, though. Where had she hidden it?

His eyes fell on the bed. Knowing that she slept there made his loins tighten. He could imagine her, soft with sleep, her long, dark lashes brushing her cheeks. He would love to wake her, his weapon needy to bury itself in her body. . . .

Back to the bed. The mattress was about six inches thick laid over the wooden drawers.

She wouldn't have put it in the most obvious place, would she? He leaned over and felt under the mattress.

She had.

He pulled the scabbard from under the mattress, triumph circling in his belly.

"Hail the *Camelot*."

Galen jerked around at the male voice coming from the dock.

"Permission to come aboard . . ."

Galen didn't understand. But he knew danger when he heard it. Would the ones who came for him call out to announce their presence? He pulled the sling over his head and slid his arm out, gripping the eight-inch knife. With his left hand he tore the strap from around his ribs.

Footsteps thunked on the deck above. Choices. Go up

to meet the danger or wait in ambush? But the quarters
were tight here. No room to for his sword to swing, biting
flesh and hacking bone. He slid the blade from the scabbard with a hiss. He'd have to fight left-handed. More
reason to fight in the open. He wasn't as precise with his
left hand. He gripped the knife with his right hand. It had
no strength, but if it got to close quarters, he might do
some damage.

There was a knock at the hatch up to the deck.

A knock?

That changed things. He stood under the hatchway,
deciding.

"Anybody home? I saw your lights last night."

"*Gōd mergan*," Galen called up. But he didn't put his
weapons down.

"Oh, you must be German. . . . Sorry. I don't speak the
language."

Galen didn't understand the man, but the voice was not
threatening. He stepped up onto the ladder, shifted his
sword to his bad hand along with the knife, and unlatched
the hatch. He pushed it up. One set of legs was visible on
the forward edge of the square trough through which you
entered the cabin. He hadn't heard more than one set of
footsteps. He shifted the sword back to his good hand,
letting it drop to his side where it was less conspicuous,
and put down his knife. Hacking up innocent visitors
would only draw attention.

Galen stepped up the ladder cautiously into the square
trough in a brisk wind. A doughy man with sparse, pale hair
was outlined against a blue sky edged with fast-moving
dark clouds. It would rain soon. The man stepped back in
surprise as Galen emerged. His pale eyes widened. Galen
watched as they roved over Galen's hair and beard, settled for a moment on his bandaged shoulder, darted to the

other bandage on his thigh, registered the fact that he was naked.

The man started to turn his head away, then saw the sword. He raised his hands, palms out. "Wow, didn't mean to . . . to interrupt anything here." He backed across the small deck.

Galen smiled and shrugged, all the while examining the pudgy man for signs of deceit. "*Ic ne understand Englisc.*" Not their kind of Englisc anyway. He stepped toward the ladder up to the main deck. He did not want to be at a disadvantage, even with this pudgy man.

The man's Adam's apple bobbed under his fleshy neck as he watched Galen climb the ladder. "Your neighbors . . . well, one of your neighbors, just wanted to know who was here. This boat . . . well, no one's ever taken it out. And no one has ever stayed aboard, either."

Galen raised his brows politely at this torrent of anxious words. Sweat had broken out on the man's forehead. Now that they were on the same level, Galen towered over him.

"Well . . . well, if there's anything you need, just let me know. I'm almost always at the Quik Stop up on the highway."

Galen watched the man back awkwardly over the line railing. He raised his right hand as far as he could in what he hoped the man would interpret as a friendly salute, ignoring the stabs of pain that shot through his shoulder. The man turned and walked down the dock, glancing back over his shoulder often. Galen registered another figure, tall and angular, browned by the sun, coiling rope down at the far end of the dock near one of the boats lighted last night when Galen was up on deck. As the pudgy one hurried to the gate, the brown man glanced up, then stared down at Galen before calmly going back to his work. He was a man who would not back down from trouble. Galen had known such men all his life and he recognized one of them instantly now. Galen watched the pudgy man until he got into a cart that was not cared for as well as Lucy's and drove away up the dirt road. Galen retreated below decks. He got the hatch secured and collapsed onto one of the soft benches across from the table, breathing raggedly. Curse his weakness! If that small excuse for a man had been the lean and brown one down at the other end of the dock—or even if he had meant harm and had a weapon—Galen would have been in dire straits. He'd better get his strength back fast, before Lucy's lover and his friends came calling. . . .

Lucy pulled into the parking lot in the strip mall on the edge of Novato, now dressed, courtesy of the bathrooms at the Safeway, in jeans and layered T-shirts, a pink elbow-length-sleeved one with lace at the neckline over a white long-sleeved one, a windbreaker, and tennies. She didn't smell like blood at all. Things were looking up. The clerk two registers over at the Safeway had heard Lucy asking about pepper spray and recommended a store called Surveillance Unlimited, right on her way to the freeway. This wouldn't take but a minute, just to check and see if they had it. The store lurked in the corner. She swallowed. The guys who hung out in places like this were mostly semi-loons. But then that included Jake, and she liked Jake just fine. She screwed up her courage and got out of the car.

The store had the kind of windows where you can see out but not see in, which made it look a lot like Darth Vader. She pushed open the door. A buzzer sounded. The place was filled with fancy binoculars and telescopes, cameras with long lenses, tape recorders, and electronic equipment she didn't recognize. A skinny guy behind the counter wore a T-shirt that advertised some long-completed 10 K run. He looked surprised to see her. Probably didn't get many women in here who didn't wear fatigues or camo cargo pants and Doc Martens.

"Uh . . . can I help you?"

"I'm looking for pepper spray." God, she hated that her voice sounded small.

The guy, who was only marginally creepy looking, gave her a big grin. "Sure." He rummaged around in a drawer behind the counter. "You know this is serious stuff."

"Good. I'll feel safer just knowing I have it."

He drew out several tiny spray cans. "I recommend the 'Halt' brand myself."

"That'll be fine."

"Pepper spray is no substitute for a weapon, of course."

This guy sounded like Galen. But he wouldn't be able to even hold up the sword Galen swung to such deadly effect on the battlefield. "I have a gun."

The guy gave her a patronizing smile. "Twenty-two pistol?"

"Glock nine millimeter." She enjoyed the look on his face, but it only lasted a second.

"So, why do you need pepper spray?"

"I . . . I don't feel comfortable using a gun when pepper spray would do the job."

"Well . . . I can see how you wouldn't feel comfortable with a Glock." He didn't think she could handle a gun like that. That made her mad. But there was nothing she could say. She'd already told him she wasn't comfortable with it. "You ought to put in some time at a range."

"I just might do that." Like hell she would.

"You live around here? I could take you over to Home on the Range for a little practice."

Uh-oh. A come-on. "How much is the spray?"

"Thirty-five. Sorry. The good stuff is hard to get these days."

"No problem." She laid two twenties on the counter and wandered away to the bookshelves in the back to avoid further conversation. Like he was going to be deterred.

"Take a look around," he called. "We got all the standards. *The Anarchist Cookbook, Revenge Unlimited.* Mostly stuff about how to use the system against itself."

Lucy scanned the shelves. "Isn't that *Cookbook* one about how to make bombs?"

"No big deal. Everybody knows how to do it these days."

That was a comforting thought. Wait. Lucy spied a big orange book about three inches thick, right next to a book about emergency war surgery. *Medical Surgical Nursing.* Now this might be useful. She pulled it down. It was some kind of textbook. She flipped to the index. *W. Wounds. Dressings, debriding infection, stitches, removal of—* She flipped to page 360 and scanned. *Yup.* Just what she needed. She turned back to the counter. "Can I get this, too?"

He raised his eyebrows. "Sure. That's sixty bucks."

"Sounds about right."

He rang it up. She waved away a bag, gave him a salute, and ducked out to the Chevy.

Chapter Nine

The sky behind her in the west had grown dark and threatening. They were in for some rain. This whole thing had taken longer than Lucy thought. Galen had been alone for hours. What if he overdosed on Vicodin or something? She pushed her speed up to seventy all the way to the turn-off from Highway 37. Past the Quik Stop, she took the dirt road at more like twenty but still faster than was probably safe and parked in the gravel lot. She gathered an armload of bags and let herself in through the gate. Down at the other end of the dock from the *Camelot*, a very suntanned, older, sailor-looking guy worked on his boat. He looked up but didn't greet her. Just as well. She and Galen weren't supposed to fraternize. A kid maybe sixteen came up on deck from a boat about halfway down, followed by a huge black wolf-looking dog. Who kept a dog that big on a boat? She hurried past as they played tug with a piece of old rope.

At slip eighteen she stepped aboard and climbed down into the cockpit. The hatch to below decks wasn't locked. Had she forgotten to lock it? She groped for the ladder juggling her bags. No sound of the television. At least Galen had learned to use the remote. Unless he just threw the television against the wall when he got annoyed with it.

At the bottom of the ladder one very naked Viking brandished the very naked blade of Jake's sword in one hand and a carving knife in the other. She gasped and froze. Where was her pepper spray? Somewhere in the bags . . . But his glower turned to obvious relief.

"You return," he said in Latin, laying the knife on the table.

She breathed again. For a minute there . . . "Well, yeah," she muttered, trying to still her thumping heart while she stacked her bags on the table. Maybe the mattress wasn't an entirely original hiding place for the sword. Now it looked glued to his hand. Not a chance she'd be able to pry it away. She glanced at the sling, its buckle torn from the strap, lying on the floor. "Why are you not in bed?" she managed in Latin.

"A man came here." Galen sat on the sofa.

She turned on him. Oh, this was bad. "What man?"

"A small, soft man."

Well, that let out the sailor she'd seen working on his boat and even the kid. And you couldn't say either Brad or Casey was small or soft. "Did . . . did he attack you?"

"No. I think he wanted to be a friend."

"Did you attack him?" She nodded to the sword, imagining fountains of blood, a body hacked to pieces and thrown overboard.

Galen looked affronted. "I did not attack him."

"Well, what . . . what came to pass?" Boy, this Latin thing was sure getting annoying.

Galen lifted his chin. "He grew frightened and left."

That sword would frighten anyone off. As a matter of fact, Galen, seen through a stranger's eyes, was pretty fearsome with his naked, muscled frame, his wild hair, his barbarian braids, and his beard. Who could it have been?

"He had a cart also, but with more dirt than yours."

A car. Someone not from the marina then . . . It was the nosey man from the convenience store Jake had warned her about, dollars to doughnuts. Galen would cause talk, and she didn't want the man spreading stories of wounded Vikings from here to next Sunday.

"Okay, okay." She had to do something about this. *First things first. Get the rest of the bags in from the car, give Galen something to eat.* She needed to think anyway. "I will return."

She carried in two more armloads of supplies while she thought. The man at the convenience store would tell everyone who came in and they'd tell someone, who'd tell someone, and pretty soon . . . Well she didn't want to think what would happen if the police heard about Galen. Brad and Casey had to have the word out. *Okay. Okay. Just stay calm.* This was bound to happen sooner or later. *First see the man from the convenience store. Make up some story to keep him from gossiping. And what would that be?*

Galen watched her rummage through the bags. She pulled out the three-pack of boxer shorts, one in black-watch plaid, one plain navy blue, and one hunter green. She tossed him the plaid. They hit him in the belly and slid to the floor, since he was still hanging on to that sword for dear life. "For you. Put down your sword." She said it in English without thinking and was amazed to see that he understood. He laid his sword down and painstakingly reached for the boxers. Fierce as he looked with a sword in his hand, he was still injured. It had been less than forty-eight hours since he'd had surgery on his shoulder. He should be flat on his back. That he was not spoke to the fact that he came from an age where weakness was rewarded with death.

He turned the boxer shorts around. His eyes widened

as he found the elastic waistband. He examined the fabric. "*Es ful gōd. Hwāer . . . ?*" Then he found the slit for relieving oneself. One corner of his mouth turned up. The smile softened his face. He looked up at her under one arched brow.

She blushed. "Put them on." She spoke in English because she couldn't recall the Latin for "dress yourself."

He got the idea. He laid his sword reverently on the sofa. He put his bad leg into the boxers and marveled that the elastic stretched to accommodate his other foot. "*Hwaet es this?*"

"Elastic," she said.

"Elastic." He pulled the boxers up to his knees and then stood, a little shaky, and pulled them over his hips. The elastic snapped against his ribbed belly.

Lucy sighed. No more X-rated scenery. That should be a relief. She would never have gotten used to it. Was it a relief? She rummaged in another bag and pulled out a pair of sweatpants. "If you are cold." She handed them to him.

Again he examined the cloth. He pulled it and marveled at the stretch. He looked for the elastic at the waist and pulled it. "*El*astic." He put the emphasis on the first syllable.

She chuckled. "Yeah."

"*Ne cyld.*" He laid them aside.

Hmmm. That was pretty clearly "not cold." The words they understood together were mostly one syllable—the Old English roots of the modern language. The basics lived on. She'd heard the *f* word was Old English, and the *c* word for female genitalia, too. *Bet you won't find those in any modern Old English dictionary.*

He watched her put groceries away. She popped open some herring and sour cream and a package of crackers.

"Lunch," she announced, and handed him a plateful and a fork. It had seemed a very Viking kind of food when she'd bought it.

"Herring," he said. "*Es gōd.*" His attention turned totally to his food, and he stabbed it as though it were still swimming.

Enough delay. There was no use putting off her trip to the Quik Stop any longer, even though she had no idea what she would say. Every moment she wasted was time the guy could be telling people about the crazy naked guy with the sword down on the boat in slip eighteen who looked like a Viking. She switched to Latin. "I go. I will be back. With greatest haste . . ."

Galen barely glanced up from his food as she left. It was less than a mile to the convenience store, but she took the car. She didn't want to be away longer than she had to be. *Look what trouble Galen had gotten into already.* The sky was really dark now and the wind had kicked up. They were in for some Northern California March weather.

She had no idea what she would say to the Quik Stop guy. If he was gossip central, he'd for sure tell the other people at the marina. Only two boats had been lighted last night, but that didn't mean only two were occupied. Jake said anyone who stayed on a boat in the winter was hardcore. The lean, brown sailor looked like just the kind who would know someone like Casey. She felt a shudder start down her spine and stifled it. She was getting as bad as Jake.

She got out of the car in the little asphalt parking lot outside the Quik Stop. Cars whizzed by on Highway 37, mostly trucks going over to Vallejo and Richmond and locals in their pickup trucks. The area was really rural and agricultural until you got up into the wine country, and that was just a more touristy kind of agriculture. The Quik

Stop probably made its money off wine tourists in high season.

She pushed into the store, still not knowing what she'd say to the guy. She couldn't stop the rumor mill. *Hmmmm.* But maybe she could use it. What would keep hard-core types from ever wanting to bother her and Galen? If she said he was a soldier, they'd want to trade war stories. If she . . .

Wait. Oh yeah. She knew what would keep hard-core types a hundred miles away.

The little man behind the crowded counter could be described as small and soft. The radio blared with pop music. He gave her a big grin. She glanced around. There were mail slots behind the counter. This was where their passports would show up tomorrow. She'd better buy something to give her an excuse to talk. Unsurprisingly, the store came equipped with a deli counter to sell unconscionably expensive picnic supplies to tourists. The goods looked a little thin and not quite fresh this time of year.

"Hi there," she said. "Can I get a pint of the olives and some goat cheese?"

"Sure," he said, rising. "You on your way up to the wine country?"

Here we go. "Nope. I'm staying down at the marina."

His eyes lighted up. "With the German guy?"

She let her eyes go soft and gave the sappiest smile she could muster. "Yeah." *Don't even tell him Galen's a Dane.* She cleared her throat. "He's my husband." An image of what a wedding night might be like with Galen started winding itself down her spine. She couldn't help the blush that rose to her cheeks. *Oh, well. That works.*

"Newlywed maybe?"

She nodded. He cut off a slab of goat cheese. "We were in Acapulco on our honeymoon." *How did he get hurt? Shark attack? Too dramatic.* "We were powerboating. He went overboard and got sliced up in the propeller pretty bad." *Was that even believable?* "The first day we got there."

"Wow. You hardly had time to . . . uh . . . get to know each other."

This guy was quaint. Most people these days had "gotten to know each other" in the biblical sense long before their wedding night. She gave a pronounced sigh, as though what he said was completely true. "My uncle lent us his boat as a honeymoon hideaway until Galen feels better. Flew us up here and everything. It was really nice of him."

"Bet you're making up for lost time now."

The blush rose again. *It's okay. Goes with the story,* she told herself. "Well, no, not yet."

The guy laughed as he ladled olives into a plastic container. "But soon. Your husband looked like he was recovering fast when I saw him today."

"You . . . ?" She feigned ignorance.

"I went down to welcome you. Saw your lights last night. I . . . I guess I surprised him."

"Uh-oh. I hope he didn't frighten you with that Japanese sword of his."

"Not . . . not really." The guy looked away and then bustled over to the cash register.

"Oh, I am so sorry. He's really very sweet."

"I'd hate to see him riled up, I'll say that." The register spit out a receipt.

Lucy pulled out a twenty, smiling. *Sixteen dollars for some olives and goat cheese. Sheesh.* Then she sobered. "I hope we can get a little peace and quiet up here. If people start dropping by . . . It's just that Galen not speaking the language and being a little protective of me, well, he . . . might react badly and then there'd be trouble."

"Normally, I'd say he looks fierce enough to keep any-body away. But believe me, those crazies here all winter are tough nuts themselves." He counted out her change. "Nope. The way to keep them away is to let them see you canoodling."

Canoodling? Who said that? Still, it was just what she'd hoped. *But wait. How to explain Galen's fierce looks?* "He's not really fierce, you know. Well, except about me. He's a little shaggy right now. Wanted to have a traditional wedding with all of us dressed like . . . like Druids." *Hope the guy is ignorant enough not to realize that Druids were Celt, not Germanic.* "He won't be quite so intimidating when we get him shaved and those braids out of his hair."

The clerk just laughed. "Lady, if you think that is go-ing to make him look less scary . . ."

"If you only knew how kind he is," she said as though sharing a secret.

"Don't worry, miss. I'll let everyone know you're new-lyweds. The last thing any of those crazies holed up on their boats want is to put up with some cooing turtle-doves."

She gave him one more smile she hoped looked inno-cent. "Thanks."

As she ran to her car, it began to pour.

Galen peered out the thin horizontal port holes into the rain. He should have forbidden her to leave. Why go when she had just returned? Where had she gone? Had she left him forever?

Or she might betray their location to her lover and his warriors, either willfully, because she had a change of heart about disobeying her man, or in innocence. Who would not recognize that red hair? Even now it was all he could do to stand and watch for her. He was dependent on her. She brought food and clothing when it was a man's place to provide for his woman. . . .

Of course, she wasn't *his* woman. She was just *a* woman. Any woman. Any woman who was a sorceress in a time of magic. When he bedded her she would belong to him, at least until he left for his own time. He must bed her soon in order to bind her to him. His thoughts were scattered by fatigue. He wanted to return to his soft bed. But he held himself on watch for her.

There! She scurried down the little dock through the pouring rain, her coat pulled over her head. He went to stand at the bottom of the ladder. Her hasty steps thudded across the deck. The hatch above him opened, letting in spray and wind. She came down the ladder, dripping and breathless, and turned to latch the hatch.

"Oh, *my*, but it is wet out there," she panted. When she turned at the bottom of the ladder, she was very close to him. She was so tiny, so delicate. She wore small gold rings pierced through her ears as though she came from the lands east of the Danube River. Her head came only to his chest. Her eyes were that clear green again. Her face was sprinkled with drops of rain. The red wisps, damp and dark, clung to her cheeks, her forehead. She had a dusting of freckles across her fine, pale skin. He felt a pull in his loins in spite of his exhaustion. It would not be a trial to bed her. She looked up at him and stilled. He imagined her naked body writhing under him, thrusting up to meet him as he plunged inside her. Did she feel that same tightness in her woman's core? Her eyes grew big.

"*Hwāer wert thu?*" he growled, not bothering with Latin.

She pulled back. But she understood him. "I saw your little man." She pushed past him. "You frightened him."

She caught herself and repeated in her halting and badly pronounced Latin. "He must not tell all of a fierce Viking."

"*Hwæt spekest thu to him*?" Galen couldn't seem to muster Latin. But she understood.

She blushed. "That we were new wed. He will tell others. No one will come here."

Galen caught himself imagining the first night after plighting their troth. Would she blush all over her milk white body? Would she be shy and try to cover herself, even though she routinely flaunted her body in skimpy clothing? Mayhaps, at least until he made her moan when he suckled her breast.

Where was his mind? He set his jaw. She had taken care of him yet again by lying to the soft man. That made Galen angry. She should have left it to him to confront the soft man.

"Go to the bed. You are sick."

He wanted to shake her until her teeth rattled for giving him orders, for being right, for his dependence on her, for being so sure of herself. He wanted to make her lie that she belonged to him into a truth. But as he glared at her his vision swam. He felt his knees wobble.

"Don't you dare collapse," she muttered. He didn't understand. But he understood the blackness in his field of vision. She grabbed his arm and half-hauled him, staggering, through the passageway until he collapsed upon the bed on his good side. She pulled the bedding out from under him, lifted his legs, and covered him. He lay gasping like a hooked fish. She brought him more of her vile tablets. He wanted to sweep away her tablets and her flagon of water, along with the concerned look on her face. But only his wounded shoulder was outside the blankets, and almost any movement made pain wash over him. He could do nothing as she sat beside him and rolled him gently to his back.

"Leave me, woman," he ordered, mustering Latin to be sure she obeyed. But she didn't. She lifted him and presented the pills. All fight went out of him. What choice did he have but to obey her? Disgusted with himself, he took the tablets (there were many this time) and gulped water from the flagon she held to his lips. He could not even turn away from her.

Chapter Ten

The man was certifiable. Why did he fight her even when he was ashen and wavering on his feet? She stood, glaring down at him. He turned his head away. *Just great.*

Well, she had other things to do.

Lucy left him in the dim cabin. The *Camelot* rocked more than usual in the water. Rain beat down in waves across the deck above. Rivulets obscured the windows. A worry intruded to crease her brows. The bandages on both his shoulder and his thigh were pink and yellow and wet again. Was that a bad sign? He'd certainly looked ill.

She sheathed his sword and laid it on the sofa. It wouldn't do any good to hide it from him. He'd find it if he had to tear the boat apart. Was he dangerous? Maybe when he got his strength back. He'd been angry with her for some reason just now. The man was incomprehensible. She rummaged in her shoulder bag under Leonardo's book and pulled out the pepper spray. Too big for her jeans pocket. In the end, she put it in the spice rack bolted to the galley cupboards, where it was accessible from the table or the galley itself. She'd have to remember to take the spray with her when she changed bandages or used the head.

Leonardo's book.

She flipped on a cabin light. The day was dim. She

went to her shoulder bag and pulled the book out. The leather with its tooled image of angels ascending to heaven gleamed in the light of the lamp swinging over the table. That book had exerted a power over her for months and now . . .

Now, nothing. It was just a marvelous book, a precious historical object written in the hand of a great man long dead. But she hadn't thought about it since she'd shown it to Jake night before last. When had she *ever*, in the time she'd owned it, not thought about it for even an hour? It had owned her more than she owned it.

She felt like a jilted lover. Whatever had been between them, her and the book, was over, a memory of passion that seemed incomprehensible, even amusing, now that she'd moved on.

Or it had moved on.

What a thing to think! She must be losing it. She put the book in a cupboard above the sofa. That was the first time Leonardo's book had been out of her shoulder bag, except when she handled it, in several months. There was a time when she would have felt anxious. But not now. Now she felt . . . right. Things were as they should be. *How odd.* The feeling this morning at Target of not being panicked about anything had grown even more intense.

She snorted and closed the cupboard. Who was she kidding? She was hiding out with a probably murderous Viking from her own friend. She'd probably changed history. And some CIA type was maybe after her. Things were *way* not right.

She glanced at her watch. Nearly two. She had some time before she needed to start dinner. She'd always been chief cook and bottle washer for her father when they sailed up the coast each summer to cruise among the San Juan Islands off the Washington coast. You could cook a decent meal in tight quarters if you set your mind to it.

Funny. Her father had tried to make her into a physicist, but he was most content to let her do the woman's work on their trips. *Can't have it both ways, Daddy.* She sighed. The experience would stand her in good stead now, though. Not that the stupid Viking would appreciate her efforts. She grabbed the newspaper, sat at the table, and flipped it open. No mention of the time machine or a search for her and/or her Viking. Good.

Wait. . . . An article in the metro section said San Francisco General was doing some construction on the parking structure.

That couldn't be coincidence. Her mind churned. Of course. They'd have to dismantle either the machine or the parking structure to get it out. She read the article carefully, only a couple of column inches. It said only that the residents nearby could expect construction between the hours of 7:00 A.M. and 9:00 P.M., with a quote from the hospital administrator apologizing for a few days of noise and dust. Why had something like this even made the paper? Maybe to keep people from complaining to city hall or loitering. The world beyond Jake's boat was taking its own direction. That made her heart thump. Brad and Casey wanted the machine enough to dismantle a parking garage. They must know that without the diamond they could never make the machine work. They would pursue her to the ends of the earth.

She thought wildly of just mailing Brad the diamond and the book.

But that thought nearly made her ill, it felt so wrong. Jake was right. Casey would use the machine for his own purposes, and those were guaranteed not to be in the best interests of the world at large.

They were in a Mexican standoff. If Brad and Casey couldn't find her and her Viking, she and Galen couldn't get back to the machine to return him to his time, either.

To do that, they had to have a working machine, and that meant giving Casey all he would need to use it. It was a trap, a horrible trap, and she couldn't see any way out of it.

Okay, she told herself. *Just calm down. There's nothing you can do right now. Just take it one day at a time.* She thought back to that time in Jake's apartment when she'd looked into Galen's eyes and known for sure that all they needed was time for him to heal. She wished she had that sureness now.

Speaking of healing, she pulled out the book she'd bought on nursing. The stupid Viking wouldn't appreciate her taking care of his wounds, either. But Jake's blithe instructions to change his bandages and remove his stitches when they were ready didn't provide anywhere near enough detail. Was his wound infected? When exactly should she try to take the stitches out? She read through the whole section on the care of wounds, then read it again.

Well. Interesting. Seepage was normal. You bandaged the wounds primarily to absorb draining fluid. Once the wounds had stopped draining there was some controversy over whether you should bandage them at all. The only other reasons for bandages were to reassure the patient and keep the stitches from catching on clothes. In fact, after her second reading, she kind of came down on the side of those who said you shouldn't bandage at all after the wounds stopped seeping if you could get away without it. The wounds healed better and were easier to keep clean. It was okay to get wounds wet, once they were sealed if you patted them dry, but not the dressings, because they held moisture and collected germs. Pulling the bandages off to disinfect the area just pulled at the stitches. And the book said you should take the stitches out in five to seven days, not the ten she'd thought. At least she still had some time. And she had a plan.

She put away the book and bustled around the kitchen,

marinating some whole snapper, peeling asparagus. Would he know asparagus? There was so much she didn't know about life in tenth-century England. She found a pan large enough to fry the snapper. Fresh bread and butter—he'd be used to those for sure.

A couple of hours later she whirled to find him behind her. For a big guy, he moved silently.

"Stinks good," he said "Ic am hungry." At least that's what it sounded like.

She nodded to the sofa. "Sit. We eat soon," she responded in English.

He nodded. Had he understood that? "After we eat, you will teach me your Englisc," he said, reverting to Latin.

She nodded. The sooner the better. Latin was getting to be a real strain.

The woman could cook. The fish was delicious and the vegetable, too, whatever it was. The bread was sour, but he liked it. She said it wasn't spoiled. It was supposed to be that way. And when he had insisted on mead instead of water, she had reluctantly produced beer in a glass bottle. Not mead. Not beer as rich or flavorful as he was used to, but better than nothing. She would allow him only one, though. It had something to do with the tablets that kept away pain.

He sat now and watched her cleaning up. He had been shocked this afternoon that she wore breeches that showed the rounded curve of her buttocks, but at least her legs were covered. Her torso was covered, too, but so tightly that every swell was clearly visible—a contrast to her tiny waist. Did women always dress to provoke a man in this time? And the shirt clearly showed the cleft of her generous breasts. This Brad was a lucky man.

She did not seem to long for her lover to come to her. She was, in fact, hiding from him with the very man he wanted to imprison. That meant she did not value him. *Good.* This Brad was not man enough to bind her to him. Galen could make her forget him. He would show her what belonging to a man could mean.

When she was finished, she got some large parchment from a cupboard aft and laid it out on the table. She patted the padded bench beside her. It was almost a command.

But it was easy for him to obey her in this small thing. She had something he wanted. He went and sat. She was very close. He could smell the soap she used on her hair and feel her heat. He watched as her nipples peaked beneath her thin, tight shirt. She held a strange wooden stick that appeared to have a charcoal center, for its tip left marks upon the parchment. She drew a line down the center before turning to him.

"You speak Danish and English very well," she said slowly, in Englisc.

He got most of that. *"Min moder is Englisc,"* he said, also slowly. *"Min fæder, Danir."*

"Do you read?"

"Ic raede and wrīte." He was proud of that. He was a rarity, if not in the way his mother had wanted, at least in some things.

"Good." Here Lucy pointed. "Write your words here and I write my words there." She pointed to each side of the parchment

He nodded. *"Werds. We beginnen."*

She was so excited she nearly let him work at it too long. She sat back when she noticed the lines of strain around his mouth and eyes. "Enough. You are tired." He didn't understand that. "You work too hard."

"I wyrce heard." He wrote the words on his side of the makeshift ledger and gestured to her to do the same with

her version. They had been through four pieces of chart paper, both sides. He already understood that modern English had simpler verb forms and he got the fact that the sentence order dictated whether the noun was a subject or object—you didn't need a different word ending. He had the pronouns down cold and could name most everything in the boat. She'd gotten through conjugating the basic verbs, "to be," "have," "do," "speak," "know," a few others.

Galen was really intelligent, maybe brilliant. She was nothing short of amazed.

"You are very good at this."

His smile could only be called smug. "I learn swift."

"Swiftly."

"Swiftly," he repeated, frowning in annoyance. She had seen that several times tonight. He was smart but also driven. He demanded more of himself than anyone had a right to expect.

They resorted to Latin sometimes, but it wouldn't be long before they could stick pretty much to English. What a relief *that* would be! There had been some surprises in how he spelled the words. His "cn" was like modern "kn" sounds. "G" sounded like her "y" sometimes. "Wh" sounds were spelled "hw" in his time. And there were two letters to indicate the "th" sound that didn't exist at all anymore. But on the whole, it was starting to make sense to her, too.

"Bed now. It is late." She rolled up the charts. "I will tend your wounds."

In his cabin he pulled off his sweatpants and lay on the bed. She turned on the bedside lamp. It cast a golden glow over his body. Outside, the rain still beat on the deck and ports. The boat rocked in its slip. She had never felt so alone with a man. The world was far away beyond the darkness. Brad and Casey and Jake, even the convenience store guy, were all irrelevant. It was only she and Galen in the watertight cocoon of Jake's boat, safe and dry, at least for now.

She got the hydrogen peroxide, the Betadine and bandages. She pulled the adhesive on his shoulder wound in toward the incision so she wouldn't tug at the stitches (thanks to the book's instructions). Then she pulled the sodden gauze away. He peered down at his shoulder.

She tossed the gauze and tape aside. The wound was still shocking, but it had pulled together and tightened. The drain in the lower end seemed even more a violation of his flesh than the black, uneven track of stitches. "It's better."

"*Hit hāeth swift.*" He was staring at her. "It heal swiftly," he corrected.

Forget the dropped *s* on "heals"—no use overcorrecting him. "You are wonderful with words." She turned to her disinfectants. He'd understand that. "Wonderful" was a word they shared.

"I was meant to be more," he said in Latin.

She glanced up to him and saw a look of shame flicker across his exhausted face. She had seen that expression before. What had he to be ashamed of? A potent warrior, a man who could read and write several languages in a time when literacy was almost unheard of . . . why would he be ashamed? "What more? More than warrior? More than leader? More than intelligent?" She spoke in a mixture of English and Latin, whatever occurred.

His expression flattened. "You *ne understandeth.*"

Well, if he was going to retreat to being the strong, silent type, two could play that game. She focused on her dressings. As well as she could. Her hands on his body were sending signals to parts of her that shouldn't be taking the call. In fact, she wasn't sure the boxers helped much. They were bulging over his generously constructed male . . . area, which only drew her attention to what she knew was underneath. And the rest of him was bare, except for bandages of course, and so her hands touched hot skin at every turn. Was he fevered? Or maybe she was the one who was hot. Either way, the result was the same. Signals. Shuddering, tingling signals.

Focus, she thought. *Not on that! On the wound. Just tend the wound.* New bandage. *Lay it out.* But the crisp hair on his chest brushed her knuckles and his nipples were soft. They made her want to rub her thumbs over them until they peaked. How had his left hand gotten to her thigh? She looked up. His blue eyes were communicating in a language that didn't need words. She got the message loud and clear.

And she was really afraid her eyes would be speaking just as clearly. What was the matter with her? *This is a probably murderous Viking, remember?* She'd bought pepper spray just to thwart unwelcome advances. Only her body was sending out signals that the advances weren't unwelcome. And she was going to be cooped up on this boat with him for a while. At the moment it seemed like forever. So she had to deal with this whole attraction thing head-on.

She sat back and took his hand from her thigh. Her heart was thudding uncomfortably in her chest. "Look," she said, then started again in Latin. She wanted no misunderstanding. "I am not interested . . ." She wasn't sure that was the right word. *More direct.* "I do not want you."

Those blue eyes blinked, slowly. Was there a hint of a smile around those lips? There'd better not be. "*Thou haban . . .*" He started again. "You have lust for me."

"I . . . I do not . . . lust for you!" Why did "lust" have to be a word from Old English?

"*Ja.* You have lust for me." He reached his good hand around her neck, under her braid.

And she let him. His calluses felt coarse against her

skin. She was throbbing and wet between her thighs. What would it be like to let a man like this have his way with her? Would it be her way, too? Would she give in to him? The word "yield" sounded in her mind.

"*Gield* to me," he said clearly, echoing her thoughts.

She started and sidled out from under his hand, to stand above him, panting. *Yield* was an Old English word? Oh, she hated that. "I will *not* yield to you." *Or to my feelings.* She switched to Latin. That seemed more . . . impersonal. But she was so flustered it was difficult to find the words. "You will be . . . be . . . good."

"I be good." He smiled, slowly. He did not switch to Latin. "Very good for you, Lucy."

"You will not touch me," she continued firmly in Latin. "Or I will leave you."

"You . . ." He searched for the right word. "You want to *cyssan* me."

"I do not want to kiss you." *Much.* At least her brain didn't. She could no longer vouch for her body, betrayer that it was. She searched for purchase on a very slippery slope. She stuck firmly to Latin. "I do not want a lover." Did she?

But this Viking didn't love her. He was looking for an easy conquest. That thought gave her the purchase she needed. "Women now do not live only for the kiss of a man. We have our own lives. We *choose* our lovers." She would have gone on, but the language barrier was just too tough. "Do you want help for your wounds or no?"

He searched her face. "*Ja*, Lucy. You heal mine wounds."

"Okay then," she muttered, losing her Latin entirely. "But you keep your hands to yourself." She sat back down and made sure all her movements were extremely brisk as she taped the bandage over his shoulder.

* * *

Out of half-closed eyes Galen watched her secure the bandage. Why had she refused sex with him? Galen was not used to rejection. Women looking for a man thought themselves fortunate to attract his attention. But not this one. Perhaps he had mistaken her. Could she possibly be a virgin? He never trifled with maidens. She said she had male "friends." Not possible. Women had male relatives who protected them, a husband or a betrothed, or lovers. Jake was more like a father or an uncle to her. Galen had seen that. But what about this Brad?

She said that women of her time chose their lovers, that they did not need a man. Danish women, too, were strong and independent. But, Galen had to admit, not until they were married and widowed. Their fathers chose husbands for them. And many were bought for their bride price and their comely bodies more than for lifelong companionship. When they were widowed, they could inherit land and run their own lives. If Lucy ran her own life, mayhaps she was a widow who had taken this Brad as a lover. That would explain much.

But what would keep her then from a little enthusiastic sex?

Ahhh. She was afraid she would want to deny this Brad after Galen had *swived* her well and thoroughly. That made sense. It would be hard for another to follow in his footsteps.

And yet . . . Could it be she loved this Brad? The thought rankled. What if, no matter her transient lust for Galen, it was he who did not measure up? He imagined this Brad a warrior with dark hair and steely eyes. Did she writhe under him as he claimed her, night and morning? Did she moan his name as he suckled at her breast?

Then, too, Brad was very important if he could imprison anyone he wanted. Galen was nothing here. What matter that he was the king's trusted commander when that king had long since turned to dust? He must push his body back to health. He would have to face this Brad to get back to his own time. And when Lucy saw Galen bring her lover to his knees, when this Brad begged for mercy, then she would be sorry she had not taken Galen to her bed.

She bent over his thigh, not looking at him. She made an apologetic face as she pulled the bandage fastener away from the hair on his thigh, though he did not flinch. Her lips pouted in concentration as she daubed at the wound with her stinging orange-yellow medicine. That wound was already drying and pulling together. The flesh around it was still reddened but not hard and hot with rot. She sat back and cocked her head, studying it.

"No bandage." She spoke in Latin even though it was hard for her, just so she would not speak words their languages shared. She rejected even that intimacy. "It is better."

He grunted assent.

She rose. *Ahhh.* Her blush betrayed her. She lusted for him whether she would or no. She hurried from the room. But soon she returned with her cursed tablets and a glass flagon of water.

"Here."

He took the tablets. His fingers brushed her hand. He managed to touch her fingers as he took the flagon, too. She practically snatched her hand away. She would not meet his eyes as he swallowed the tablets.

"Good night." She switched off the light. The little, rocking room went pitch-black.

He sighed. Whatever happened, he could not afford her fear. "Lucy." He could feel her uncertainty in the darkness. He spoke carefully in Latin to make sure she understood. "I will not try to . . . kiss you again. You need not be afraid of me."

The silence stretched.

"Thank you," she said, in English. Then she was gone.

The whole parking structure reverberated with jackhammers and the bone-jarring crash of front-loaders dropping hunks of concrete into waiting dump trucks. This would have to be the last load. It was long after dark. The smell in the air was a curious mixture of diesel fuel and powdered cement. They'd cleared away the little kiosk and the striped gate arms at the entry.

Brad stood still while Casey paced the sidewalk. His head ached with the noise. Or maybe it was the fact that he wasn't sleeping. He couldn't stop thinking about what a fool he'd been with Lucy. Why had he been so obsessed with her? A bookseller, for God's sake, when he deserved someone as brilliant as he was himself. She wouldn't take up science. She wouldn't run marathons with him, even though it would have made her leaner. She wasn't his ideal of a woman at all. Who knows what some hulk from the past saw in her?

He wasn't the only one upset. The hospital administrator was livid. Especially since no one would tell him exactly why the machine in the parking structure was so important that hospital routine had been shattered, or how it had gotten there if it was too big to fit through the entry. Patients had to park two blocks over in the public lot. Employees were walking five blocks. Only ambulances were allowed to use the driveway and even they had to pull in about fifty feet from the ER doors and run their gurneys up the sidewalk. Cops manned the barriers out at the street where gawkers milled.

And now the engineer said it was going to take three or four days to get the machine out.

Casey stopped in front of Brad, fuming. Casey looked worse than Brad felt. "I need a cup of coffee," Casey muttered in a normal voice, which meant Brad had to read his lips.

Brad followed, squinting, as though to shut out the noise.

The hospital felt as silent as a tomb after the din of construction, in spite of intercoms and conversations and heels clicking on the linoleum floors. Down in the cafeteria they filled Styrofoam cups with sludgy coffee and paid the cashier before finding a table by the window. An elderly woman was crying in the corner. A father tried to keep a boy of about seven from zooming around the room like an airplane. Casey didn't even seem to notice. He stared out the window at a little courtyard garden, ignoring his coffee.

"Any news of them?" Brad blew on his coffee. No use burning his lips.

Casey turned cold blue eyes on him. "What do you think?"

Brad just sipped his coffee. It burned in spite of his efforts and he sputtered.

Casey ignored him and turned those eyes out to the garden again. "Won't get anything useful out of her shop assistant now, because she'll say whatever we want to hear."

Brad shuddered. He didn't want to think about why.

"They didn't use cabs," Casey continued. "No hotels. No other hospitals. We've checked surgeons and primary-care doctors to see if they had anyone showing up for aftercare for shoulder surgery. Nothing. We've got the pictures and the artist's renderings spread out over airports from San Diego to Seattle, BART and Amtrak stations. We're blanketing the surrounding counties."

"That sounds . . . promising," Brad offered. Casey's eyes were scary cold.

"No, it doesn't," Casey snapped. "It's as if she and the Viking disappeared into thin air."

"So . . . uh, the Stanford guy confirmed the guy is Viking?"

Casey seemed to notice his coffee for the first time and took a gulp. It must have been hot enough to scald, but he didn't register pain. Casey was one big callus. "Hard to tell. Clothes are tenth century. Sword is Saxon workmanship, but the etching on the blade is in Danish runes. Apparently, it says: 'I was made for the son of Valgar, for whom the world waits.' "

"What the hell does that mean?" Anger welled up in Brad's throat.

"It means the guy has a high opinion of himself."

Lucy had a high opinion of him, too. *Stupid bitch. She falls for someone with empty boasting on his sword.* Brad only realized his grip had tightened on his coffee cup when the Styrofoam broke and hot coffee spewed over the table and onto his lap. "Jesus!" He jumped up and grabbed napkins from the dispenser on the table to scrub at his Dockers.

"Maybe the landlord is the key," Casey muttered. "If you expect to get into your apartment after four months of not paying rent, you've got to have an in with the landlord. She was probably boffing him, too."

Brad swallowed. That couldn't be. "Maybe the damage made the machine bring her to the wrong time. Maybe she didn't know she was four months late."

"Then she'd be surprised she couldn't get in. And where might she go?" Casey dripped condescension. "Landlord's lying about not having seen her. We'll work that angle." Casey rubbed his jaw. "Then we have the problem of how they got away from the building, landlord or no. They didn't take a cab. There's no car missing from the parking lot. *We* have her car, and they can't have walked with him in such bad shape."

"Rental car delivery?"

"Checked that."

"You need a witness. Maybe there was a homeless person outside her apartment."

Casey stared back at the garden, jaw working. Okay, he'd checked that. Brad resolved not to offer any more suggestions. But Casey wasn't giving him a choice. "There's got to be something about her we're missing . . . some skill, some . . . something that might tell us where she was." He looked at Brad.

"I told you everything I know months ago. She hangs out in libraries and bookstores. She walks—a lot. She knows lots of languages."

"Okay, that's now. What about things she did as a kid?"

"Well, she used to sail, and I think she had horses once."

Casey's eyebrows rose. "You never said she sailed. That has possibilities." Brad was relieved he'd said something useful. "Jensen find any diamond big enough to substitute?"

Brad shook his head. "There's a new one from India about the right size. But it's still in the rough. The cutters in Amsterdam are studying it before they take a chisel to it."

"I'll tell them to get on with it."

"It isn't that easy. They have to eliminate the flaws by using them to split the stone. By the time they get it cut down, it may not be big enough."

Casey rose suddenly and drained the last of his coffee. "I'm going to get some sleep." All eyes in the room followed him as he strode from the cafeteria. He looked like danger incarnate. Rumor had it that the last job he'd been on, a guy who'd reported Casey's tactics to his superiors had gone missing. Well, all except a couple of fingers. Brad wondered if he should just go back to the lab and stay as far away as possible from Casey.

But if anyone could find the fugitives Casey could. Brad wanted to be there when he did.

Chapter Eleven

Friday

Lucy dragged herself out of bed. She'd slept badly. Maybe it was the pepper spray under her pillow. He might have promised he wouldn't try to kiss her, but you could rape someone without kissing. *Whoa. Cynical.* Did she really think he structured his promise so he could keep it and still rape her? The kind of guy that rapes a woman doesn't care if he breaks a stupid promise. The problem was that deep inside she believed Galen was an honorable man. She might be losing it, but . . . but there was something about the look in his eyes . . . Maybe that was naïve. Too cynical or too naïve? The endless tape of uncertainty had played over and over in her mind last night. So, she took the pepper spray to bed. Cold comfort that.

Speaking of comfort, she couldn't find any. And definitely not anything cold. Her thoughts, waking, and her dreams, asleep, all had a temperature north of a hundred, involving one raping, pillaging, and very attractive Viking. Not comfortable at all. Even now she was wet between her thighs, left over from the dream she'd had just before being wakened by thunder and the pelting rain of a fresh shower.

Maybe pepper spray wouldn't protect her from what she really feared: that she was the one who would end up running her hands over his body, inviting a lot more than kissing.

He was *wounded* for God's sake. That sure didn't seem to stop him last night.

And he wasn't her type. *Viking? Hellooooo.*

Well. She wouldn't think about any of this anymore. The best thing to do now was take a shower, for a lot of reasons. She got up, hugging her arms around her fake-satin sleep shirt. It was emerald green, her favorite color. The boat was cold. The ports were fogged opaque, the rivulets of rain on the outside only faintly visible. She pulled out her jeans and some fresh underwear and T-shirts from the drawers under the bed. Best dress before the Viking was awake and rev up the electric heater. She'd forgotten all about dying her hair yesterday in her panic to do damage control with the guy at the Quik Stop. Now the guy at the Quik Stop and the kid and the brown, hard sailor on the other boats had all seen her red hair. If she dyed it now, wouldn't that just scream that she and Galen were hiding?

She slipped out the door to her cabin on the way to the head. She was too late to avoid Galen. There he was, in all his half-naked glory, limping out of his own cabin.

His eyes dropped to her bare legs, slowly. She was acutely aware that she was not wearing a bra and her too-ample breasts were free underneath the sleep shirt. He tore his eyes upward to her face. "Lucy, what day is today?" She hadn't taught him "today." It must be like so many other words—the same in both Old and modern English.

She had to think. What had they told her at the hospital? It was a quiet night because it was Tuesday. That meant today was . . . "Friday."

"Friday." His brow creased. "Danir take bath on Thorsday. I am one day late."

"In there." She nodded to the head. A shower would

make him feel better. "No bath. Shower." He didn't know what that meant in these times, even if he understood the word. "I'll show you. First take off the bandage. We have to see if your wound is ready for a shower."

He sat on the sofa and peeled at the tape. He was doing it wrong. He'd only pull too hard and tug at the stitches. She cleared her throat.

"Let me." At least the bandage wasn't wet with seepage. She peeled away the tape and gently pulled back the gauze, touching him as little as possible. It wasn't little enough, of course.

The wound looked much improved. The edges had lost puffiness. He healed quickly. Still, no way would the stitches be ready to come out Sunday no matter what the book said. "The wound is good."

He peered down at his shoulder. "*Ja*. I tell you this *beforan*. I am mighty." It was a mixture of what she had taught him and his own words, but it worked.

"Okay. You can have a shower."

She turned away to get him a towel from the drawers set into the cabinet next to the head. When she turned back, he had the plastic tubing at the base of his wound between two fingers. "No," she started . . . but under her shocked gaze he pulled it out with a grunt.

He looked up at her. "It is time."

She sighed. Well, at least *she* didn't have to pull it out. She took it from him. It was maybe three inches long. Was his wound that deep? She peered at the stitches. A little blood and the drain left a bit of a gap, but it was probably okay. She tossed the tubing into the trash compactor and handed him the towel, pushing past him toward the head.

Opening the narrow shower door, she turned one of the faucets. "Hot. Understand?"

He nodded.

"Cold." She turned on the other one. "Soap." She held

it up. "Soap for hair." She pushed open the top of the shampoo bottle and squeezed so he could see how it worked. If he couldn't soap his hair with one hand, she'd have to do it in the little sink. "Be quick. The water tank is small." He looked blank. "Water?" He nodded. "Tank?" *Not getting that. What was sort of a primitive tank?* "Barrel?" Yep. *That did it.* She could see it in his eyes. "Small? Little?"

"*Ja. Lyttle waeter byrla.* I be swift. Am swift," he corrected.

She squeezed past him. *Much* too close. He seemed to fill the tight doorway. He stepped inside and stripped off his boxers without bothering to close the door.

"Do you *like* to be seen naked?" Without waiting for an answer, she pulled the door shut.

But she heard him say, "*Ja,* Lucy. I like naked." Great, "naked" was the same word in both times. She might have guessed. He obviously had much less concern about his body than she did. Why would he? He must have about 2 percent body fat. Not that he was stringy. A better description would be "packed with muscle." Lovely, round butt, heavy shoulders, a broad back that rippled with every movement, an eight-pack, not six-, and thighs . . .

She turned on an electric heater in the salon. She might not need it long. She was definitely feeling warmer. She sliced bread and put it in the oven to toast and slapped some bacon into a frying pan, got out some eggs. Water beat against the fiberglass shower stall. She wouldn't think about him soaping his . . . No. Definitely wouldn't think about that.

The shower went silent. Jeez, he'd probably rip open his stitches drying himself with the towel. She gritted her teeth and opened the head door. "Come here." He stepped, dripping, out into the passageway. His hair was wet, too, the blond color darkened. He smelled clean, but there was still something masculine about his scent. It made her want to bury her face in his chest. She grabbed his towel and glanced up at him. Speculation flickered in his eyes.

Great. Now he thought she was coming on to him. "I don't want you to harm your wounds," she muttered, not caring if he understood. She patted his shoulder dry. "Like this." She was not going to do his thigh. That was way too close to . . . well, she just wasn't. She handed the towel back to him and nodded toward his other stitches. "You now."

He took it from her, his eyes fixed on her face. "*Thonc to thu.*"

"Yeah, well, it was nothing." She turned away. *Think about something else. Like his hair. And his beard.* She was going to have to do something about those. She backtracked to the head and found the razor. Then, since she didn't want to prolong her agony, she retrieved another set of boxers (the navy blue ones) and sweats from his closet in the bedroom, along with one of Jake's shirts. When she emerged, Galen had finished drying his body and was toweling his hair, braids and all. He'd managed to lift his bad arm a little. The nursing book and said he ought to start moving it as soon as possible, so that was good.

"Here," she said, shoving the boxers in his general direction.

He grinned at her. "These *bēoth* for me *othe* for you, Lucy?"

She rolled her eyes and went to retrieve the toast. "The word is 'or,' as in 'me or you.'" She slathered all four slices with butter and quartered some of the pears while the bacon sizzled. She saw him slide into the bench around the table out of the corner of her eye and chanced a glance. Whew. He'd managed to get Jake's shirt on, though it wasn't buttoned because it was too tight across the chest, and the sweatpants. Better for her sanity all the way around.

Galen seemed to like the food. He went through three

slices of bread, four scrambled eggs, two pears, and all but two slices of the bacon. When she had cleared away the plates, she picked up the razor.

"Now. Your beard." She pointed and held up the razor. She'd tackle one thing at a time.

He looked wary. "I like *min* beard."

"We are hiding," she said. "Yes?" She waited for his wary nod. "Then no beard."

He thought about that. "I have no beard if . . . you . . . are not . . . *wundenlocc.*"

What?

He pointed to her braid. "Okay. Point taken. Braids are recognizable." She handed him the razor and gestured toward the head. He glared at her. "Oh, all right," She flipped her braid over her shoulder and pulled out the band that held the end. She ran her fingers through it to separate the strands.

A small smile tugged at his lips. "Better."

"Now you," she said firmly, handing him the razor. "Use soap."

He took it, suppressing his smile, and retreated to the head, examining it carefully.

Did Vikings shave at all? If they did, it certainly wouldn't be with a Gillette four-bladed Skin Saver. They *probably use a knife the size of . . . well, a really big knife.*

She busied herself washing up the dishes and putting things away. You couldn't afford to be untidy living in so small a space. She got out the nail scissors she'd bought. They'd have to do to cut his hair. But her attention was all for the quiet in the head. What was taking so long? Could you accidentally cut your throat with a safety razor?

When the head door opened, she whirled around and was confronted by a stranger. Beneath that beard had lurked a chiseled chin that sported a cleft. And now that it wasn't obscured, his mouth was fuller than she'd thought, his lips soft looking. He seemed younger than the hardened warrior who had gone into the head a few moments ago.

"Lucy *likath* . . . likes no beard?" His eyes were sly.

Oh, God, she was staring. She turned away and shrugged. "You look different." She glanced to him. "Not the same." *Nope*. That wasn't getting it, either. "You are a new man."

He rubbed his jaw. "*Ja*. New man."

She brandished the small scissors. "Now for your hair."

His head jerked in her direction, registered the scissors gesturing toward his locks. He stilled. "No. Not hair." His lips were a grim line.

"No men have hair like you. We are hiding, remember?"

"No." He drew himself up. He looked like the Rock of Gibraltar. "Not hair."

She frowned. She couldn't cut his hair if he didn't want her to. Unless she pulled a Delilah and did it in his sleep. *Right*. She'd never believed that story. Samson would have wakened and just pitched Delilah across the room. Like this Viking had nearly done when Lucy had tried to wake him in the car the other day. Maybe the Samson/Delilah story applied in other ways, though. In Samson's time men thought long hair was what made them a man.

"Okay. You can keep your hair." She put the scissors in the head. "But no braids for you, either. They're just too . . ." Well, just too everything if it came to that. She retrieved her brush from her bag and handed it to him. He was probably used to combs carved out of antlers, but he got the idea. He sat and pulled the leather ties from the narrow braid at each temple, glaring at her. She couldn't help but grin. "Turnabout is fair play. Sauce for the goose?" She reverted to Latin and repeated the sentiment.

The corners of his lips tugged upward against his will. He dragged the brush through his hair. It got stuck. Too many tangles. She rolled her eyes.

"Silly." She strode over, extracted the brush, and started from the bottom.

He went still. She worked at the tangles, trying not to break the strands. It was such beautiful hair, thick, a dozen colors of light brown and blond. Untangling it took a long time. She couldn't help but touch his neck, his cheek, but at least Jake's red and black plaid flannel shirt covered Galen's upper body. Brushing his hair this way was strangely peaceful. When at last the brush ran through the strands freely, she stood back and put her hands on her hips.

"There."

He pushed his hair behind his ears. It promptly fell across his cheeks, too thick for such confinement. Guess that was why he braided the temples, to keep it out of his eyes.

"Okay." She took one of the leather thongs, gathered a piece from each temple at the back of his head, and tied them firmly. "Better."

He nodded, examining her face. "Now you," he said, standing.

"Me?"

"Sit," he ordered. "Sauce." The tiny smile appeared at the corners of his newly revealed mouth. He had a sense of humor. It made her think it might be okay to do as he said. To yield.

Don't go there.

But she sat. He knelt beside her and took the brush. He started at the bottom of her hair and worked his way up until he could brush with long strokes from the crown to the ends. "Is good hair. You are *fȳrfeaxen.*"

He probably wasn't talking about faxing fire.

"Hair *mid fȳr.*"

It dawned on her. "Red-haired." She smiled. How could she not? "You can write it for me." She got up and got out their chart paper.

Shoulder to shoulder, heads bent over the chart, puzzling out a common language felt . . . natural. Mayhaps even right in a way Galen could not explain. He could smell her hair, the woman's scent of her. Her breasts moved freely under the fine smooth green shirt she had slept in. When he first encountered her this morning, she had seemed self-conscious. But now she had forgotten herself in the task at hand. Her hair was thick and wavy from her braid. It cascaded down her back and over her shoulders like a molten river of lava. Was it the same in her time— that a woman's hair was left unbound only in the presence of her family or her man? If so, then letting him comb it was for her the incredibly intimate gesture he'd intended. They had combed each other's hair. He felt his manhood stir. It was as well she had brought him the baggy breeches that stretched. He didn't want to frighten her and spoil this moment. He repeated the word she spoke.

This language would come easily. It was much like his Englisc, only more simply constructed. The words that were different he would learn. Some of them seemed related to Latin, which made those easier, too. He had an excellent memory, almost as good as a scald's. And he had learned much harder tongues under much less comfortable circumstances. The prison in Kiev flashed through his mind. Learning the language of the wretch in the chains next to him was the only thing that had kept him sane.

He had suggested that they try to speak only English so he would learn faster. She agreed, with the proviso that she could revert to Latin for words that were difficult to explain. Just now only half his attention was engaged in learning the action words she was teaching him. The other half studied the delicate tint washing the fine, pale skin of her cheeks and the long, dark lashes that hid her green eyes as she wrote the word "sail" on the parchment. The smattering of freckles that dusted her nose made her look vulnerable.

After last night, there were things he wanted to know about her. The intimacy of learning her language just might afford him an excuse to find out.

"I want a new word," he said. "*Widewe*. You understand this word?"

"Widow? Yes."

"Are you widow, Lucy?"

She looked surprised. "No. Why do you ask?"

Any woman in his time would have known exactly why he asked. He was glad she didn't. But he didn't like her answer anyway. If she was not widow but had no man, she would be virgin. A virgin was off-limits. But how could she be a virgin when she consorted with this Brad? Galen didn't like to think she might have given her maidenhead to this Brad without the protection of marriage. Galen chewed his lip. Was she promised but not yet married? Not as good but some protection. He didn't like that, either. Again, she would be off-limits to him. Why get bad news? Still he had to know if she had a protector. Even in this world that must be important. Would she understand the word for promise? "This Brad *weddast* you?"

Her cheeks went red. She looked away. "No."

This was bad. Brad had not promised her, yet her blush said clearly that she had bedded him. In spite of her clothing, Galen had grown certain she was not a prostitute. But she would never call this Brad her friend if he had raped her. That meant she had given herself to him in spite of

the fact that she was not betrothed. Galen's gut churned.
There was only one reason for that. Why was this so important to him?

"What is the word for *lufian*?"

"Lufian?" Her delicate brows creased. "I don't know."

He pressed ahead. "You *lufast* Brad?"

She got that one. She flushed to the roots of her hair.
"No. I told you. He is a friend."

Galen frowned. "Is he very old?" Maybe this Brad was
like Jake, more a father or an uncle.

"No. He is about my age."

"He has your years?" This was bad. "No man of your
years is friend. He lusts for you, Lucy. Do you lust for
him?" The thought made Galen's gut churn.

"No!"

"Do you allow him—?"

She didn't let him finish. "No! And that is not for you
to know anyway."

"When he wants to imprison me, it is for me to know."
He had to admit to himself that was not why he asked.
"What is he for you?"

She was silent for a moment, thinking. Then she took a
breath as if for courage. "It is hard to explain. To make
you understand," she corrected herself when he didn't get
the gist of it at first, "I will speak Latin."

She wanted to change to a language they didn't share
to push him away. "No. English. Speak more slow."

She looked down. "My father liked Brad. Much."

Was she using past tense? "Your father is dead?" Galen
made his voice gentle.

She nodded and her eyes filled. She managed a small
smile. "Nine months."

Well, "dead" was a word they shared. "I am sorry for it.
Do you have kin from your mother?" He raised his brows
and waited quietly. She stared at the word charts.

"No. I have only Jake. And Brad. My father wanted me to marry Brad." She glanced up at Galen. "Marry? Wed?"

He nodded. Her word for marry was the same as his word for promise. Not surprising.

"I do not love Brad. I want to love the man I marry. But Brad can speak of my father. I like to speak of my father with Brad. It makes me remember him. Like he is not dead."

Galen saw it all. This Brad only waited for her to recover from her father's death. Would Brad ask her to wed him, or would he just take her virginity so that she would have no choice but to wed him? Galen liked the fact that she did not love Brad. But perhaps Brad would worm his way into her affections and convince her that it was love, and she would go to him anyway.

"Do you know love?"

"No. I have known men." She was bright red now. "But I do not know love."

So she was not a virgin. Galen blinked rapidly. That meant she was available. That was good. It meant she might have been a prostitute at one time. He didn't care about that. And now he knew why she wanted to be her own person, away from men who might have victimized her.

She looked up at him expectantly. Her eyes asked him a question. He grasped for what it might be. *Ahhh.* She wanted to know if he knew love. He couldn't enlighten her on that one. He had loved his mother, of course, and his father in a different way. Galen treasured companions for their loyalty, their wit. He owed fealty to his king. Galen liked women, respected them sometimes even. But love?

"I do not know love also, Lucy."

She smiled at that, a little sadly, and he returned in

kind. That felt good on some deep level, to share a smile. A slinking, uncomfortable thought wormed its way into his brain. She might not love Brad, but without her maidenhead what place in the world could she have if some man did not promise for her and make her his bride, or at least agree to protect her in return for exclusive use of her body? Jake would try to protect her, but he was old. He would die soon. Her only choice might be prostitution without the protection of a man. She had disobeyed Brad. He was angry with her. Mayhaps he would not protect her. She was vulnerable. Something inside Galen stirred.

But she was so beautiful surely another man would protect her if this Brad did not. "You have other men friends, Lucy?"

She blushed again and shook her head. "Not now." She held her chin up. "I am not what men want. Fyrfaexen. Not thin. Not tall."

They wanted a woman to look like a starving peasant? What were the men of this time, that they did not tell this woman that she was beautiful every day of her life, with their eyes, if not with their words? Even this Brad, who lusted after her, had not made her feel the power of her beauty. Galen could make her feel beautiful, if he was to be her protector. . . .

Fool! He was in no position to be her protector. But Brad was.

If Galen had his way, this Brad would be *made* to promise for her. He should be flogged until his back was raw and bleeding if he made her unhappy for a moment in time. Galen wanted to be the man to do it. He grimaced and shrugged his shoulder, trying to loosen it. The swelling made it tight and painful. Curse his weakness . . . He didn't like to think of her belonging to this Brad, but she needed someone to protect her, and this Brad was certainly powerful.

Galen had no standing in this strange world to make Brad do anything or to protect Lucy himself. That thought rankled like a burr under his horse's saddle.

But there was another thing he wanted to know. "Why did you go to my time, Lucy?"

"To your time?" She looked uncomfortable. "I had the book. Brad had the machine." Galen didn't understand the word "machine." He signaled as much to her. Why could he not learn *faster*? She switched to Latin. *Ahh*. The bronze wheels were called a machine. She went back to English. "I thought it was . . . fate. You know fate. Destiny?"

He shook his head, and she had to resort to Latin again. Frustration made him want to stand and pace the room. But that would only take him away from her, and he didn't want to lose their contact. "*That* was stupid." She tried to laugh and resorted to Latin to explain the word "stupid" again. "Enough of this." She tried to make her face hide her feelings. One of the best things about her was that she failed. Her eyes told her soul, like the color of the ocean that varied with the weather and the health of the sea. "We must work."

He let her go back to their lessons. He needed language if he was ever to be independent.

" 'Sail,' " she said again, writing it in her column. "Like 'sail a boat.' "

He nodded and wrote *seglian* on his side of the ledger. "I sail. You sail. He sails. They sail. Sailed. Sailing. Will sail." He would learn her English if he had to work day and night.

She must know her vulnerability in angering Brad. Did she have any options at all? "Lucy . . . ," Galen began.

She shook her head. "No more questions. Just the lesson. 'Walk.' " She wrote it down. And then she suddenly said, "I have not yet had my bath." She rose and hurried to her cabin.

The moment of intimacy had passed. He was sorry. But he was not sorry for what he had learned. He wanted to know more than action words. He wanted to know, for instance, why this Brad had let the woman he lusted after go into the middle of a battle alone and unprotected.

Chapter Twelve

Lucy let the hot water sluice over her head, trying to keep her balance as the boat rolled in the wind that had kicked up after the rainsqualls of the morning.

Why the hell had she answered Galen's questions about Brad? And admitting that she slept with men? Waaaay too personal. Was she an idiot? She had blurted out her life story to a Viking she'd known for—what? Three days?

She poured a handful of shampoo and began scrubbing at her head. All she really knew about him was that he was insufferably sure of himself with women. He probably bedded everything in sight in his own time, whether they were attractive or not. Which was the only reason he'd come on to her. She wasn't anybody's idea of beautiful. She'd so forgotten herself she sat next to him clad in nothing but her sleep shirt for hours while they studied this morning. Was she out of her mind?

Or did she subconsciously want to provoke another attempt to kiss her?

Absolutely not. She'd just gotten carried away with teaching him. He was not her type. She liked a refined man. Brad was refined. Well educated, knew good wine. Liked to take her to the Exploratorium to try to change her into a woman who loved science as much as he did . . .

Enough. She rinsed her hair and soaped herself. There were other refined men besides Brad. It didn't mean she'd fall for a guy who practically dragged women around by their hair.

She was at a fragile time in her life. That was how she'd let Leonardo's book become such an obsession. That was why she felt such an attraction to Galen. And why she had dashed back in *time* for God's sake, looking for answers about a life to which she no longer seemed connected? She should have told him she loved Brad and Brad loved her. That might have made her off-limits, even in his Dark Ages mind. Why hadn't she?

Because he asked her for the truth.

As if that mattered when it came from a man like him. She pushed open the shower door and grabbed a towel. He'd just been looking for a chink in her armor. He wanted her to admit she was free and desired him so he could slake his lust without actually raping her. He must know he was dependent on her right now. He wasn't unintelligent.

Far from it, actually.

She pulled on her clothes and dragged the brush ruthlessly through her hair. That brought back the moment of closeness they'd shared while he brushed her hair. Surprising in the extreme. She could still feel his big, calloused hands lifting her hair, his breath on her neck . . .

Get hold of yourself.

Right. Right. Well, it was good that his English would improve so rapidly. Two could play this game of eliciting uncomfortable admissions. Because he wasn't the only one with questions. Why, for instance, did he look so ashamed of himself sometimes? That was so at odds with his insufferable sureness. Why had he been fighting Danes when he was half Dane himself? And did he have a woman back in 912? She snorted to herself. He probably had dozens, eager to welcome him to their beds. Why not, with that body and that smile?

But still there were things about himself he wouldn't want to reveal.

She'd ask him, if for no other reason than to see him squirm. Sauce for the gander.

Lucy returned to the salon after bathing and dressing and found Galen with his boots on. "We walk out," he said, standing. "We are on this boat too many days."

He had cabin fever. Frankly, so did she. "Are you well enough?"

He nodded. "*Ja*. We walk now."

She wrinkled her nose. "What is this smell?"

He didn't have to ask what that word was. "*Min scōen* . . . Nay . . . my boots. Blood."

"Well then," she said, pulling on a heavy knit sweater and grabbing her bag. "We will go find you new boots."

"A quest?" He grinned at her.

"A quest." She grabbed Galen's pills and some more of Jake's cash. Lucy's bag was practically featherweight without Leonardo's book. She felt lighter, too. Galen would probably collapse in the middle of the store. Or maybe not. The Viking seemed pretty hardy. Three days and already he was much better.

Maybe her blood donation had helped him.

Stupid. It had probably been one of many pints of blood he'd gotten. But the thought of her blood running in his veins and helping him to heal was strangely . . . intimate.

She pushed open the hatch and climbed out into the cockpit. The wind was brisk off the bay. It took her hair and whipped it around her face. She gathered it in both hands and twisted it into a knot at the nape of her neck. Torn clouds raced across the blue of the sky. At least it wasn't foggy. Movement caught her eye and she turned to see a heron lifting off the marsh, out of the reeds. It glided out over the bay, its passage causing other birds to whirl up in anxiety. She recognized some mallards among the confetti spiral of smaller birds.

Galen shoved up through the hatch and climbed up to the deck, looking up at the sky. Jake's flannel shirt flapped away from his rock-hard body.

"Why is the sky *brun*?" he asked, pointing over to the industrial area of the east bay. "Is there a great fire?"

"No." How to explain smog? "Many cars and . . . and . . . smithies?"

He frowned, but it wasn't because he didn't under-stand. "The sky is sick, Lucy. I feel it." He peered over into the side, frowning. "Water sick, too."

"Yeah. Too many people now." But there was nothing you could do about it, short of wiping out enough of man-kind to go back to the population level in Galen's time.

He shook his head and began moving around the deck touching the halyards, the nylon lines the fiberglass, the metal I-bolts. *How strange this must all be to him. Jake is out of his mind if he thinks Galen will be able to sail a modern boat.* He might be able to crew for her and follow directions if she taught him words for everything. He'd really hate taking orders from her. He might just refuse. What would she do then?

"Is she fast?" he asked, staring up at the mast.

"Not the fastest," Lucy admitted. "These are boats for pleasure not for very fast."

Galen peered over the edge into the water again. "She sits high." Maybe compared with a Viking warship loaded down with men and weapons and supplies for a four-month journey, including cattle. She'd seen illustrations. He climbed down into the cockpit. "What is this?"

"The wheel." He looked his question. True. Boats would not have had wheels in his day. "Tiller," she said, making the motion back and forth of holding a tiller. "To the rudder."

That he understood. "From here?"

She nodded and motioned under the boat. "From the wheel to the rudder."

"We sail this boat today."

Lucy frowned. "Your shoulder." She touched her own.

He clenched his jaw, looking disgusted with himself. It must be hard for a man used to his strength to accept limitations. He climbed up and limped over to the back of the boat, leaned over the aft rail, and nodded in satisfaction at the sight of the rudder. "What is the iron under there?" He pointed to the cockpit.

Hmmmm—oh, he must have seen the engine room. She blew out a breath. *How to explain?* "Like the car. It makes the boat sail when there is no wind."

He frowned at her. "Boats do not sail without wind."

"This boat sails. Like the car goes."

"Show me now," he commanded.

"No. We are on a quest, remember?"

He looked rebellious. "Show now, then quest."

"I have no desire to go sailing, with or without the motor," she said, exasperated.

"A . . . a woman does what a man speaks." Galen was glowering now.

"Not in this time." *Well, some did, to be fair.* "Not me." That, at least, was true.

Galen was about to retort something when his eyes sharpened and fixed upon a point over her right shoulder. Lucy turned. It was the tanned, hard-looking guy down the dock, coming topside on his boat. He stared at them.

Jeez. Here they were facing off like two boxers. That didn't match her and Galen's cover at all. Could the guy hear what they'd been saying? It didn't matter. She'd better make this look like a lovers' spat. Oh, boy. She was going to regret this.

She held out a hand to Galen and softened into a smile. "Come, darling, you know you'll be worn out, what with all the exercise we've been getting."

Galen didn't get much of that, if anything, but he heard the tone of her voice. He glanced to her hand as she moved forward and then up to her face. The man was a picture of suspicion. Not good. Lucy took his good arm and sidled in against him, so she could keep an eye on the hard guy. A guy and the kid who'd been playing with the dog yesterday emerged from their boat about halfway down, dressed in shorts and boat shoes even in this weather. The dog was with them. *Great.* Everyone seemed to be coming up on deck to enjoy the respite from the rain. Now they had three witnesses to a tiff.

"Don't be angry," she cooed. Galen's eyes widened. "Kiss me," she whispered. She was going to regret this bigtime.

Wariness crept into Galen's blue eyes. His chin lifted.

"Kiss me," she hissed, moving her head slightly to indicate the others down the dock. "Just for show."

Wariness was replaced by that light in his eyes. "*Ja,* Lucy. I kiss you for show."

"Make it good," she whispered. "We are new wed." She looked up at him and suddenly she was afraid. Not that he would ravish her. She was afraid of something worse. Or better.

Galen dipped his head. His breath was warm on her face. His lashes brushed his cheeks. His beard and mustache, gone, had freed his lips to reveal a sensuality that was dangerous. They brushed her lips softly. His arm came round her waist, holding her to his hip. She felt the bulge of his biceps as he tightened his embrace until she could hardly get her breath.

How had her lips opened? They did it without her will. He took ruthless advantage, his own tongue slipping in to caress hers. How dare he be so tender with her? He was a Viking, for goodness' sake. But there was nothing of goodness about it and she found herself loving the moist sensuality of his mouth, the faint taste of bacon still lingering from this morning. Slowly he plunged deeper and then, somehow, their tongues entwined and she was kissing him back, even though she never meant to make it a true kiss on her side. Her hands slid around his ribbed torso, under Jake's flapping flannel shirt. The contrast between Galen's muscled hardness and her breasts and belly pressed against him made her feel vulnerable. That wasn't bad, exactly.

She'd begun to feel light-headed by the time he broke the kiss. All her blood was pooled between her legs, and she was throbbing. He didn't let her go. His arm still held her pressed to his hip. His eyes weren't icy now. Definitely not.

"What means 'for show'?"

So . . . so that was the problem. She felt a little shaky. Her chest was heaving as she sucked in air. Her lips felt the imprint of his lips still. "Pre-pretend—not real," she stuttered. She resorted to Latin and repeated.

"Ah," he said, nodding. "I understand. I will know this better when I kiss you again."

Oh no. "There will be no 'again.'"

"I did not break my vow, Lucy," he warned. "You wanted kiss."

True. No, false. She wanted *a* kiss, not *that* kiss.

She extricated herself from his arms. He let her go. She looked around hoping her knees would hold her up and resolutely refusing to think about soft lips and hot eyes and hard body. The very tanned guy was checking the condition of his boat after the storm and pointedly ignoring them. The man and his son were giving each other disgusted looks. They had tied the dog's leash off to a cleat. People kept cats on a boat maybe, but not a big black wolf of a dog. These reclusive, gun-toting types were really too much.

Galen leaped over the line railing and the gap to the dock, sure-footed, and turned to stretch out his good hand. His eyes heated her more than her jacket in the cold bay wind. She couldn't refuse his hand in case the others were looking, and with the rocking of the boat she wasn't sure she could just jump the line railing and the little gap as he had. She looked up and saw him laughing at her with his eyes. So, with no other alternative, she pressed her lips together and took his hand. The calluses against her soft palm should have been repellant. They weren't. A shock shot through her, making her knees even shakier as she stepped across.

He gathered her into his side as they moved down the dock. Somehow she let him, but she looked up, questioning, whether herself or him she didn't know.

"For show," he said seriously. But she didn't think his eyes were quite serious. *Smug bastard.* He knew exactly what he was doing to her. But she couldn't break away, just in case their neighbors were watching. She took a deep breath and let it out. Okay. So she might as well enjoy it.

No, you don't. This is one slippery slope.

Okay. She wouldn't feel his hip moving against hers, or the bare ribs pressed up against her side, or the bulky muscles in the arm around her shoulders. She wouldn't feel . . . safe. Right.

Rightness coursed through her. A part of the universe thunked into place inside her, as surely as when she had realized that Brad's secret project was Leonardo's time machine. The very rightness of it all made her afraid. She shook off both the fear and the feeling of rightness. The guy was a Viking. He was going back to 912 as soon as she could figure out how to do it. With no access to the machine, the fact that it was broken, and . . .

She squinched her eyes shut. Their heels thudded against the boards of the dock. The water lapped in from the bay in unaccustomed enthusiasm after the storm. She might have been trembling against his side.

"Quest, Lucy," he whispered. "You think of quest only." And then the bastard kissed the top of her head and her trembling stopped. What right had he to quell her fear?

Casey's mouth turned down as he surveyed the human refuse milling around the interview room through the one-way glass. The anonymous brightly lighted room was painted institutional green and served by its own elevator, just so "guests" such as these didn't mingle with the government workers who occupied the rest of the high-rise. One woman just rocked obsessively and moaned. They were a colorful lot, from one guy's red and white high-tops to the multicolored knit cap on that woman in the corner, ballooned out by her Afro. The only thing they had in common was a veneer of greasy dirt and dead eyes.

Damn that poncey little scientist, Steadman. He was nearly useless. But he *had* realized that a homeless person might have witnessed the Viking and the girl leaving the apartment building. Casey hated to admit he'd missed that angle. But you moved on.

Casey was checking the landlord's background. He wanted to get some leverage on the guy before they tried to interview him again. Casey's people were scouring marinas around the city with a picture of the girl and the artist's rendering of the Viking. But the homeless riffraff on the other side of the glass still constituted at least a tenuous shot at finding the fugitives.

Casey grabbed a pack of cigarettes from his jacket

pocket and tapped one out as Evans led one of the interviewees out of a room. He flipped open his lighter and inhaled until the tip glowed, then snicked the lighter shut. He'd been exiled to supervise a stupid joint research project between a lab and the fuckup Italian government about a machine that still had gears, for Christ's sake. God knew how the Italians convinced the NIATF to put money into the project in the first place. Even his superiors thought it was a bust. He was exiled to the fucking North Pole, and why? Because his assignments tended to be a little messy. He got what they wanted, didn't he? That's why they hired people like him, who could do things to people nobody else wanted to do. They wouldn't have had that lawsuit if they'd let him clean up loose ends after the guys broke. And that last village was a totally expendable rat hole filled with bad narco-targets and a few basket weavers. But some jerk-off general got squeamish.

So they gave him a crappy assignment. But lightning strikes. He'd lucked onto a fucking time machine. They didn't believe him yet. And that was fine. Now he'd have choices. He could go back and shove it in their faces and get whatever assignment he wanted.

Or he could use it for himself. *Khrushchev. Now there's a mo-fo who could have used killing. Castro? Toast. Economy in the tank? Go back and fix it. Nothing you can't do with that machine. Save the goddamn, pathetic world. Or create a better one. In your own image. Visit the future, find the new Microsoft, and come back to invest in it today. Find your enemies and cut their fathers' dicks off.* He'd had months to think about the possibilities.

That machine can make you a god.

And it was broken. *What a bitch.* He needed the fucking diamond and the book. And then the world would be his oyster.

Pollington stuck his head out of the nearer room and beckoned to the glass.

Shit. Can he have something? Casey pushed himself off the desk and stubbed out his cancer stick in an almost empty Styrofoam cup. The end hissed in the sludge of old coffee at the bottom. He strode out to Pollington.

"Mr. uh, Smith here was in the right location, just across from the apartment building all night on Tuesday." Pollington spoke in an undervoice.

Casey just pushed past the younger man and into the interview room. Mr. "Smith" was black, looked sixty, was probably forty-five. He wore layers and layers of shirts under one of those big sweaters from Tijuana. Gray fuzz covered his head and face, and his hand shook as he clutched a cup of that sludgy coffee. Great witness.

"Mr. Smith, I'm Colonel Casey. I'm in charge here." He sat down opposite the man. The reek of unwashed bodies clung to the walls. They'd have to fumigate the place.

"Pleased, Colonel." Smith probably once had a honeyed bass drawl, but now he was hoarse, his voice cracking. He cackled. "Only colonel I knowed before you made chicken."

Casey smiled grimly. "You were on Filbert just off Van Ness Tuesday night?"

"That's my regular place, yes sir. They's a overhang on one a them buildings there, and a hedge blocks the wind. Pretty good place. Yes. Pretty good."

Well, at least the guy was more coherent than the rocker. "You know the building just across from your digs?" The guy nodded. "Did you see anything there that night?"

Smith shrugged and shook his head. "Like what?"

Casey snapped his fingers and Pollington handed him the pictures. "Like maybe these two people coming out? It would have been—maybe four in the morning."

Smith's eyes opened wide. He began to nod. "Yeah.

Yeah, I saw red hair. Just kind of a gleam in the street-light. She was driving the car. Somebody big in the passenger seat."

Casey tried not to get excited. "What kind of car was it?"

"Kinda old. Maybe a Chevy. GM anyway. Blue."

Not bad. The guy was observant. "Was it parked at the curb? Did somebody bring it?"

"Naaah. It came outta the parking garage."

Casey sat back, mind humming. That meant someone in the apartment building had failed to report a stolen car. Maybe someone had loaned it to them. Casey rose in one motion. Time for a little visit to the residents of 1632 Filbert.

Evans tapped on the door with a clipboard.

"So what's the deal on the landlord?" Evans's expression gave Casey a thrill.

"Jake Lowell," Evans intoned. "Bought the apartment building for cash in '77. Tenants say he got the limp in 'Nam. But there's no service record for a Jake Lowell, or Jacob, or Jackson, or any of those as a middle name. No records at all, military or otherwise, before the purchase." Evans cracked a smile. "Jake Lowell is not what he seems."

"Excellent," Casey muttered. "Just excellent. Let's have a talk with Mr. Lowell, while you find out just where he got such a big payout, and for what services."

"Could be mob money, drug money."

"Maybe." Casey doubted it. He was beginning to smell something much closer to home.

Chapter Thirteen

"So, you ready for the car?"

Galen took a breath and let it out, remembering how fast the thing had gone when they rode in it before. He pulled the lever that opened the door and got in. *"Ja.* I will learn how to drive this cart as you do." He set his jaw. "You will teach me, Lucy."

"That's a disaster waiting to happen," she muttered as she slid behind the wheel. He didn't understand those words. But he got her tone.

"You think I cannot do this?"

"Can we go on our quest first?" She was giving him that look of exasperation. He knew why. It was the kiss. It had unnerved her. He swallowed. It had unnerved him, too.

"Ja," he answered. For a single instant, she had been so soft, so yielding. He had wanted nothing more than to protect her from her world. For an instant on the deck, she had revealed most clearly that she wanted him and that, even more important, she might let him protect her. When had that become important to him?

He cleared his throat and sat up, grasping the handle on the door to this car with the hand of his injured right shoulder. "We will now go fast." He braced himself for that unnerving speed.

She reached around him and pulled a thick strap with an iron tongue on it across him and snapped it into a kind of a buckle on his left side as she had before. "Seat belts, everyone."

The car backed up, slowly, turned as she turned the wheel, then started up the dirt track. As they approached a crossroads, other cars tore by, very fast, in both directions. Lucy took her foot from a lever on the floor and pressed another pad. The car stopped. She pulled a lever by the wheel with her left hand and a rhythmic sound began. He craned to see what she was doing. A little green light blinked, pointing left. She looked both ways, waited for some other cars to whiz by, and then pressed the lever on the floor. The car went onto the slicker, black road. She pressed down harder and the car sped up. He was ready. He braced himself with his good hand on the seat and pushed his feet against the floor. Marshes and reed beds flew past.

He steadied his breathing. *Not so bad.* How many leagues could you go in one day with a cart such as this? No horses to feed. No need to worry about their stamina. Was there?

"Does the cart grow weary?"

"Weary?" She glanced from the road to him. Her mouth tried not to smile.

He nodded. "Weary." He liked it when she tried not to smile. Someday, maybe she would not try. She would just smile many times in a day.

"No. But you must give it gasoline. Like food. It goes until it has no more gas."

They came to a very large village, though its halls were not as high as the ones the first night. She pulled the cart in among many others standing in rows in front of a huge building that looked like a squat castle stretching away into the distance. At several points huge stacked towers stretched even farther into the air. Carts roamed the aisles, pulling in and out. It was a maze of confusion. Did everyone in this time have such wonderful carts?

"Since I don't want to become familiar, let's try Macy's this time." She unbuckled her own thick strap and got out of the car. He pressed the metal buckle as she did, and the strap snapped back into a little, hard house at his shoulder. He unfolded himself from the car. People were walking in and out of doors made entirely of glass into total darkness within a huge tower of the castle. The young women wore breeches and tight, revealing tops like Lucy or tiny skirts that left their legs bare, the older women were clad in baggy breeches and voluminous smocks. The men shoes that laced and tight breeches and shirts in bright colors. Many were blue. This must be a rich time to have enough woad to dye so much cloth blue.

As he and Lucy approached, the doors opened by magic. He followed Lucy, who was striding toward the open maw of darkness. He straightened his shoulders and tried to breathe. This was an everyday thing for her. She was not frightened of this magic or the darkness. Quests demanded courage of a man. Was he not the first of his king's warriors?

Galen tried not to limp as he followed her into the darkness. It wasn't dark. He froze. The interior of this castle was lighted without lamps, like the place in which he had first wakened, but not so brightly. Small round moons in the ceiling glowed. The floor was hard and smooth, with earth-colored tiles much finer even than the tiles the people made in the lands around the southern sea. People were everywhere, walking briskly, or strolling to look at more goods than he had ever seen. Shelves and tables stretched away into the distance. A stairway moved upward of its own accord, taking riders with it. He swallowed.

"Move it, buddy. You're blocking traffic," an old man said, pushing by him.

He swallowed again. He could do this. He took Lucy's arm. That felt better.

"It's okay," she said. "Okay" was the word she used to indicate that all was well. He'd heard her use the word to reassure herself. "Let's find you some clothes and shoes."

He took a breath and let her guide him. She seemed to know her way.

Lucy headed down to the men's department. Galen was holding her arm, and she didn't shake him off in spite of the nagging trill that sent down her spine. The look on his face was half wonder, half fear, and she couldn't help but admire the way he faced such a foreign situation. He was a brave man. She wouldn't deny him the solace of contact with a friend.

A friend. That's what she'd be to him, for as long as it took to get him back to a time he understood. Now if she could just get rid of the nagging trill. Well, the first thing was not to kiss him again. They'd more than convinced the other marina dwellers they were besotted with each other. Mission accomplished. So no more kissing.

She stopped at a rack of jeans. "Here we go."

"These are like the cloth of your *brec*, Lucy."

"Yes. Jeans. Men wear them, too." She flipped through the rack.

"I look like other men. Good for hiding."

"Not if you talk about hiding so loudly," she whispered, frowning.

He examined the jeans. "The cloth is for *ceorls,* yet it is dyed with woad."

"Ceorls?"

He repeated in Latin.

"Peasants? Oh. Because it's rough. But it wears many

years." Woad was what they used to get blue color back then—some kind of a rock they ground up or something. She held a pair up to his backside and blew out a breath. She knew nothing about men's jean sizes.

"Can I help you?" A young man with slicked-back black hair, a red satin acetate shirt, and pointy-toed black boots approached. Lucy sighed in relief. Here was someone who could help. Good ole San Francisco.

"My friend doesn't speak English very well. He needs a new wardrobe. Can you help us figure out sizes?"

The kid's eyes slid over to Galen. Up. Down. Lingering on the important aspects. "Gladly, mademoiselle," he said. No one said that anymore. His nose wrinkled at Galen's smelly boots, sweats, and plaid flannel shirt that wouldn't button. "Obviously time for a makeover."

The kid's name tag said: *Brendon*. "I leave him totally in your hands." *Oops.*

Brendon's eyes slid over to her for one shocked moment. Then he sighed. He must know Galen was never going to be in his hands. On the other hand, he got a chance to dress Galen. "Mais oui, mademoiselle." His head swiveled as he scanned his stock. "He has a rugged look, which we will accentuate with traditional five-oh-ones. Buttons or zipper?"

"Zipper." Better keep the buttons to a minimum. Though Jake's shirt was a little small, Galen hadn't tried buttoning a single one.

Brendon scanned Galen once again. "I think . . ." He tapped his chin with one finger. "Thirty-four/thirty-fours." He picked a pair of jeans from the rack. "I'll pick out some shirts."

"No *hemeth* like this." Galen pointed to the red acetate shirt that shimmered on Brendon.

"No, no, no." Brendon rolled his eyes. "You couldn't carry this off in a million years." He gave Lucy the jeans

and indicated the dressing rooms. "But never fear, I shall
provide."

"Can you find him a jacket, too? We need something
waterproof."

Brendon grinned. "I'm on the job."

Galen was stiff and glowering as she took his hand and
drew him to the dressing room. "Don't look like that," she
said. "He's sweet."

"I do not wish to eat him." Galen's brow grew even
darker.

" 'Sweet' sometimes can mean 'kind.' 'Good.' " She
drew him into the big dressing room and closed the curtain. " 'Vulnerable.' Like the Latin word."

She watched Galen's face take on a rueful cast. "We
have such ones as he in my time."

"Then you know he needs protection, not hate." She'd
bet anything "hate" was the same in his time as in hers.
Galen's lips pressed together in a grim line and he nodded.

"He will help us." She handed Galen the jeans.

He kicked off his smelly boots, peeled his shirt off,
and pushed down his sweats. Lucy tossed his boots out
under the curtain. When she turned back, Galen stood in
his boxers, unbuttoning the jeans, but he was nonplussed
by the zipper.

"Here," she said, pulling it down.

His intake of breath was sharp. He pulled the zipper up
again. He pulled it down. His eyes lifted to her, stunned.

She couldn't help the giggle. "It's a zipper."

He pulled on the jeans over the stitches on his thigh and
his boxers, jerked up the zipper tab, worked at the button.
She swallowed. The jeans rode his hips. Which left ridges
of muscle that disappeared into the waistband and the
vee of light brown hair that pointed downward. The only
thing that kept his body from perfection was the horrible
stitches across his shoulder.

"Is good," he said, looking at his reflection in the long mirror. "I look like your time."

"How are they with your stitches—your wound?"

Galen shrugged. "Good enough." However he spelled it in his mind, it sounded the same.

Steps sounded outside the dressing room. "Excusez-moi," Brendon trilled. He peeked through the curtain with an armload of shirts, sweaters, and socks. "G-goodness. Well, those fit." Galen turned and Brendon saw the stitches. "Ouch!" he exclaimed. "That's one nasty wound."

"Car accident," Lucy improvised. "Which is why he only has the clothes on his back. His luggage was destroyed in the fire."

"Car fire?" Brendon looked horrified. "He's lucky to be alive." Brendon averted his gaze, suddenly shy. "Well, uh. Here are some shirts that might work. I'm guessing seventeen-and-a-half collar with thirty-three sleeves and extra large for the sweaters and pullovers. He's . . ." Brendon cleared his throat. "He's a pretty big guy."

Lucy sorted through the booty and picked out several. A work shirt, a pullover sweater with a collar and a zipper at the neck, a couple of thick waffled Henleys. Brandon had brought soft blues to match Galen's eyes, a kind of gold/beige to match his hair, and chocolate brown. "Put on one of these," she said to Galen, and slipped out to speak to Brendon.

"Can you dispose of these boots?" she asked, making a face. "And find us some Nikes."

"Certainly, mademoiselle." He picked them up with two fingers.

Lucy thought she probably owed him an explanation. "Gutting fish. A bucket overturned." She was getting tangled up in her lies again. "Uh . . . before the car accident. You know how Scandinavians are about fish."

Brendon rolled his eyes. "Herring. They all eat herring."

His eyes slid over to the curtain. "Apparently makes them big and strong, though. I'll get him all the accessories."

Brendon disappeared with only one longing backward glance. *Sheesh, as bad as the nurse.* Anyone would give their eyeteeth to hook up with this guy. Anyone except her of course.

Lucy returned to Galen. He was pulling his hair from under the collar of the work shirt. She held up the shirttail. "Inside your breeches." While he unfastened his jeans and tucked, she buttoned all except the top two buttons. Her knuckles couldn't help but scrape his chest hair. She chewed her lips and worked fast so she could step back. He fumbled at buttoning the jeans again. It took all his attention. That allowed her to look her fill. *Whoa.* The tenth-century Viking had disappeared, and in his place stood one hunk of a modern man. This guy would turn heads anywhere. Not good for hiding, but at least the beard and the braids were gone.

Brendon returned with a lined windbreaker that was just what she'd had in mind and a bomber jacket in chocolate brown, another pair of jeans and some brown cords, some Nikes, and a pair of Frye boots. A couple of belts in both brown and black leather with brass buckles hung over his shoulder.

"Leather," Galen said, his eyes lighting up at the sight of the bomber jacket and the boots. He pulled on both carefully. She helped him get his other arm in the jacket. This might be the garment most familiar to him. Lucky he hadn't spotted any leather pants or she probably wouldn't have been able to talk him out of the sleazy rock star look.

She glanced back to find Brendon watching in fascination. "That should do it. We don't have much space on the boat."

Brendon bustled out ahead of them, his arms filled.

"Hey, I've always wanted to live on a boat. Just sail away if you get tired of one place."

"Storage is a problem. And then there's the mold," she said. "Boats are just plain damp."

"Hmmmm. That couldn't be good for my poster collection. I may have to rethink."

She was betting Marilyn Monroe movie posters. And the fact that he could consider having a poster collection aboard a boat showed how little he knew about living aboard.

Brendon checked them out and distributed the many bags, Lucy thanking him profusely.

She was fuming by the time she and Galen got to the parking lot, though. He turned heads all right. Women were undressing her Viking with their eyes at every turn. And Galen might be exhausted, but he was looking smug. He had just discovered that women were women, whatever the millennia. But once in the car, he eased his shoulder against the car seat, letting out a breath.

"So, we will go back to the boat and you will sleep now." Her speech had taken on an unfamiliar rhythm as she strove to use words they shared or that he had learned. Who was changing more, Galen or herself?

"*Ja,* Lucy," he muttered, closing his eyes. "You speak sooth."

But there was one more stop to make. They rolled into the parking lot of the Quik Stop about half an hour later. Lucy got out, motioning Galen to stay, and practically sprinted into the little store. The sooner she got him back to the boat and some Vicodin the better.

"Hey," she greeted the clerk. The radio was blaring. Sounded like a basketball game.

"That package you were expecting showed up." He turned to the boxes behind the counter, took out a key that unwound from a clip on his belt, and retrieved a thick package. There was no name at all in the address. It just said: *Occupant, Slip 18.* Talk about discreet.

She glanced up to find that the guy had a really curious look on his face. "It was delivered by messenger," he said.

"Oh. Well . . . thanks." She turned to go.

"Wally," he called after her. "The name is Wally Campbell. And you are . . . ?"

She laughed in what she hoped was a carefree way, glancing over her shoulder at him. "The newlywed in slip eighteen." Then she escaped, the bell of the door dogging her heels.

When she got to the car, she ripped open the padded bag and pulled out the contents. Two passports lay on top of a sheaf of papers, one the familiar navy blue with gold lettering and one red. She flipped open the navy blue one and saw her picture—the one Jake had taken in the apartment. Her name was now Lucinda Jane Gilroy. *Great, Jake. Couldn't you have thought of a nicer name?* At least she could still be called Lucy. That prevented slipups. Today her name was short for "Lucia," but "Lucinda" worked just as well. Her passport had some official-looking stamps in it, the latest from . . . Denmark. The other passport turned out to be Danish. And the picture was clearly Galen. The hair was short, the beard trimmed and neat. Good old Photoshop. He didn't look fierce at all. Someone had retouched the circles he'd had under his eyes that night and given him a complexion that wasn't ashen. He looked like a modern, very civilized denizen of Copenhagen. You'd never know he was a Viking from more than a thousand years ago. His passport was stamped with a U.S. entry.

Galen peered at the passports. He started when he recognized himself. "What is this?"

Of course he'd never seen a photograph. "That is a photo. It captures your reflection. Like the far-seer, or . . .

like a mirror." She took her compact mirror out of her purse.

"Ahhh. Like a *sceawere*. Mirror." He peered more closely at his picture.

"It tells people who you are." She pointed to his name. "See? Galen Valgarssen."

"I can tell people who I am."

"Everyone needs one of these in our time. People want you to have one."

"Then I have one." He peered over at the other documents.

Jake had been thorough. A U.S. visa for Galen. Two birth certificates, one in English for her and Galen's in Danish, and a California driver's license for her, registration for the Chevy in her name, even some letters from a fictional mother, saying how happy she was at Lucy's marriage and wondering whether she would be taking Galen's last name. There were pictures she couldn't even tell were faked that showed her and Galen against the backdrop of a busy Mexican market. She looked like a real person. A different person, with a different life, but real.

Impressive. If she had ever wondered whether Jake was really some bad-ass dude who did dirty work for the government, her doubts had just been laid to rest. Jake was the real deal. And he thought she and Galen were in big trouble.

Now that was frightening.

Chapter Fourteen

"Well, look who's up and about," Lucy said, looking over her shoulder at Galen. He looked tousled and soft with sleep. He'd been out like a light for several hours. Now, in the fading light, barefoot in jeans and a Henley pullover, he looked good enough to eat.

"No wind," he remarked, easing himself carefully onto the bench around the table.

The boat rocked gently in its slip. "Fog tonight." She glanced her question to him. He shook his head. "Mist?" she tried.

He quirked his lips and nodded. "*Ja*. Mist."

"New storm . . ." She raised her brows. "Storm?"

"It is *ilca* in my words. Storm."

"The word is 'same,'" she said automatically. "New storm comes tomorrow night." Of course the basic words for weather were the same. Weather endured. The Earth endured, though it might be embattled just now.

"How do you know this?" he asked.

Uh-oh. That was a tough one. He'd think she was a witch again. She bent to the refrigerator and opened the door while she thought. Pulling out the sour cream, she scooped out a cup for her dill sauce. "Wise men can learn to know what weather will come. They tell us."

"They know *weder*? Storm? Wind?"

"Weather," she corrected. "They are not always right." Galen gave a look of frustration that he didn't know all the English words. *He's been at it what, two days? He pushes himself so hard.*

He frowned. "Were they here that they tell you of this?" He obviously didn't like to think others had been on the boat while he had slept.

Well, she might as well show him now as later. She reached over to the radio on the bar and turned the knob.

"And now, the marine forecast," the announcer's voice said, right on cue, sounding slightly tinny. Galen lurched to his feet in a crouch.

"It's okay." She raised her hands, palms out. "It's okay. It's like the far-seer." She pointed to the small flat screen mounted on the wall in the salon. "Men in other places speak. We hear them through this." She pointed to the radio and turned it off.

He heaved a breath and sat back down. She could see he was troubled. "Your time is not the same as mine. I do not *belimp* here."

Belimp . . . belimp. Limp? Context was wrong. "Belong?" He looked away. What could she say to that? He *so* did not belong here, no matter that he looked the part now.

"I am like a *bearn* . . . a *lytling*." He looked disgusted with himself. "Not like a man."

Those words she understood. She turned down her sauce and went to sit beside him. His analogy was pretty good. He was like a child learning a new environment. But that meant the problem was temporary. "We all learn about radios and TVs and cars. You will learn, Galen." She knew the word for learn was the same—they had been through that this morning. He turned his head away. He must not want her to see the pain in his eyes. And why wouldn't he be in pain? Far from all he knew, all those he cared about. Not sure whether he would ever get back. "I do not belong in your time, either. I was there only a moment, and I almost died."

He was silent for a moment. "You are not a *duguth*, Lucy."

She shook her head, signifying she didn't understand.

"Wigend?" He sighed and used the Latin.

"Warrior," she supplied. "I understand. But there are many ways to fight. Fight?"

He nodded.

"You fight to learn the words. You fight to heal your wounds. That is enough for now."

"It is not enough." Before he turned his head away, she saw the look of shame flicker across his eyes.

That right there was what she wanted to know about him. Why he got that look in his eyes. He had opened the door. She could ask him why he said that. But wanting a tit-for-tat revelation because she'd said things about herself she hadn't meant to say was petty revenge. She patted his forearm instead. The contact made her thrill even through his shirt.

"You are too hard on yourself." He looked up, a puzzle in his eyes. They seemed to see right into her. She broke the moment by standing. "What you need is food. Yes?"

"*Ja*, Lucy. I am hungry. Like *hors*. You have *horses*?"

"Ahhh. Beautiful horses. I rode as a child. *Lytling.*" She liked that word.

"I have a strong horse. No, *had* a strong horse. He is long dead." Galen sighed. "His hide was *fȳrfaexen*."

"We would call him a chestnut."

"You have horse now?"

"No. No horses in the city." She got up and went back to the tiny galley.

"*Hund*?"

"No. No dog."

"Mother?"

She shook her head. "Dead when I was *lytling.*"

"You have women who are friends?"

"I have kept much to myself since my father died."

"Only Jake and this Brad." Her lips would not behave. Galen said Brad's name with such disdain. "You need more friends, Lucy."

He probably had lots of friends. Female friends. She didn't like the feeling that brought on. "Perhaps you're right." She had thought just this afternoon that he might become a friend.

"Oh, I have the right of it? You *besyrwast* me."

She could tell by the sarcastic tone of his voice he probably meant "surprise." She checked with him in Latin. *Yep.* "The word is 'surprise.'"

She was surprised herself. Who knew Vikings could be sarcastic? She couldn't help the crinkle in her eyes as she bent to take out the salmon. As she moved around the galley, he kept it light, asking the words for food, for the actions she took. She turned on the lights, and the gently rocking boat was bathed in a soft glow. The feeling of rightness washed over her again, unrelated to kisses and the almost constant pull she felt to his body. It was a deeper, more satisfying rightness, comfortable, certain. Lucy had never felt anything like it, not even when her mother was alive. It was as if this was where Lucy belonged, talking softly to a half-Saxon, half-Viking warrior as she made him salmon for dinner. Brad and Colonel Casey were far away. Her fears and doubts seemed almost foolish.

Sated, Galen watched her wash up the dishes. She had made him a fine dinner. Beef and a bowl of lettuces and a roasted *wyrt* she called potatoes. It was a woman's place to cook, but she had provided even the food, much to his shame. Her red hair glowed in the light of the lamps, the movements of her body endlessly fascinating. What a kind woman she was, generous. In other times, if he were another man, he would have felt . . . content.

He puzzled over the thrumming rightness he had felt sometimes in the last days. Was it some kind of a call? He had felt it when he kissed Lucy today. Her mouth was sweet, yielding. He had felt her nipples peak against his ribs. She was a tiny thing but strong of spirit. Still, she had trembled as they walked down the dock. She was not afraid of him physically, in spite of the differences in their strength. Was she afraid of what she felt for him?

He understood that. He was drawn to her. He wanted her as he had never wanted a woman, not because he had not spilled his seed of late, not because he was dependent on her. That was abhorrent to him still. He needed Lucy in such a deep way that . . .

It was if some foreign thing possessed him, growing inside him and straightening his cock. Even now, as he watched her reach to place a dish in a high cupboard, the curve of her breast made a drumbeat in his loins. He had desired many women in his life. But this was something else, growing more urgent, more insistent every moment. He *needed* to make love to Lucy. He needed to protect her. Claim her. Something inside him said that if he did, everything would be all right.

As he watched her silhouette, he saw her nipples peak again. She was aware of him. Her eyes slid to his. He saw both lust and fear there, echoes of the unfamiliar emotions circling inside him. She stared at him, and he could not look away.

He sucked in a breath, almost a gasp. A thought chased itself around inside his head. This was no ordinary lust. It felt like a force on its own, apart from him. Was she a *wicce* indeed? Did she bespell him? He barely suppressed an outraged laugh. Not what his mother wanted for him when she named him Galen, meaning "bespelled one."

This spell was making him lose his way. He belonged in another time. Lucy was only a means to an end. Contentment was a trap. He must go back as soon as he could to a time when he had value that he might fulfill whatever destiny he had left.

Or maybe he had a new destiny. To be imprisoned by this Brad and his friends, tortured as in Kiev. Only a fearful outline of Galen's destiny was visible, as though a beast approached through mist. The threads of the Norns, who wove men's destiny, had been broken by Lucy's time machine and might never be put right again.

He shook himself. All men had fear. But men of value pushed down their fear and acted. His action now was to learn the language and get back to strength.

He jerked his gaze away from her witch green eyes. He mustn't lose his soul to her.

He stood abruptly. "I must sleep."

She blinked, as though coming to herself. "Yes. Of course. Rest well." She turned away, her blush creeping up her throat into her face. It made him want to kiss away her embarrassment.

And mayhaps to lose himself forever.

He stumbled aft and shut the cabin door, fumbled at his jeans, pulled his shirt over his head with his left hand and down his injured shoulder, and struggled out of his jeans and boxers. His erection, hard as an oak staff, sprang free. He eased himself down, naked on the bed, on his back so not even the blankets could touch his rod and aggravate his condition. The throb in his shoulder and thigh was pale in comparison to the tight beat of need in his loins. He was sweating, Loki take him, just at the thought of Lucy in the next room, practically outside the door, blushing, wanting him.

He thought of other things. Guthrum's son. The battle. It didn't matter. Lucy fought her way into his brain—the way her naked breasts moved beneath the green shirt this morning, the way her lips opened to his on the deck in the wind for all to see.

He groaned.

There was nothing for it. He grabbed his rod and jerked at himself without mercy until his loins contracted and he spurted hot semen across his belly. That would keep him from losing his soul to the green-eyed witch.

But all it did was make him miserable. An emptiness crept into his belly as though he had desecrated his destiny.

Saturday

Lucy was out of the shower and dressed by the time Galen got up. She'd been so relieved last night when he went to bed early and removed the temptation to march over to where he sat and kiss him again that she hadn't even tried to disinfect his wounds.

And if relief left her feeling bereft, well, at least she'd won the battle with herself. She *had* won, hadn't she? Then why did it feel like a devastating loss? She'd tossed her pepper spray into the nightstand drawer in disgust. Not only would she probably not resist if he came into her bed, but he obviously wasn't going to come. And he didn't.

Now he came out of the aft cabin like a tousled Norse god, naked and glowering, and marched into the head with a grunt of "good morning." He carried a batch of clothes under one arm. His genitals were full, if not fully erect.

Lucy blew out a breath and tried turning her attention to the sizzling bacon whose smell was no doubt what had brought him out of his lair. That probably didn't conceal her blush. Damn her fair coloring. And damn the feeling that seeing him naked and rising put between her legs.

She was almost in pain, so suddenly that it seemed that
someone had just flipped a switch. *Great.* How was she
going to deal with this constant response to him?

The head flushed. The shower started. Her imagination kicked into high gear. This was just untenable.

She realized that the stitches on his thigh had been
slightly red. Probably from the irritation of rubbing on his
jeans. She sighed. *Okay.* She'd cut some bandages for his
thigh and give him the Betadine and the hydrogen peroxide solution. He was well enough to take care of himself
at this point. She gathered materials, waited until she heard
the shower shut off, then opened the door a crack and
thrust the supplies into the steam.

"Bandages for your thigh." She cleared her throat to
get the gravel out of her voice. "You can tend your wounds
yourself today."

Did his hands have to brush against hers as he took the
supplies?

"*Thonc* . . . Thanks, Lucy," he growled, then cleared
his throat. They seemed to be afflicted with the same
problem this morning.

Lucy snatched back her hand and shut the door with a
bang. A month until she heard from Jake? Well, more than
three weeks. She was stuck here with Galen until then.
*And after? There must be some way out of this predica-
ment.*

Galen's progress was truly amazing. Agatha Christie's
phrase "mind like a bacon slicer" occurred to Lucy. He
remembered all the words she had taught him with very
little repetition. He seemed to be able to use them almost
immediately in sentences. He had gotten the hang of using Latin roots to understand the meaning of many
English words. His accent was still pronounced, but he
was pretty much talking in whole sentences without a lot

of stopping to figure out words anymore. She swept the crumbs from their sandwiches off the chart and rolled it up. They had hardly used it all morning as he progressed faster and faster.

"Enough for now."

He sat back. The ports had condensation on the inside. Probably from the heat he and Lucy generated between them. If only her attraction to him would fade as fast as his language progressed. She kept what distance she could in the close quarters, but she couldn't stop her blushes, or the feeling between her legs. She couldn't not look at him, or smell his sweet, clean man-scent after his shower. And the cords and blue sweater he'd put on were . . .

Well, she wasn't going to think about how they made him look.

And he wasn't helping, either. The heat in his blue eyes when he looked at her, the fact that he couldn't keep them off her as he repeated her words . . . Well, the whole lesson had been torture. Breakfast was torture. Lunch was torture. She was practically squirming in her seat with the desire to kiss him, feel his soft lips and his hard muscle. Squirming only made things worse.

"Do you feel up to a walk?" she asked.

He looked as relieved as she felt when he answered "*Ja*. Walk is good."

Jackets were taken from lockers. She got her bag, just in case. "I saw a trail along the bay when we drove out yesterday." He wrote "yesterday" with lots of *g*'s.

Then they were out into the brisk air. Clouds piled over the coastal mountain range to the west, but for now the day was crisp and clear. No one seemed to be about on the other boats. Only one car in the lot besides hers. Just as well. She locked the hatch. After all, there was a great big diamond behind the trash compactor and a book she'd been offered a fortune for on the shelf over her bed. Her hair whipped around her. She stopped to twist it into a knot while Galen surveyed the top of the bay. About halfway across you could see where the Petaluma River came in, bringing with it a brown fan of silt from the Sonoma Valley after the storm. Small on the horizon, the San Rafael Bridge arched toward the ship-yards of Richmond.

"Storm tonight," Galen remarked as he swiveled to watch the clouds grow. "We listen to your voices wise in weather later."

"Radio. It's a radio."

"Radio." He looked as though he was going to hold out a hand to her. But he thought better of it and shoved both of them in the pockets of his leather jacket.

Disappointment again swirled with relief. Did she want him to touch her or not?

They walked up the dock, out the marina gate, and across the parking lot before picking up the little raised trail through the squishy marsh. As they walked single file, Lucy in front, there wasn't much chance for conversation. That was a relief, too. Too much talking this morning. Galen's presence tugged at her, but it seemed all wound up in the lucid day, the wind pinking her cheeks, the sky a blue that made you hurt, the wetlands teeming with tiny flowers of white and pale yellow, rough saw grass, and taller reeds where the water was deeper. Herons stalked among them, and smaller birds swam and flew and fluffed their wings. The marsh smelled like the salt water of the bay and the rich rot of plants giving their nutrients back to the earth. It wasn't a bad smell. As her limbs loosened, her gait swung more freely. Walking felt good. She'd missed it. As her body warmed, that right feeling returned, as if she and Galen and the day were all in tune.

They'd walked for a while when a rough plank bench appeared, set on an earthen platform encouraged by railroad ties fitted together into a square like Lincoln Logs. She'd felt Galen's strength flagging even though she hadn't turned to look at him. She glanced back now to see that his expression was determined and a little grim. She'd been so enjoying the walk she'd allowed him to overtax himself.

Chagrined, she sat on the bench, patting the seat beside her. "Let's rest here."

He did not resist but sat at the opposite end of the bench. That was good. As far away as possible. A small disappointment flashed inside her. He'd obviously thought better of his attraction for her. He didn't want to kiss her now. While kissing him was almost all she thought about. And the rest of her thoughts were filled with more than kissing. He eased his shoulder against the back of the bench. His pills with breakfast were obviously wearing off.

"How do you feel?" He wasn't getting that. "How are your wounds?"

"Wounds are enough good," he grunted in that baritone voice that seemed to rumble in her chest as well as his.

Yeah, right. But what is a Viking warrior going to say? He'll never admit he hurts.

Either inside or outside, she thought with some surprise. Which meant he would never want to tell her why he looked ashamed sometimes. *God knows Vikings probably have enough to be ashamed of. Raping and killing and pillaging and all.*

But a Viking wouldn't be ashamed of that.

So what was it that so hurt him? She wanted to know. She rolled her lip between her teeth as she gazed out over the marsh. Some would call this desolate, but it was quintessentially alive. He called it quick. Okay. He wouldn't tell her all at once. So she'd start obliquely.

"The battle . . . the one you were fighting when I first saw you . . . why did you fight?" Was it for home and family? She'd always assumed he had many women, but maybe he was married with children. Just because a Viking made a pass at her didn't mean he wasn't married.

He looked out over the marsh as well, not at her. "I fight for Guthrum, king of the Danelaw, against Egil and his men."

"Egil seems like a Danish name. I thought the Vikings were fighting Alfred the Great and the Saxons about that time, not each other."

He glanced to her sharply. "Alfred called is the great king?"

She nodded. "Is called," she corrected. "The only English king given that honor."

"He was dead many years by my time. His son Edward the Elder is king of Saxons now."

"So weren't the Danes fighting Edward?"

He looked back out over the sea of reeds and saw grass. "I told my king that Edward would make a good friend to the Danes. Friend who fights together?"

"Ally."

"Yes. Ally." He let out a breath. "I thought when the Northmen come from Gaul, Edward and my king, the second Guthrum, could fight together to save their island. But to do that, the Danelaw must remain strong, or all is lost. Egil—he was just a *wearg*. Galen glanced to her. "*Wearg*?"

"Probably traitor." She couldn't remember "traitor" in Latin so she tried, "Betrayer?"

He nodded. "Traitor. I led an army to stop him. To keep the Danelaw whole." He frowned out over the marsh to the bay beyond. The water was perhaps thirty yards away. There was a little chop from the wind but no waves to speak of this far north.

"You . . . you have a woman there, *lytlings*?" Lucy tried to make it sound casual.

He glanced back to her. His eyes gleamed a little. "Nay,

Lucy. Not a woman. Many women, but not *a* woman. No *lytlings*."

She shrugged, hiding her relief. "Just wondering." Why was she relieved? He'd just told her he slept around. As she suspected. Of course, to put it in perspective, what man who looked like Galen wouldn't sow wild oats? These days they called themselves "not the marrying kind."

He looked back out over the bay. "You know the name of Alfred. Know you Guthrum?"

"No," she had to answer. "I know the Danelaw, though, and that England was ruled by a Danish king." His head lifted sharply at that. "Cnut the First."

He nodded, thinking. "Only one?"

She nodded in her turn.

He shrugged. "The people of my mother prevailed. This is why you remember Alfred."

"It must have been hard, being a son of both Saxon and Dane."

He shook his head. "Not so hard. There were many and many. Danes took Saxon wives. We made villages beside the Saxon villages. We traded and spoke. Had sons and daughters."

"I thought you just burned the Saxon villages and raped the women." At his incensed look she said hastily, "Sorry, but I did."

She saw him working at the thought a minute. "Sometimes, what you say is sooth. Good men there were and *yful* or stupid. That is a way to take the land, if there is no choosing of another way. But it is not the way to hold the land. My father did not take land thus."

"And the women were wives, not concubines?" She used the Latin word for "concubines."

Now he looked really insulted. "Saxon women come to the bed of Danir men freely. Why not? We bathe many more times than Saxon men."

She tried not to smile. "Well, that would do it." Yeah. What was she thinking? Like any Saxon woman with half a hormone wouldn't jump into bed with Galen. Sitting there, all glowery, with his hair blowing back from his face and his blue eyes burning, he was making Lucy's body react in its usual way. She had to think of something else. Anything else. But she couldn't think of anything else but Saxon women coming to his bed. He'd be naked, because he seemed to like to be naked. . . .

He cleared his throat. "You say there were many English kings?"

"There is one today. Well, a queen."

He looked astonished at that.

"And her husband," Lucy hastened to add. "But she is the queen. Elizabeth."

"She rules, and not her husband?"

"Oh yeah," Lucy chuckled. "No question about that."

He nodded after a minute. "This is good. King or queen, it is good that they are *Englisc*. The kingdom is still there. I . . . what is action word for 'fright?' "

" 'Fear.' "

"I feared the kingdom would fall to the North-men who settled in Gaul."

"North-men?"

"From Northway."

She blinked. *Norway, settled in Gaul. North-men . . . could he mean . . . ?* "Normans? Normans were actually from Norway? "

"*Ja.* They have that name. But they did not take the island. This is good."

She raised her brows in apology. "But they did. Normans conquered England in 1066."

His jaw worked and he looked away. "All I fight for is like nothing."

He must love his island much. He had certainly sacrificed for it. He was not only a brave warrior but also a principled one. She had to give him comfort. "You kept them away for a hundred and fifty years." That wasn't doing the trick. There it was again, that look. Was he ashamed that he had not single-handedly staved off the Norman invasion? "It was bad to be Saxon for a time. But . . . but England just . . . absorbed them." She looked to see if he understood. "Ate them? They became English just like Danir. Their words are in our language just as Danish words are today."

"What Danish words do you have today?"

" 'Skirt'? 'Skill'? 'Gate'? 'Law'?"

His expression grew thoughtful and not quite so bleak. "*Ja*. Danish words."

"Same with Norman words. But now it is all English. Just a bigger English."

He thought about that.

"Same here in America," she continued. "Men and women of many lands are here. But all are American. And we all speak English. Well, most of us sooner or later. We were once in thrall to English kings. We fought many battles to be free. But we still speak English."

"The words are quick."

He meant "alive." She nodded.

"They *wefan* us together."

Did he mean weave? He must.

"Is this a big kingdom?" he asked.

"Very big. Not a kingdom, though. The people here choose who leads them. We call the king a president. Every man and every woman has a choice who will rule. We call it a vote."

"This is a strange time. Choosing kings." He looked bleak. He must be feeling lost.

"Not so strange. Men and women haven't changed. We still want the same things."

Oh, *that* was a bad subject to raise. His eyes grew heated, if blue could burn. But instead of sliding closer to her, he actually pushed himself farther into the corner of the bench. She didn't understand. One minute he seemed to lust after her, and the next he was acting like she had the plague. Or maybe he was trying to keep his promise.

Like she could be attractive to a man like Galen. But he was a Viking. He'd been in a war. Probably hadn't . . . hadn't *fucked* anybody for a while. She cringed at the word. But that would be all it was to him. She was just available.

That made her feel small. Before she knew what she was doing she had risen, just because she'd become uncomfortable in her skin. "Are you rested?"

"Nay, Lucy. Sit." She sat with some anxiety on the edge of the bench. He swallowed, trying to work up to something. "What will be . . . what happens here, Lucy? We hide. I heal. Then . . . what? Do you know where is this Brad? Will he make the machine work again?"

This was what she hadn't wanted to think about for the last days. She took a breath. "I know where he is. He will fix the machine if he can. He will understand that you must go back to your year to make time right. But the others who are with him . . . they are unknown." Again she looked out over the marshes, as though to absorb some of their peace and vitality. "They took all I have. Had. They are looking for me. I don't know what is in their hearts."

"They are *yful*?"

"Maybe not evil. Just angry at me."

He looked a question at her. "Wrathful?"

She nodded, feeling a little forlorn. "Maybe they think I stole the machine."

"You did not steal this machine. It was the Norns who set your course and mine."

"Maybe I should go to Brad and his friends and tell them what happened. Maybe then you could go home." Something almost like pain snaked its way from her belly to her heart at that. "It is not good for you to stay here." Was it? Confusion rolled around in her stomach.

"Jake is wise man. He thinks you should hide from Brad."

"Jake is mad." She tapped her temple. "He sees enemies everywhere." She had to use the Latin for "enemy" before Galen understood.

Galen shook his head, thinking. "Jake is not mad. Our way is not yet clear, Lucy. For now we will not seek this Brad. Or his friends."

"I wish I knew what to do. How will we get the machine? If Brad's friends want to imprison you, then you can't get back to your time, and who knows what will happen when you are not where you were meant to be?"

He pushed himself up from the bench. She could feel the fear in him. They had that in common. But he straightened his shoulders gingerly and set his jaw.

"The Norns have not yet shown us their threads. But we will know them, soon or late."

That was hardly comforting. She wished she had his courage.

Chapter Fifteen

Casey watched the old guy stroll across the interview room like he didn't have a care in the world. Lowell didn't look around at the hive of activity, didn't acknowledge Evans and Jameson at his side. Huaraches, torn jeans, a suede jacket with ridiculous amounts of fringe. Went with the gray ponytail and the beard. Guys stuck in the past were pathetic.

Casey pointed to the interview room and Lowell strolled inside and took a seat on one of the folding chairs, legs crossed out in front of him. Casey motioned Evans and Jameson out. He remained standing. That always intimidated them. "Jake Lowell?"

"Yup."

"You the manager of 1632 Filbert?"

"Yup. Owner, too. You already know that."

Lowell's eyes were appraising. Not afraid. Not even with being dragged down to a federal building with a special elevator and into a busy beehive of hard men in suits. *Interesting.* There was one kind of guy who wouldn't be intimidated. Casey felt himself getting excited.

"Wanted to talk to you about a car that was down in the parking lot of the building."

"What car was that?"

"Tenants say it was an old blue Chevy, maybe a Pontiac. Say it never moved."

"I might remember a car like that. . . ." But he only *seemed* to consider.

"Your tenants have assigned spaces?"

"Nah. It's every man for himself. Or woman."

"Do you have records of your tenants' cars, since they're parking on your property?"

"Not much into keeping tabs on people. Too much trouble."

Casey pulled on his upper lip with his teeth. "So you don't know who owned it."

"Doesn't anybody claim it?" Lowell looked surprised. "Guess you could break in and see the registration, seeing as you're who you are."

"And who is that, Mr. Lowell?"

"You tell me. Something with lots of initials. CIA. NSA. Branch of the military. Maybe NIATF, even. Not retired and selling yourself on the street corner, or you wouldn't be using this building."

"You have a lively imagination, Mr. Lowell." That nailed it. Nobody would guess NIATF. No one even knew about it. "To get back to our point. The car is missing."

Lowell glanced to the one-way glass. "All this trouble over a stolen car? Law enforcement must be rolling in dough these days. Well, I guess murders were down in the city last year. Gotta have something to do."

"You're a real comedian, Mr. Lowell."

"Nah. I'm not smart enough. Lenny Bruce. Now *he* was a comedian. Richard Pryor. Sam Kinison. They were comedians." Lowell folded his hands across his thighs and waited.

Casey called on his well-known control. "Was that your car, Mr. Lowell?"

"Don't have a car. Walk or ride the cable cars. Better for the earth."

"Do you know who took the car?"

"Say, does this have anything to do with that former tenant you were asking about?"

"Lucy Rossano, Mr. Lowell. Don't pretend you don't remember who we were looking for. And yes, it does."

Jake shook his head. "Well . . . maybe the car was hers then and it's wherever she is."

Casey turned his back so Lowell wouldn't see his frustration. How did you break someone who had probably played this game a thousand times?

After a minute Lowell said, "So, anything else I can do for you? It's getting late."

Casey took a moment before he replied. He didn't turn around. "No. You can go. I wouldn't leave town if I were you."

Casey heard the man stand. The chair scraped back. "You seem to have extra help, so feel free to set a tail on me. Better get some good walkers, though. I'm spry for my age."

The door opened and closed. Casey stood for a long minute more. The guy was a spook, or had been. He'd either blackmailed somebody or been paid off with a lot of cash and a new identity for very dirty work. He was involved in the Lucy Rossano mess up to his eyeballs.

But did you ever retire? Did anyone ever let you? Maybe Lowell was working for a rival agency. The CIA would kill for a time machine. Maybe the NIATF had a leak. Or maybe Casey's bosses were only pretending not to believe him about what it was. Maybe they didn't trust him to bring it home and were running a shadow operation. One thing was certain. It was too much of a coincidence that Lucy Rossano was living in an apartment building with an ex-spook.

"Hey, Colonel, did you mean to let Lowell go?"

"Of course I meant it," Casey snapped without turning around. "We can pick him up again whenever we want."

"Right." Evans did a disappearing act.

Casey wanted Lowell in the worst way. Nobody was going to get that machine but him. But it was more than that. Jake Lowell thought he was better than Casey at his own game.

So Jake Lowell was going down. But first Casey had to find out what he was up against, who Lowell was working for. Time to call in some very old chips.

By the time Lucy and Galen got back to the marina, the clouds had spilled over the coastal range and were racing, dark and low, across the bay. Lucy took out her key and fumbled at the lock. Galen loomed close behind her. The electric feeling in the air echoed some feeling inside her. Down the dock, the hard guy was out on his deck screwing down something. Boats took a lot of maintenance. The *Camelot* was impeccable. Jake must hire a service to do it. How did he pay them without leaving a trace?

The father and his son were out on the deck of their old Catalina, too.

"Goddamned dog," the father slurred, his voice loud enough so she and Galen could hear him clearly over the creak of boats rocking in their slips. "Get him up here, Kevin." The father had a lined and pinched face, his eyes narrow, whether from squinting against the sun or just because he didn't want to take in very much of what he saw she didn't know.

"He didn't mean nothin' by it, Dad." The kid was surly, his hair brush-cut like his dad's, his jacket worn out at the elbows. "They was my socks. I didn't care nothin' about them."

"Him or you," the father threatened. "Leavin' crap

all over where he can get at it . . ." The father's fists were balled up at his sides. "You think money grows on trees?"

The kid took a couple of heaving breaths, thinking about rebellion before he slumped and disappeared down the hatch. The man looked around and stumbled over to a stout stick with a hook on it used for hauling in big fish like marlin or tuna and picked it up. Lucy had a horrible image of spurting blood until he grabbed it by the hook end and stood there, tapping the long handle against his palm. That was bad enough.

Lucy's pulse raced. The boat loaded with impending violence was several down to the right. She and Galen should be turning left to get to the *Camelot,* but Lucy couldn't just walk away. She glanced to the hard guy, maybe five boats farther down from the boat in question, but he studiously turned his back. He'd seen this before.

The kid came up the hatch dragging the big black dog behind him, rope around his neck.

"Get him over here," the father slurred. "Teach him to chew socks."

The dog knew what was up. Maybe he had seen this before, too. Or felt it. He sat down and the kid had to drag him over, the dog pulling and shaking to get out of the rope noose.

"Damned dog."

The dog whined and cringed, pulling against the rope as he rocked back on his haunches. The boy had gone flat and emotionless. He held the rope about halfway down its length so the dog had nowhere to go. The sound of the dog's nails scrabbling against he wooden slats of the deck mingled with his whining. The man raised the handle, a gleam of satisfaction in his eyes.

Lucy wasn't going to sit here and watch a dog get hurt. "Hey, stop that" she yelled. The handle paused. She started forward.

Galen was around her and off at a run. "Stay here," he growled.

"No, Galen!" He was in no shape to take on a guy like that. She hurried after Galen.

The father raised the handle again. Galen leaped aboard the boat and strode over to catch the handle with his left hand before it came down on the dog. He wrenched it away easily, holding it by the hook end, as his adversary had. The kid looked like Martians had just landed.

The father staggered back. "What the *hell* do you think you're doing?"

"You will not beat my *hund*."

"Not your hound. Not your business. Get off my boat."

"I take my *hund* now." Galen held out the hand of his bad shoulder to the kid for the rope.

"Like hell you will." The man straightened up. The shock had sobered him. He wasn't swaying anymore. Oh, this was bad. The kid took a step back, eyes frightened.

"Galen," she called, not knowing quite what she wanted to say but sure she had to stop what might happen here.

He ignored her. Instead he just tossed the fishhook into the air and caught it by the handle, so the hook end was available for business. He grinned, his eyes glittering. A kind of sureness radiated from him. He swung the hook backward without looking and put it through a port in the cabin. Glass shattered. Shards tinkled to the deck. "You come now. We fight."

The guy's eyes shifted around, looking for a weapon. He thought about reaching for a pole lying on the deck. Lucy saw his changing mind reflected in his face. He held up his hands, palms out. "Dude, take the damned dog. He's a shit-ass dog anyway. We're better off without him."

Galen looked to the kid. Lucy saw the fear in the kid's eyes replaced by sadness. He handed over the rope. "He's a good dog, purebred and all," the kid whispered. "He just chews socks."

The dog didn't move. Galen didn't pull on the rope. He just held it. Keeping one eye on the father, Galen spoke to the kid. "You are like him?" He indicated the father with his head.

"No," the kid said hastily. Then a spasm crossed his face. "I don't know."

Galen nodded. "I understand. How many years you have?"

"I'm seventeen."

"Enough." Galen nodded to the hatch. "Get clothes. You go from here. Or not. You choose." She'd never taught him the word "choose," so it must be a lucky confluence of the language. Who knew how he was spelling it in his mind. Galen's accent was a little thick, but the kid got the idea.

"Boy, you leave now, I'll see you in hell before I let you back."

The boy gave a frightened glance from his father to Galen.

"Make a new life," Lucy said from the dock. "I'll give you money."

The boy's eyes gleamed for a moment. Then the light in them dimmed. "Haven't got nobody but Dad. When the money runs out, what am I gonna do, work at some McDonald's?"

"Go to school," Lucy suggested. She couldn't take him in when they were on the run. Could she? She'd be putting him in danger. . . . But she could see him wavering.

"I ain't much for school."

"We'll help you. You can stay with us." How could she not offer?

But she lost him. He frowned and looked away. "I guess I know who I am."

Lucy knew then. He couldn't see any other life but what he had. He was trapped.

"Good boy," the father said. "You don't need no dog. What I was thinking to let you keep a dog on a boat anyways I'll never know." He turned to Galen. "Now git off my boat."

Galen looked around at the boat. It was old, but that wasn't the problem. It was not well kept, unlike most others in the little marina. Old rags were scattered around the deck. The fiberglass was porous from never being sealed, and greasy. The sails flapped where they hadn't been properly stowed. "This boat does not . . . belong here. You sail it to another place."

The guy started to protest, then eyed the fishhook. He swallowed. "Been meanin' to go over to Richmond anyway. Slips are cheaper there."

Lucy doubted that, but it didn't matter.

"You go by dark," Galen said to the father. He glanced to the boy and spoke carefully. "You come to that boat," here he pointed, "if you choose other street before he go. Goes."

The kid nodded, but Lucy didn't hold out a shred of hope.

"I keep this," Galen said, hefting the fishhook. He leaned down, slipped the rope over the dog's head, and tossed it onto the pile of rags by the hatch. What was he doing? That dog was going to bolt for the Canadian border after how he must have been treated. Galen backed to the edge of the boat and stepped over the side to the dock.

"Come, *hund*."

To Lucy's surprise the dog got up, limping a little, and managed to leap over the line railing. He touched Galen's hanging right hand with his nose. "Good *hund*," Galen whispered. Then he lifted his gaze to the father. "You go . . . now."

Lucy's heart thudded in her chest. Galen took her arm and turned her up the dock. The hard guy five boats down looked on impassively. Lucy craned around. The dog was, miraculously, trotting behind them, though his gait was a little off.

"What do you mean, sayin' you aren't like me, you little creep?" the father hissed at the boy. "Now see what you done with that dog you had to have."

"Sorry, Dad," the kid mumbled. "Real sorry."

"Now you take the truck over to Richmond. I'll motor over, moor in deep water. Call me when you got a slip. It better be cheap. And don't be long about it."

Lucy hoped the kid took the dilapidated truck and drove to Oklahoma or Wisconsin or somewhere, but she didn't hold out much hope. Maybe he couldn't help being like his dad after all. Galen would say the Norns had already woven the kid's fate. But she didn't believe it. He had a choice. He just wouldn't take it. But *did* he have a choice? There was nobody to show him life could work any other way. As she and Galen walked down to their own boat, the kid trotted up to the parking lot, brushing at his cheeks. She and Galen stepped onto the *Camelot*. She paused, in spite of the first pelting drops of rain, and watched the truck roar out of the parking lot. Then she unlocked the hatch and scooted below, just in time to avoid the downpour. Galen came down the ladder and beckoned to the dog, who hesitated for a long instant, then plunged into the cabin.

Galen felt better all around. His thigh was throbbing and his shoulder was even worse. But that was "okay," as Lucy would say. He felt more like a man.

The *hund* sniffed his way to the aft cabin, exploring. The creature looked like a black, long-haired wolf, but more elegant, with feathered tail, hindquarters, and front legs and a ruff around his neck. He was young, not filled out in the chest yet. He was much like the dogs Galen had as a child. His mother had gotten the first from a great *wicce* in Suthfolc named Britta. He had grown up with that dog's progeny, a long line of intelligent companions. They were tricksters and thieves, fiercely protective, easily trained to herd sheep and cattle or guard sleeping babies and grain harvests. Was this dog descended from those ancestors so long ago? Only the Norns could know for certain.

"What are we going to do with a dog on such a small boat?" Lucy asked, hands on her hips. She was more bemused than exasperated.

"This is a big boat, Lucy. The *hund* will live here well. We have much food. We will take him off the boat to shit."

She rolled her eyes. "I might have known that word would be the same."

He raised his brows.

She sighed. "I know. What else could we do?" A small smile drew her lips up. "You were fearsome. Mighty." Then she frowned. "But you could have been wounded again. Very stupid."

He liked the fact that she thought him brave. "That man wound me? No, Lucy." And she worried for him. That was good too. The *hund* came up and nosed Galen's hand.

Galen went down on one knee and took the *hund*'s ruff in both hands. Lucy and the others had called him a dog. Galen looked directly into the dog's face. He got concerned, started to struggle, and then relaxed as though he were melting butter. "You are safe now," Galen rumbled. "You are my *hund*." He glanced to Lucy behind him. "And you are Lucy's dog."

The beast's tail gave a little thump on the floor. Galen's smile broadened. This was a good dog. The moment broke and Galen gave him a pat and rose.

"He came right with you," Lucy said. "Why didn't he run for the hills?"

"*Deōrs* are my friends, always."

"*Deōr*? Dog? No, you call them hounds."

"*Swine, hors, lamb,* all these."

"Oh. Animals. Beasts."

He nodded. Beasts liked him. They came to him naturally. "You will name this dog, Lucy. He be your friend."

"Will be," she corrected, looking doubtful. "Well, let's get him some water. He probably has fleas."

"No fleas."

"How do you know?" She frowned at him.

"If other beasts are here, I know." It was just true. He could always sense other life. It was part of his warrior's senses. No one could waylay him from a hiding place.

She gave him a wide-eyed look and got down a bowl, not made of glass but of something she had told him was plastic. She filled it and put it on the floor. The dog lapped eagerly.

"Poor thing," Lucy said, looking down at him. His fur was worn away where the rope around his neck rubbed. His skin was raw. "And that poor boy." She sighed. "I don't think he'll ever escape his father."

"Mayhaps not." A father could twist a boy's soul as a mother could not. Galen was lucky in his own father, who had been honorable and stern but loving. It was he who had made Galen a warrior and a leader of men, when he could not be something more.

Lucy knelt and examined the dog. She made soothing sounds. It occurred to Galen that this was the sound women made when they crooned to their babies. "He's got some raw places, but no wounds. And nothing's broken. Maybe he's just sore from getting hit recently."

"*Ja,* sore. Same word." Watching her, there, caring for the dog as she had cared for him, made him remember her hands on his flesh. His loins tightened. His *scamlan* began to swell as well as his *wǣpen*. Odin's eye, but she could raise him.

She must have felt his gaze on her. She glanced up and reddened. He found her blushes inflaming. And her eyes. So green. And her hair. *Fȳrfaexen*. And her breasts and the buttocks the breeches she called jeans revealed so clearly. Dear Freya and her maidens, this woman was attractive to him. So attractive he was like to lose his soul.

"I'll brush him. We'll feed him good food. He'll heal and his coat will shine."

Galen nodded, swallowing.

"You . . . you want some Vicodin?"

He shook his head. He had forgotten about his shoulder and his thigh. He pretended he didn't want to raise her to her feet and drag her to his bed. Instead he peered out the small, high windows. The rain had brought twilight early. The boat that had been the dog's home was making a noise like Lucy's car as it moved out from the docks. "He goes."

Galen heard her clear her throat. "How about pork for dinner? Swine?"

"*Ja*. Is good." Now how was he going to get through the night without ravishing her?

Chapter Sixteen

Sunday

Lucy had lived through another rainy evening, trying to focus on the dog rather than the pull toward Galen that was becoming unbearable. Worse, it seemed that the attraction was as much emotional as physical. The man practically radiated the fact that he had a core of goodness and honor. But how could you reconcile that with the fact that he was a Viking, with his smug looks that said he knew he was attractive to women and used it to his advantage, or with that look of shame that crossed his face sometimes? What in God's name would a Viking, who had probably done *everything*, be ashamed of? She resolved not to think about him. Again and again.

The dog was settling in nicely. Galen took him out before they went to bed last night and first thing this morning. A clever creature, young and playful, the dog threw himself into everything with total gusto. He nipped at your heels when he wanted to relate or nosed his way under your elbow for petting. Definitely a sheepdog. He was still worried, though. He would return anxiously and touch Galen's thigh with his nose to reassure himself that Galen was still there. And if you made a sudden movement with your hand or your foot, he'd cringe away. Maybe someday that reaction would fade, but for now, it was a reminder of the kind of life he must have led. Lucy caught herself vowing that she'd make him forget that life. She was not in a position to make promises.

She'd lived through another morning sitting next to Galen as they studied, trying to control her responses. But her nerves were much the worse for wear. They'd walked up to the convenience store during a break in the weather. They bought overpriced dog food, though the dog was more than happy with the scraps of pork and gravy from last night. He gamboled beside them as if they'd always been a threesome. She'd picked up a can of tennis balls. Galen insisted on carrying the supplies home in his good arm and she let him. A Viking had his pride after all. The look of shame she'd grown to watch for had flickered across his face as she paid for their purchases. She'd have to teach him about money. He needn't be ashamed he didn't have any. She didn't, either. They were both living off Jake at the moment.

On the way back to the boat, she threw a ball for the dog, who trotted after it, a little gingerly. He'd soon be racing after it when he felt better. Galen marveled that the ball bounced.

"Plastic inside," she explained.

"Like the bowls?"

"Not really. I can't explain. I don't understand it."

"You live in a world you do not understand?"

"Yeah. Get used to it, guy." He might have to get used to it if she couldn't get him back to his time. "And don't believe everything people tell you." She showed him the can the tennis balls had come in. " 'Miracle bounce,' " she read. That took some Latin to translate. "Not true. It's not a miracle. Just plastic."

"Men lie to you about your world?"

He was serious, as she had not been. "All the time. That hasn't changed."

"Men do not lie about balls in my time."

"Only because they didn't have tennis balls." The dog brought it back, a little soggy. She threw it out again and the dog trotted into the green weeds blooming with small yellow flowers. "Men lie and trick and steal." The man was a Viking, for goodness' sake. Vikings weren't naïve. "What do you call conquering the east of England but stealing?"

He looked indignant. "Mighty people are meant to spread over the world."

She raised her brows. "Doctrine of manifest destiny if I ever heard it." She sighed. "Not that America is any different. Bush doctrine of preventive wars and all. And the Mexican-American War. And the War of 1812, now that I think of it." The dog brought back the ball.

"So, Lucy, your people are like Danir." Galen's voice was sly.

"Do *not* think that's anything to brag about." She threw the ball with two fingers. *Yuck*.

"Danir are a good people. They do not lie about what they want."

"Of course they do," she protested. "Look at Leif Eriksson." His expression was puzzled. *How does he not know one of the most famous Norsemen of all time? Oh.* "You were before his time. But he is known by all. He discovered a great island west of Iceland and even colder. He named it Greenland so he could get settlers to go there. Real estate scam if I ever heard one." Now how would she explain "real estate scam"?

But Galen didn't ask what it was and indeed seemed unfazed by the accusation. "Who would take his woman and *lytlings* to 'Ice and Snow Land'?" He watched the dog go after the ball. "This Leif Eriksson is a wise man."

"What about Danegeld? Your people asked for payment to leave a kingdom in peace."

"We took the silver. We went away." He shrugged and looked his question.

"But you didn't *stay* away. You came back the next year."

"It was the choice of the king. Pay again, we go away again. Or we settle there."

"So that's what you call it." She grinned. "*Settling.* I'd call it conquering." A disturbing crinkle around his eyes made her sure there was no use arguing with him.

But he came back to being serious. "No land in Denmark for second sons. Only land in England, Iceland, Brittany, the lands around the Volga River. My father was second son. You think we are thieves? We do not take the land of the English. We make villages beside them. Often the land of our village is not so rich as their land. But we do not fear work."

She sighed. "I guess it's the way of the world, anyway. That's how America was settled, too. We *did* take land from the people who were here." Vikings had nearly been the ones to settle North America. Their settlements in Nova Scotia, way before Columbus, didn't take. She had to admire that they'd crossed the North Atlantic in boats that couldn't even tack before the wind. "Your people were good sailors."

"We know the sea."

Lucy noticed that he used present tense and she used past tense to talk of his time. Another signal of the barrier between them. They walked on in silence. Lucy was worn-out. Maybe it was all the lessons or the constant electric arc of attraction between them. He felt it, too, even if it was just desperation for a lay. But he didn't act on it. Was the only reason because he had promised not to kiss her? He was an honorable man, but was that all?

She knew why *she* didn't act on this growing urge. Because he didn't. She wasn't going to risk rejection. And because he was from another time and would soon go back.

God, how? How will I get him back? She tore her thoughts away. *Don't go there, Lucy.*

If he couldn't go back, he'd be devastated. Indeed, so much stood between them conversation was like shouting across a chasm that grew wider by the hour.

When they got back to the boat, she could see he was tired. She showed him how to work the DVD recorder, so he could listen to words, and she put in a copy of *The Searchers* from Jake's collection. A cowboy movie wouldn't overwhelm Galen with dialogue at least. The dog plopped down at his feet with a sigh. She went out to make dinner.

This was the most domestic she'd been for four days in a row in forever. At least since her father died. At home her fridge was filled with Lean Cuisine dinners and pre-washed vegetable packs. Why cook for one? But this . . . it seemed . . . peaceful. At least when she wasn't thinking about Galen's dilemma, or whether Brad and Casey would find them. That underlying core of . . . rightness was growing. Was she getting sentimental? Was she . . . ?

Hell, she didn't know what was happening to her anymore.

She took a bowl in to Galen. It was a stew, but home-made this time.

"Right kind of you, little lady," he said in a perfect John Wayne drawl. The guy did have an ear for accents. His accent had been growing less pronounced as he listened to her speak.

She laughed. "You are dangerous."

"What means this?" He looked askance.

"Uh . . . something or someone who gives others fear that something bad will happen."

"Ahhh. *Plihtlic.*"

She considered. It sounded like "plight." "Yeah, probably."

"I am dangerous." He looked up at her, his bowl forgotten. "You are dangerous."

"Me?" she asked with a half laugh. "I am sooooo not dangerous."

His gaze roved over her face. "I like laughter. Your laughter."

He said it without an "f" sound in it and who knew how he thought it was spelled, but she knew what he meant. She felt herself blushing. "Laughter is always good." She got her own bowl and sat beside him. The dog begged shamelessly, nosing her bowl and licking his lips. "You go away," she ordered. Her words fell on oblivious ears. "You have food in the galley. Free feeding means your bowl, not mine. Now go away." Nothing.

"Go." Galen flicked a finger. To her astonishment, the dog went to the other side of the bed and lay down.

"Boy, you do have a way with dogs."

He nodded. "It has always been so." And then the look of shame flickered across his face. His expression went flat to hide it, and he turned to his stew. But he was still thinking about something. She could see a muscle work in his jaw.

How she wanted to know what caused that look. How she wanted to relieve whatever pained him so. She wanted to reach out to him, touch his shoulder. The feeling was almost overwhelming. It didn't feel natural. She was losing herself. Or at least her self-control.

They grew silent, pretending to eat without thinking or feeling. What a lie. When she heard his spoon scrape against the bowl, she rose. He handed it to her and their eyes met and Lucy felt as though she were falling a long ways into icy blue waters that burned they were so cold. It took all she had to jerk away and hurry out the door.

Odin's eye. What was he going to do?

She was a *wicce* and she had ensnared his soul. And it

felt *right*. That was the worst of it. He wasn't sure he cared to keep his soul, if giving it to her would make him feel thus. He was glad Egil's axe had found his flesh, because only his wounds could possibly make her feel safe around him. And he wanted her around him. All the time.

So, what was he going to do?

He could feel she wanted him in spite of this Brad. But he couldn't be her lapdog, dependent on her, answering to her beck and call, because she was more powerful than he in this time. He could have no value to her except what pleasure his body could provide her.

He grimaced to himself. When had that stopped his frolicking in bed with a winsome widow, or even a married woman whose husband was *vikingr* and who needed the services of a man? They took their pleasure of each other in bed and were done with it.

Mayhaps he could do the same with Lucy and be done with it. Once he had plunged himself inside her and loosed his seed, then she would not have this hold on him.

He knew then that she had been right. Danir did lie. He was lying to himself. If he bedded her, he would be lost. He began to throb as thoughts of bedding her had their usual effect.

He could hear her moving about in the little place for cooking food. He'd just shut the door. There was no use releasing his seed himself. He'd already proved that did not help. He'd have to just wait out his violent erection.

He felt the moon rise.

Could you feel the moon rise? But he did. Moonlight bathed the cabin through the small, high windows. It twisted inside him, a cold fire. His loins throbbed almost painfully inside his tight breeches. He rose from the bed against his will and went to the small passageway. A feeling of incredible urgency washed over him. Something was required of him. Something immediate and real. Things were wrong, somehow, and he had to set them right. He saw Lucy, standing in the moonlight, frozen, staring at the hatch. His gaze moved to the hatch and was caught, too.

The lights in the boat fizzled and went out. They were bathed in darkness. Galen's gut trembled. Lucy must be trembling, too, because she dropped the pot she had been washing. It clattered to the floor. Galen knew that if he moved, he would race toward that hatch.

And his brain told him, whatever his heart and his loins were shouting, that he should not go out in the moonlight.

The lights in the cabin went out with a fizzle, leaving only the clear, pale moonlight streaming in through the ports. Lucy couldn't get her breath. She was hurtling toward something that had been growing inside her, around her. It felt like destiny. She could refuse it. She had a choice. But she was standing on a precipice and everything would soon be very wrong if she made the wrong choice right here, right now. Her certainty was stark, as though illuminated by lightning.

But the sky had cleared. No storm, except the one inside her. So what had doused the lights? She felt Galen behind her. His physical presence overwhelmed the small space. Her thighs were wet and she throbbed, her pelvis aching. She didn't know what to *do*. But she had to do something. She just stood there trembling until finally she couldn't hold the pot in her hand.

It crashed. She held herself still for one long moment more. And then her head moved of its own accord. She turned to look at Galen. He shook, alternately flushing and going dead pale in the moonlight. His gaze jerked to hers.

Conflagration.

And she knew what she must do. It wasn't what she'd thought.

She held out a hand. "Let's go on deck."

He looked alarmed, confused.

"You know it's right." *She* did. All would be well if they could but see the moon.

A taut invisible line stretched between them. She saw him struggle. She smiled, hand still extended. He closed his eyes, took a breath. She moved to touch him. He flinched under her hand. She didn't flinch. She expected the firestorm of feeling that shot through her. It was just a more intense version of what she'd felt each time she touched him since he'd fallen against her on a battlefield in 912. His eyelids fluttered and opened.

"I fight no more," he whispered.

She opened the hatch. They climbed the ladder single file, the dog wriggling out ahead of them. The moon was rising over the bay to the east. It had cleared the horizon, golden from the pollution in the air. It shone in eerie serenity. Clouds still laced the sky. The moon would be obscured soon, but just now it was sure of itself, eternal. It spread that sureness to her.

This moon had shone over Galen's time, just as it shone now. He came up behind her.

"What month is it?" he whispered hoarsely.

She shivered, only half from cold. "We call it March. Third month."

"What day? What day?" He sounded as if it was the most important thing in the world.

She had to think. *What had the woman at the hospital said?* The day before St. Patrick's Day. Yeah. That would make this the . . . "Twenty-first." She held up fingers.

He rolled his head as though in pain. "Ostara's day. Change of season."

"The . . . the vernal equinox . . ."

"*Ja. Ja.* Day same long as night." His voice held half wonder, half fear.

The beginning of spring. The day that signaled a

change in the world as it quickened toward the plenty of summer. "Who . . . who is Ostara?"

He seemed most agitated. "Norse goddess of . . . ," he went to Latin, "fecundity. Like Saxon Eostre," he added. "Very mighty day."

So powerful that Christian priests had borrowed it, moved the date and made it the celebration of Christ's resurrection to spread their faith among the pagans. Druids, who believed that the elements of the Earth, its plants and animals, all were incarnations of the gods or the force of the universe—they celebrated the first day of spring, too, didn't they? But the moon couldn't always be full exactly on the twentieth or twenty-first of March. That must be pretty rare. . . .

She turned to him under the full moon of the vernal equinox and knew in her bones and her belly that something special was supposed to happen here, something bigger than her or even bigger than her and Galen together. The full moon, the tides, the earth's axis that rotated through space, all those could be explained. But in their confluence, they became something more. She ached for completion and she *knew* what would complete her. *Could something be bad that feels so right? Yes, if the universe lied to you, as men lied.*

God, she sounded like a loon, even to herself. The universe was *not* talking to her. Next she'd start believing in astrology or numerology, and she'd open up a shop that sold crystals and incense and tarot decks.

But Galen was here, big and real in the cold March air of the vernal equinox under a full moon. She felt his physical presence, the essence of him clearly. This was real. This was right.

"Lucy," he whispered, and it was a plea or a prayer, maybe for deliverance. Whether from what would happen here or from the pain of resistance she didn't know.

He reached out with his good arm and drew her tight against his body. His chest was hard, his biceps were hard, and the ridge under the zipper of his jeans was very, very hard. It made her dizzy. The ache inside her made it difficult to think.

"Lucy." His lips had found her hair. Her *fȳrfeaxen* hair. His hands ran over her back, down to cup her buttocks and lift her slightly against him, so her belly pressed against the ridge of his erection. She turned up her face and his mouth found hers, not gentle this time but hungry. She returned that kiss with all the need she'd been suppressing for the past days. His tongue searched her mouth, and she pressed her breasts into his chest as though they could get closer. Which they could. . . .

His thoughts must have been tending the same way. He broke away and held her by the shoulders. The moon was bright enough so she could see how blue his eyes were. "You are cold. We go below."

He pulled her toward the hatch and the warm cabin where they could get naked and closer still. She wanted to melt into him. The dog was ahead of them. At the bottom of the ladder Galen reached up and simply lifted her down. Was he hurting his shoulder? You'd never know it by his expression. How selfish she was to be using his small strength this way. Did she have a choice? No. She'd made her choice when she drew him out into the moonlight. She wasn't sure she could be careful of his wounds. She'd try. She'd try.

He pushed her toward the aft cabin, leaving the dog staring after them. Galen turned and firmly shut the cabin door on him. Lucy heard him sigh and settle down in the passage. The only light in the room was the dim glow of the moon through the high ports on each side.

Lucy knew what she wanted. She grabbed the bottom of both layers of her tees and pulled them over her head.

He pulled off his Henley, surprisingly deft with an injured shoulder. His stitches were black across it. His hair streamed over his shoulders. She unclasped her bra and tossed it to the floor. Galen groaned and reached for her breasts. She wanted that. More than she had ever wanted anything. She moved closer to slip her hands across the hard muscle of his belly and unbutton his jeans. His hands cupped her breasts and his palms rubbed the nipples lightly. Sensation ripped straight to her core. She lifted her face to give him access to her lips, and he took her mouth in a kiss as thorough as the one up on the deck. She worked his zipper as she moaned into his mouth. She wanted him naked. She wanted to touch all of him. She'd wanted that for days. By the time he broke away to kick off his boots and push down his jeans, her body was screaming for gratification. She fumbled at her own jeans as she watched his cock spring free. She sucked in a breath. It was big and straight and thick. She'd never had a man with equipment like this. Could she even do this? She pushed off her own Nikes and jeans. He kicked his clothes away and moved back toward her, a beast coiled to spring.

She reached for his erection, satisfied with his ragged breathing, and ran her hand along the shaft. It was rock hard under the silky skin and straining with need. He backed her the single step to the end of the bed. The edge pressed against the backs of her knees. He lowered her carefully onto it. He had that much control. But then he was on top of her, his body fitting over the length of hers as he braced above her on his elbows. His erection prodded at her entrance even as he kissed her thoroughly. The head of his cock must be drenched in her juices. But he didn't thrust inside her. He raised himself on his good elbow and kneaded her breast gently with his other hand, leaning in to kiss her throat as softly as he could. But his breath was still ragged and his teeth nipped at her as though he could barely keep from devouring her. He made his way down to her breast. She thought she might burst. He was trying to make sure she was ready. But she didn't want it gentle. She wanted it *now*, as fierce and demanding as she could get it.

So she spread her legs under him and thrust her hips up a little, undulating against the head of his cock, showing it the way in.

"Odin's eye, Lucy," he breathed, pulling his head up. He was throbbing at her entrance, still straining for control.

"Kiss me," she whispered, whether entreaty or command she couldn't tell.

He did. His lips were soft. The day's stubble rasped against her chin. She opened to him, and he thrust his tongue inside her mouth in an echo of the thrusting they both wanted even more. He groaned again into her mouth, and she couldn't wait any longer. She reached down, took the thick length of him in her hand, and pressed him down slightly to achieve the right angle.

"Lucy," he said, and this time her name was a capitulation and he pushed inside her with one powerful thrust.

Filled. Right. True. Necessary.

She reached to clutch his buttocks as the muscles in them bunched with each thrust. She wanted him as she had never wanted a man before, as she had never wanted *anything*. Thrusting to meet him, the friction rubbing at her clitoris, his big cock touched places inside her she'd never felt before. He slipped an arm under her shoulders as they rocked together and clutched her to his chest, his tongue still thrusting and questing inside her, his cock impaling her. They seemed to be melting together in the heat they generated into something entirely new, separate from what they had been, not to be separate from each other ever again.

She felt it coming from a long way off, like a wave at sea, building momentum from somewhere deep and unseen, inexorable. Their bodies were slick with a light sheen of sweat, both of their chests heaving now as if there were not enough air in the world, let alone this tiny cabin. He withdrew until only the tip of his cock was inside her. He was trying to prolong it for her. Sweet. But wrong.

"Galen," she moaned.

He pulled away from their kiss, his brows drawn together in concern. Could he possibly mistake that moan? How could she make him understand what she truly wanted? *Needed.*

"Fuck me, Galen."

She'd never said that word in her life. But it must be Saxon all right. Because his eyes darkened and he thrust inside her, his eyes never leaving hers. And now they watched each other's faces as the wave was there again, more urgent, more powerful for the pause. She saw his eyes glaze over.

And then the wave crashed over her, drawing her under. Every muscle in her body contracted. Her eyes squeezed shut and a shriek, coiling up from her loins, was squeezed from her by the weight and the power of the wave. Through it all she felt Galen's own orgasm take him. He didn't scream, but a series of grunts matched the spurting she felt inside her. They were under the wave, no breath, no air, just the immense sensation squeezing them, squeezing them . . . until they popped to the surface.

Bobbing on the subsiding sensation, she gasped for air, and Galen did the same. Galen looked into her eyes for a long moment, blinking, as she did the same. The moonlight through the line of ports near the ceiling was cool and kind, bathing them in a silver iridescence. There was a breeze inside the room, from somewhere, nowhere, because the ports and the doors were all shut. It cooled their sweat and felt . . . comforting. That's what it was. The room was filled with comfort and rightness.

It was almost frightening.

"What the hell was that?" she whispered. She had *never* had an orgasm like that.

He gave a tiny, dazed shake of his head and swallowed, hard. "I know not, Lucy." It had been different for him, too.

He was still inside her and that felt right as well. Her breathing began to steady, as did his. The moonlight was just . . . moonlight. What had she been thinking? And there was no breeze in the room. How silly was that? It must just be that orgasm had unhinged her there for a minute. *What an orgasm.* She hadn't known it could be like that. *And that spooky feeling of rightness . . . well, that is just the lovely afterglow of sex.*

Isn't it?

"Lucy," he breathed, and kissed her head, cradling it against his shoulder.

Stitches! "I didn't hurt you, did I?"

"Nay, Lucy. I am okay. Very okay." He lifted her chin. "Are you okay?" He looked contrite. "I was . . . I know not the word . . ." He switched to Latin. "Crude? Rough?"

"You were wonderful. Just what I wanted."

"You are what I want also." He kissed her hair again. "I like *fyrfeaxen*. You are beautiful."

She looked away. She wasn't beautiful. Red hair and freckles and way more curves than were fashionable. "I bet you say that to all the women."

"Nay. The other women know they are beautiful. There is no need to say it."

Great time to remind her about all the other women in his life. And that they were beautiful.

He must have felt her contract, in spirit if not in body. He put a finger under her chin and turned her face up to his so she could not help but look into his eyes. "You are the one for me. Do you not feel it? I want you, Lucy. The night wants us together. You know it is sooth."

God, but she needed that to be true. The night might be the only thing that wanted them together. He was from another time. And both their former lives were lost to them. What were they doing here, waiting on this boat, for what they did not know? He rolled to the side, keeping her with him, still inside her. She scanned his face, her doubt in her eyes.

"This was always the thread of the Norns." He said it solemnly. He meant their joining was preordained. That was his explanation for why it felt so right. Tragedy could be preordained, too, though. Maybe this was just the taste of what could be before it was all jerked away from her in some cruel twist of fate.

"Do you believe in fate?" she asked.

That look of shame flickered over his face, and the peace that had hung heavy in the air was torn a little more. What made him look like that? She wanted to help. Whatever he had done, he could get past it, and so could she. No matter how horrible. This was Eostre's night. And wasn't Easter all about forgiveness, at least for Christians? Lucy had felt the goodness in him. She wanted to be part of his healing. She knew very well that she wasn't the most beautiful woman he'd ever been with. But she put her own feelings aside. She wanted to know all of him as she had known him physically in the last moments. She wanted to help him. Taking her courage in her hands as she took his face, she turned it up. A man like this would not give up the secrets of his soul easily.

"Why do you look like that?"

He shook his head. The look flashed across his face and was suppressed. "I do not understand you, Lucy."

"Don't give me that. You understand."

He eased out of her. The peace in the room ebbed a little farther. He looked around, as though he felt it, too. He scooted up to sit against the teak headboard. "It is of no matter."

She felt the loss of his body inside hers so acutely it was almost pain. She wanted to sidle up under his good arm and curl against him. But she didn't. She wanted the peace, the feeling of rightness again, but it had to be about more than just fantastic sex. It had to be about who she was, not just that she was close at hand. That was the only thing that could make up for not being the most beautiful woman he knew. And that meant it had to be about who he was, too. She looked at him. He swallowed. Would he bare himself to her in more than body?

"Your will is as thick as a priest of the Christ Cult," he complained.

"Is it bad to want to know you?"

He closed his eyes. "What is cannot be . . . otherwise." His eyes opened. They were bleak.

She wanted to comfort him, but such a man couldn't bear that. So she said, "But the burden can be shared. Burden?" she asked in Latin.

He looked away but not before she was sure he understood her.

Another time, without the waft of sureness still hanging in the moonlight, she would have backed down. But not now, not when she had a dreadful feeling that there was only this night to bind them together and that this night was one of few they might have together.

"Now or never, Galen Valgarssen. Whatever makes you look like that, I will always think you are mighty and smart and honorable. You might even have a sense of humor." She didn't stop to explain. He might not have gotten all of it. But he got the challenge and the gist. Pain flitted into his eyes again, and now she could not resist. She scooted up and curled beside him, head on his chest, listening to the thump of his heart and feeling the peace seep into her with his warmth. His arm slipped around her and held her tight against his side.

"My mother was a mighty *wicce*," he said above her after a moment. She heard it as a rumble low in his chest. "She was from the Old Ones of the west, though she lived among the Saxons. She served the goddess of horses, Epona. She speaks to horses. Nay, spoke," he corrected himself. "And other beasts. She is dead now. Her kind always had only daughters. But she loved my father, a Viking warrior, against the law of her kind. On Sahmain night in the circle of stones he got her with a *lytling* to be the priest of Epona after her. But it was a boy. My brother, Eric. The kin of my mother thought he was a sign from God and he would be a mighty priest, perhaps the most mighty, to lead them against their enemies. But Eric died. My mother cursed the goddess. My father mourned him. Later, I was born."

He heaved in a breath. Lucy held hers. "My mother named me Galen in the words of my father. It means . . ." He searched for the English word, then said it in Latin.

"We would say 'bespelled.' "

"*Ja,* bespelled. She hoped I would be mighty in *drȳcræft* like my brother."

"Drycraft?"

He used the Latin.

"Oh, magic. Your mother thought you'd have magic powers and take your brother's place." *Boy, is that a lot to put on a kid.*

"But I have no magic. Beasts love me, but I do not speak to them as my mother did. I am not Eric. The magic died with him. Always I was not what they wanted. I saw it in their eyes. "

"Your . . . your parents were disappointed in you?"

He heaved another breath. Her head rose on his chest and fell. "They loved me. They were good kin. But I knew. And wherever I went in the land around, all knew."

"How did you bear it?"

"My father teached me to wield a weapon. I watched him bind the people together, Saxon and Danir, and learned from him. But I was unstill. When I had seventeen years, I went *vikingr,* first to trade up the Seine and then up the Volga to fight for the king there. In the language of the Volga, we are called Rus. The land we controlled, they called Russia. It was a hard time. I was put in a *carcern* in Kiev."

Carcern. Incarcerated. "Prison."

"*Ja.* I was gone many years. When I *gewend* to the Danelaw, my mother was dead, my father feeble. I labored for that part of the Danelaw that held my mother's people and my father's. At first Guthrum does not trust me. It is hard. I am half-Saxon. But I fight good. At last Guthrum takes my counsel. The scalds sing of my deeds. Yet still the songs tell of the one the Norns say will save his people, the one I am not. And will not be."

What a thing to live with. Belonging to neither people, living in the shadow of a dead brother, knowing people expected you to be magic and you weren't . . . Her heart went out to him. What could she say? She had expected him to be ashamed of some terrible act of carnage. The scars on his body said he'd lived through many. But he was a product of his time. He was proud of fighting and killing for the king of the Danelaw.

She had wanted to go back to a time when magic was possible. Galen certainly believed it was possible. He was ashamed he didn't have any. Maybe there was no magic in the world, then or now. You couldn't count on anything outside yourself to save you.

"Being a good man is enough," she said quietly. "There are too few of those."

"Nay, Lucy. Life is hard. Men need . . ." Here he had to ask in Latin the word for "hope." "Men looked to me to make life better. To protect them. I could only fight like other men or help in little ways: a bridge, a new saddle for horse." He had to ask the word for "saddle." She could feel him getting impatient with himself for not knowing all the words. "They ask me to say the right of the matters they bring to me. So I say which thing is right." He held her more tightly to his side. She made the leap in her mind. He could not protect his people with magic, or a woman. Was that why he had leaped so blithely from bed to bed, lingering in none? He wanted no responsibility. Yet he fought for Guthrum to unite the kingdom against the invasion only he foresaw coming from the Normans. He struggled to do what he could do, far more than most men could, always believing he was not enough. Was that not the definition of courage?

She glanced up. His expression was so bleak. What comfort was there for such a man? And then she knew. "There are all kinds of magic, Galen Valgarssen. What we had here tonight is magic." She scooted up to look him in the face, surer now. "You said the night wanted what happened here. Is that not magic? Is finding each other across a thousand years not magic?"

His eyes softened. Then the heat started in them. "You are magic, Lucy." She realized her breasts were pressed against his side, his good arm around her shoulders. She breathed in the feeling of peace as it hovered in the room again. The light had dimmed in the cabin. Clouds must have obscured the moon. But she and Galen were still here. His gaze roved over her, hungry for her. And she felt . . . beautiful. Who cared if it was a lie?

"No." She smiled. "But we can make magic together."

"Now," he rumbled, kissing her forehead. "More slow this time. I will show what I know of women." His hand found her breast. "You will yell for me tonight many times."

"You may yell yourself, big fella," she murmured into his mouth as he kissed her. The throbbing had begun between her legs, insistent. She was suddenly very glad that the vernal equinox meant there were twelve whole hours of night.

Chapter Seventeen

Brad watched the cranes move into place on the asphalt between the parking structure and the hospital, anxiety churning in his breast. The army engineers had determined just where at the base of the machine to hook in and winch it up onto the flatbed truck over the rollers set in front of it. But that didn't mean the torque might not still damage the machine further. They'd waited until dark to attract as few eyes as possible. But still gang members, old people, and the local prostitutes were way too interested in the goings-on. Arc lights nearly eclipsed the light of the full moon rising over the bay.

Brad turned to where giant I-beams formed a new entrance to the parking structure. The rollers clattered, signaling the movement of the machine out into the glare of the arc lights.

Now if only he was sure he could fix it. They might never find Lucy and the diamond and the book. She was probably busy fucking that Viking hunk's brains out. The thought made Brad sick and strangely excited. If he ever caught up with them, he'd do what they did in Viking times with women like her. He'd have her stripped naked and whipped through the streets with crowds yelling, "Whore!" and pelting her with stones and refuse.

Or maybe he was just imagining that's what they did back then. It didn't make a less attractive prospect. And as for the Viking . . .

"Watch out there!" he yelled as a workman who was pushing the machine across the rollers stumbled and went down. "You damage that, you're . . . you're toast."

The guy in overalls picked himself up, glaring.

"Bet he's frightened of that threat. I sure am."

Brad whirled to find Casey standing, haggard and hard-eyed, behind him.

"Well, at least I'm holding up my end of the bargain. I'm getting the machine back to the lab. I don't see you finding my little whore of a girlfriend and her tenth-century boy toy." He wasn't quite sure how he had the courage to talk like that to Casey. But then Brad had changed a lot since he found out Lucy had betrayed him and ruined his career into the bargain.

"I know who knows where they are," Casey said. "That's something."

"The manager?" It seemed impossible that an old guy wearing huaraches and a serape had made them disappear into thin air. "That old coot?"

"He's more than that." Casey stared at the machine as it was pushed up to the base of the ramp that led to the flatbed.

"What is he?"

"Not quite sure. But he's not working for any government agency. Had to call in some favors to find that out. Some coincidence that he happened to be the girl's landlord. But since he's not official, I can ask him directly where the girl is."

"I want to be there." Brad was already breathing hard at the possibility of finding Lucy.

"Might be kind of messy. Better take a pass."

Brad swallowed. "Well . . . I should supervise the machine getting back to the lab anyway. Call me when you find out where she is. I want to see her face when the marines come over the hill."

"Will do," Casey said. Then he turned and walked to a waiting black Escalade beyond the army barriers.

Brad shivered. Casey wouldn't call him. He knew that. *Damn it*! He had a right to be in on this whole thing. He wanted to see Lucy squirm. And the Viking? Whipping wasn't enough. But Casey would know how to make him suffer.

"Well, Mr. Lowell, this interview is going to be a little different than the last one."

Lowell was tied to a chair bolted to the old boards of a ramshackle building down by the industrial side of the docks, not the tourist side. It was being redeveloped, but the permits were hung up in red tape. Permanently. Made a convenient interview site.

"Yeah. I figured."

Lowell didn't look scared. He should.

"You disappeared that girl and her Viking, Lowell. I want to know where they are."

"How would a broken-down old apartment manager who likes jazz know anything about disappearing people, Colonel?" He made the title sound like an epithet.

"Like that's what you are." Casey paced around the chair. Pollington stood in his shirtsleeves in the shadows. He had a billy club dangling down the seam of pants that broke perfectly over his tasseled loafers. Too bad that nice white shirt was going to get ruined tonight. "I don't want to spar with you, Lowell. I just want some answers."

"If wishes were horses . . ."

Casey nodded to Pollington, who hit Lowell in the belly and left him retching all over his knees. "Now this can be easy or hard, Lowell. Easy or hard."

"Do your worst," Lowell spit when he could get his breath. Then he smiled. Like he knew something more that Casey didn't than the whereabouts of the girl.

Monday

Galen watched Lucy sleeping beside him, on her belly, the swell of her breasts clearly visible as they pressed into the bed, her *fȳrfeaxen* hair spread out over the crumpled white linen. Light leaked in through the windows around the cabin, and sun lit her hair with shiny copper threads. The dog lay sleeping in one corner. Galen got up and fed him last night after he and Lucy made love again, and let him out to relieve himself. He was a good dog. When Galen brought Lucy bread and cheese and beer, the dog had begged, of course, in spite of his full belly. But when Galen had seen Lucy's eyes light yet again, one word and the dog retreated beyond the cabin door while Galen *swived* her well and thoroughly until she screamed her climax. She was a generous lover, a generous person. She had tried to comfort him by telling him he was enough for her.

Not true. He did not deserve her. But somehow he had been granted a time with her, the Norns only knew how long. He would take it and be grateful to the gods. And he would protect her, in his poor way, as well as he could.

He lay on his good side, his elbow propping up his head, and watched her breathe. He felt good. Whole. Perhaps for the first time in a long time. Maybe ever. Lucy did that for him. He closed his eyes. He felt Lucy's breathing, his breathing. His shoulder didn't ache as much now. He could almost feel it sealing itself together with each breath. The boat seemed to breathe, too. No, it was just rocking. It was the water that breathed. He could not help the smile that curved his lips. How right that felt, that the earth breathed. Water breathed into the air; the plants breathed; the land warmed and cooled with the passing of the sun. He felt the bay stretch beyond the boat, out under the marvelous bridge they called the Gate of Gold and away to other lands stranger than he could imagine, teeming with life. Down into deep trenches darker than night went the water and up shallow estuaries to meet the rivers. And below the water was the earth itself, the muck of all existence, fertile and quick, and below that was a seething core of molten glass, fiery, like Lucy's hair. He felt the ice that crept over the earth in places, colder even than the lands north of the Volga, and hot barren sands blowing in fury. They were all connected. They all breathed as one. . . .

But there was a sickness in the earth. The cities, like cankers, breathed out smoke. He felt a shelf of precious ice fall into the sea somewhere. The earth shuddered beneath it. He felt the fishes suck for air and gasp and die where rivers ran, yellow and noxious, into the pure blue-green of the sea. . . . Something was wrong, terribly wrong. . . .

"Well, sleepyhead, are you going back to sleep?"

His eyes snapped open, his feeling of connection gone. "Lucy." He smiled, blinking. Had that been a dream? It was a strange one.

She sat up, clutching the sheet to her breasts. The dog rose and stretched and wandered over. Galen gathered Lucy into his chest and fondled the dog's ears. "*Yful hund*," he said.

"He's not a bad dog."

"You must name him, Lucy, if he is to be your friend."

"You could name him," she said, snuggling into Galen. She was so soft, so absolutely female. He held her more tightly to his body. He couldn't imagine how she could not know she was beautiful. Had the men in her life never showed her what her beauty, inside and out, must do to them? He had thought to bind her to him by bedding her. But it was he who was bound. He only hoped that if and when this Brad came to claim her, she would not choose the man who could provide for her better than he could. That struck him to his heart. How selfish he was, to think to take her from a better life than he could give her.

He left off stroking the dog and stroked Lucy instead.

"I'm not sure what happened last night," she murmured, sleep still slurring in her voice. "But I liked it."

"You love my *wǣpn*," he chided, smiling.

"Weapon?" She looked up at him. "You're kidding." She lifted the sheet. "Tell me that's not what you call your . . ." She nodded to his *pintel*.

"*Ja*. We call it *wǣpn*. Like sword or spear. Same."

"Technically it's called a penis."

"*Pintel* is my word."

"But we call it cock, or shaft. I guess that's like a spear."

"Cock, like the bird, cock?"

"Uh-huh. Cockerel. Rooster."

He tried to keep his mouth serious. "That is a very stupid name."

"*I* think it's because cockerels are so proud of themselves, just like men are of their. . . ."

"Their *wǣpns*."

"Weapons." She pretended to capitulate. But he knew her better than that now. "Okay, so tell me what you call other parts of your body." She touched his chest.

"*Breast, bosom*." He'd play this game all day if she would touch him.

She touched his eye.

"*Eye*." Then other parts. "*Chin. Shoulder. Elnborga*."

"That's sort of like elbow."

"*Mūth. Tunge*." When she touched his tongue, it made him shiver in places that had nothing to do with his mouth. "*Hype, thēoh*," He cleared his throat. Touching those was like to have consequences. "*Hearthan*."

"Those are testicles. We call them balls."

"I will remember that." He kissed her hair.

Suddenly the dog came up beside them and shook one of Galen's stockings fiercely to get their attention. Lucy laughed. "He still likes socks." She turned to Galen in surprise. "I know. I'll call him Vandal."

"What means this word?"

"They were a people from around Germany, I think. It has come to mean 'thief.' You understand that?"

"*Ja. Thēof.* Word is same. And we call those men *Wendalls*." He turned it over in his mind. "*Ja*, Vandal is a good name for this dog."

"I think this dog needs to go out."

"Nay, Lucy. Vandal can wait." Galen pulled her closer.

She put both palms on his chest. "We can wait. We have all day."

He liked that. He wanted to spend the day making love to Lucy. It felt so right. They might not have very long. But they could make it a time that scalds would sing down the ages. He let her get out of bed, enjoying the sight of her rounded bottom and narrow waist, just touched by the ends of her long hair. She went to the little locker where she had her clothing and pulled on jeans and those tight shirts she called T-shirts.

"I'll take him out. You did doggie duty last night."

"I will shower, Lucy, to prepare for *swiving* you all day."

Damn it! Casey was nowhere to be found. The goons fielding calls this morning at Casey's lair downtown hadn't seen him all night and professed not to know where he was. Brad slumped in a folding chair. The industrial green of the bullpen made his stomach turn. There were only a couple of guys there so early in the morning. The calls hadn't picked up yet.

Brad had nowhere else to go. The machine was en-
sconced back in the lab down on the peninsula. He'd spent
the night replacing parts in the power source. But without
the diamond, he couldn't even test the thing. Who knew
whether they'd ever get a substitute diamond or whether
that diamond would work in the same way as the one Lucy
had stolen?

He picked up one of the handbills with the artist's renderings of Lucy and the Viking guy on it. *This is all
Lucy's fault.* The anger coiled in his gut, hemmed in by
impotence until he thought he might explode. He crumpled up the handbill and tossed it overhand toward the
wastebasket. It bounced out and across the floor. He didn't
like to think what Casey might do to that landlord, but
whatever it was, it damned well better work.

The telephone in front of him rang. He glanced up to
see the guy in shirtsleeves point to him. The other two
were busy murmuring encouraging noises into the micro-
phones on their headpieces and taking notes.

What the hell? He might as well take some crank calls.
What else did he have to do? He picked up the receiver,
fitted it over his ear, and hit the button.

"Special Investigations Unit," he answered. That's what
the other guys had been saying. He pulled over a notepad
and removed his number two mechanical pencil from his
shirt pocket.

"Hello? Is this the place where I report if I saw those
two people you're looking for?"

The guy sounded gay. *The one bad thing about living
around San Francisco.* "Yeah."

"They aren't in any trouble, are they? She was so
nice . . . and he . . . well, it would be a shame if they were
missing or something."

"Well, with your help, they won't be missing long."
What bullshit. How many calls had Casey said they'd

fielded already? Hundreds. Everybody had seen Lucy and her Neanderthal. They were in Oakland disguised in Afros and in Santa Cruz smoking pot. All at the same time. "Where exactly did you see them last?"

"Macy's in Novato. She came in to buy him clothes. He'd lost his luggage in a car fire."

"Novato. Check." Nobody hid out in Novato. Suburbia. Small-time suburbia. Brad looked at the top handbill on the pile. Lucy and the Viking stared back. "Are you sure it was them?"

"Well . . ." *Now we'll get to it. It* kinda *looked like them.* Brad could practically hear the guy's certainty waning. "Well, the picture shows her with her hair back, so you can't see how long it is. But it fell to her waist." Brad glanced to the picture. You actually couldn't tell she had long hair, but this guy knew she did. "And it's not in color of course, so even though it says 'red hair,' you might miss that it's really, really red hair."

Shit. This could be it.

"How about the guy?"

"Well, he didn't have a beard when I saw him, or those braids. But he did have long hair. And you don't mention that he didn't speak the language very well. He was Danish or something. *Really* well built. You can't see that from the picture at all."

Double shit. Novato. Now what to ask?

"Did . . . did they have what they bought delivered? We're . . . we're looking for the place where they might have been abducted."

"Abducted? Oh, that's just terrible. Well, let's see. They took everything with them. Paid cash." There was a long pause. This was going to be a dead end, like everything else. Just a dead end in Novato. "She did say they were living on a boat."

A boat? He'd been right!

"Thank you, that's helpful," he said as calmly as he could. "Did she say exactly where?"

"No." The guy's voice fell. "No, she didn't."

"Well, that's more than we had yesterday." Brad glanced around. No one was paying any attention to him. That was good. A little plan was hatching in his mind. "Let me get your name and address. Be sure to contact us if you think of anything else."

He clicked off his headphones. They were living on a boat in a marina. Casey's people probably hadn't worked their way up to Novato yet. They might never get there. It didn't spring to mind when you thought about marinas. Not like Oakland or Sausalito. How many marinas could there be near a suburb like Novato?

Let Casey get what he could from the landlord. Casey always dismissed Brad like he was nothing. Maybe Brad would be the one to find them. He glanced around. Everyone was busy. He had the whole day to himself. Time for a trip to Novato.

Watching Galen come out of the shower was like watching Triton rise from the sea. Droplets clung to his body. His hair was damp around the edges and that wonderful cock of his was half-swollen as though remembering last night.

She'd taken Vandal out to race around the parking lot and the marshy area just to the northeast. The weather looked iffy, but just now, though damp, it wasn't actually raining. The dog was a bundle of energy this morning. Unlike herself.

What a night. She'd thought the direct approach she and Galen had taken the first time would be a Viking's only repertoire. Wrong. He knew women all right. Including how to use his mouth. She hiked in a breath and closed her eyes as her body shuddered in memory. He said he got it from the women in Gaul when he'd gone *vikingr* up the Seine. She'd begun to think more kindly of the women he'd had in his life if they were the root of her current pleasure.

It was more than pleasure.

She had never felt so right, so calm and sure of herself.

That stuff about a full moon on the vernal equinox was ridiculous, of course. Moonlight had been luring lovers into each other's arms since time immemorial. It didn't mean there was any magic to it, even though she'd told him that the night had wanted them together. That was just to comfort him, because he so wanted magic in his life. And also for her comfort, maybe, because she'd been looking for magic, too, to take her away from a life she didn't care about. Everyone craved magic. They wanted to believe you could eat all the calories in the world but not gain weight, that you could exercise while you slept, that God paid attention to your prayer for a Mercedes-Benz. Easy results without any effort from you.

But so what if she'd lied to him? There might be no magic, but she had gotten closer to Galen last night than she'd ever been to a man. That was miracle enough. Of course it wasn't love. Not in six days. But it was . . . something.

With a Viking, no less. Who knew?

Galen dried himself with a towel, but his eyes never left hers. When he was done, he didn't feel the need to wrap it around his hips. He let it fall to the floor. That didn't annoy her now. She wasn't afraid of the effect his nude body had on her anymore.

"Do you like to go around naked?" she whispered as she took the few steps across the salon toward him.

"*Ja.* Naked is good. You be naked, Lucy." He reached for her.

It was only then that she noticed his shoulder. The

wound was entirely sealed. Yesterday she'd thought it would be days yet before she could remove the stitches. This morning it looked like she might be late.

"Galen, look. . . ."

He peered down at his shoulder, then stared back at her, questioning. She had no answers. "I . . . I heal good."

"That couldn't happen overnight. . . ." Was she talking to herself or him?

"Mayhaps last night, it could."

She pulled away to look at his thigh. It was the same. Really almost healed entirely. "Well, we'd better get those stitches out." The moment she'd dreaded was on her. And now those stitches were in there tight. She retrieved her supplies and the little nail scissors. She could do this. She could.

He sat on the sofa. She got the disinfectants from the head that opened on his cabin. Chewing her lip, she bore down on him.

"Lucy, I will do this thing."

Had she looked that uncertain? Well, she wasn't uncertain. He needed her help, and she could do this for him. "You will *not*. I took care of these wounds, and I will see this through."

He raised his brows and held up his hands, palms out, in surrender. "*Ja*. You will do this thing."

She'd start on the thigh. That one was the most healed. Pulling out the stitches would probably make him bleed. But it had to be done. She made her mind small as she knelt in front of him, steadied his thigh with her left hand, and cut each stitch with the little scissors. That was the easy part. She let out a breath and grabbed the knot end of the first stitch between the nail of her thumb and forefinger. She pulled. God, she could feel the stitch pulling through the flesh. Blood seeped out in two bright dots. She let go as though burned and glanced up to Galen. He hadn't flinched, but this *must* hurt.

He smiled. "Is okay, Lucy. Swift. Like this." He made a plucking motion in the air.

Taking her lip between her teeth, she grabbed the knot again and just . . . jerked. *Oh, dear. Oh, dear, dear, dear.* She realized she'd been holding her breath. Okay. She'd done it. She patted away the drops of blood with a cotton ball soaked in Betadine.

One down and about a zillion to go.

She was so afraid to hurt him. It took all she had to keep at it. Galen wanted to protect her from that. He could have pulled the stitches out faster. But she needed to do something she was a little afraid of, to make her sure of who she was. He knew she was strong. But he wasn't sure she knew it of herself. He sat, watching her concentrate, murmuring apologies he only half-understood. The bond he shared with this woman made him wonder at himself. Had he changed so much that she could capture and hold him so securely, without even trying?

Perhaps. Or maybe he had always had it in him to bond with a woman. He had just never met the woman with whom he was destined to bond.

He had finished healing, nearly. If he listened, he could feel the knitting of the muscle and sinew inside his shoulder, slow, inexorable. And if he listened to that, then other sensations crept in. Wind, whirling across land and sea. Far away the rumble of an angry earth as the hot liquid iron pushed up through a mountain. An island, its strange trees tossed in a mighty wind like green hair, as a storm battered it. All . . . all wove together into a kind of singing, bass and high, like men and women sang together. A song of the earth.

Something had changed last night. Perhaps many things. Maybe he himself had changed.

"That's it," Lucy said, jerking Galen from his reverie. The song subsided.

He glanced down at the scars, now accompanied by a line of dots on either side. Lucy swabbed them with the yellow-orange of her *acetum*.

"You do good, Lucy," he said. She tried not to smile. She was proud of herself.

"Now I'm going to feed us some steak for breakfast," she pronounced, rising. "Or, uh, lunch as the case may be. Then I have something I want to do to you."

He raised his brows. "*Ja?* What is this something?"

"You'll see. Can't let that shower go to waste." And with a smug look he found most appealing, she turned into the tiny galley, Vandal sniffing at her heels and poking her, to remind her that his bowl was empty.

Galen could hardly wait to find out what she had in mind.

Chapter Eighteen

Lucy had Galen backed up to the bed, stark naked, or *nacod*, as he'd showed her he spelled it. She'd just finished kissing him thoroughly and had the satisfaction of feeling his weapon stiffen against her before she took both hands and pushed his chest until he fell backward, grinning in surprise. The grinding sound of Vandal chewing on the beef bone she'd given him echoed comfortingly from beyond the safely closed door. Scars still wound redly over Galen's shoulder and thigh, but all trace of bleeding from removing the stitches had disappeared. The man was really a remarkable healer.

All last night he had taken the lead in their lovemaking. Vikings probably expected that. But she was a modern woman and she expected reciprocation. Would he allow that? He was still a man of the tenth century. But she had no desire to be a tenth-century woman.

"You are hungry for my body, Lucy?"

Oh, he had no idea. "Yes, my big, buff Danish warrior," she said, crawling onto the bed between his splayed legs. "I am going *vikingr*."

He lifted his brows. "You know what means *vikingr*?"

" 'Plunder. Pillage.' " She translated in Latin.

"Or 'trading,' " he corrected.

"I will plunder, pillage, or trade. My choice."

His eyes darkened. "It is for man to plunder, not woman."

She shook her head. "Not in my time. You are here now."

He reached for her, grinning again, his eyes alight with his need. "*Ja.* I understand."

She pushed him back down and waved her finger at him, mocking. "Woman is a partner in this time. Equal. Same."

"You were . . . partner last night," he said, reproach in his voice.

She smiled. "*Ja.* And you are partner now. Yet I will say what we do."

He thought about that for a moment, then reached up above his head, easily, even with his bad shoulder, and grasped the brass railing that lined the box where Jake stored books and DVDs with both hands. There was a lustful glow in Galen's eyes.

"My body belongs to you, Lucy. Do what you will."

"You might be sorry you said that," she threatened. But she'd make sure he wasn't. This was probably a pretty big step for him. "Hold tight, no matter what I do." This was going to be fun. She was wet between her thighs just thinking about it. From the looks of things, Galen was looking forward to it, too. His cock lay along his belly, close to bursting. She spread his ankles farther apart and scooted in between his thighs, bracing herself on elbows placed on each side of his hips. Rolling to one elbow, she cradled his balls. She felt him brace himself. She was going to go slowly and enjoy every second of this. She rubbed the place just behind his testicles with three fingers, in little, firm circles. He was having a hard time breathing. *Thank you,* Cosmo, *for all those "Ten Tips to Drive Him Wild" lists.* She'd never gotten a chance to try those things.

Strangely enough, she hadn't even cared to drive the men in her life wild.

But Galen . . .

By the time she took the head of his cock in her mouth and sucked it gently, he was gasping like a beached fish and the knuckles grasping the brass rail were white. The bulge of biceps, the hair under his arms slightly darker than on his head, and the ripple of abs were making her grind her own hips against the bedspread. He sometimes closed his eyes tight and sometimes watched her handling his genitals. He couldn't keep his hips from moving. She loved that. She alternately sucked the head and licked along the large vein that ran along his shaft.

Occasionally she stopped for conversation, to let him calm down and prolong the pleasure. "Do you like this, Viking?"

"*Ja*. I like it." He was breathless. *Good.*

"Do Saxon women do this to you?"

He shook his head.

"Would you like more?"

"*Ja,* Lucy. More is good."

And she began again.

Before he went beyond the point of no return she scooted up and straddled him, grasping his cock and angling it so she could settle onto it. She'd never done it this way before. It felt free and a little dirty/sexy to know he could watch her as she moved on that thick shaft.

"Ahhh," she sighed as she was filled. That's what she'd been waiting for.

He broke his hold on the brass rail to reach for her.

"Uh-uh," she warned. "You said I could do what I wanted with your body. I want you to hold that rail."

His lips were mobile with an incipient smile as he nodded acquiescence and gripped the brass again. She was glad for all that walking as she raised and lowered herself, reaching forward to thumb his nipples. Strong legs came in handy. His hips bucked under her in counterpoint. She was not going to come until he did. She wasn't. But he'd better come soon, because she could feel the underwater volcano building to an explosion. She'd never been this responsive before. Orgasms had always been elusive, and she'd faked more than a few in her time. Now they seemed inevitable, and the fact that she and Galen had made love several times in the last twenty-four hours didn't seem to dull her appetite. Or his.

He wanted it faster. He was practically bouncing her on his hips.

And then he stilled, groaning, and she felt his cock inside her throb and spurt.

A sense of fulfillment washed over her as he twisted his body, arching, trying to get deeper inside her. It was long moments until he lay back, gasping.

"There," she panted. "I hope you feel plundered."

In answer he swung up to sitting and rolled her over onto her side, withdrawing. He kissed her, tenderly, first on her mouth and then on her neck. She arched to meet him. He kissed his way down to her left breast and suckled there as his hand found her mound and delved into it to spread their mingled cream across her clitoris, starved for release. He swabbed it expertly as she arched toward his hand, all the while suckling and licking at her nipple. Lucy thought she might come apart, the sensation was so great. It seemed unrelated to any sex she'd ever had. And the volcano was building, and building. . . .

Galen rubbed and teased until Lucy was begging for release. He watched her come apart under his hands and his mouth and was very proud of himself.

He had never let a woman have her way with him before. To submit to a man was a woman's place, and while he had always rewarded them for their submission, he had never experienced what they felt. It was strangely . . . erotic, to give yourself over to another, to trust that you would be treated as important and valued. There was no question he had felt valued. And mad with sensation, and bound by lust and love. To think that she would do that for him. To him. This opened up whole new possibilities he wanted to explore.

She turned into him, gasping, and he cradled her against his chest.

Yes, this new time had possibilities. He closed his eyes as Lucy's breathing steadied. Her breathing was part of the natural order of things. And that was something he was beginning to understand, down in his very bones.

"It will storm again tonight," Galen said as they walked out over the marshes late Monday afternoon.

"How do you know?" Lucy asked, looking around. Vandal was only a black speck in the distance as he splashed after some poor ducks. The day was blue as only March days could be. The salt wind off the bay was so brisk she tied her hair in an unwieldy knot.

"I . . . I know these things. Like your wise-in-weather men." He bent to pick up a broken Styrofoam cup. In his leather jacket over a sky blue Henley and jeans as yet unfaded over boots, he looked like any other stunning guy who might grace the cover of *GQ*. Except hunkier. Okay, maybe the cover of *Men's Health*. Without a shirt on. *Yummm.* How lucky was she?

"Ahhh. The sailor in you. Or do you have a knee that predicts the weather?" She was feeling lighthearted as well as entirely sated. Or maybe she'd never be sated again. Maybe that was what was making her feel lighthearted.

"No. Not the same. Since last night . . . A thing happened, Lucy."

He sounded very serious. He'd stopped, so she turned to face him. "What thing?" She didn't like his tone.

"I am not certain. But I hear the land." He seemed to be listening now, head turned into the damp salt wind. "I hear wind and water, ice and steam." He turned to her, his brow furrowed. "I know when the air hurts from too much smoke." He looked down at the ruined cup. "Too much of this." He took a breath as though gathering his courage. "I . . . I think it may be the *drȳcraeft* my mother wanted for me. It came with the equal night." He examined Lucy's face. "It came with you."

Oh, dear. He wanted to be magic so badly—to fulfill his parents' expectations of him, to be the dead brother to whom they always compared him, to be the hope of his people, their protector—that he was making the fulfillment he and Lucy had found together into something that would transform him. She understood completely. But it wasn't true. And that way lay madness.

She put a hand on his arm. "Sometimes we want something so much we think it true. But it's not, and to believe it is to lose our way in life." She paused, thinking. "Maybe Jake is like that. He has lost his way."

A flash of pain crossed Galen's face, then vanished. He looked away, across the marshes to where a heron stood, one legged. "You are right, Lucy. I will not speak of it more."

She sat on the bench they'd sat on before. For the first time she noticed a small brass plate on the side. *In loving memory of Miriam Bostick, from her beloved Ernest.*

Some other couple had sat here, connected over years, looking out on the birds and the marsh grass and the bay beyond, but not as many years as stood between Lucy and Galen. Her hair escaped its knot and blew across her face.

"Here," Galen said, coming to stand behind her. "I will make you like Danish woman."

He divided her hair in half, separated that half into three parts and deftly braided it. Then he did the same with the other half and pulled each braid across the top of her head and tucked them securely in, even braiding the ends into the base of the other braid.

She felt her head tentatively, smiling.

He came to sit beside her, nodding seriously. "Now you look like a Danir queen."

She felt like a queen. And he was a man she wanted to stay with over many years. The thought slapped her. Then an overwhelming sense of loss washed through her in its wake.

She couldn't stay with him. He belonged in his own time. She couldn't go back with him without changing the world's destiny. She had proved that already. And if he didn't get back, who knew what would happen?

Maybe something had already happened. It had occurred to her, belatedly, as she cleaned herself up after their lovemaking and a very satisfying nap, that she had used no protection during four sessions of wild, abandoned sex. She was probably safe. As far as she could figure, she wasn't ovulating. But it was stupid to take such chances.

So she would have nothing left of him when they were parted. They *had* to part. And she had to find a way to get them parted. They needed the time machine. She felt sick. Her eyes were full. She turned into the wind. Let him think they were just watering. She looked down and cleared her throat. She must have courage. He wanted to go back. He might have feelings for her, but he must miss his own time terribly. So it was up to her to make him okay with leaving, if and when they could find a way to do that.

Was she that strong?

She had to be. For the integrity of time.

Bullshit. Integrity of time . . . blah, blah. It was really for him. She touched the crown of hair he'd braided. He should be where he could belong, where this was only a frightening dream.

So. About the time machine . . .

And then it all came clear. It was if the scales fell from her eyes. She'd been living Jake's delusion—a paranoid vision that everyone was out to get everyone. Of *course*, Brad was trying to find her. She'd just disappeared, for heaven's sake. And of course he'd call in all the help he could get—FBI, police, whoever. Amy, her shop assistant, was sensitive. Of course she'd cried when they questioned her. Lucy would just explain what had happened and give them the diamond. The book, too, if they wanted it. Brad would understand why Galen had to go back. They'd send him back to a time after she came, healed, so he could continue his life. They'd just have to take a chance that no one would think he'd been resurrected.

What if he was meant to die in that battle?

But you couldn't start thinking about that stuff. Nothing changed the fact that she had to get Galen back where he belonged.

She took in a gulp of air and let it out slowly.

"I've been thinking, Galen."

"Not good, Lucy," he said, and put his arm around her. "Sometimes thinking is *yful*."

"Well, I've been thinking anyway. Jake is a little paranoid." Like Galen would know that word. "He sees evil everywhere."

"Mayhaps he is wise."

She shook her head. "I don't think so. He has lost his way, wanting to believe in things that are not true." Like Galen had a moment ago, but she wouldn't mention that. "Galen, you have to go back. You know that, and I know that. You don't belong in this time."

His brows drew together and he looked out over the marsh.

"We should just take the diamond and the book to Brad. He will fix the machine and you can go to your own time."

He looked at his hands. She couldn't tell what he was thinking. Was he sorry to lose her, just a little? "You say his friends will imprison me."

"That was my fear speaking. Casey and Brad are not stupid. They will know you must go back."

"I will think on this, Lucy. Until tomorrow. Let us *gewend* . . . I mean, return to the boat."

He rose, and there was a new tension in his body. She was sorry for that. But it couldn't be helped. There was a new sorrow in her, too, as though she already missed all the closeness she might have felt in the years ahead with him. She touched the little brass plaque on the bench.

"Good-bye, Miriam and Ernest."

Galen whistled for the dog, who raised his head from where he was snuffling after some animal spoor and bounded through mud and water. Lucy started off along the path ahead of Galen.

She wanted to send him back.

He had wanted that from the start of this adventure. Then why did it feel so wrong?

Because being with Lucy felt so right. She would not return with him. He could feel it in the regret that raced across her eyes like clouds across the sky. Why would she want to leave her world, where carts ran without horses and voices told the weather?

And she did not believe what he thought might have happened to him last night. She believed her voices about the coming weather, but not him. Him she thought only mad. Had she not seen the healing? He had healed more in one night than in the days before altogether. She *might* believe something happened to him if he was struck by lightning.

That's what it felt like—that he had been struck by some force of the gods and now their whispers echoed in his mind. He hardly dared hope that his new connection with wind and earth and water meant that his mother had been right—that he had a destiny that was important to the world. He knew not what to do with the gift from the full moon on the vernal equinox. But he knew that destiny had to involve Lucy, or it would be but barren comfort that he was fulfilling his mother's prophecy at last. And he was fairly certain that it was Lucy who had brought on this new connection he felt with the world and all that was in it. Lucy, and the moon.

They swung along the path toward the marina, the dog racing in huge circles around them. That dog needed some sheep to herd. When they came to the flat, paved part where the cars were left, she stopped and sighed.

"If we are going to be on that boat another night, there's something we need." She turned right, up toward the little store. "You go on back to the boat with Vandal."

She did not want him with her. Doubt had opened a chasm between them. He watched her walk away. The dog followed her. "Vandal," he called, and pointed to his side. The dog barked excitedly and circled round to Galen. "She does not want us now."

Still he froze where he was, torn. He wanted to go to her, command her to come to the boat with him. He would make love to her again and show her how right it was that they should be together. Even as he thought about her, that feeling of being full and drained together pooled in his loins. He didn't just long for her body. He longed for the feeling of completeness he had when he held her.

Why did she have to bring up going back to his time? Women. Always they wanted to decide, to talk things over when talking could do no good, only harm. Could she not live with him on this boat, without deciding? He would let this new thing inside him grow and tell him what he was to do with this connection he felt to the world around him. He and Lucy together.

He watched her grow tiny as she walked into the paved area in front of the little store.

He started walking toward her. The problem with Lucy was that one couldn't command her. The image of her riding his weapon in wild abandon as she controlled their *swiving* did really interesting things to his body. So, equal partners could be . . . good. Very well. He would meet her as she came out of the store and walk back with her. He would not obey her commands, but neither would he command her. She could not resist him, and he would show her that they were meant to be together and that she could not resist the forces that drove them to be together. Then she would not talk of him going back. They would just be.

When he was about halfway to the store, a car pulled into the paved area, sleek and black. A man got out and walked into the store. Galen wasn't sure why, but he broke into a run.

Chapter Nineteen

The radio was blaring inside the Quik Stop, as always. The clerk waved as she came in. This was going to be embarrassing, but if Lucy was to spend even one more night with Galen, she was in need of some condoms. The fact that their time was running out made her feel positively ill inside.

"That storm on the north coast is going to miss the city. But you folks up in Mendocino will get yet another bout of rain and wind tonight . . . ," the radio announced.

"Hey, how are you?" the clerk called.

"Uh, fine . . ." *What was his name?* "Wally."

She went aisle by aisle finding nothing until she realized they probably kept condoms up by the register to prevent shoplifting. No doubt under lock and key. *Great.* She wasn't even going to skate by without having to ask for them. Well, she was a big girl. She'd survive asking for condoms. If only she could suppress the blush that was all too inevitable.

"And now for some local news," the announcer said. "Cable cars came to a standstill while forty arrests were being made at the protest in Union Square yesterday. . . ."

She marched to the counter. *Yep.* There they were in a plastic case with a lock right behind the clerk. *Oh, dear.*

Pleasure Pack. Thintensity, Magnum. Skyn. Do they have to be named things only guys would ever say? She'd have to yell over the radio. "Uh, can . . . can I buy some condoms please?"

Wally gave her a smirk. "Guess he's feeling better."

She gave an embarrassed smile and felt the blush creeping up her neck. "Yeah. Newlyweds and all."

"The City Supervisors voted to help make case for same-sex marriage in the Supreme Court by filing a brief as a friend of the court. . . ."

"Well, what's your pleasure, so to speak? We got your flavored kinds. We got the special ribbed ones. And the ones that vibrate." He lifted his brows and wiggled them.

Yuck. "Trojans will be fine."

His hand hovered over several of the boxes labeled: *Magnum.* "Size?"

"Uh." She swallowed. "Extralarge?"

"Lucky man," Wally said wistfully, handing her a box.

The door behind her must have opened. She heard the bell.

"The murder rate is climbing again in the city. . . ."

"Lucy?"

Oh, God. She knew that voice. *Brad.*

A thousand thoughts flashed through her brain. Fear predominated, though. *Stupid.* She was going to seek him out tomorrow anyway. He was just a little early.

"Brad." She turned. It was Brad all right—pressed chinos, sage green IZOD golf shirt, Bruno Magli penny loafers with no socks, and all.

"Where have you been, Lucy?" he asked, his brow darkening.

"Oh, Brad, I have been so silly. I started thinking all sorts of things. That you . . . and Casey . . . well, never mind. I got over it. I was going to come and find you tomorrow."

Brad's gaze roved over her face, as though he couldn't actually believe it was her. It fell on the packages of condoms in her hands. He flushed, and it wasn't in embarrassment.

"You're fucking him. Of course you're fucking him, you little whore. You weren't coming to give yourself up. More like you were figuring out more ways to screw him while you screwed my career." He was so mad he was sputtering.

"Brad!" Confusion, then outrage washed over her. What right had he to talk to her like that?

He strode forward and gripped her by the arm. "I've got the machine. Now you're going to give me the diamond and the book and then you're coming with me."

"Hey!" Wally shouted, coming out from behind the counter.

"Butt out, creep," Brad hissed, and jerked Lucy to the door. The clerk hovered uncertainly.

Lucy struggled. "Get your hands off me!"

"And in other news, the body found this morning floating in the water near Pier Forty has been identified as Jake Lowell, owner of the apartment building at 1632 Filbert . . ."

Both Brad and Lucy froze.

". . . beaten to death, Mr. Lowell's death is attributed to gang violence. The Chief of Police has vowed to stop the gangs from terrorizing . . ."

Lucy looked at Brad. "Jake?" She couldn't breathe. *"Jake?"*

Guilt flashed across Brad's face. He might not have done this. But he knew who did. So did she. Casey.

And that meant they'd killed Jake to get to her . . . and Jake had been right all along.

"Come on," Brad said through gritted teeth, coming to himself. She tried to pull back, but he dragged her toward the door.

"Hey!" the clerk yelled. "I'll . . . I'll call the police."

"Go ahead!" Brad yelled over his shoulder. "You'll be up on charges of harboring a fugitive."

"A fugitive!" Wally hustled back behind the counter. "Hey, I don't know who she is."

"Keep it that way." Brad shoved out the door, dragging Lucy with him. Fear coiled in her belly. Why had she come up here alone? She staggered across the parking lot behind him, twisting to loosen his grip.

"You're not taking me anywhere. I'll give you the diamond. But then Galen and I—"

"*Galen* and you?" Brad turned, his face twisted into a mask of fury. "You two-timing . . . and to think I was about to ask you to marry me. . . ." He took her other arm above the elbow so tightly it would leave bruises and shook her. She'd never seen someone so angry. It was frightening on some elemental level. She couldn't speak, couldn't even think, as her teeth jarred and her head snapped. "You took my love, and you pissed on it."

Brad *loved* her? "We . . . were friends," she gasped. "I thought we were friends."

"Like hell you did. You played me. You *made* me fall in love with you." Somewhere she heard a dog barking. Brad paused for breath and raised his arm.

"Brad . . ." She tried to get a hand up to block the blow, but she was too late. The arm came down. At least he hit her openhanded. Her head snapped, her whole face stinging.

A presence loomed behind Brad. A big hand on his shoulder jerked him away. Lucy staggered back as Galen whipped Brad around. Galen. Relief swamped her. A look of stunned surprise flooded Brad's face just before Galen's fist connected to his cheekbone and he went sprawling on the pavement.

Vandal barked, deep in his chest, as he circled Brad.

Galen's face didn't show the same blind fury as Brad's had, just grim determination. But Lucy's relief vanished nonetheless. Galen's blue eyes were hard as ice chips. He glanced to her to make sure she was okay, then bore down on Brad, who scooted away on his butt.

"Hey," Brad said. "You can't—"

Galen leaned down, grabbed Brad by the throat with one hand. His left hand joined his right and lifted Brad off his feet. "You harm my Lucy?" he growled.

Lucy saw his fingers tighten around Brad's throat, digging into the flesh. Brad kicked ineffectually and started to gurgle, clawing at Galen's fingers. Vandal pulled on one of Brad's pant legs, growling. Lucy scrambled up from the asphalt. "Galen, Galen, you'll kill him."

"*Ja*," Galen said through gritted teeth. "I *ācwell* him." He shook Brad, whose face was now turning violent red, shading into purple. Veins stood out on his forehead.

Lucy pulled at Galen's shoulder. "You can't."

He shook her off. Obviously, he thought he could. At that moment a dark stain bloomed over the fly on Brad's pressed chinos and the smell of urine flooded the air. A stream of it ran down his leg and pooled on the asphalt. Vandal leaped back and began his circling bark again. Brad's tongue jutted out through his mouth. In another moment it would be too late.

"I'll never forgive myself if you kill him," Lucy said quietly.

That seemed to get through to Galen as her shouts had not. He grunted in disgust and tossed Brad to the pavement. Supporting himself on shaky arms, Brad heaved in a breath and then another. At least he wasn't dead. His first breaths were followed immediately by heaves as the contents of his stomach spewed onto the asphalt.

Galen stood rooted to the earth, clenching and unclenching his fists.

"Vandal, come," Lucy said. The dog stopped barking to look her way; then, to Lucy's surprise, he actually came to her side, panting.

"You are not enough for Lucy," Galen growled at Brad, his own chest heaving. "You live by her *mild-heartness* only. You go now."

Brad didn't need encouragement. He scrambled to his feet and tottered to his car. He was going to have dandy finger-shaped bruises around his neck. "You were just a charity case," he croaked, rubbing his throat as he leaned against the Jag. "Like a rescue dog. I took you on because I felt sorry for you when no other man would have you."

Lucy hoped he didn't have a gun in the car. She tried to pull Galen away, but he was still making like "pillar of Stonehenge."

"You could have had everything," Brad said in a hoarse half voice. A glimpse of sadness rushed up into his eyes. He looked as though he might have said more, but then a kind of hatred engulfed the wistful look. He shook his head in disgust and slammed the door. If he had a gun, he didn't have the courage to use it. His swung the Jag round and squealed out of the parking lot onto the highway, causing another driver to slam on his brakes and give a long protesting honk.

Galen stared after the retreating car.

"Hey, that was quite a show you put on." The doughy clerk hurried over.

Great. He'd seen the whole thing. As a matter of fact, any cars passing on the highway would have gotten an eyeful, too. With her luck they'd be calling the highway patrol or something. "Old boyfriend," she explained. Vandal looked at the clerk with interest but didn't growl. Apparently the clerk's aura didn't scream "threat."

"He said you were . . . uh . . . fugitives. Some diamond? Are you hiding out?"

Well, *that* was closer than she'd like him to get. She made her mouth rueful. "I guess he thought I should have returned the ring, even though *he* broke up with me."

"Crazy." The little man shook his head. "Bet you haven't seen the last of him."

"You're probably right about that," she muttered.

"Looks like your husband can handle it, though." Wally's eyes were wide with admiration. "Never seen anybody just . . . pick somebody up by the neck."

Galen turned to her, ignoring the clerk entirely. "You are well, Lucy?" His eyes roved over her face. It felt swollen. She'd probably bruise, but it could have been way worse.

"I'm fine," she said. Which was a total lie, since she'd started to shake.

Galen's face softened. "We go now." He picked up her bag that had fallen to the asphalt and put his arm around her. Wally returned reluctantly to his post, all the while casting longing glances out to the road, hoping for more excitement. Galen guided her back down the road, Vandal at their heels.

"You were r-right," she stuttered. "He . . . he did lust after me. How did I not see it?"

"Because you did not lust after him."

"He . . . he called me a whore."

Galen probably didn't know what that was. But he didn't ask. "This Brad is *andig*. Think not on him."

"Andy?" They had to use Latin to sort that one out. "Oh, jealous." Galen spelled it for her. *Andig*. Somehow that seemed funny. Lucy got the giggles. Galen chuckled with her, a rumble in his chest, right up until she started to cry. Then he just stopped and held her.

"Shhhh," he said, kissing her hair until her sobs turned to hiccups.

He didn't know. She had to tell him. "We have to get out of here," she said. "Brad will bring Casey."

"*Ja*," Galen said, his voice soothing. "We sail."

"That isn't the worst." It seemed natural now to have to tilt her head so much to look up at him. "Jake's dead, Galen. They killed him." Her eyes welled with tears. "He died . . . for me. For us. They . . . they must have tortured him, but he didn't tell them anything or Casey would already be here." The words poured out, and she couldn't stop them. "I don't think Brad did it. But he knew. He *knew* about it. And he didn't stop it. So he's not who I thought he was. And he has no control over Casey. And Casey is exactly what Jake thought he was. Jake was right. He was *right*. And it cost him his life. *We* cost him his life." Tears coursed down her face as the words dried up.

Galen's mouth went grim. "Jake is in Valhalla now. He drinks and eats and fucks the Valkyrie."

She gave a watery chuckle. "Hope that's his idea of heaven."

"How not?" Galen smiled. But she could see more sober thoughts flickering behind his eyes. "We go now." He glanced to the sky, which was still blue as blue. The wind was rising, though. "It will storm tonight."

"The radio said it would miss us."

"It will not." He sounded so sure she was taken aback.

"I don't know if I can sail in weather," she said. Her voice was smaller than she'd like.

His eyes crinkled. "Viking boat sails in all weathers when we are far from land. We will not let this Brad and Casey come to us." He paused. "They have the machine, yes?"

"Yes. They got it back to the lab." She looked up at him, realizing she'd been insensitive. *What must he be feeling?*

His time was lost to him now. "I'm sorry you can't go home."

"No one *awyrcs* the machine now." He said it thoughtfully.

"Not without the diamond." *Hmmmm.* "Maybe they can get another one." A thought occurred. It made her almost ill. "Maybe you *can* go home, Galen. It's me Brad hates. I'll give you the diamond. You wait here for them. They'll fix the machine and send you back. I'll . . . I'll take the car and go."

Would they send Galen home? Would they imprison him to "study" him? Would they kill him when they'd finished just to make sure no one knew about the machine? Was anyone safe around someone who could torture and kill Jake?

"*We* sail, Lucy." Galen took her shoulders. "Together. Always together. That is right and true."

She blinked. Uh . . . was what she'd just heard a kind of Viking commitment? All she could do was nod, because it did feel right and true and she didn't know what else to do.

Galen took off toward the boat at a trot, holding her hand and pulling her beside him.

"Dog," he called to Vandal, who had ranged off to the west of the road. Vandal came at a dead run.

Lucy raced around the boat, stowing everything that wasn't already secured, while Galen changed into his Nikes and got out their weather jackets. They'd have to leave Vandal below until they were sure he had sea legs for the deck. Better safe than sorry. And hope he wasn't seasick. Lucy got out the diamond and the gun and put them in her bag, which she stowed in the locker right by the hatch. She'd told Jake she'd never use a gun in this lifetime. But that was before someone had beaten him to death. *Oh, God.*

What was she saying? She'd never have the courage to shoot anyone. She should have taught Galen to shoot. He was the ruthless Viking.

She wouldn't *have* to shoot anybody. They were going off the map. She went to the chart locker and got out the sea charts, flipping through to the ones for the bay and the coast. Galen came up behind her. "Here." She pointed. "We are here. Island. Island. Strong wind through the Golden Gate. That's tough sailing."

Galen studied the map. "*Deop*?" He pointed to the channel.

She nodded. "Deep. Strong current."

"I understand. We call it *stream*. Boat cannot fight wind and stream, Lucy."

"In your time you couldn't sail against the wind. But this boat does. We call it tacking. The sails move at an angle to catch the wind. I will show you."

She weighted down the maps and left them out for reference. Galen studied them a moment longer and nodded as though he was committing them to memory.

"First we get off the dock," she said. She went up to the cockpit and got the engine started while Galen made sure Vandal was tied safely below decks. The dog wasn't happy about it, but there was no time for dog-overboard exercises today.

Galen blinked once or twice at the motor's noise but jumped off and untied the fenders and dock lines. "Bring those aboard," she called, "and get them below." She pointed. Galen followed orders like a seaman. No questions, no rebellious looks. One hurdle passed.

She glanced up to see the hard-looking tanned guy out on his boat, watching them rig up. If he was surprised at all their haste or that they were going out so late in the day, he didn't say anything. He wouldn't, she guessed. He had a beer in his hand and was wearing shorts with his jacket. Real hard-ass. Just like Casey. She was sure they'd be meeting, as Casey returned in a couple of hours to "interview" everyone in sight. This guy wouldn't be able to tell Casey much, except they'd sailed down the bay.

Galen came up from below. Lucy throttled up gently in reverse and they backed out of the slip. As she turned the wheel, the boat swung out into the bay.

The hard guy gave them a casual salute and, hesitating, she waved back. That was probably the biggest show of emotion he knew how to give.

Twilight was about an hour away. She swallowed. Was she up to this? She'd sailed at night only once, when she and her father had torn a sail and come in late. And she'd never sailed in weather in the dark. *Let's hope Galen is wrong about the storm*, she thought. She turned the boat directly into the wind to keep them from moving, and cut the motor.

"Time for a quick course in sailing words while we rig her up."

Galen was an even quicker study than she expected. He obviously knew lines and sails, and some words were the same: "mast" and "starboard," for instance. The biggest problem was, of course that back in his day ships didn't have advanced hull design and triangular sail configuration that allowed modern boats to tack or sail close-hauled. And they had no wheel. They used tillers. That meant she was going probably to have to captain this thing. If he would let her. She pulled the mainsail out of its bright blue canvass housing. *Woad. He'd say it was dyed with woad*.

They put the battens in, fastened the tack and the clew, attached the halyard. He hauled it up the mast. No sign of stiffness in his shoulder. Or he concealed it well. She pointed to the other winches used to haul and hold the sails in place when they were filled with wind and told him they were called grinders. She showed him how to grind and feed the line in at the same time. Galen got the idea immediately. In a racing boat there'd be a crew person for each of those tasks for each grinder, but he was going to have to do it all. She had him practice a couple of times. He had it down in no time. With those shoulders, he'd be a great grinder. If his strength lasted.

Was he up to this? "Are you well?" she asked, putting a hand on his shoulder.

"I am mighty." He grinned. "Better than before."

Well, she had to trust him. There wasn't anyone else. She tossed him the outhaul line and pointed to the cleat on the side. He tied it off with several deft wraps and moved automatically up to the jib, asking questions about what things were for, how the sails worked. Jake had the jib rigged on a roller furler, so all they had to do was haul one line. He'd planned for fast getaways, never knowing they wouldn't be his own. She wasn't going to imagine what Jake looked like after being beaten to death and left in the water overnight. Too many episodes of *CSI*. *Not fair*, she wanted to scream.

She pushed down thoughts of Jake. He would have to wait for mourning.

She tried to explain to Galen about the points of sail and how tacking worked to let you sail into the wind. You always had to tack out of the Gate. A wind was rising from N-NW ahead of what might or might not be a storm. He listened, nodding, asking a question or two.

The feeling that this was just impossible was getting stronger. Two people sailing in weather through the treacherous currents of the Golden Gate with night coming on?

But there was no choice. No choice at all.

It was barely twenty minutes later when she put her hands on her hips and scanned their work for anything she'd missed. They'd made good time getting her rigged in view of the fact that one of them was inexperienced at modern sailboats. Both the mainsail and the jib were luffing, making a soft, ruffling sound as they flapped, head into the wind. Tiny storm sails were stacked where she and Galen could get at them in the cockpit next to the hatch below. Jake had, of course, outfitted the *Camelot* with foul-weather gear. Lucy stood at the wheel. Galen had accepted that without complaint. Points for him.

"Okay," she said. "Back the jib." She motioned to the forward sail and pointed to the left. He trimmed the sail with the line that would pull the jib over to the left. As the wind filled it, the muscles in his shoulders and arms bunched under his Henley shirt where he held the line. She turned the wheel. The bow moved to starboard on the port tack, out of the no-sail zone. Things must happen quickly now. "Trim the mainsail," she called, and pointed right. He nodded, a smile lighting his face. He winched the mainsail just taut enough as the wind came full on the jib.

He was already on the move to the jib line when she called for him to trim it. He slacked the line that held it in the backed position, switched lines, winched it tight until it caught the wind in the new position. That was one perfectly trimmed sail, just off luffing to maximize the use of the wind. Guess he did know wind and water. The boat began to pick up momentum. She'd keep it on a wide reach for maximum speed. *Damn Jake for keeping the boat up in this backwater.* It was a long way down and around the point to the Gate. Full out, how fast could this size boat go? Maybe nine knots? And that only until they started having to tack against wind and current in the Gate. The Gate was tough in the best of times.

She wouldn't think about that. Because they had to get out of here and they had many hours of sailing ahead of them. Just because they were on a boat didn't mean they were safe. She wouldn't win a chase with Coast Guard powerboats. She wouldn't feel safe even after they were out in the open ocean.

But if they made it—if they escaped Casey's clutches—then what? She wasn't sailing across the open Pacific to Hawaii, probably not ever, but *definitely* not in March with Pacific storms still slamming Northern California. Mexico maybe, or South America, where they could keep close enough to land to assuage her nerves. Galen would get a chance to learn Spanish.

That didn't feel right.

Of course it didn't. Even though she had Galen, it was her responsibility to sail this thing out into open water in heavy weather. She knew better than anybody that she probably wasn't up to that.

They were sailing south down what was technically called San Pablo Bay toward the narrows between Richmond and San Rafael that separated it from San Francisco Bay proper. They were practically on a run, with the wind filling their sails from just off their rear. Clouds rolled up over the hills behind her. She had Galen pull both the jib and the mainsail out almost like wings to catch that rising wind.

Galen was grinning like he'd just seen a Valkyrie as he looked up to survey his handiwork. "This boat is fast, Lucy. She sails sweet."

Lucy just hoped it was fast enough.

Chapter Twenty

Damn pussy scientist, Casey thought. *He goes off on his own without telling anybody when, wonder of wonders, they finally got a real tip. He tries to play the hero. And he doesn't even take a gun. So the Viking beats him to shit and sends him packing. How stupid can you be?*

Now he'd spooked the quarry. Right when they had been about to close in.

Not that it hadn't already been a frustrating day. That bastard Lowell had a heart condition. He knew he could sneak out of the interrogation session by fucking dying. "Sorry, Colonel, gotta go," he'd said when the chest pain hit him. His little smile as his eyes rolled up in his head made Casey want to stab someone again and again. They'd tried like hell to revive Lowell. But it was no good. Still, assuming he had spirited the fugitives away, Casey figured they'd need false documents. There were only a few guys around whom someone like Lowell would trust. It had taken all day, but they'd found the forger. They were just about to sweat him.

And Steadman screws it all up.

It was dark and raining hard when Casey's little convoy pulled into the parking lot of the Quik Stop. No way the fugitives would still be here. Sunday traffic on the 101 had been pretty bad. It had taken Brad almost two hours to make it back into the city and Casey's team an hour to make it back out. *The guy couldn't just call in? Too embarrassed. Probably only his anger at the girl and the Viking made him finally fess up. So he notches up another stupid move.* Brad wanted to tag along for the confrontation, but Casey exiled him to the lab to watch over the machine. He should never have let the lab rat out of his cage.

One of the SUVs flipped on a searchlight. It illuminated the little marina down at the end of the dirt road, maybe three-quarters of a mile. The light caught the white of boats and rocking masts through the pelting rain. Two cars were still in the parking lot. Casey couldn't make out if one was an old blue Chevy.

"Get down there and secure the area," he ordered Pollington. "Evans, see if the clerk on duty is the one that saw the altercation. I want to know whether they left by car or by boat."

He stayed in the car, thinking. Either way it was bad. If they had left by car, the marina manager might have done a better job than Lowell at keeping track of occupants' license plates. If they had gone by boat, Casey needed to know what kind.

The wipers squeaked back and forth across the windshield. The rain was almost horizontal. He was betting they had left in the blue Chevy. No one would sail in this weather.

Pollington, in his hooded slicker, waved at Casey from the marina parking lot and he rolled the Escalade down the dirt road. As he got closer, he saw the Chevy in the parking lot. The fools had taken the boat out. With his luck the weather would scuttle the boat and the diamond and the book would be somewhere out in the bay under one lot of water.

Jesus.

He climbed out of the car and stalked through to the marina. Two slips empty. Only one boat with lights on. Pollington was already hailing the occupant. Casey strode down the dock.

A head poked out of the hatch to the rear deck.

"Yeah?" The guy had a crew cut and looked like he ate nails for breakfast.

"We'd like to ask you a few questions." Pollington had a hard time sounding menacing with water dripping down his face.

"I'm not in the mood for questions."

Casey pushed by Pollington. "Look, we don't care who you are or what you've done. We just want to know where the big blond guy and the red-haired girl made off to. If you talk to us, we just leave. If you don't, then we start digging. Your choice."

The guy thought about it, though you'd never know it from his flat eyes.

"Did you see them go or not?"

The guy said nothing, but he opened the short doorway wider, and Pollington climbed down inside, dripping. Casey followed. The guy shut the hatch on the weather.

"They left about five," the guy said, not inviting them to sit down.

"Bad time to go for a sail," Casey said noncommittally.

"They'll be okay. They headed for the Carquinez Strait. Probably wanted to do a little river cruising where it's a little more protected."

"Still, stupid to go out with only an hour of light."

The guy shrugged. "She was the one at the helm. Didn't look real experienced. Maybe she misjudged the weather."

Casey looked at the wet floor. "Got anything else?"

The guy shrugged. "They kept to themselves, all

lovey-dovey like. Maybe Wally up at the store knows something. He usually knows everything."

Bet he doesn't know who you really are, buddy, Casey thought. "Name of the boat?"

The guy shook his head. "Never noticed."

"Okay. Thanks, man. We'll leave you to your meal." How could the guy eat with the boat rocking like this? They pushed out into the rain and climbed up to the dock.

"Shall I get the Coast Guard to go up the Carquinez?" Pollington asked.

"Yeah. Get the name and make of the boat from this guy Wally at the Quik Stop. But I want the Coast Guard on the lookout by the Gate, too. The Carquinez dead-ends in the Sacramento delta. That's a trap for a sailboat with a keel."

"That guy didn't have any reason to lie to us," Pollington protested, maybe hoping the fugitives would be cornered as the river went shallow.

"That guy lies every day of his life," Casey said. "Get on the horn and pull some rank."

Rain spattered Galen's face as the wind changed and he ducked to avoid the swing of the boom. He surged up to the winch and wound the handle with both hands as fast as he could. He felt Lucy adjust the rudder with her wheel. Through the boat he felt, too, that she was tiring, and fighting the mighty current here at the mouth of the bay took strength. She feared the weather and the night. She was not used to sailing so. He was. Weather on the North Sea was treacherous, and one could not avoid the night when one was far from land. He tried to reassure her, if not in words, then with his own assurance. Her voice was raw, but she no longer had to shout instructions. He knew this small ship now and what she needed. The rigging had more sails than he was used to, but he understood their purposes. She could run fast, this boat, and steer precisely. She was a fine vessel, if very different from his shallow-draft, dragon-prowed craft. The giant bridge loomed ahead, dimly orange in the dark and the slanting rain. It looked like a sea monster arched between the spits of land. To be able to construct such an enormous thing, men must surely command magic. The lighted towers of the huge city were off to the left, winking through the weather. Magic. Magic, all of it.

He was cold and wet and his shoulder ached from winding the winches, but he would last. He had to last. Lucy was counting on him.

He glanced back at Lucy, leaning into the wheel, her braided crown of hair dark with water, its fire quenched. She had thrown back the hood of her coat. Her face was pale and bruised; her eyes squinted against the slashing rain. Lucy would not last.

As he turned back to scan the sails, he saw lights ahead. Directly ahead, under the bridge and high in the air.

"Jesus!" Lucy shouted as the lights resolved themselves into the largest ship he had ever seen. No sails, all black iron, it drove straight across their path out of the storm.

"Starboard!" he yelled, and sprang into action. They'd never make it past the boat on their current course. They'd have to turn about almost into the wind to skirt disaster.

He felt Lucy pull on the wheel. The current fought them, pushing them toward the huge ship that now tow-ered above them. The boat tilted wildly. The sails flapped as he loosened the sheets so they could swing to the other side. The boom came across and he ducked, then spun and hauled in the mainsail tight to the other side and cleared the line. He scrambled up to do the same for the jib sail.

A growling whistle rent the night. The ship came on. They weren't going to make it. The boat needed to come around even more.

He slithered aft to Lucy and braced against the side of the cockpit, leaning into the wheel beside her, putting his back and shoulders and thighs into the spokes. The mast bent. *Let not the jib sail tear, dear gods.* His muscles strained to breaking.

"Njord!" he shouted into the wind. "Spare your seafaring children!"

The bow wave of the mighty ship caught them almost across their flank, just where it should not, rose under them, and for a long moment Galen thought they would go over. The boat teetered, half out of the water. But the wave pushed them out of the way of the ship and they were off, skimming almost northwest just on the edge of the wind. Galen jumped to the mainsail and hauled it tighter.

The huge ship powered on, seeming unaffected by the storm. Giant white words spelled *HANJIN* on its side. High above, tiny figures lined the deck and shouted.

Galen breathed. Lucy might be crying. He couldn't tell in the rain. They passed under the span of the giant bridge. The unstill open sea stretched before them into the night. But there were still the stern waves of the giant ship. Galen was ready. Lucy turned the bow slightly into the stern waves. The sea was a mass of roiling currents as the stern waves countered the rolling seas of the storm. The turmoil waited to capsize them. He raced back to help Lucy pull on the wheel, both of them leaning back and heaving. Waves slapped their stern quarter. Water rolled over the boat. But they held to the wheel.

The boat came around and headed out to sea. He trimmed the sails again. Weariness had seeped into his bones along with the cold salt water. He felt apart from himself. The bridge and the city and the other ship faded behind them. It was only wind and sea out here, and through his weariness, or because of it, he could feel the swell of powerful water surging under him and the breath of the gods in their sails. It filled him with peace in the middle of the choppy midnight ocean. He sipped from the strength of wind and water until it filled his chest. And there, underneath, he felt a scraping deep down in the earth, the pressure building under the seabed. *Tomorrow*, it whispered. *Tomorrow will the world right itself and become true again.*

Galen listened and heard it clearly through the silence inside himself, in spite of the wind and the creak of the boat.

When he came to himself, they were out to sea.

"South!" he yelled to Lucy, and saw her shove against the wheel spokes. *Poor Lucy.*

But it was decided now. They would go where they must go. South. He saw in his mind's eyes a quiet bay, south facing, smaller and shallower by far than the huge body of water they had left.

He set the sails. They would not need changing now. Scrambling back to Lucy, he took the wheel. "I sail now, Lucy. I know where we must go."

She looked up at him, her pale cheeks wet, her lashes spiked together. She scanned his face. And then she let him have the wheel. "The wheel works opposite of a tiller I'll tend the sails."

He nodded. He had already figured that out.

"*Ja.*" But the sails would not need tending. The boat would run before the steady wind out here, south to the bay he saw in his mind. That felt right.

It must be two o'clock in the morning, Lucy thought through a haze of fatigue. They eased into the south-facing curve of Half Moon Bay up behind Pillar Point where they were protected from the wind by the curving spit of land. All Lucy had to do in the last couple of hours was sit on the windward side of the boat, though what her weight could do for such a big boat was doubtful. Galen sailed the *Camelot* like he was born to it. He knew how to keep a boat straight in the following wind, no mean feat as well she knew. They had gone faster than she had ever sailed before. It was frightening but also exciting now that the treacherous currents of the Gate were past and they'd narrowly avoided that tanker. *God, but that was close. Thanks be to whomever Galen prayed in those last moments.* Only divine intervention could have saved them.

The wind was dying, almost as though it had blown them to safe harbor and done its job. The rain only spit fitfully. A cluster of lights showed along the shoreline across from the cove.

"We anchor here," Galen said.

"There's probably a marina near the town," she said. *Oops.* "Bad idea." Showing up in a marina where people could identify them or their boat would be stupid.

"We anchor here," he repeated.

She nodded. They took down the small weather mainsail and stowed it. They furled the jib. Lucy's limbs moved sluggishly, as though disconnected from her will. They were about a half a mile from shore, she figured, maybe less. She hoped the *Camelot* had enough anchor line. They needed five to seven times the depth. Galen loosened the anchor winch and let it out. It reeled off for a long time. She started the engine and backed down on it at "slow" to set it, then nodded to Galen to release some more line. He leaned over the side to feel the line. She didn't have to tell him you could feel whether the anchor was just bumping along the bottom through the line. Embarrassing that she'd not had faith in his assertion that he could sail. He was way better than she was, and on a strange boat, too.

When he was satisfied, he straightened and looked around
at where she'd been stowing the mainsail and furling the
jib.

He nodded once. "We go under, Lucy."

She had never heard anything so welcome in her life.
She thought briefly of lighting the lights on the top of the
mast that told other boats there was a craft anchored there
in the dark and then decided against it. Better run the small
risk of getting rammed in this out-of-the-way anchorage
than reveal their location to prying eyes.

Vandal greeted them with eager whines. She'd forgotten about him totally. The poor thing had probably gotten
tossed about pretty badly. She stumbled around and lighted
the lanterns in the salon. The boat was still rocking. She'd
never tried to sleep in an open mooring like this. She
checked the floor. Not a seasick puppy. They were lucky.

Galen looked like a drowned rat, but he grinned at her,
peeling off his dripping coat. "You sail well, Lucy."

"You are even better. Your shoulder okay and your
thigh?"

"Ja." He rotated his shoulder and suppressed a wince.
"Good."

"Oh yeah. Just peachy." The roll of the boat was getting less all the time. "Let's get dry."

They stripped and toweled each other off. Galen was
very gentle with the livid bruises Brad had left on her arms
and her cheek, and she in turn was gentle with his
healing wounds. The scars were only lines now. They
had really healed fast. Lucy wasn't ready to think about
that just yet. Her mind was numb. She unbraided her hair.
When every towel in the boat was wet, but they were not,
they dressed. Dry clothes were heaven. They needed
something to eat, but you couldn't really cook on a rolling
boat. She rummaged through the galley and got out bread

and cheese, a beer for Galen, some red wine for herself. Galen sat at the table in the salon.

The future loomed ahead, just like that Hanjin tanker tonight. Just because they'd gotten out of the bay didn't mean they were safe. It didn't mean Galen could get home again, or that she would ever be able to stop running from Brad and Casey.

"So, I guess tomorrow we head south. Go off the map like Jake said, where no one can find us. We'll just have to hope that the world isn't changed too much by you staying in this time." That plan didn't make her happy. As a matter of fact, it felt very wrong. She sat beside him and handed him a knife for the cheese. He didn't look happy, either. Of course he didn't. She wanted to think he could get used to being in the twenty-first century. But maybe he couldn't. Maybe it was a tragedy that would stain his life and twist him into a bitter man.

"I am not sure of this," he said, cutting off a slab. Vandal scooted up to the table.

She blew out a breath, then broke off a hunk of sourdough and handed it to Galen. "We can't get to the time machine to take you back. I'm sorry. Brad and Casey have it. And we know they're capable of killing." She stared at her hands, thinking of Jake. She'd lost a friend. Two if you counted Brad. Galen had lost life as he knew it. Hell, she'd lost life as she knew it, too.

Galen chewed, lost in thought. His brows were drawn together as he tossed a piece of cheese to Vandal.

Lucy's thoughts strayed back to Brad. "Was Brad always so much of an asshole?"

"What is this, 'asshole'?"

She pointed at her buttocks. Galen suppressed a smile. "*Earse. Ja.* This Brad is asshole. He tells you that no man wants you, that you are not fair. Is a word, 'fair'?"

She nodded, blushing. She didn't think he meant "fair-minded."

"He is a stupid man." He tossed another piece of cheese to Vandal. "Are you sorry that this Brad is asshole?"

She chuckled then grew serious. "Maybe I did know, somewhere down deep, that he wanted to be more than friends. Women know. But I thought I could skate over the top and keep it just friends." She looked up. He understood "skate." Of course. That was a word from Danish. "Maybe I wasn't fair to him."

"You do not know men, Lucy. Men lust, always. Many men lust for you. I know this." He took a swig of his beer. "I am glad you do not lust after Brad. I am *andig* for you, Lucy."

The boat had nearly stopped rocking. He was jealous? She'd thought it was just protective. He hadn't liked Brad hitting her, of course. But jealous? She wanted to dismiss it. She wanted to disapprove. But it made her feel . . . good.

"No rolling," she remarked to give her thoughts new direction. "At least we'll be able to sleep tonight."

"It will be still until morning."

"I guess I have to believe you. You sure were right about the weather today." She exchanged the cheese he handed her for another hunk of bread for him. "How did you know it would storm? The weatherman said it would miss us entirely."

She thought he would say something about obscure Danish weather lore, sailors' warnings, or some old injury that told him the barometer was dropping. Instead he got quiet. He tossed another piece of cheese to Vandal and took another swig of his beer. When he remained silent, she raised her brows at him. "Galen?"

"I tell you before. Why should I speak it again?" He took a bite of bread.

Oooh. That hurt. She wasn't very good at leaps of faith. "I promise I will listen."

He took another swig of beer and cut more cheese. She wasn't sure he was going to answer at all. At last he said, "Something happened, Lucy, in here." He touched his chest. "In my heart. I know things, about the land, about the sky and water. They tell me things."

Lucy pushed down her clamoring protestations. She had promised to be open to his answer. She doubted she could believe what he was saying in the end. He still believed that gods of the sea granted prayers, and she only called on hers in some half-mocking way. His was a simpler time with more direct beliefs. But she'd promised.

"Okay," she said, nodding for him to continue.

"I think I become like a brother to the earth."

He actually used the word "brother." His longing to be special like his brother was at the root of all of this. But she hadn't thought he'd be so blatant.

"I know things now about the world. In your time the earth is sick. Ice melts. Air stinks, like with many fires." He looked at her.

"Smoke," she said, a little stunned. "It smells of smoke." He could see the pollution over the east bay, but how did he know about the melting of the ice shelves at the poles?

"Your bay is sick. Evil things flow into it. Fish die. The *wyrts* of the sea die." He looked to see if she understood.

Wyrts? Like Saint-John's-wort, maybe. Plants? She understood all right. Or maybe she didn't. "How . . . how do you know this?"

"I listen. Since we lust together, they speak to me."

Whoa. She wasn't sure she could go there.

"I feel when the world is right and when it is not right." That struck a chord. She'd been feeling that rightness herself lately. Like being with Galen. Like when they made love. "I . . . uh . . . I have sometimes felt that rightness."

"You have, Lucy?" His eyes lighted.

"Yeah. When we're together, mainly."

His face softened. "*Ja*. Then you know what I say is sooth." He heaved out a breath in relief, though she hadn't actually said she believed the whole "brother of the earth" thing. Suddenly she wasn't sure exactly *what* she believed. She blinked at him as thoughts rolled around in her head as though the boat were still pitching. Did she believe she'd fallen in love with an honest-to-God Viking in six days? The pull toward Galen had been so strong, in retrospect it was almost uncanny.

She *was* in love with him. She wanted to be with him, enough so that the prospect of giving him up to his own time, knowing she couldn't go back with him without changing everything, made her almost physically ill. She wasn't sorry they couldn't get to the time machine, no matter the consequences. That was the bottom line. And she didn't care that he believed he was connected to the earth since they'd made love. If that made him feel whole and happy, fine. Hell, she felt more grounded since she'd been with him, too.

Guess she'd finally found out what love was.

She was in for a rough ride. He was a Viking. Probably not a monogamous bone in his body. They'd be stuck together on a tiny boat for weeks at a time. Their money would run out and they'd start to quarrel. In broken Saxon English. What a farce. It would be like a bad French movie where the plotters all ended up hating one another after they'd committed a crime, and got caught and thrown in prison in the end.

Just dandy.

But it couldn't be helped. She loved him, whether he really loved her or not. And she'd try to keep him out of Casey's hands, and Brad's.

And to hell with the time machine.

Now why didn't that feel right?

They ate in silence while Galen's mind spun with possibilities, all more outlandish and impossible than the last. Somehow he had to protect Lucy. He had to make her world safe for her, even if he had to sacrifice himself.

He looked over at her. In the lamplight, her drying hair made a cloud around her face. She looked like the Valkyrie he had first thought her when he woke in that white room. Or an angel of the Christ Cult. An angel who still wasn't sure she was beautiful, a Valkyrie who blushed.

He felt a surge of life course up his veins, as though it came from the very center of the earth. He reached his arm around her and tucked her in close. "Lucy," he said, "we can do nothing until morning."

She looked up at him, and he saw that she flowered with his thought as well. "We should sleep." She didn't mean it.

"We will sleep. After we lust."

She grinned and slid out of his arms to rummage in her bag. "Then I have a surprise for you." She pulled out a box and from it a small circle of strange material stretched across a ring.

"What is this?"

"A condom." She unrolled it over her finger. "For your weapon." She grinned.

"Why?"

She blushed. "No *lytling*."

She didn't want to make a child with him.

The thought struck him like a blow. He straightened

his shoulders. Why should it? It didn't matter. He wanted to make her happy, whether she wanted to make a child with him or not. "*Ja*, Lucy. I will wear your condom."

Freya, the goddess of his father, who watched over the fertility of the earth, rose from a fiery chasm and spoke to him. The blast of hot air from below carried the stink of sulfur.

"The Earth is sick, Galen. And you will make it right. Go, into the jaws of death, and snatch it back from the brink of ruin. Time is a vortex. Now is your time."

And Baldur, the sacrificed god, so fair of form he was blinding, strode through the blackened forest all around the crevice to stand on its edge. "You must go in my name, Galen. You must brave losing all."

"Will I be sacrificed, as you were?" Galen called to him.

"Time will tell the sooth of things."

"Will I make a child with Lucy?" That was not important to the gods, but it was to him.

"Time will tell . . . ," Freya echoed. She and Baldur began to fade, both of them.

"You speak in riddles!" Galen shouted.

"You know what to do." This last from Baldur just before he disappeared.

Galen was left alone in the searing heat from the crevice of the earth and the smoking, blackened ruin of a forest.

Galen woke in a sweat, gasping. Lucy lay beside him sleeping like the dead after their lovemaking. What kind of a dream was that, where gods spoke in riddles?

But it wasn't a riddle. He knew what to do.

Chapter Twenty-one

Lucy swept the results of Vandal's morning constitutional into Half Moon Bay and rinsed the deck. Oh, well, at least it was natural. But she felt guilty after Galen's speech about the ailing earth. They'd slept late. The sun was already up over the coastal hills, lighting the boat, though the town of Half Moon Bay, stretched along the coast, was still in shadow. *Must be about nine.* The cold sea air stung her lungs in a good way. Today they would start south, never touching a wharf until they were past San Diego and into Mexican waters.

Why didn't that feel as good as the air in her lungs? She motioned Vandal below. If they were going on a long haul, she'd better check the equipment one more time. Spare parts for the engine—had she seen those anywhere when she was exploring that first day? She didn't think so. She vaulted down through the hatch and jumped off the ladder. How could she feel so good with so few hours' sleep? Probably had something to do with that Viking bent over the charts. She sobered. She had felt some reticence in him last night. He'd looked almost tragic for an instant when she'd rolled the condom over that lovely big weapon he owned. Probably mourning for a time when there were no such things as condoms. He might be mourning his time for the rest of his life. And that might stand between them.

A cup of coffee steamed on the chart table beside Galen. "About ready?" she asked.

He nodded with a sad little smile. *Oh, boy.* Something was wrong. She sighed and gathered herself. Engine parts. She checked the locker under the chart table. Not really big enough. She opened the lockers across from the head. Nada. Engine room? Not enough space.

Where else could they be? A man like Jake who thought of everything wouldn't have neglected spare parts. She looked around.

Hmmm. The very bow of the boat, where it came to a point, was closed in. The headboard of the bed that was once half a V-berth was up against it. Was there a way into that?

She headed fore and crawled up on the bed to examine the headboard.

Latches!

She undid them and pulled the whole thing down like the writing board of an escritoire. There were the spare parts, all sealed and labeled in neat plastic bags to guard against salt water. And two really big duffel bags. For extra rope maybe? She pulled one zipper.

She couldn't help the gasp.

There, in equally tidy plastic bags, were bundles of hundred-dollar bills. A really, really lot of them. Like maybe millions.

Galen came up behind her. "Lucy, are you okay?"

"Oh yeah," she managed, a little hoarse. "Jake left a little something for us."

Galen peered over her shoulder. "This paper you can trade like gold coins. Is it much?"

"We're rich." She cleared her throat. "Assuming these aren't marked bills and nobody comes looking for them."

"Jake is not stupid."

"No." Jake wouldn't have left marked bills. Well, no matter what else happened, their money wouldn't run out.

"This is good, Lucy. We sail south now."

A pain wrenched her gut. She looked up at Galen and saw him wince as well.

"A little south," he amended.

There, that was better. Must have been the pears she ate this morning.

They'd gone only about twenty nautical miles or so when Galen called a halt.

"What?" she shouted. She was at the wheel again today, though she was still stiff from yesterday. In smoother water it didn't need his strength.

"We go in close here." He came over and took the wheel before she knew what had happened. "I will be helmsman today. You trim sails."

"There's nothing here," she protested, scanning the shore. As far as she could figure, this was that uninhabited area between Half Moon Bay and the natural reserve where elephant seals mated this time of year, Año Nuevo.

"This is the place."

"What place? Galen . . ."

"*Triēwe* me, Lucy." And the look in his blue eyes was half-pleading, half-commanding.

She raised her brows and he said it in Latin. Trust. He was asking for her trust. She blew out a breath. Well, this was what love was all about. She nodded. What else could you do?

She wasn't so sure as he actually ran the boat aground on the beach. The keel struck sand and trembled. She came racing up from below where she'd gone to get some sunscreen.

"What now?"

"I heave it out," he called as he pushed past and went below.

He came back with his sword slung around his chest and a leash for Vandal, which he handed her. "Keep hold of dog."

A horrible suspicion circled in her belly. Galen threw one leg over the railing and slipped into the water, chest high. He jumped up with a wave and settled back, making his way to the bow. "What the hell do you think you're doing?" she cried, running forward.

She looked up at the cliffs. This was . . . probably . . . just west of Stanford's Super Collider Lab, if you went inland about fifteen miles and over the mountains. How the hell had he known just where to beach the boat? Did he even know where he was?

He looked up at her, and it was there in his eyes, a sadness, a determination. He knew.

"You are *so* not going to do this."

"If Brad and Casey use the machine, it is not good for the earth, Lucy," he said, putting his good left shoulder into the bow.

There wasn't much time to convince him. "You can't do anything about that. They will kill you."

He chewed his lip. That small gesture of uncertainty told Lucy all. "Mayhaps I will be like Baldur, sacrificed. But it will serve the world. This I know."

She was not going to let him sacrifice himself if it was the last thing she did. He heaved on the bow again, timing his shoves with the waves to help lift it. She felt the boat shudder. He was going to get it off the ground. "You're only one man!"

"The earth will help. At the right time."

"They can't use the machine without the diamond."

"I must take them the diamond now."

What? So wrong. He can't make it easy for them. "You

have the diamond with you." He must have taken it from
her bag. "Will you use the machine to go back?" Maybe
that was what this was all about.

"I do not know what the Norns weave, Lucy." He stared
up at her with those blue eyes, water washing around his
chest. "I only know I must go across the hills to the
machine. That I must take the diamond with me. And that
I cannot let Brad and Casey own it."

How did Galen *know* just where the machine was?

All the things he knew, about the earth, about the
weather, his connection with animals, all came together in
her mind. Or somewhere deeper, in her bones maybe and
her gut. He healed too fast. He knew where the lab was
even though he'd never been there, never seen it on a chart.

She believed. He *was* something more than just a half-
Viking warrior from A.D. 912. He was what his mother
always wanted him to be.

Shit. Damn. Hellfire and brimstone.

He was going to go.

And she couldn't let him go alone. Certainty flooded
her. She wasn't certain what would happen, just that she
would go with him. Maybe that was enough.

"Just a minute!" she yelled. "Don't you move until I get
back." She disappeared into the cabin. She felt the boat
shudder again as he heaved it off. It rocked with the movement of the water as it floated free. She grabbed clothes
and their spare Nikes and stuffed them into a waterproof
duffel. She got the book . . . and, God help her, the gun
and put them both in her shoulder bag. She stuffed that in
the duffel, too, and scrambled up on deck.

"Take this. Dry clothes for you." She tossed the duffel
and he caught it and held it above his head. The bow
of the boat was protecting him somewhat from the rolling
surf. "Return to the boat if you can." She wasn't going to
tell him what she had in mind until it was too late.

"Thank you, Lucy. For all you do for me." His eyes were serious. He thought he might be going to his death. She thought so, too. Damn it, not if she could help it.

"Have done," she corrected, because she didn't know what else to say. She watched him turn and stagger toward the shallows. Vandal strained at his rope, whining. "Not yet," she whispered, fondling his ears. When the waves washed shallowly at Galen's feet, she turned aft and winched the anchor out. Not waiting to test if it caught, she slipped the rope from Vandal's neck and let herself over the side into the water. She was enough shorter than Galen that she had to swim for it until she could find bottom. She struck out for shore. Behind her, Vandal whined and turned in circles on the bow.

"Come on," she called. He looked for another way out and then finally scrambled through the lines and leaped into the waves. She saw him safely swimming and then turned toward shore again. Galen had spotted her. He waded out to meet her and pulled her up when they were both thigh deep.

"Lucy," he growled. "What do you?"

She was dripping and cold. "What do you think?" she crabbed, shivering. "I'm coming with you." Vandal splashed to the beach beyond them and shook himself violently.

"Too much dangerous," Galen said, gripping her shoulders. She winced, still sore from Brad shaking her.

"It sure feels right to me."

Galen froze, examining her with a frown, maybe examining his own feelings. He knew it was right that she come. She saw him give in. He finally rolled his eyes. "Woman, you are too much partner," he grumbled.

She grinned. "Partner needs dry clothes." She spotted the duffel where he had thrown it into dry sand.

They changed in silence. But Lucy couldn't stop thinking. As she stood, she said, "It will take us too long to walk over the hills to the lab. I don't think there are any roads inland in this area. Just Highway One that runs north and south. Maybe we can catch a ride up to Highway Eighty-four and around that way."

"No roads. Not safe. But we will not walk."

Right. Like maybe they'd fly? She didn't question him further, because she wasn't sure she'd like the answer. She got out her bag and he put the duffel behind some big rocks. She sure hoped they'd get back to claim it. And the boat.

He walked up into the dunes that lined the beaches here. Wispy sea grass poked up out of some of them, as though they were giant old men with sparse hair lying on the shore.

Galen stood, still, his hair ruffled by the breeze, facing into the sun. After a minute, he lifted both arms, as though praying or . . . or sacrificing himself. Vandal whimpered at her side. Galen turned and beckoned. When she reached his side, he just turned and strode off across the dunes.

"I thought you said we wouldn't walk," she grumbled.

"Not long, Lucy."

Good, because struggling across the dunes was hard, slow work. They crossed the Pacific Coast Highway, not a car in sight mid-Tuesday morning, and headed out across an open meadow dotted with California oaks. The hills were green this time of year. Birds twittered in among the oaks, and they flushed a rabbit that gave Vandal a good time until he lost it. Then he discovered that the oaks were home to squirrels. Ahhh, dog heaven. Not so much for the squirrels. They had to run up their trees, scolding him, to escape.

Lucy and Galen had walked for nearly an hour. It was getting really warm. She had begun to think his promise was just wishful thinking.

Watching Vandal dash from tree to tree, she almost missed the main event. It was left to Galen to take her elbow and point to a gap in the hills where a stream wound into the meadows.

There, the thunder of their hooves faint with distance, came a herd of horses, galloping into the meadow.

Galen looked smug. "See, Lucy? We do not walk."

"There are no wild horses around here. This isn't Nevada. We couldn't ride wild horses anyway." She realized she was muttering to herself. "Where did you get these horses?"

"They live over the hills, in barns." He said "barns" with a couple of extra syllables. "They come to me."

Indeed, they trotted up, maybe twenty of them, and it was apparent that they were local show horses from the expensive homes in the hills of Los Altos. Warmbloods and thoroughbreds mostly, their shiny coats told their story. Some had braided manes and others wore leather halters with brass plates engraved with their names. They stopped, snorting and blowing. Vandal barked, once, until Galen shot him a quelling look.

She was . . . uh . . . really going to have to rethink the whole thing about Galen and what had happened on the night of the vernal equinox under a full moon. He wasn't indulging in wishful thinking about being like his brother. Because if this wasn't some kind of magic, she didn't know what was.

"Choose one, Lucy."

She swallowed and got hold of herself. "I'm not sure I can ride bareback, Galen. And these are hot-stuff horses. I'll be on my butt on the ground in about a minute."

Galen shook his head. "They want to carry you."

She looked at the multicolored hides jostling around her and thought horses had never seemed so huge. She took a couple of steps back, shaking her head. "I don't know. . . ."

"Pick one, Lucy. This is okay."

The herd milled around. Not one drifted into grazing. They seemed to be waiting for her to make her choice. Dear God, was she going to do this?

She didn't have to choose. A bay mare with a kind eye and a broad back stepped forward from the crowd and nosed Lucy's shoulder. She had been chosen. She looked around. No mounting block in sight. But Galen came up behind her, took her by the waist, and tossed her up. She managed to get her leg over the mare's back. Lucy expected sidling or fidgeting, but the mare stood rock steady. Oh, Lucy's muscles would hurt tonight. She hadn't ridden in a long time. But the mare's broad back was easy on Lucy's crotch. It felt funny not to have reins in her hands. She grabbed the base of the mare's mane instead. Galen better know what he was talking about here. Lucy had no control over this horse. She was a beauty, though. Lots of thoroughbred in with the warmblood. Probably Trakehner.

Galen beckoned to a big gray with an ice brand barely visible on his haunch. A Hanoverian, seventeen hands at least. The creature trotted forward, almost prancing in anticipation. Galen ran palms over the big horse's shoulder and back, softly, soothing him. Then Galen grabbed mane and vaulted on, pushing himself up until he could sling a leg over the horse's back. Lucy had never seen anything quite like that.

Galen and his partner turned up the meadow and the gray broke into a gentle trot. Her bay mare followed, and the rest of the herd milled along.

"We must hurry," Galen said. The trot turned into a canter, which was actually easier to sit. The herd followed easily. Vandal loped alongside, barking encouragement.

So they were going over the hills to the lab with a herd of horses Galen had rustled up out of nowhere. And after that . . . Well, after that, she didn't know. Galen had magic. He had *something* anyway. She only wished she didn't feel like she was being pulled along in his story. Would he use the machine to go back to his time? Maybe that was best. It would be tragedy for her. But he seemed sure of his destiny, something that eluded her. And he was a brave man. She loved him. So she would go with him now, unsure as she might be, even if it was his story and not hers they were telling.

It was nearly dark. They had rough going over the mountains Lucy named Santa Cruz. As the horses tired, they walked only. Galen and the great gray horse had led the herd through open spaces with no houses. Where it was steep they had to zigzag. Since they had crested the spine of the mountains, houses were everywhere, like a solid village for miles and miles. The earth had no room to breathe.

They stopped now, the herd crowding round Galen's big gray and Lucy's sturdy mare, just above the stone and glass building that held the machine. In the distance, perhaps half a league away, many cars with glowing eyes sped down a wide road, raised on a berm as though it crossed a marsh. There were lights on in the recesses of the big hall, though other halls in the area were dark. Three cars only sat in the wide paved place.

Now what to do?

Galen had tried to display quiet certainty all day, without answering any precise questions, and after a while Lucy stopped asking. He wasn't sure just what his role was or what the likely outcome. He was only sure he should go to the machine where Brad and Casey were. Galen hadn't wanted to bring Lucy. The thought that he had taken her into danger when he should have been protecting her had eaten at him all day. And yet the wrongness of being parted

from her had made him want to vomit as he tried to push
Jake's boat back out to sea this morning.

Galen would die to save her if it came to that. Her presence made the "Baldur outcome" for this adventure even
more likely. When Galen thought of Brad hitting Lucy,
his blood still boiled. He should have killed this Brad
outside the little store. If not for Lucy, Galen would have
done so.

He hoped he got another chance, where Lucy could not
see.

He glanced to Lucy, who was looking at him, not at
Brad's building, waiting for him to say what to do. He
swallowed. He could feel the earth bunching under itself.
But it was not yet ready to help. They could not wait here.
The herd would draw attention. Better he face his enemies
like a man than wait for them to come to him.

He nudged the gray down through the trees and onto
the paving. The herd followed. They jostled together, their
shoes clopping on the hard surface. Through windows two
floors high, Galen saw a man dressed in a dark blue with
gold braiding push back from the table where he'd been
sitting, wide-eyed. He touched his ear. They could see
him speaking, apparently to no one, though they could not
hear him.

In moments, four men burst through a doorway
from the back. One was Brad. His cheekbone was cut and
scraped, and his throat was lined with colorful bruises.
Good. Two other men wore white coats that flapped against
their legs. The fourth? Well, the fourth must be the man
Lucy called Casey. His short blond hair was almost white,
his pale eyes hard. He looked lean and stringy strong.

Casey pushed out through the doors. Brad followed.
Brad stared first at Lucy, then at Galen. He was very, very
angry.

Not so Casey. This man knew that anger made you

weak. He nodded to Lucy and Galen. "To what do we owe this honor?" Galen felt rather than saw other men coming around the outside of the building. Casey would not be stupid enough to come with only four men and no visible weapons.

Lucy looked to Galen. Her eyes were frightened. Galen swung his leg over the gray's neck and slid to the ground. He fished the diamond from his jeans pocket. "You *forleose* this?"

Casey glanced to Lucy. "Yeah. We lost it. Thanks for bringing it back. Why don't you come inside?"

Galen went to lift Lucy down, but she had already slid off the bay mare.

"I hope you know what you're doing," she muttered under her breath.

He smiled with what he hoped was reassurance.

"Thank you," he said to the herd. "Go home now to your barns. You have served the earth today." The big gray threw his head and pawed the pavement. Vandal whined. "Go, dog, back to the sea." Then, as one, the herd wheeled and disappeared into the trees at the edge of the pavement. Vandal circled at the corner of the pavement once. Galen motioned him away and put in his mind a picture of the boat. If they made it through, if the dog made it through what was coming, then would there be time to reunite. The dog stood like a figure of clay for a long moment. Then he, too, whirled and was gone.

Galen turned to Casey and Brad, nodded once.

Casey made a gesture toward the door with a smile that did not reach his eyes.

"Somehow I thought," Casey said conversationally as they moved to the back of the building, "that we would have to come to you." The doors opened to a long corridor. "The horses were a nice touch, by the way. And the way you sent them away? How exactly did you do that?" Galen glanced back to Casey and saw that his eyes were alive with thoughts. He wanted Galen now, too, as well as the diamond and the machine. Galen did not answer. Beside him, Lucy was wound tighter than the lines that held the sails on their boat. Brad seemed as though he were about to burst with anger like a rotting pig's bladder. That one was dangerous because he was not in control of himself.

The men from the outside came into the building. Galen could feel them behind him. Again he glanced back. They were shadows in the shadows behind Casey. No swords. But they carried long, heavy metal clubs oddly wrought and ungainly, swinging from straps on their shoulders or held at the ready. Galen did not know what these were, but he recognized the ready stance, the brandishing. They were weapons of some kind. Of that he was sure.

Chapter Twenty-two

They were walking into the mouth of hell. At least that was what it felt like to Lucy. The lab doors opened. Leonardo's time machine sat glittering on the platform of the two-story lab.

It was really beautiful.

"I'll take that diamond," Brad said through gritted teeth.

Galen held it out.

She wanted to shout that they should never have come, that this was all wrong. But it was no use now. Even as Brad snatched the huge diamond from Galen's palm, a dozen men in military gear crashed into the lab behind them. Lucy whirled. They carried machine guns. She wished she'd told Galen about guns, how easy it was to kill from a distance. He mustn't think his sword was any protection.

He didn't move a muscle at the entrance of these ominous reinforcements. It was as though he wasn't surprised.

Brad muttered to himself as he strode across the lab to the machine. He fitted the diamond into the newly repaired prongs at the head of the control lever. One of the lab-coated guys handed Brad what looked like a giant jeweler's pliers. They must have been made specially, because they fit right over the diamond. He clenched the prongs tightly around the diamond.

He stepped back looking triumphant. Relief and anticipation coursed through the room.

Casey turned to Lucy and Galen. "Now, if you will give me your shoulder bag. That square outline means you've brought the book as well." When Lucy hesitated, Casey gestured impatiently. "It's not as though you have a choice here."

She swung the bag over to him. He picked it up and fished out the book. That smile again. He glanced over to the machine. "Steadman, I have an urge to try it out. Just to see if your repair job worked. Ahhhh, but with whom? Our little bookseller isn't trustworthy."

This was it. This was her test of character. Could she embrace the tragedy for Galen's sake? "Send Galen," she said, her heart contracting. "He's got to go back. The fact that he's here has probably already changed things." She refused to look at Galen. If she did, she'd cry.

Brad pushed past Casey, his eyes flashing. "You think I'm stupid? He takes it and brings it back to somewhere else in a month and you've got control of it again. If anybody is going to try the machine out, it's me. It should have been me in the first place."

Casey raised his brows at this outburst. "You didn't have the guts the first time, Steadman. As I recall."

Brad's face was mobile with emotion.

"Not our Viking, either. I have some . . . questions for him."

"Me, too." Brad's eyes were a little wild. "And I'd like to beat the answers out of him, twice a day, for a long time."

"Steadman, you surprise me. You're getting a backbone. A little late, maybe."

Brad wheeled on Lucy. "And you, you slut—"

"Will you use the machine or nay?" Galen rumbled, cutting off Brad's tirade.

"Okay, you." Casey gestured to one of the assistants, a slight Hispanic guy. "You're our lab rat." The guy looked like a rat. A cornered rat. Panic surged into his eyes. He didn't move.

"Casey, it's got to be me. I want to go." Brad looked to Lucy in triumph, as if that proved he was a better man than she was worth.

Casey looked disgusted. "You we need in case it doesn't work. You're the expert, the one who can fix it, remember?"

Brad stood, his chest heaving. His glance darted around the lab. Then he stilled. "Okay. Yeah." He seemed to get some control back. "Get over here, Rodriguez." Brad turned to face the machine. When the assistant didn't move, Casey gestured to the military guys. Two moved up and pushed Rodriguez forward with the butts of their machine guns.

"This *is* going to change the world," Brad said. "And I provided the power." He knelt and flipped switches on the lunch box–sized power source. He didn't seem to recall that it was Leonardo who built it. "Jensen never gave me credit for the quality of my research," Brad muttered. "Fuck him. I'll have his job."

Brad stood in front of the machine. "Christ. I won't need his job. I'll have my own institute. 'Multiphasic Research.' That's catchy." He pulled the lever down. The machine began to whir. He grabbed Rodriguez. "Now where shall we send him?"

"You could see Alfred the Great change the world," Galen suggested. The gems began to throw colored beams around the ceiling. Behind Lucy the military guys gasped.

Brad's eyes lighted up. "The event that made us what we are today . . . the fall of the Danelaw to Alfred . . ."

The machine seemed to pause. "Yeah, Rodriguez. Think about that."

Casey tossed a gun he took from a holster under his jacket. "Just in case."

Rodriguez didn't catch it; Brad did. The assistant looked paralyzed with fright.

"Think of the twelfth day, fifth month of A.D. 912," Galen called above the hum of power in the room. "The hill to the south of the plains outside Whitby."

"Yeah," Brad murmured. "Bet those cretins have never seen one of these." The sound of his voice was almost lost in the hum. Whether he meant a time machine or a gun Lucy didn't know. Galen took her hand. His calluses grounded her against what was about to happen here. Didn't Casey see it? Brad was going back. Maybe he'd take Rodriguez with him, or maybe he'd shove the assistant out of the way at the last minute. But apparently everyone in the room was too ignorant of history to know that Alfred was already dead in 912. The battle between Alfred and the first King Guthrum was long won, and it had not eliminated the Danelaw, just controlled its spread. Brad was going back to the battle where Galen had fought Egil.

Suddenly the machine snapped into action. The gears all whirred into a blur. Casey darted forward, realizing Brad's intent too late. Brad shoved Rodriguez, who stumbled back.

Brad and the machine both disappeared.

There was a long moment when the only sound in the room was the gasping of lungs and the click of weapons being readied against a foe that wasn't corporeal but time itself.

Galen put his arm around Lucy's shoulder. Casey looked around wildly. Rodriguez lay on the lab floor, gasping in relief.

"God damn it!" Casey yelled. "The fucking idiot."

"What . . . what happens now, Colonel?" The lead military guy was lost.

"We wait," Casey snapped.

They waited. If Brad was successful, he would be back within minutes, and even if—

The lights went out in the lab. What sounded like thunder boomed all around them, as if lightning had struck the building.

And then the machine was sitting on the platform once again.

Alone.

The lights blinked on. No Brad. But the machine's bright surface was splashed in several places with red-brown. Lucy put her hand over her mouth.

Casey strode to the machine and examined it. "Looks like Steadman bought the farm." Casey didn't seem concerned.

Lucy's imagination was working overtime. Brad set down in the middle of Galen's battle. Slashing swords and swinging axes, the smell of blood and smoke—all as she remembered it. Brad would start shooting wildly. He'd kill people, but the clip would run out sooner or later. Then those left standing from both sides would fall on him. . . .

"At least it works," Casey said, turning to them. "And Steadman was really no longer useful." Casey's pale blue eyes still roved over the glinting brass and jewels of the machine, possessively. "He was unreliable."

Brad had just been a little insane. Casey was major insane, the cold kind, not the hot kind. He'd made a mistake, letting his chief scientist and bottle washer get killed, and now he was justifying it, making it seem as though it weren't a mistake at all.

"So that's the second man who died for this machine. The first one you killed."

"Honey, I've killed more men than I can count." He glanced over his shoulder at her. "Oh, you mean Lowell. Yeah." He shrugged. "Guy had a bad heart. He sneaked out on our little party early. Knew it, too, the bastard. But we got the guy who did your IDs. He would have told us where he delivered them. Now we don't need him, of course."

Why did she think that meant the forger was a dead man, too? She glanced to Galen. He was tight, about to burst it seemed, maybe . . . waiting for something.

"And anyone can run the machine at this point. So," Casey said, as if deciding. "Time for a little cleanup." He picked up Lucy's bag and rummaged around until he found the gun. He held it up. "Thought Lowell would make sure you had something like this. Glock nine. Bet you don't even know how to use it."

Casey snapped it up and put bullets in the foreheads of Rodriguez and the other lab assistant. Lucy gasped in shock. Galen jumped back, dragging her with him. The military guys behind them took a step forward, brandishing their guns as if to hold Galen and Lucy in place.

"What weapon spits fire and kills from a distance?" Galen muttered.

"A gun," Lucy answered. "You saw them in the western and just didn't know what they were." She'd begun to tremble as she stared at the lab assistants, collapsed on the floor, gaping holes in their heads. Funny. There wasn't much blood.

"Jake gave you this weapon?" Galen sounded outraged. "You had it always?"

"Sure beats a sword, doesn't it?" Casey had turned the gun on them. Galen pulled Lucy behind his body.

"Come on out, honey. No use putting this off." Casey motioned with the gun.

"Kill me," Galen growled. "You let Lucy free."

"No, no, no, no. *You* I want to keep for a while. I want to know how you can talk to animals like that. You might even know where some Viking hoards of silver are buried. She's the expendable one." He motioned to the guys wearing camo. Two came up and grabbed her while three tried to seize Galen. He twisted a gun out of the hands of the nearest soldier and used it as a club. The stock part of it came up and caught the guy under the jaw, dropping him in his tracks. Galen was already swinging for one of the guys who held her. She twisted away, but the soldier had her arm. For a minute, and then he went down, too.

Galen pulled out his sword and sliced at another one, who clutched one hand to a spurting neck and fell to his knees. A gun went off in a short burst. It caught one of the remaining soldiers bailing into the melee. He bloomed with blood.

"Don't fire in these close quarters, you idiots!" Casey shouted.

Another soldier hit Galen with a baton from behind. Galen managed to duck and spare his head, but the blow caught his shoulder. He staggered and then there were four of them hitting and hitting. He sank to his knees.

"Galen!" she cried, pulling her remaining captor off balance as she lunged toward Galen.

Another gun went off. A single shot. "Enough!" Casey yelled. All motion stopped. Two of the camo guys were groaning. One lay still in a pool of blood from his slashed neck. One of the guys still standing around Galen kicked his sword away. It spun toward Lucy and the guy who held her by both elbows from behind.

"Cuff him or tie him up or something," Casey said, disgusted. "Before you let him cut you to pieces with that sword." He walked over to Lucy. "You want to do her, or shall I?" he asked the guy who held her. He was a black guy, with dead eyes and a white scar on one cheek.

"Be my guest, Boss," the black guy growled.

Galen had gone still, kneeling on the floor, his hands jerked behind his back. Casey came up and held Jake's gun to Lucy's head. The muzzle was cold at her temple.

"Say good-bye to your girlfriend, Viking."

"You will freeze in Hel's kingdom," Galen growled.

That wasn't the only growl in the room. From a distance a powerful grinding sound thrummed up through the floor. It buzzed in her chest, coming closer.

"Shit," one of the camo guys said. "I know that sound—"

But before he could say what it was, the whole place was shaking like Vandal shook Galen's socks, sharp and fast. The men around her staggered.

"Earthquake!" one shouted.

Casey fell backward. The gun went off and skittered from his hand. Glass shattered and tinkled. The floor heaved like someone was shaking out a rug. Men scrambled toward the exit.

"Get out. Get out!"

Galen crawled toward her. Ceiling tiles crashed to the floor and broke over the gears of Leonardo's machine. Galen covered her with his body as a rending sound squealed through the lab. A broken girder poked through the wall toward the machine.

Galen had recovered his sword. "Lucy, come away!" he shouted over the din.

They staggered to their feet, reeling. The grinding sound was passing on. "We can't leave Casey with the machine!" she shouted.

They looked around and saw that Casey was staggering toward one of the abandoned machine guns just in front of the machine. *Would he rather kill us than save himself?* It was as though someone else from far away was thinking that. The west wall of the lab leaned slowly in.

And then it was still. The grinding sound was gone. The silence was deafening. Casey got to his feet. Galen shoved her behind him and readied his sword, his face grim. He'd be cut down by that machine gun.

But there was Jake's gun. At her feet. The one she swore she'd never use because she wasn't that person.

But she was all they had. She reached for it. Casey was turning, machine gun in hand, his face a mask of hatred and greed. She stepped out from behind Galen and brought Jake's Glock up. She pulled the trigger again and again and again. She braced her feet against the kick, but it was so much more than she expected. Her shots went wild and high and then she wrestled the gun down again and—

Casey's face disappeared. It just shattered in blood and white splinters of bone.

The machine gun clattered to the floor. Casey toppled forward.

Lucy was heaving sobs. She didn't remember starting to cry. Galen held her, whispering soothing sounds.

"You are *dēor,* Lucy. Brave."

"I . . . I just killed a man." She couldn't get her breath. There was so much dust in the air.

An aftershock ripped through the lab. The west wall buckled. This whole place was going to come down. It might destroy the machine. Leonardo's lifework. The key to time itself.

But what if it didn't?

"Boss?" The camo guys were making their way back into the building.

She looked up at Galen. "We've got to get the machine out of here. And there's only one way to do that."

"It will *gewend* back here as it did for Brad."

Debris crashed behind them. Casey's men would be through the wreckage any minute.

"Yeah." She chewed her lip. "Leonardo said it comes back to where it left because time is bent too far and bounces back into its track." She looked up at Galen. "But what if you didn't take it far in time? Just to the next second? But to a different place. Maybe it would stay where you took it."

She picked up her bag with the book in it and ran to the machine without waiting for an answer. "Okay, okay," she reassured herself. She flipped on the power. It whined up the scale.

She positioned herself in front of the lever. Galen came and put his arms around her. She pulled the diamond down.

Where to take it? Where was there room for fourteen feet of time machine, where no one would find it? The lights began to play across the wreckage, coloring motes of dust. The gears ground to a halt. In seconds they would slingshot forward.

"You okay, Boss?" More crashing from behind them. She couldn't think. *Where?*

And then she knew. Why it should come to her like that she didn't know. The Palace of Fine Arts. Her favorite place. The place she had shared picnics with Brad. In the empty, secret room they'd found under the Rotunda. Now it was sealed again. Would they be sealed in, too? But the *Chronicle* had said there was a passage into the Exploratorium.

She smiled up at Galen as the momentum of the machine threw them into the vortex.

Lucy sat up, coughing. Galen stirred beside her and shoved himself up to hands and knees. She felt the machine looming above them, though she couldn't see it.

Are you okay, Lucy?" He felt for her in the darkness. His hands skimmed her face. They were trembling.

"Yes. Yes." She was just a little breathless. "And you?"

"I am sore from where they *bēateth* me, no more." He paused. "Where are we?"

"Under the Palace of Fine Arts in San Francisco. No one will find the machine here." He gathered her into his arms. "You knew the quake was coming, didn't you? That's what you meant when you said the earth would help us."

"*Ja.* I can feel the earth, Lucy. I speak this to you before."

"Your mother was right after all." Lucy thought about his connection to animals. "I think you had it in you all along." He could now be to his people what they expected of him. He could take his brother's place. It was what Galen had wanted all his life. And she must not keep him from his happiness. This was his story, after all, not hers. She was just along for the ride.

She had never felt so small, so insignificant, so wrong.

"The Norns wove it," he agreed softly.

She was glad she couldn't see him. That meant he couldn't see her. All she had to do was keep her voice steady and he'd never know that sending him back was like ripping out her intestines. "You can finally go back to your own time. The machine is safe. It will come back here now when you are done with it, where no one will find it."

"*Ja.*"

One word. Flat. That was it then.

"But that would not be right," he whispered.

She tried to breathe. *Don't push him. He's not the kind of guy who can be pushed.*

"I was thinking, Lucy, while we ride the horses. You came to my time because you thought the Norns wove that for you. You speak this to me. I remember. You name it 'destiny.'"

She nodded.

"We both look for our fate. I think we have it, Lucy."

"You . . . you certainly found yours."

"Both. Did we not both lust until we were mad with it? Did we not lust under the moon of the vernal equinox? It was then that I hear the land and water and air."

"So use your gift. Be what your people need."

"But the land and the water, they were not sick in my time. They are sick now. I think my destiny is here, with you and your time." His words came out of the dark, hesitant. "The land and water need protection."

She wanted nothing more than for him to stay, whether he loved her or not, whether he was constant or not, difficult or not. But what did she contribute? "You may be right."

The silence hung between them.

"Lucy?" His voice had gotten even more tentative.

She cleared her throat and tried to sound brisk. "It sounds to me like your powers come from a connection with something the Greeks called Gaia. They thought the world was a living being. Not like a god or goddess, more like a person. It breathes and thinks and plans."

"*Ja.* That is how it is to me."

He wasn't touching her. That was good. If he touched her, she might break into tiny shards like the glass in the lab.

The silence stretched.

"If we aren't going to use the machine, I . . . I guess we should go." *Go where? Do what?* She shoved herself up.

He grabbed for her hand. "Lucy," he said, his voice raw. "I hear what you say not. Know this. I cannot do this thing without you. You think you are not enough, Lucy, like I did. I know not who told you this. My brother spoke from his grave to me. But it is not true. We are enough."

"You are . . . wonderful," she managed, though he had hold of her wrist and that thing was happening where jolts shot to her loins. "Magic, even. But what do I bring?"

"You jest with me." His brows drew together like they did in those first days when he was in pain.

"I'm not jesting. You need help with the language for about another week. I know you're disappointed that a sword is not the weapon of choice here, but you'll be a charter member of the NRA in no time. You've got all the money you need, assuming the boat is still anchored off Pescadero Point. I . . . I'll just be a drag on you."

He got enough of that speech to get the drift. "You drive carts. You sail. You killed a man. You saved the machine, Lucy. You are brave and strong. You are so beautiful a man's eyes are sore. And you have mildness in your heart for man and dog. How is this not enough? At first, when I come here, I yearn for a time when I do not need you. Is this the way to be a man, to need a woman for everything? But I need you, Lucy. And now that feels right and true. How can I use what the gods give me when I know nothing of this world? You will know how to use what I am. Together we are wonderful. Without you, I can do nothing. The world is lost."

"Great. I'm the practical one."

"*Ja*. You feel when things are sooth like me. The earth calls to you, too. No scalds will sing our story each by each. We are only enough together, Lucy. My destiny. Your destiny also."

He was saying that his story *was* her story. But he offered a business partnership that came with a haze of marvelous sex. Valhalla, where sex and feasting and drinking were supposed to be enough to satisfy you. Did they?

And he was wrong about her being the strong one. That was just the problem. Jake, too, had believed she was a person she was not.

Yet, she would never have believed she could find the courage to go back in time to look for a different kind of life or that she could lie to the police or pull stitches out of a Viking's flesh or kill Casey. Maybe she *was* that person Jake and Galen thought her.

"Faugh," Galen said into the dark and her considering silence. "You demand yet more from me. You would tear out a man's heart to see it beat? Then hear this. You. You are my fate, as much as the gift. I will wed you, Lucy, if you would have a warrior with no weapon of value, a man who has no time, one who needs you. I am little enough to protect you. But I will give my life trying. You want equal partners. I will try. This I vow. Can you ask more, woman?"

The disgust in his voice was so . . . Galen. And the declaration was Galen, too. He did not make it lightly. He made it with the power of his heart, and the honor in his soul. No woman could want more.

She had gone back to find a time where magic was still possible. Who said that magic wasn't possible in this time? Galen thought cars and elevators and zippers were magic. Maybe they were. Maybe we missed the magic that happened all around us every day. Maybe the real magic was the work you had to do to make yourself into the person who could push and shove the world forward. No easy answers. No eating all you want to lose weight. Galen had a gift that could only be called magic, and it was not like to be an easy answer for him. His way in this time would be hard. But she couldn't deny her world could use a man who heard what was right for the earth. And maybe there was another kind of magic at work here, the magic a man and woman made between them. Lord, that wasn't any kind of an easy answer. But she had felt the rightness. She could understand him, as perhaps no other woman could.

"I cannot ask more."

She felt him holding his breath. What was he waiting for? *Ahhh*. She had not matched his vow. "I will love you, Galen Valgarssen, until the day I die. Don't you dare break my heart."

He took her into his arms in a crushing embrace. His scent engulfed her. She would know that scent until the day she died as well. Her heart beat against his, not in unison but in delightful counterpoint. It seemed right and true.

"If I wound your heart, I wound my own," he breathed into her hair.

They stayed like that, feeling the rightness wash over them. Lucy listened to their hearts and felt another presence there. She squeezed her eyes shut. A woman couldn't know she was pregnant after only two days. Or maybe she was different from other women now. . . .

"Come," he said after a moment. "Know you the way out of this darkness? We must go for dog and boat before I can fulfill my vow."

"There is a passage." The *Chronicle* article better be right, or they were going to die a slow death. But she didn't believe that. "Help me feel for the door." She scrambled to her feet and put her hands out in front of her. Taking cautious steps, she felt her way around the girders that now supported the Rotunda floor. He went in the opposite direction. They made their way toward each other around the outside wall. She was the one who found the passage. An empty space turned out to be a long corridor.

"Door," Galen grunted as they reached the end of the corridor. A bar crossed the door to open it. Pray it wasn't locked or they'd starve here. The bar did nothing. *Uh-oh*. Maybe there was a bolt lock that worked by hand from the inside. She felt around. What she found was a large button about chest height, like the kind on the inside of walk-in freezers to prevent people from getting locked in. She pressed it in relief.

The door swung open. Lucy sucked in fresh air. Work lights glowed from somewhere. The exhibits of the Exploratorium loomed in the shadows. Now she saw her way. She turned and pushed the door shut on the time machine. The lock clicked into place. A large sign plastered across the door said: *Danger. No admittance. Unsafe conditions.* Excellent.

Now they'd find a night watchman, plead that they'd gotten locked in after hours, and get him to let them out.

"Lucy," Galen said, putting a hand on her arm. "In one thing you must submit to me."

She raised her brows. He was glowering, an expression she found strangely comforting. "So much for equal partners. What is it?"

"I want no condom on my weapon when I *swive* you."

She tried to make her mouth serious. "It will mean making a *lytling*." It already had.

"Good," he grunted. "Mayhaps he will come on Sahmain midnight like my brother."

Epilogue

It was late afternoon, though you could not tell the time inside the Exploratorium. Pony was too young for any but the simplest of exhibits, but Lucy had to admit that the Exploratorium was way more fun with a child in tow. Galen bent over their daughter's flaming red head, showing her how to look through a lens at some fish that glowed in the dark. She giggled and shrieked with delight.

Galen and Lucy had traded in the *Camelot* for a fifty-three-footer, better for a family with a dog. Apparently, no one at whatever agency Casey worked for believed that there had ever been a time machine, or maybe everyone was just engaged in a gigantic cover-up. A brief note of apology from the Secretary of the Navy no less had been waiting for them in Santiago, noting that some rogue operatives had expressed some strange ideas that were officially non-sanctioned and that any inconvenience would be compensated. That was scary because someone knew where they were and who they were. But nothing more materialized. And that was that. No one was after them.

Galen's hair was shorter and streaked blonder from the sun since they had been in San Francisco last. He was as gorgeous as ever. He could still send her spinning with a touch. He now spoke English with barely an accent.

Tanned from their years at sea, he looked like the sailor he was.

What he didn't look like was a prominent environmentalist. His papers on how to manage population density had gathered quite a following. Using the identity Jake had provided, Galen had become the face of a new environmental consciousness. He sponsored conferences and refereed feuds between factions, even authored legislation. It had as much to do, Lucy suspected, with his strange magnetism as his sensible ideas. He was a natural leader. They figured out together which issues to tackle and how to use his new "talents." She doped out the right agencies and NGOs to enlist in their cause. Galen had been right. She had a lot to offer. They were better together than either would have been by him- or herself. They'd worked for four years to establish Galen's credibility.

So they were ready for the latest challenge.

They'd met yesterday with the head honchos from the Berkeley Seismological Laboratory and the U.S. Geological Survey out of Menlo Park to propose a private/public partnership establishing a serious earthquake prediction center. The only thing that had gotten them the meeting on such a crackpot idea in the first place was Galen's reputation.

What got them the commitment was a demonstration. Galen had told the scientists about every earthquake—both the intensity and the site—that would occur in the next two hours around the globe. Then he and Lucy had gone down to the cafeteria for coffee and to get Epona an orange juice. Quite an exit. They'd left everyone sputtering. But two hours later, Dr. Magnussen himself had sought them out in the cafeteria, his tone all humble pie, and it looked like serious efforts were going to be made to fund this venture. Galen could give people enough notice to leave the quake zone. He was up to predicting three to five days in advance for serious quakes. Millions of lives could be saved. Maybe they could use his predictions to discover a way to predict quakes on their own. It would give him even more credibility as he tried to get the peoples of the world used to working for the earth, not against it.

Or maybe it would be her daughter that completed Galen's mission. Epona had been conceived on that very first night, the vernal equinox, as far as Lucy and Galen could figure out. Lucy sometimes looked into Pony's blue eyes and saw something stirring there. It frightened her. But Galen had learned to live with his gifts, and she supposed Pony could learn to live with her own, if it turned out she had them.

"Mommy," Pony shrieked. "Come and see the fish."

Lucy smiled. Galen looked up, his expression soft. Hardly like a Viking warrior at all. He was a good man and true, constant in his love for her and patient with Pony. He'd never once said he wanted a boy after Pony had arrived and been named for his mother and her horse goddess. He'd get one now, of course. Lucy patted her stomach. In about another five months. That was one reason why they'd decided to come back to live in San Francisco again. No more babies delivered in Thailand. It was time to come home from the sea.

Jake, as it turned out, had left the apartment house to her in a hastily made will before Casey had gotten to him. And she happened to have a gift for the stock market. You can trade from anywhere with a satellite phone and an Internet connection. So she and Galen were more than set. They could fund his efforts to save Gaia from mankind till the cows came home.

She leaned over, and the weight of Leonardo's book in her bag jostled Pony. "Sorry, honey," Lucy said. "Oooh, those are great fish." She'd taken to carrying the book around with her again ever since they hit land last week. It was a little worrying. She thought she'd left that whole obsession thing behind her. Other than her obsession with Galen, of course. That hadn't abated one bit. Nor had his for her. She'd had to unlearn some prejudices about Vikings.

The Exploratorium was emptying out. Galen glanced toward the door marked *Danger, No Admittance* in the hallway beside the gift shop.

They were here to check that the machine was still secure.

They drifted toward the gift shop, Pony in tow.

A little docent with mousy brown hair and big eyes hurried over. "Closing time, sorry," she announced.

"Okay," Galen said. "We'll just stop at the restrooms before I take my two girls home."

The docent smiled.

And Lucy shuddered. The echoing Exploratorium around her seemed to pulse in and out. She couldn't get her breath. She could feel Leonardo's machine behind that door as though she could see right through the metal. And she could feel his book under her arm, almost . . . quivering. Was that possible?

"Lucy, are you all right?" Galen was at her side, supporting her. She staggered against him. "You need to sit down." He looked around.

"Over here, ma'am," the little docent said. "Here's a bench."

"Thank you," Lucy murmured as Galen helped her to sit.

"What's wrong with Mommy?" Pony asked in a small voice.

"Nothing, honey," Lucy managed. "Maybe Mommy didn't eat enough at lunchtime."

The museum was empty now, all the noise now concentrated out by the doors.

"I'm fine," Lucy insisted as both Galen and the docent hovered.

"You look . . . uh . . . pretty pale," the docent said. There was something about her . . . had Lucy seen her before?

Galen looked around. "Can you look after Pony?" he asked the docent. "I'll buy a coffee mug at the gift shop and get a glass of water."

The docent grabbed Pony's hand, and Galen strode away.

The presence of the time machine at Lucy's back was palpable. Leonardo's book seemed almost to . . . yearn for something. That sounded crazy. Better take her mind off this.

"Have you been a docent long?" she asked.

The girl turned her attention up to Lucy and . . . and a connection sparked between them. The girl's eyes were really quite beautiful. Hazel maybe, with long, thick lashes.

"A few years. It pays the bills while I wait for my ship to come in."

"And what exactly would your ship look like?"

The girl smiled, a self-deprecating, self-aware smile that said she was smart and knew well enough that being so was not always an advantage. "Well . . . I write books. You know how it is." She looked up to see Lucy's expression of sympathy. "Oh, I'm published," she assured Lucy. "But it doesn't come with health insurance or a four-oh-one(k). Working for the city of San Francisco does that."

"What do you write?"

"Romances. Well, they aren't the usual romances," the girl assured her. "They're very carefully researched."

"Historical?"

She nodded. "Premedieval. The origins of the age of courtly love."

What would this girl do if she knew she had a Dark Ages Viking not twenty feet away collecting water from her water fountain in a cup that said . . . Lucy peered over at him . . . *Explore today at the Exploratorium*? She'd probably wet her pants.

The girl sighed. "That was a time to live in." Longing drenched her voice.

And Lucy knew.

Just as Frankie Suchet must have known that day nearly five years ago now, Lucy knew.

Sureness. Rightness. The feelings coursed through her. Galen came up, a worried frown creasing his brow.

She smiled, first at him and then at the girl. "I have a gift for you. You're just the person to appreciate it." Lucy hauled Leonardo's book from her bag and handed it to the girl.

The girl glanced from the book to Lucy and back again. "This is old. . . . I . . . I couldn't take this."

"Of course you can. I want to give it to you, just as it was given to me." She glanced to Galen and stilled his protest with a look.

The girl opened the leather binding gingerly. "It's . . . it's written backward."

"Yes." Points to her for seeing that. To most people it just looked like gibberish.

"What language is it in?"

"Archaic Italian, some Latin."

The girl looked dubious.

"Take a class. It will be worth your time. Or have it translated. There's a guy over at Berkeley, Dr. Dent. He could do the job."

Galen swept up Pony in one arm. Lucy rose, feeling better than she had all week. She couldn't keep from smiling. "I'm feeling okay now. We can go." Galen looked disturbed. He glanced significantly at the *Danger* door.

"I've done what I came to do," she assured him. Turning to the girl, Lucy said, "What's your name? I'd like to pick up some of your books."

The little mouse blushed charmingly. "Diana Dearborn."

"That's a great name for a romance writer."

"I didn't change it. That's what my mother named me," she said defensively.

"Lucky you." Lucy pressed Diana's hands. "Have a wonderful time. I did. It will change your life. Maybe it will transform you. And when you're ready . . ." She leaned forward and whispered in her ear, "Look behind the door."

Diana Dearborn looked shocked, puzzled. Yeah. She would. But not forever. She'd figure it out.

Galen downed the rest of the water and gave the cup to Pony. He took Lucy's arm and guided her protectively out into the night. "What about the machine?" he whispered into her ear.

"It's there. I felt it. It's fine. And we're done with it. The book needed to go to someone else. I think it needed to go to Diana Dearborn."

"You look as though a weight has been lifted."

"An obsession, more likely. One of them. I still have obsessions." She rubbed his arm, feeling the hard muscle through his sweater.

He looked down at her, a smolder rising in his ice blue eyes. "Pony really likes that nice lady who babysat the other night, don't you, sweet one?"

"Yesss," Pony said carefully. She was newly aware that she had a sibilant *s*. "S-she is very nice. She likes Vandal."

"Vandal likes her," Galen said, talking to Pony but still looking at Lucy. "Even though he's very protective of you."

"And they're doing Wagner at the opera . . . ," Lucy

added. Galen was wild for Wagner. All that Germanic Sturm und Drang must be pretty close to his own experience.

He gave her a warning look. "You know that Wagner always puts me in the mood for . . ."

She sighed, trying not to grin. "Something to do with pillaging? I guess I can handle it."

"*Ja*," he said, his accent coming up a little, just as it always seemed to do in the bedroom. "You handle it, Lucy." He bent to kiss her ear. "And I will handle you. Equal."

"I warn you, you're likely to feel equally pillaged."

"Ahhh, I'll try to bear up," he said sadly. "My proud Viking spirit has been broken."

"Sometimes I wish," Lucy laughed. But she didn't. She liked him difficult and protective and even demanding. He was a match for her in so many ways.

Galen opened the door for Lucy and bundled Pony into the car seat of the black Escape Hybrid. Vandal lavished her with kisses. Lucy slid into the passenger seat. The car smelled like new leather and wet dog. It had been raining earlier.

"Vandal," Pony cried, laughing as the big black dog washed her ear. "What an *yful hund*." What would Pony's kindergarten teacher think of her mixture of Old and modern English?

Galen came around to the driver's seat. He loved to drive. In fact, he loved to drive fast, but he didn't with Pony in the car.

"Why do you like opera so much?" Lucy asked when he had settled behind the wheel.

"Because it seems magic, of course. The singing, the music of so many instruments joining together into another thing altogether, the way they make you think the stage is so many different places . . ." He pulled out of the parking lot under the arch of the Golden Gate.

Galen had brought a simple joy and wonder to so many aspects of the world she'd always taken for granted. What had life been like before Galen? Maybe she'd gotten the magic to transform her life in more ways than one. Not easy, any of it. But worth it, every day.

"Then Wagner it is. Let's go and find a little magic tonight."

Read on for an excerpt from the next book
by Susan Squires

THE MISTS OF TIME

Coming soon from St. Martin's Paperbacks

The machine that lowered the casket into the ground
made a grinding noise. They really ought to oil the mech-
anism. Fog rolled in as the light faded. She pulled her
black wool cape tighter around her shoulders. Spring in
San Francisco still seemed far away in March. A guy
waited in a small tractor-thing to scoop dirt back into the
grave. Indoor-outdoor carpet was draped over the exca-
vated pile, as if that would camouflage the finality of dirt.

The other mourners had gone after they said all the
prescribed words about the "unfortunate event" being a
blessed release since her father had Alzheimer's, and how
he was going to God's bosom—that sort of thing. She
couldn't quite muster the will to take her eyes from the
coffin. If you'd watched as many horror movies as she had,
you couldn't help but wonder what he'd look like after a
year or five or ten or fifty in there. Maybe she should have
opted for cremation. But her father had wanted to be buried beside his wife of thirty years. They were the reason
she could write romances. She knew at least one couple
who'd found love.

The thunk as the coffin hit the bottom of the grave was
like a slap. She heaved in a breath and jerked her eyes up.
Her gaze was drawn to the grove of redwoods up the hill

from the gravesite. The shadows between their trunks were filling up with mist.

She knew he was there before he stepped out from the trees. Dark hair, fair skin, bulky shoulders. She might have been mistaken when she'd seen him across the lake at the Palace of Fine Arts. He could just have been someone who looked a little like the guy who pushed past her in the corner liquor store near her apartment.

But this time, there was no doubt. It was the same guy all right. If she got closer, she'd see the blue-green eyes (or maybe gray?) and classic features she'd glimpsed in the liquor store. Was he stalking her? *You can't stalk somebody if you look like the cover model for a romance novel*, she wanted to shout. *People notice a guy like you.* Women, anyway. And while she might not be someone guys ever noticed, she was still a woman. In that liquor store, as his whatever-colored eyes had met hers, she'd experienced some thrill of . . . well, of the sort she only wrote about. Spooky, really. You couldn't be attracted to a man you didn't even know. Not like *that*. But it meant you'd recognize him when you saw him again.

A thrill of fear found its way into her stomach. She couldn't look away from the stalker now, as though staring at him could solve the mystery of why any man would be stalking someone like her. Romance writers sometimes acquired stalkers. The guys who wrote all those fan letters from prison sometimes got out. But she wasn't a big name or anything, though she'd had a score of books published. She wasn't rich, and she wasn't beautiful. He just stood there, maybe fifty yards away, letting her look. Did he *want* her to know he was stalking her, just to wring maximum fear out of the situation?

He looked . . . familiar, somehow. More than just the two or three times she'd glimpsed him. He couldn't be . . . and yet . . .

"Miss Dearborn?"

Diana gasped and jumped.

"Oh, I am so sorry, honey. I didn't mean to scare you."

Diana heaved breaths while she patted her palm against her breast as though that would start her heart. How had the woman surprised her? She always heard what people would say just before they said it. That was her gift, or her curse. The world was like an echo chamber for her, people forever repeating what she had just heard them saying. Like singing a constant "round robin" song. She must have been distracted by her stalker. "Don't mind me," she said breathlessly. The woman was a candidate for "portly short" clothing. Her hair had been dyed what hairdressers called "menopause red." She glanced up to the redwood grove, but her stalker had disappeared. Was she imagining him?

Now the familiar echo of what the woman would say reverberated in Diana's mind. "I don't mean to interrupt your hour of mourning." People in the funeral business used those formal phrases to mask the fact that they no longer gave death any but the most cursory attention. "Perhaps you'd like to continue your meditation in the comfort of our reception lounge while our associates put the final touches on your father's resting place?"

Diana tore her eyes from the redwoods, now enveloped in mist. "No, thank you. I'd better go." She put her head down and squished away over the damp grass inset with flat headstones. *Thank goodness I wore flat shoes.*

Diana turned before the woman could call after her. "You don't have to send the flowers to my apartment." The woman looked shocked. Diana usually didn't reveal herself that way, but she couldn't stand any more formal sympathy. The tractor engine ground to life. "You just . . . do whatever you do with them usually." A big dumpster crouched in back of the reception building.

She stumbled down the gentle slope. Her car looked lonely in the visitors' parking lot because the employees parked around back by the dumpster.

Fitting. She'd always felt . . . separate. Not only because she lived in an echo chamber but because she had had no childhood. At least until she was thirteen. That was about how old she was when they found her wandering around the suburbs of Chicago, dressed strangely and speaking in tongues, with a big gash in her scalp and a king-sized knot, unable to remember anything about where she came from or where she belonged. No one came forward to claim her. After some disastrous foster care, she'd been adopted by a wonderful older couple. Her adoptive mother died in a car accident a couple of years after the family moved to San Francisco. Now her father was gone, too.

She had no one.

She sloshed across the gravel parking lot to the old Honda Accord that had been her father's. She slid into the driver's seat and closed her eyes, hugging the shoulder bag that held her treasured antique book. Maybe the book was all she had now.

She couldn't even write anymore. She had only twenty-five pages done on the novel that was due next month. She dreaded telling Jen, her editor. The whole thing made her want to rip her hair out. Much as she loved the setting of Camelot and her hero, Gawain, the romance just wouldn't come to life. She'd give back the advance and call it a day, but the money had gone to pay the deductible on Dad's insurance this year. Happy endings seemed to be in short supply right now, even fictional ones.

She put her bag on the passenger's seat beside her. The priceless book inside had been taking up more and more of her thoughts. That was just because she needed an escape. It was hard to visit her father every day and wonder whether he'd recognize her or not. But the obsession had really ramped up since her father's death. She knew why. She just didn't want to admit it. At least she wasn't imagining the book. It was real. And it was by Leonardo da Vinci.

Yeah. *That* da Vinci. She'd have enough to set her up for life if she sold it, let alone enough to give back her advance, but the horror at even the *thought* of selling the book made the word "obsession" seem inadequate.

Whoa. Probably imagined stalker, obsession over a precious book, writer's block, all on top of her little natural proclivities . . . Maybe she needed a therapist. As if she could afford one.

She took two deep breaths and started the car. Okay. It wasn't crazy to feel bereft on the day your father was buried. Adopted father, but still. . . .

She headed west on Waller, to hit Delores south. Time to go home to her little apartment just east of the Mission District. Unable to help herself, she reached over to touch the book. The way it had come into her life was a little surreal . . .

Diana had been coming out of the office at the Exploratorium, the children's science museum where she supervised docents to make ends meet when she practically ran into the family. The woman had very green eyes and very red hair and that translucent, perfect skin that goes with them. Her baby bump was just beginning to show. The little girl was a paler version of her mother. The father was a looker. Anything in range with a female hormone was casting surreptitious looks at him. He ought to be standing at the prow of a Viking ship, preferably stripped to the waist.

"Closing time," Diana announced. The Viking's next words echoed in her mind.

"Okay." He gathered the little girl into one big arm. "We'll just stop at the restrooms before I take my two girls home." He took his wife's elbow protectively.

The woman took one look at Diana, gasped, and slumped against her husband.

"Lucy, are you all right?" The Viking hauled her in against his free hip with one massive arm. "You need to sit down." He looked around, frowning.

"Over here, sir." Diana guided them to a bench beside the door marked with a large sign that said "Danger. Keep out." The little girl was worried.

"What's wrong with Mommy?" she asked in a small voice.

"Nothing, honey," the woman called Lucy managed as she eased down on the bench. "Mommy didn't eat enough at lunchtime." She laid her large shoulder bag down beside her.

The Viking's gaze swept the area. "Can you look after Pony?" he asked Diana, setting the little girl on her feet. "I'll buy a mug at the gift shop and bring some water."

Diana grabbed Pony's hand, and the Viking strode away. Pony. Odd name, but cute.

The woman grabbed her shoulder bag again and clutched it to her chest, her green gaze fixed on Diana's face. "Have . . . have you been a docent long?" she asked.

Diana glanced up from the little girl to the woman her husband called Lucy and . . . and a connection sparked between them. Did Diana know her? "I'm actually a supervisor. It pays the bills while I wait for my ship to come in." She never told anyone about her father's illness.

"And what exactly would your ship look like?"

Diana mustered a smile "Well . . . I write books." She looked up to see the woman's expression of sympathy. Everybody and their brother was a failed writer these days. "Oh, I'm published," she assured the woman. "But it doesn't come with health insurance or a 401K. City of San Francisco provides those." That was her standard line. People always thought you were rich if you were published. Only a few, like Stephen King and J.K. Rowling and Nora Roberts made millions at writing. Almost everybody else just survived.

"What do you write?"

Diana sighed. Now she'd see the flash of derision or the uneasy shifting of the eyes. "Romances. They aren't the usual romances." Did she sound defensive? "They're very carefully researched. They're well-reviewed, too."

"Historical?"

She nodded. "Premedieval. The origin of courtly love."

Not even a hint of eye-rolling. Emboldened, Diana continued. "That was the time to live." She couldn't help the longing that drenched her voice. "Right now I'm researching Camelot. I think that was the start of everything."

Diana watched as Lucy gave a sharp intake of breath and examined Diana's face as though she'd just had a revelation. The Viking strode toward them with his cup of water, a worried frown creasing his brow. The woman smiled, first at him, and then at Diana. A look Diana could only describe as sureness suffused her expression. "I have a gift for you." She hauled a very large leather-bound book from her bag and handed it to Diana.

"This . . . this is old. I . . . I couldn't take this." The tooled leather binding was beautiful.

"Of course you can. I'm giving it to you just as it was given to me." The woman glanced to her husband and stilled what Diana was sure was an incipient protest with a look.

Diana opened the book gingerly, scanning the pages. "It's written backwards."

"Yes. It's in archaic Italian and Latin."

Diana frowned. "I have some Latin but I'm afraid I don't read Italian."

"A professor over at Berkeley, Dr. Dent, translated it. He'll confirm its authenticity."

Authentic what? The woman rose, looking strangely serene. "I'm feeling fine. We can go." Diana caught her husband's pointed look at the "Danger" door. "I've done what I came to do," his wife assured him. To Diana she said, "What's your name? I'd like to read your books."

Diana blushed. "Diana Dearborn."

"That's a great name for a romance writer."

They always thought it was a pseudonym, "That's what my mother named me." In a way it was *a pseudonym, since it certainly wasn't the name she'd been born with.*

"Lucky you." The woman pressed her hands. "Use the book. It will change your life. And when you're ready . . ." She leaned forward to whisper in Diana's ear. "Look behind the door."

Diana drew back in shock, then glanced to the door marked "Danger."

"Yes. That one." The woman smiled. And then she and her family strolled out into the San Francisco fog. The whole scene looked like the fade-out happy ending to a movie.

Diana jerked her head around as a car honked at her and sped by on her left. She felt a little shaky. Maybe she'd just pull over. Dolores Park loomed to her right. It was easy to find a parking place at this time of night. The park was cool and black. She'd just get her breath.

But the feeling of anxiety in her chest was ramping up into panic.

The red-haired woman called Lucy thought there was something behind the door marked danger that would change Diana's life, apparently for the better. Once she'd read Dr. Dent's translation, Diana knew what Lucy thought was behind that door.

Ultimate craziness. The very fact that Diana could half-believe it was a sign that she was going a little round the bend. The book was a hoax, even if it was a hoax by Leonardo da Vinci. The manuscript recorded Leonardo's effort to build a time machine. It said he succeeded.

There was a picture on the last pages, after all the diagrams and calculations, and all the scientific stuff she didn't have a hope of understanding. In the illustration the machine seemed to be just a bunch of gears. Appropriate for 1508 when the book was written, but not exactly the kind of thing that could manipulate the time/space continuum.

It would be easy to check it out. As a supervisor she had a set of master keys. But in the five months she'd had the book, she'd never used them on the door. Opening it, thinking there might be a time machine behind it, seemed like crossing some line toward insanity.

Like it wasn't crazy to carry the book around all the time. Or to sleep with it.

Okay. A little crazy. And it had gotten so much worse in the three days since her father had died. It was like the book was shouting at her now, where before it had only whispered. But you had to draw a line somewhere. She wouldn't believe there was a time machine hidden in a children's museum. Bad enough that she thought she had a stalker. The fact that she'd been researching Camelot was research for the novel she couldn't seem to write. She'd brushed up on her Latin because it gave her something to do as she sat with her father.

Oh, hell. She brushed up on Latin because that was what they'd spoken in Camelot as a second language to Brythonic Proto-Celtic. Because she *wanted* there to be a time machine behind that door and she wanted it to take her back to Camelot, far from this stark reality. She'd always had an affinity for Camelot. She wanted to live in a time when things were simpler, when anything could happen, and people believed in love and magic and honor. She felt like she belonged there, and she, who had no childhood, wanted so *much* to know where she belonged.

Her chest heaved and she couldn't seem to get air. She glanced over at the book. It exuded hope. It almost seemed to be pushing at her. Like maybe it could make her happy, like the red-haired Lucy said it could, like maybe stalkers and deadlines and obsession and grief were what was unreal and there was some new reality just waiting for her.

That was dangerous. Sanity was knowing reality for what it was, no matter how stark, and learning to cope with it. If there was no machine that could change your life behind that door, then she'd be able to go home to her empty apartment, make an appointment with a therapist at some free clinic, and face her future. So she knew what she had to do.

She was going to the Exploratorium tonight and look behind that door marked "Danger."